THE FATE
OF SILENT GODS

ALSO BY SCOTT DRAKEFORD

THE AGE OF IRE

Rise of the Mages

THE
FATE
OF
SILENT
GODS

SCOTT DRAKEFORD

TOR PUBLISHING GROUP
NEW YORK

THE FATE OF SILENT GODS

Maps by Jennifer Hanover

A Tor Book
Published by Tom Doherty Associates / Tor Publishing Group
120 Broadway
New York, NY 10271

www.torpublishinggroup.com

Tor® is a registered trademark of Macmillan Publishing Group, LLC.

Library of Congress Cataloging-in-Publication Data

Names: Drakeford, Scott, author.
Title: The fate of silent gods / Scott Drakeford.
Description: First edition. | New York : Tor, Tor Publishing Group, 2024. |
Series: The Age of Ire ; 2
Identifiers: LCCN 2024025251 | ISBN 9781250820167 (hardcover) |
ISBN 9781250180216 (ebook)
Subjects: LCGFT: Fantasy fiction. | Novels.
Classification: LCC PS3604.R36 F38 2024 | DDC 813/.6—dc23/eng/20240610
LC record available at https://lccn.loc.gov/2024025251

Our books may be purchased in bulk for promotional, educational, or
business use. Please contact your local bookseller or the Macmillan Corporate
and Premium Sales Department at 1-800-221-7945, extension 5442,
or by email at MacmillanSpecialMarkets@macmillan.com.

First Edition: 2024

Printed in the United States of America

0 9 8 7 6 5 4 3 2 1

For Violet, my very favorite reader

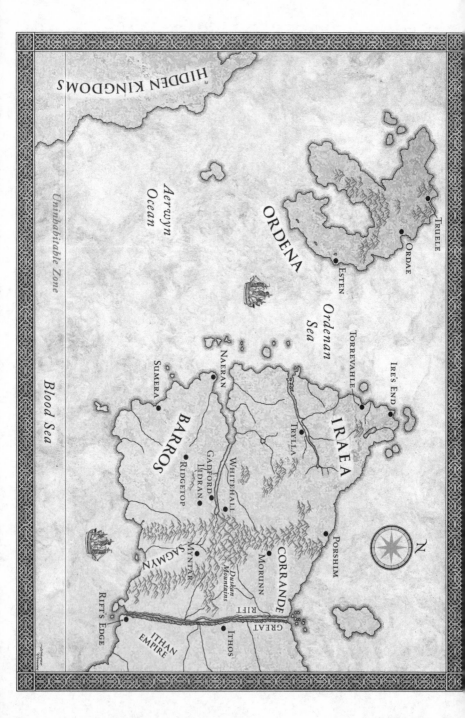

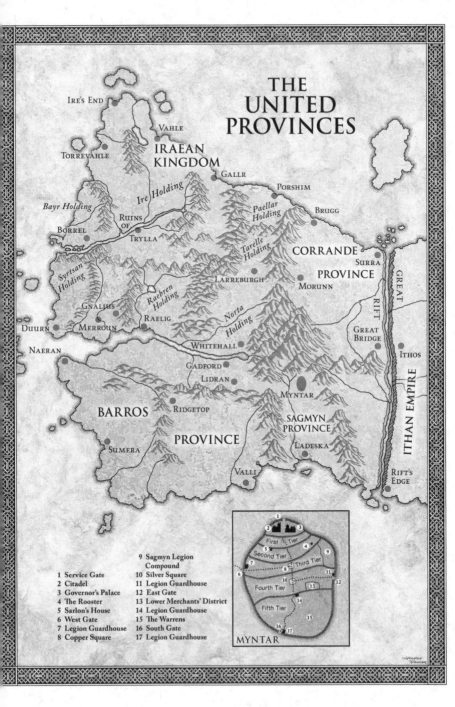

THE UNITED PROVINCES

IRE'S END

VAHLE

TORREVAHLE

IRAEAN KINGDOM

GALLR

PORSHIM

Ire Holding

Bayr Holding

Paellar Holding

BRUGG

RUINS OF

BORREL

TRYLLA

Tarelle Holding

CORRANDE

SURRA

Syrtsan Holding

LARREBURGH

PROVINCE

Raebren Holding

MORUNN

GNALIUS

RAELIG

Norta Holding

DUURN

MERROUN

GREAT BRIDGE

NAERAN

WHITEHALL

ITHOS

GADFORD

LIDRAN

MYNTAR

BARROS

RIDGETOP

SAGMYN PROVINCE

PROVINCE

SUMERA

LADESKA

VALLI

RIFT'S EDGE

GREAT RIFT

ITHAN EMPIRE

9 Sagmyn Legion
    Compound
1 Service Gate   10 Silver Square
2 Citadel   11 Legion Guardhouse
3 Governor's Palace   12 East Gate
4 The Rooster   13 Lower Merchants' District
5 Sarlon's House   14 Legion Guardhouse
6 West Gate   15 The Warrens
7 Legion Guardhouse   16 South Gate
8 Copper Square   17 Legion Guardhouse

First Tier
Second Tier
Third Tier
Fourth Tier
Fifth Tier

MYNTAR

THE FATE
OF SILENT GODS

PREVIOUSLY IN THE AGE OF IRE

Emrael Ire and his brother, Ban, are students at the Citadel, a school of military arts and *infusori* Crafting, studying for their Master's Marks. They are the heirs to the Iraean Kingdom by blood right, or would be if Iraea hadn't been conquered and subjugated by the Provinces fifty years earlier.

Governor Corrande, the leader of a neighboring province, attacks the school in a bid to control the Citadel's *infusori*-Crafting resources as he launches a war against the Ordenan Empire. Emrael's mentor, Jaina, manages to get him and his friend Elle Barros, the daughter of Governor Barros, and Elle's mentor, Master Yerdon, to safety. She is aided by her fellow Ordenan mages, called Imperators, Sarlon and Yamara. Jaina and her friends are citizens of the powerful Ordenan Empire; more than that, they are trained *infusori* mages placed in the Provinces by their Order of Imperators. In the course of their escape, Emrael discovers his own budding mage powers, much to Jaina's chagrin.

Emrael and his friends are tracked down and attacked again by the forces that attacked the Citadel—the United Provincial Legion, more commonly known as the Watchers. Emrael and his friends are separated, but Jaina finds him in the woods outside the city, and together they recruit the help of Emrael's old friend Halrec, an officer in the Barros Legion.

The Watchers catch up to Sarlon, Yamara, Elle, and Yerdon on the road to Elle's home city. They grievously injure Yamara during Emrael and Jaina's rescue attempt, and Emrael just barely manages to survive a fight with Darmon Corrande, the son of Governor Corrande, and the sinister Malithii mage-priests from the faraway Westlands who have allied themselves with Corrande and the Watchers.

Emrael and his friends are detained when they seek medical aid, and shipped to the Barros capital for judgment, save for Sarlon and

Yamara, who are granted leave to remain for treatment from the Barros Legion healers. En route, they are attacked again by the Malithii, who have brought their monstrous undead slaves, their soulbound. The entire Barros Legion party escorting the captives is killed save for two men. Jaina, very familiar with fighting soulbound and their Malithii masters, manages to shepherd Emrael, Elle, and Halrec to safety once more. In the midst of their escape, they encounter an ancient Ravan temple in the forest, on their way to the city of Whitehall. Their enemies catch up to them before they reach the city, and they encounter an unlikely ally in Toravin, an Iraean soldier turned smuggler, who helps them fight off the soulbound and Malithii attackers. Emrael puts his life on the line to protect a helpless woman and her children from the soulbound, and Elle is forced to sacrifice the life of her mentor, Master Yerdon, to save Emrael.

Upon reaching Whitehall, Emrael attempts to leverage Elle's status as daughter of a governor to negotiate with the Lord of Whitehall, Lord Holder Norta. Instead, they and Sarlon, who catches up to them after his wife, Yamara, dies, are thrown into Whitehall Keep's dungeon. Lord Holder Norta doesn't count on Emrael and Sarlon's mage abilities, however, and they quickly escape. On the way out, they also liberate a fellow prisoner who turns out to be Lord Holder Norta's traitorous son, Dorae Norta. Dorae immediately resumes his bid to overthrow his father upon his escape, and Emrael et al. use this as their chance to raid the location of the captive Citadel students held in the city.

Alas, Ban isn't among the students they free, and they must now attempt a rescue back at the Citadel in Myntar where their adventure began. Luckily, Dorae's revolution has been successful this time, as he had retained many friends and followers from a failed coup three years prior. He raises an army of retired Legion soldiers and home-trained craftsmen for Emrael, primarily to deflect the attention of the Provincial forces away from himself but ostensibly with the aim of resurrecting the Iraean Kingdom.

Emrael and friends lead this ragtag army to Myntar and are successful in their assault, save for Emrael's own raid into the Citadel, where the Watchers and their Malithii allies are more prepared for the attack than he was led to believe. His men are killed; he is captured, and subjected to excruciating torture at the hand of a mute madman working under Malithii priests. When the Malithii begin to torture his brother, Ban, in the same room, Emrael breaks the bounds of what he has been told is possible and draws *infusori* directly from his environment. He frees himself and kills his torturer, only to find that the mute madman was his father, who had gone missing years earlier in a botched military operation. The Malithii had captured him and forced him to torture his own sons using a Crafted control device called a mindbinder.

Emrael is devastated physically and emotionally, but manages to carry Ban to safety. Jaina has fetched Emrael's mother, Maira, and a formidable force of Ordenan Imperators from their homeland. Maira heals her sons and the Imperators lead the Iraeans in a final successful assault of the Watchers, Malithii, and soulbound holed up in the Citadel.

But the war they have started is far from over. . . .

PROLOGUE

Raltan Gan wiped a sheet of sweat from his forehead as his squad's longboat glided smoothly through the calm, fog-shrouded waters of the bay. The fog was so thick that even in the full light of the blue moon, he could just see the keel of his small boat cut through the small moonlit waves.

Here close to the uninhabitable region in the south of the Westlands, the oppressive heat threatened to suffocate him even now in the dead of night. Before long, the hot mist filled his nostrils with the swampy marine scent of the coastal town the locals called Raalek. They were close.

He looked about him, eyeing each of his squad mates. He had fought beside them countless times, beating back hordes of poorly armed peasants, horrific *alai'ahn* monsters with their ancient *alai* binders, and even the dread black Malithii priests themselves once or twice. But none of his companions had been with him as long as Skinny Jack. Jack had joined the Ordenan Imperial Army in the Dark Nations near the same time as Raltan, and they had fought to earn their freedom for the four years since.

Raltan nudged Jack. "Hey, Jacko. You shouldn't be here. Your years are up. You are a full Ordenan citizen now, you got your tattoo. Go home and find yourself a nice willing lass. There will be any number lining up for you, even ugly as you are."

Jack chuckled, teeth bared in a smile that always seemed to charm women in moments. "You think so, you iron-faced ox?"

Raltan grinned. "I do indeed. Now me, I just got to put in four more years for Mel, and all that Ordena has to offer is ours. But you could go back now."

"I will someday soon, I will. But if I go, who'll keep your sorry ass alive? If I am not here, you'll be butchered like the pig you are the next day, most like. Then who will take care of that beauty of yours back home? Assuming she has not already found another nice bloke to cozy up to."

Raltan slugged his friend in the shoulder, ignoring the glares of his squad mates on the oars who now had to combat the sway of the boat. "Not my Melia, not while I still breathe. 'Sides, if I die in service to the Empire, she and my sweet girl are free sooner than I could have hoped and set up with plenty of copper besides." He smiled. "I would rather just liberate a few of the dread black priests of their heads to earn some years off my time, and live to see them again myself, though."

Jack shook his head, his long hair swaying. "You do have a death wish. I have told you, stay away from those Malithii bastards. They are not usually stupid enough to come into the protected zone themselves, but I have seen it once. Not pretty. You are big, and good in a fight, but not that good. Especially since the damn commander did not send any Imperators with us. Going to scout an entire *infusori* Well regiment that has gone silent and we do not have a single mage." He spat over the side of their small wooden craft before continuing. "If you want to earn extra time and stay alive, just collect binders from a few of their lifeless monsters. We already have enough between us to take a whole year off your girl's time. We will have enough for us to go home together in no time."

Raltan put a hand on his friend's shoulder, trying to keep emotion out of his voice. "Thank you, Jack."

Their captain whispered hoarsely from the back of their longboat, "Shut your damn mouths. Silent approach."

The reality of their assault was beginning to set in. They'd been on plenty of raids, but something felt different about this one. The Imperial Army command hadn't had word out of this region for some time, odd enough that command should have sent far more than ten longboats with ten men each to retake a town of this size. There were normally a hundred of the Imperial Army stationed here—or there had been. Command wanted a situation report, but only sent an equal number as what had likely been wiped out. Did not make a whole lot of sense to him. Unfortunately, his lot was to follow orders, not to understand them.

The rocky shoreline came into view just before they slid to a stop with a muted tinkle of rounded pebbles. Raltan and Jack jumped into the warm surf to help the squad pull the boat farther up shore, and started the boot-squelching two-league march toward the small but high-walled town that circumscribed the highly coveted *infusori* Wells.

The fog had thinned to be merely an annoyance by the time they joined the other two squads at the rally point, a small hill several hundred paces from the wall. The buildings within sat dark and silent in the still of the deep night, but a thimble of caution was worth a bucket of blood, as Jack was fond of saying.

The intelligence reports said that a small service gate on the northwest side of the wall provided their best point of entry, and if Raltan remembered the map correctly, it should be a straight shot from the hill.

"Raltan, Jack, Jian, Talli on point!" the Captain called quietly. "Have that gate open within ten seconds of arrival, or I'll gut you myself. You know the plan; each squad puts eyes on their targets and we meet back at the boats an hour before dawn. Reconnaissance only."

When they reached the small wooden side gate, Raltan used a small *infusori* Crafting to melt the hinges, lowering it to the ground with no more than a quiet creak. Jack and the other two ducked through immediately, short spears and shields at the ready. Raltan shoved his spear through a strap in his pack and drew his heavy-bladed short sword.

He sprang through the gate but pulled up short when he found himself alone in the dark courtyard of a compound of warehouses that reeked of fish. "Jack?" he called softly, crouching instinctively.

"Here," the reply floated through the still, thick night.

Raltan scanned the courtyard but couldn't see anything. Not a single building in the town had a light, and while the fog had cleared significantly this far inland, a slight mist still veiled the world. "Daft bastard . . ." Raltan mumbled, then raised his voice slightly. "Where?"

A hand abruptly waved at him from a shadowed alleyway, then disappeared.

Grumbling, Raltan turned back to the now-open gate, signaling the all-clear to the rest of the Ordenan troops waiting to enter the courtyard.

Each squad formed up briefly at the gate and then disappeared into the mist, marching in near silence toward their targets. If they were lucky, the forces that had attacked the Well would be regular Westland soldiers, like their commanders had claimed in the pre-mission briefing. It was going to be a long night—or maybe a short one—if any of the soulbound monsters or their Malithii priest handlers were here. What Raltan couldn't figure was where the townsfolk had gone.

Raltan fell in at the end of his squad's column this time, holding his sword ready as he slipped out of the alleyway and onto a street lined with wood-framed homes and shops.

A short and quiet jog brought them to their target, a section of the town full of older stone buildings that surrounded the two *infusori* Wells. This was where the Ordenans would be—or where they should be. He had half-expected to find the streets littered with corpses and the wreckage that always followed a battle, especially one with the Westlanders. But besides a broken door or window here and there, the entire town was just . . . empty. The Westlander civilians and Ordenan soldiers were just gone. He felt a chill roll through him, giving him goosebumps. And not the good kind.

Their task was to clear each of the warehouses. It would likely take all night. He prayed to the Silent Sisters under his breath as his squad broke into twos to inspect each of the buildings.

Jack hung back to pair with Raltan, as they always did. Their sergeant motioned them and two other pairs toward a large, dark building at the far edge of the complex, nearest the Wells. He made a big circle with one hand, telling them to work their way back to where they stood after they cleared the building.

Jack and Raltan wasted no time in moving with their four comrades, good men with whom they had fought for years. The building that was their target had most recently been used as the Imperial Army headquarters, but as they drew nearer, Raltan recognized it as an ancient church where the locals would have worshipped the Fallen God of Glory under the watchful eyes of the Malithii priests. Its ragged spires and crenellations looked to Raltan like the giant fist of some skeletal monster clawing its way free of the earth.

Raltan joined Jack in squatting behind the low wall ringing the cathedral grounds. His friend, being the most senior of the four, whispered orders hoarsely. "Jian, you and Talli take the left side once we're in. Second pair go right. Let Raltan and me through first to clear the entry. We will get the door open and hold it."

Raltan nodded. He wasn't the most nimble, but he could hold a tight spot better than most. Besides, something about this didn't feel right. It felt like a good night to be close to an exit.

Jack led the way, running in a crouch to the large metal doors at the front of the dark, silent building. He tested the door, found it open, and immediately slipped inside, weapon at the ready.

Raltan shook his head involuntarily in the darkness. He didn't like it. Those doors should have been locked at the very least. Every door worth going through in this Sisters-cursed land needed kicking down, he'd found. This felt too easy.

Nevertheless, he followed Jack inside, where they cleared the high-ceilinged entry foyer while the other four entered and cleared the rest of the building. Jack set his feet on the left side of the main doors, so Raltan crept over to the right, his sword at the ready.

A large archway gaped empty and black at the other end of the foyer. Raltan stared into the darkness intently, his mind conjuring countless horrors. He'd have liked to clear it himself, but his job was to stay put with Jack. They'd have to wait for one of the other pairs to work their way through the building.

A crash and a quickly stifled shout emanated from the rooms to the left. He and Jack started moving at the same time, crossing slowly to the left-hand doorway. Before they reached it, however, the darkness beyond writhed and became flesh in the form of two ragged figures lurching toward them.

Raltan's blood froze in his veins before it turned to fire, as it always did in a fight. He'd need it, today. He and Jack had faced the undead soulbound before, but never even numbers, and certainly not in close, dark quarters.

"Get outside where we can butcher them proper," Jack barked, readying his sword and backing toward the entryway. Raltan kept his eyes on the shambling soulbound as he followed suit, backing out the doors and into the courtyard of the cathedral.

Moonlight reflected dully off the monsters' bald pates, sharply from the enormous weapons they hefted with unnatural ease. One of the creatures was slightly larger than the other, but both were nearly Raltan's height, and he was about as tall a man as he had ever met.

The tactics drilled in Imperial Army training cycled through Raltan's mind as he drew deep breaths to help himself focus.

Maintain distance at all times. Kill them quick. Run if you must.

Jack struck first, whipping his sword at the midsection of the soulbound nearest him, retreating before the creature could react. Thick blood splattered on the stones of the walkway.

The monster stumbled and slowed as its entrails flopped to the stones underfoot, but did not stop. It swung its mighty blade overhead, but Jack nimbly stepped aside, leaving the monster's weapon to clang and spark against the stone where he'd stood. Jack struck again quickly, severing the tendons in the soulbound's arm before darting back to safety.

Raltan wanted nothing more than to watch his friend's beautiful sword work, but he had problems of his own. The larger soulbound had shuffled within striking distance. He brought his sword up just in time to catch the huge blade and deflect it to one side. A desperate grunt escaped his lips at the impact. Silent Sisters, soulbound weren't supposed to be this fast. He desperately lashed out with a front kick.

He quickly followed the kick with a thrust to the soulbound's midsection and was rewarded with a sickening crunch as his blade passed through his enemy's rib cage. He took several rapid steps backward as he twisted his blade free, knowing that the fight wasn't over. Soulbound took much longer than a living human to bleed out.

It lurched, but still swung its blade at Raltan with incredible strength. Stepping out of range just in time, he struck with a strong overhand blow that severed the soulbound's head from its corpse in an eruption of thick, putrid blood.

Jack still battled his monster, stabbing and moving, stabbing and moving. His way would work, but it would take forever. Luckily, the remaining soulbound had its back to Raltan.

He covered the distance in a few powerful strides and sheared the beast's sword arm from its shoulder. Before its arm hit the ground, Jack's sword plowed through its chest but stuck in the monster's rib cage. The soulbound's remaining hand clutched Jack's throat and pulled him close, seeking to crush the life out of him. Raltan roared as he leapt forward. Unable to use his weapon for fear of wounding his friend, he reached up to hook his fingers in the soulbound's eye sockets and pull with all his might. He felt a snap, and the monster's head rebounded violently when it hit the stone-covered ground. Still the damn thing clung to Jack, who rasped and kicked wildly.

Raltan reclaimed his sword and planted the point through one of the soulbound's ruined eyes. It shuddered and finally lay still. Jack rolled free from its grip, coughing and breathing deeply.

Sweat dripped from Raltan's brow and his breath came heavy as he leaned down to wrench his friend's sword from the beast's chest. "Might want to hang on to that in the future. No good wrestling them."

Jack gasped a laugh. "Damn things die hard. Different when we're not in a shield wall, eh, Ral?"

Raltan took a knee to recover the binder bracelets from the monsters' wrists—these two alone would take another year off the time he still owed for Melia—and to catch his breath for a moment. "Don't mention it. Just don't make a habit of it. C'mon, let's go see what our boys ran into."

He heaved himself to his feet. Jack followed closely as they stepped carefully back through the door into the deep darkness of the cathedral of the Fallen. "Talli?" Raltan called softly. "Lomar? Jian?"

Nothing.

He approached the left-hand doorway slowly, Jack swinging wide to cover him and get a better view of the room beyond. Something the size of a small man moved just inside the doorway.

"Lomar?"

Raltan caught the brief glint of moonlight flashing off metal streaking in Jack's direction. Without thought, Raltan leaped to intercept it.

Pain lanced through his shoulder and chest. He hit the ground hard. He struggled to breathe. Someone screamed with rage. A cold laugh echoed through the chamber.

Raltan turned his head feebly to see Jack spring toward a shadow, blade raised. No, not a shadow. A Malithii priest robed in black, who met Jack stroke for stroke with a much smaller blade, almost a dagger.

He forgot his pain long enough to feel nothing but fear for his friend. They were going to die—or, worse, end up as one of the mindless soulbound monsters, enslaved by evil binder bracelets. Raltan fingered the hilt of the dagger that protruded from his right shoulder. He prayed to the Sisters for death to take him before he could be turned, before he had to see his friend be killed. Everyone knew that facing a black priest alone was a sure way to die.

But to his surprise, Jack wasn't dead yet. In fact, he seemed to have the upper hand. He grunted with effort, his blade moving faster and faster, keeping the shadowy priest on his heels. The mind-numbing flurry of activity ended when Jack lunged, thrusting his blade through the priest's midsection. The Malithii hunched over and fell, clawing feebly at the blade impaling him. Dangerous they might be, but they still died like any other human.

Jack bent over to retrieve his sword, and cried out, a hand to his thigh. The bastard priest had stabbed him with a small dagger, malicious even in the throes of death. Jack hacked at the priest until the form lay still, each fall of the blade a sick squelch.

His friend limped over to Raltan and knelt, inspecting the knife stuck in him. "You saved my life, twice over, Ral. I don't think we should take that knife out of you just yet. It's already bleeding plenty. Can you stand?"

Raltan summoned what strength he had left and lurched to his feet, swaying. "Find me a wagon, Jack. I won't make it twenty paces. And get that priest's head." He already felt like he was going to empty his stomach, and the knife stuck in his shoulder ached something fierce.

Jack wasted no time on talk. He wrapped Raltan's wound as best he could around the blade, wrapped his own bleeding thigh, then hobbled away to look for a cart, a horse, anything.

Raltan must have passed out, for the next he knew, he was

bouncing along in the back of a hay cart next to the bloody tattooed head of a Malithii priest. They were already outside the town walls, speeding down the dirt road in the general direction of the longboats as fast as Jack could goad the cart horse into trotting.

Raltan watched deliriously as five hundred paces or so behind them, a mass of lumbering soulbound boiled out from the town's gates. At least two Malithii priests drove the soulbound from behind with cracking whips.

"Jack!" Raltan called in a panic. His best friend in all the world put a calming hand on his head.

"I know, Ral. There's thousands of the beasts. The whole town turned, likely the battalion stationed here too. Never seen anything like it. All our men are dead, or ran already. The damned soulbound came out of the Well compound right as I was loading your huge ass into this wagon."

Raltan lay back, closed his eyes, and tried to focus on anything but the pain radiating from his shoulder and his impending death at the hands of a horde of soulbound. His wife's face, and his daughter's, floated to him from the warm depths of cherished memory. For a time he lost himself in them, their look, their feel, their smell. It was almost as if he were with them again. He missed them so much. Maybe Jack would kill him out of kindness.

"Ral! Raltan Gan, don't you dare die after I hauled your giant ass out of that town. There's a Mage-Healer on the galley. I've just got to row us out. Just hang on."

Raltan regained consciousness long enough to realize that Jack had somehow put him in one of the longboats. The scrappy little man was stronger than he looked.

He reached out a hand after Jack pushed them away from shore and began rowing. He found Jack's leg and gripped with all the power he had left to him. He felt the blood from Jack's own considerable wound, warm as it oozed over his fingers. "Jack. Find my girls, Jack. Make sure they get their citizenship."

Jack grunted through labored breaths as he rowed. "You're not dead yet, you oaf. But if the Malithii have managed to make that many soulbound right under our noses, I'm not sure any of us are making it home anyway. The war just got a lot worse, I think."

1

Myntar City, Sagmyn Province

N o no no no no no no no . . ."
The Malithii priest knew at least one word of Provincial Common, apparently.

Emrael and Jaina sat with their prisoner in a dank stone-walled cell beneath the Citadel. The stink of mold, blood, and piss permeated the air. A single *infusori* coil sat on a stool behind them next to a bloody pair of pliers, a dirty towel, and a bucket of water turned red with gore. The coil cast its steady blue light so that their shadows danced with their captive, who hung by his wrists from a chain mounted in the ceiling.

Dark red blood oozed in rivulets from raw patches on the Malithii's arms where his angular script tattoos had once been. The Malithii believed that their tattoos granted them status with the Fallen God of Glory in some sort of afterlife, and it was evident to Emrael that this was not Jaina's first time carving said tattoos from the flesh of a living Malithii priest.

Jaina leaned down to shout in the young Malithii's ear. "*Ichta dromni aes? Oule gaberei pire ousse! Ousse!*"

The language of the Malithii was close enough to Old Ordenan that they could understand each other. The Ordenans had preserved as closely as possible the language and culture of the ancient Ravans, the people from which the Malithii had also diverged in the early days of the world.

The priest said nothing, though his body shuddered as he struggled to contain sobs of desperation. He clamped his eyes shut, knowing what came next.

Jaina pulled her knife from where she had stabbed it into the arm of the chair. With excruciating slowness, she dragged the tip of the blade through the priest's skin, tracing another tattoo, this one high on his shoulder. The young Malithii's semi-controlled whimpers crescendoed until he wept openly.

She snatched the pliers from the stool. The Malithii's breath quickened as she secured a grip on the skin at the top of her cut. She jerked the flap of skin from the Malithii's flesh.

Emrael's stomach twisted as he watched the man scream himself hoarse. It was not lost on him that the torture was similar to what had been done to him several months prior. His heart beat heavy in his chest, his breathing quickened as the memory of his father's mad green eyes flashed through his mind. He could still recall the feel of the knife parting his own flesh. He closed his eyes and drew a deep breath, repressing his own pain and panic.

This Malithii, young though he may have been, had done horrible things to earn his tattoos, and would do them to Emrael and his people given the chance. Jaina described the tattoos and the deeds done to earn them to Emrael as she tore them from the priest's body.

"This one is given to those that participate in the ritual sacrifice of young women. They cut out their eyes, their womb, and then their still-beating heart in an offering to the Fallen," she said, holding the latest bloody patch of human skin up to the light to inspect it. "Fucking barbarians."

This priest had been taken after months of bloody fighting to take the Sagmynan *infusori* Wells back from Sagmyn Legion rebels who had chosen to stick with their Malithii allies, even as the demented priests turned captives from Emrael's ranks—their former brothers-in-arms—into their soulbound monsters.

Jaina drew her knife once more and muttered a few more words Emrael didn't understand as she placed the tip of the blade beneath the priest's right eye and began to apply pressure slowly. The priest whimpered, then began to scream again as the blade pierced the skin and slid slowly into his flesh.

"*Ichta dromni aes?*" Jaina said it quietly this time, still holding the knife in his eye socket.

The priest started gibbering, and Jaina stopped pushing her knife. After the priest gasped a few sentences, Jaina pulled the knife from his eye. She turned to look at Emrael. "I believe he's told us all he knows. He believes Corrande answers to his Malithii masters, to someone called 'the Prophet.' They are gathering in the Corrande and Barros provinces, traveling through the Ithan Kingdoms as we thought. He was told that the men gathering in Barros would be here to help them if they held the Wells long enough. Though this one likely does not know much beyond his own journey and rumors he's heard. He is very junior."

Emrael nodded, staring at the young Malithii priest, who had now vomited on himself. His head drooped down to his chest, the pain of being slowly skinned alive finally robbing him of his consciousness. Emrael was surprised that he felt pity more than contempt. The young mage was fighting for the only cause, the only way of life he knew, making the best of the life he had been handed.

Just like Emrael. Tens of thousands dead because of his choices, and many more would die before the conflict was over. He had been so sure he was justified in starting the war, but it was hard to feel morally superior when staring his own torture victim in the face.

He motioned to Jaina, who drew her sword and stabbed the Malithii through the heart in one smooth motion. She cleaned and sheathed her blades quickly, her face an uncaring mask that Emrael did his best to match. They exited the dungeons to speak with three of his Ire Legionmen waiting in the hallway.

Emrael locked eyes with the man in the lead, an Iraean sergeant named Ligan. Ligan's squad were the ones who had captured the Malithii priest alive in the latest battle to liberate a Well, and they had paid a heavy price to do so. Five of his men dead, two gravely wounded.

"He's in the second row, ten cells down. Deal with the body quietly. Lady Barros cannot hear about any of this."

"Yes, sir. Thank you, sir." A few tears streaked Ligan's otherwise stoic face.

Emrael hesitated, but finally asked, "Who did you lose?"

"My cousins, sir, and other lads from home."

"And where is home?"

"A village called Four Hills, near Old Forge in the Norta Holding, Lord Ire."

Emrael nodded, feeling queasy as he remembered his own desperation to keep Ban safe just a few short months ago. Ligan was living a nightmare like the one Emrael had feared, losing his friends. And they had done it for him.

He clapped the man on the shoulder and walked on toward the Citadel proper.

Jaina caught up with him a few strides later. "Are you well?"

Emrael shrugged it off. "Yes. It's just . . . I'm fine."

Taking him by the arm, she pulled him to a stop, then stared at him quietly for a time. "I know a thing or two about what you're feeling, I think. I experienced—and did—some truly terrible things in my time fighting in the Westlands." She paused, her gaze growing distant. "What matters now, however, is that you overcome the pain."

She gently lifted his arm to peer at the bandage that covered his wrist and hand. "This, however, is inexcusable. You should never have been involved in the battles to retake the Wells in the first place. You have armies for that, now."

He jerked his hand back. "I won't sit in a palace while these men and women die for me, Jaina. Besides, this was just a lucky spear throw."

She grunted. "Well. Do not complain to me when it turns to rot."

"I'll have Elle or my mother take a look at it right now. They want to review the trade proposal we're sending to Ordena."

Her sour expression turned sly. "Good. Make sure one of them heals it fully. I will make you run laps if you are late to training, ruler of a province or no."

Jaina watched with a small group of Imperators as Emrael sparred with Yirram, an Imperator she did not know well but had quickly grown to respect. Yirram, a short, muscular Stonebreaker, didn't talk much, but fought well. Sisters be praised, so did Emrael. The shame of having trained an inferior student would have been unbearable, particularly when the student was Councilor Maira's son.

Emrael had also become a passable Stonebreaker and even showed some skill as a Battle-Mage in the several months since Lord Governor Corrande's attack on the Citadel had interrupted that training, though he was understandably nowhere near the skill level of a full Imperator. The precise control of *infusori* required years, if not decades, of experience to master.

Still, he had progressed significantly. A taste of battle these past months had done the boy a favor in that regard.

However, she worried that his torture at the Malithii's hands had affected him excessively. Emrael's scars glittered in the sunlight, clearly visible even now without any *infusori* in his system. Beautiful, and horrifying. What worried her more were the scars within—the true extent of which only she had likely felt, as he only trained the Art with her. He hardly laughed anymore, and his eyes now burned with a ferocity that had nothing to do with his use of *infusori*. She had seen that look before, and rarely did it end well, especially for mages. She herself had been in a similar state after Welitan's death, and had almost gotten herself and others killed because of it.

As she watched, Emrael escalated the sparring match with a flurry of strikes, his wooden practice blade a blur. Yirram's blade dipped too low, and Emrael ended the match with his sword pinned to Yirram's chest. The old Emrael would have gloated, or at least smiled. Now, he simply stepped back with a small bow for his opponent. The changes had not been all bad, perhaps.

"Again," Emrael barked, but Yirram had had enough after nearly two hours of sparring without rest. Sweat dripped from every inch of bare skin on both men.

Jaina clapped her hands loudly three times, ending the training session and summoning the others to her. Emrael and the Imperators quickly gathered in a small semicircle in front of her. Her fellow Ordenans had accepted her leadership easily after Maira had given her the command during the battle for the Citadel. All of the new arrivals had seen battle in the Dark Lands, but none as extensively as she.

"Yirram!" she barked. "Why did you lose?"

This had become her standard for training, whether single combat or group exercises. Train, analyze. She did not do this to shame the losers, but to teach the entire group effectively, and purposefully. Though in truth, shame was an effective teacher, as long as success was given due recognition as well.

To his credit, Yirram did not fidget or hesitate, though he took a deep breath, winded after the prolonged fight. "My stamina failed, Imperator Jaina. I did not maintain proper defensive position nor counterattack appropriately to deter my opponent. I will improve by drilling for quickness in counterstriking, and doubling my endurance training." He glanced at Emrael, who was similarly slicked with sweat and breathing hard but stood perfectly erect, and muttered audibly, "The demon bastard." A compliment, coming from an Imperator.

She turned to point a thumb at Emrael as she addressed the other Ordenans. "Now, what did he do well?"

"His balance and footwork are impeccable," one called. Timan, she thought. One of the better pure Battle-Mages Maira had brought with her, and seemed to have the Councilor's favor besides. Jaina would keep him close.

Another of the young Imperators, a Mage-Healer named Cailla, offered her critique. "The varied power behind Emrael's strikes tired Yirram more quickly than a consistently tempered attack would have."

Jaina nodded along with all of them. "Very good. That is enough, the boy's head is large enough already. Where does Emrael need to improve?"

Cailla spoke up again. "He is arrogant. His willingness to take risks in sparring often wins matches in the training yard, but creates unacceptable liability in battle. Behaviors chosen in training are sure to be repeated, soon or late."

She tried to hide a small smile and failed. She had told Emrael the same more times than she could count. Again, Emrael showed no reaction other than a slight nod of his head in recognition of the critique.

Satisfied, she turned to wave at a few dozen blocks of granite she had placed at the edge of the combat yard. "Now to truly humble him. Yirram, show us how to shear the block cleanly in two, vertically. The rest of you, gather close to watch. Feel. You especially, Emrael."

Emrael toweled off after his cold shower—cold because not enough *infusori* yet flowed from the newly liberated *infusori* Wells in the mountains above the city for use on such luxuries. This according to Elle, anyway.

He didn't have time for a prolonged shower in any case. Training had gone long, and Toravin was already waiting to take him on a tour of the Legion.

Waiting right outside his bath chamber, in fact. "Hurry your ass up, Ire. The men will be waiting. A few months as a king and already making thousands of people wait on you."

"I'm not a king, you dumb bastard," Emrael called back as he pulled clean clothes and not-so-clean armor on. Toravin had fast become a friend, his easy manner and general disdain for authority extremely refreshing. He was already sick of people bowing and saluting at him left and right. "Not yet. Governor at best. But Elle and my mother do most of the governing."

Toravin clapped him on the shoulder as he exited into the hallway. "And a good thing they do. You're good enough with a sword and with tactics, but I'd hazard a guess that civilian relations and international trade are not your strengths."

Emrael grunted sourly, but didn't argue. Toravin was right, for the most part, though Emrael made a point of spending several hours per day learning the craft of governance from his mother and Elle. Over the last months, he had sat in on scores of mind-numbingly boring audiences and budgeting meetings, contributing where possible but mostly trying to absorb as much information as he could about the day-to-day workings of a province.

Flanked by a squad of ten Legionmen, he and Toravin walked through the Citadel compound and to the second tier of the city, where Emrael's army had taken over the large compound that had housed the Sagmyn Legion. When they arrived, men with varied styles of Legion armor worn over green uniforms lined the top of the short walls of the compound. While his men still weren't outfitted uniformly, all of them now had functional armor and weapons, many pilfered from Sagmyn stores or stored away for decades by those who had served in the Barros Legion or even the Watchers in the past. It would do, for now.

The Legionmen on guard saluted them as they approached the open gate to the sudden sound of beating their swords on their shields. Emrael looked to Toravin, frowning. "Really?"

Toravin laughed. "Just wait."

They reached the courtyard and found thousands of their

Legionmen lined up in perfect ranks. They began beating their shields as well, a thunder of crashing metal.

Toravin was now laughing so hard that tears streamed from the corners of his eyes. "You should see your face! Act pleased, the men were very excited about this little display. Dumb bastards. Good lads, though, most of them. Fought well so far, for a ragtag army."

Toravin still had a smile on his face as he waved to the gathered soldiers, and Emrael followed suit. While he was uncomfortable with the constant reminders of his newly acquired status, this display gave him goosebumps and filled him with pride. He had aspired to leading men like these—he just hadn't dreamed that it would happen so quickly, or that he'd feel like a fraud most days.

As they continued their tour of the Legionmen gathered in the courtyard of the compound, the assembled men broke into companies of one hundred to demonstrate drills.

The companies paired off to form opposing ranks three deep, with shields to the front and overlapped, forming a traditional shield wall. Men pushed and shoved with their shields, shouting and cursing as they battered away at their "enemies" with clubs fashioned from seasoned wood or unbladed spear hafts. No sense in using edged weapons in training, after all.

Toravin gestured at a nearby company running this drill. "I've got them fighting properly with shields. None of that fancy sport-fighting you learned at the Citadel."

Emrael guffawed. "I started drilling with the Barros Junior Legion before I was twelve years old, and we fought with shields often enough at the Citadel. I've likely drilled in full gear more than any man here, with the possible exception of old-timers like Voran."

Toravin nodded at that. "Aye, the men have noticed. *I've* noticed. Stupid of you to risk yourself in the battle for the Citadel and the skirmishes up in the mountains, but you've earned yourself a great deal of loyalty among the men. The Sagmynans like that you're a Citadel lad, and the Iraeans have been waiting for someone like you for two generations. Fighting men appreciate a leader who takes the same risks they do."

Emrael grunted. "I'm a fighting man same as them, Toravin."

Toravin looked at him askance, a small smirk pursing his lips.

"They call themselves the 'Ire Legion' now, you know that? Not the Iraean Legion, not the Sagmynan Legion. The 'Ire' Legion. If we succeed, it will be because you made them believe you were something more than that."

Emrael clapped his friend on the shoulder fondly. "Tor, if we succeed, it'll be because you have done a damn fine job organizing and training this lot. I never would have believed that the Sagmynans would take so quickly to joining us. But are they ready for war? Real war?"

It was Toravin's turn to look uncomfortable. "As ready as they can be. I've had them training as much as I can without them killing me in my sleep. As long as we're smart about how we use the men, they'll get the job done."

"How many are ready to march? Barros is breathing down our necks—the last reports said he's got twenty thousand in Lidran already."

"Voran is the one keeping the ledgers and other paperwork. I only handle the city defenses and training. But based on the men in rotation for city duty and what I know of other stations and patrols . . . we might be able to take twenty thousand with us. Twenty-five, if you're very sure that Corrande won't try to retake Sagmyn."

Emrael just grunted noncommittally. At best, he'd have half a Legion to fight three Legions' worth of men between Barros, Corrande, and the Watchers. Not to mention the Malithii and their Glory-forsaken soulbound. If he didn't find more men, and quickly, they were doomed.

They reached the command building of the Legion compound. Emrael had expected to find Voran there, and had hoped to review some of the ledgers. They had lost hundreds of men liberating the *infusori* Wells from a small band of Sagmyn Legion holdouts, but more recruits joined their ranks every day. He needed an accurate count of their men and training statuses for what came next. "Speaking of the old bastard—where is he?"

Toravin looked at him sideways before trying to cover it. "I thought to ask the same of you, Ire. Supplies and the soldiers' pay arrive as they should, which is nothing short of a miracle, mind you. But I hardly see the man more than a day or two each week. Figured he was up at the Citadel with you."

Emrael frowned, but soon shrugged. "I'll find him later. Take me to see the men on the walls like you wanted."

The two of them and the squad assigned to accompany them were given saddled horses at the Legion stables, which they rode through the bustling city streets to several different Legion guard-houses for inspection.

The large structure at the west gate that had just recently been rebuilt—after Emrael had destroyed it in their assault in early summer—was the last guardhouse they planned to visit. As they rode their horses at a slow trot, the iron-shod hooves clopping as they struck the stone cobbles, Emrael recognized an inn. He had stopped there what seemed like a lifetime ago, though in reality it had just been a few short months.

Emrael called for a halt. When Toravin looked at him like he had gone mad, Emrael said, "Just follow me. And bring your coin purse."

"My what?" Toravin replied, confused.

Emrael dismounted without responding and made his way to the door of the inn. When he stepped inside, the same stocky inn-keeper he remembered stood behind the counter of the bar.

"Can I help you . . . Captain?"

Emrael smiled. The man didn't recognize him, despite the distinctive hair, and the fact that Emrael had robbed him just months earlier. "Yes, you can, innkeeper. I've come to repay a debt."

The innkeeper's brows furrowed in confusion, then recognition slowly widened his eyes. "You!"

The burly man's eyes darted from Emrael to Toravin, both of whom wore the armor, riveted straps, and added stars of Commanders in a Legion. No doubt he was trying to decide whether Emrael was here to trick and rob him again.

Emrael nodded. "Me."

He turned to Toravin, who stood watching in confusion. "Your purse?"

Toravin slowly extended a leather bag full of coins.

Emrael took it and asked, "What's the going rate for a Legion mount, Tor?"

Toravin looked to the Captain Third who led the squad accompanying them today, who shrugged. Toravin sighed. "Ah . . . last I checked it was three copper rounds."

Emrael stared in momentary shock. "Glory, that's triple what it should be."

Toravin shrugged. "Everything costs more when a war is on. Some bastards attacked the city a while back."

The innkeeper, recovered from his shock and confusion, grumbled, "Try running an inn with no travelers, and food costs at five times what they should be. And those Legionmen handing out free food in nearly every square. I'm nearly bankrupt."

Left unsaid but clearly communicated through his baleful glare was an accusation that Emrael was behind the economic difficulties. And he wasn't entirely wrong.

Toravin, however, objected. "Hundreds of my men are dead and thousands wounded, all to provide *infusori* to the city and the rest of the province. Food is being paid for and handed out—at our expense, mind you—to keep people from starving. It will get worse before it gets better, but we are doing right by everyone we can. War is not always so civil, good innkeeper."

The innkeeper's eyes now bulged with anger. "You are thieves, criminals! Attacking our city and then lording about as if it's your right to be here."

Toravin opened his mouth to respond, but Emrael held up his hand to forestall him.

"Governors Corrande and Sagmyn brought war to the Provinces. No doubt you've seen their monsters we strapped to the gates. But, I won't deny that I brought war to Myntar." He began counting coins from the purse Toravin had handed him, clicking them on the bar counter one by one until he had laid out ten full copper rounds. "If I were truly just, I would be in a cell right now for stealing from you. The world is not just, however, and I don't have time to be, either. But here is payment for the horse I stole and much more. Perhaps enough to ease your hardships."

The sum was likely as much as the innkeeper would have earned in several weeks of operating his inn. That silenced him, and Emrael left without another word.

"What was that about?" Toravin asked as he caught up to him out in the street.

"I pay my debts, Tor. All of them I can."

Toravin laughed. "Well, you owe me ten copper rounds."

That night, Emrael sat in a leather-cushioned chair on the opposite side of a large table from his brother, Banron. Their old, worn Reign game board and pieces were out of place on the finely finished wood of the table in Ban's new rooms.

Emrael had practically had to force his brother to take the old Master's quarters in the wing nearest the Crafting laboratories instead of the small room that they had shared the year before. The rooms were nearly as large as his own suite of rooms in the main wing of the Citadel, which had been newly repaired after he had collapsed a portion of it in the battle several months before.

On the other hand, convincing Ban to take charge of the Crafters left in the Citadel had been quite easy. Even the few Masters who had survived the Watcher and Malithii occupation now deferred to his brother readily, though he was just shy of twenty summers old. In his few months in charge, the Crafters of the Citadel had produced more Craftings than they otherwise would have in a year's time. A good thing too—Craftings were desperately needed to power cooling chambers and pumps that supplied the city and much of the rest of the province with fresh food and water. Now, they would likely be able to feed the entire province solely from their own stores, even through the winter.

The remains of their dinner—fire-roasted chicken, flatbread, and summer squash—sat on trays scattered about the table along with pitchers full of ale, both light for Emrael and the dark that Ban favored. A map of the Provinces lay on the table next to Emrael, marked with the latest information from their scouts.

Emrael pulled his gaze away from the map to stare at the Reign board in consternation. "Absent Gods, Ban, have you been doing nothing but playing Reign all day while I'm out working and training? How did you get this good so quickly?"

Ban laughed and raked his hand through his now shoulder-length chestnut hair. "You're distracted, and I still only win half our games at best."

"Half too many, if you ask me," Emrael mumbled sourly as he

swept his pieces from the board, admitting defeat. His brother laughed harder.

They were silent for a time as they reset the board. "Your move," Emrael grunted, then drained another tankard of ale.

Ban eyed the map and the empty tankard after he placed his first piece. "Worried?"

Emrael grunted a sardonic laugh. "What would I be worried about?"

Ban simply raised his eyebrows in reply.

Emrael sighed, tapping on the map. "We're in a hard spot, Ban. Barros has us pinned in the west. Corrande, the Watchers, and the Malithii are gathering to crush Dorae in Whitehall, and then us soon after, no doubt. This might have all been for nothing."

Ban met his gaze for a moment, his lips pursed. "What are our options?"

"I don't know that there *are* any options, Ban. We have maybe one-quarter the soldiers Corrande and Barros do, and ours aren't nearly as well trained or equipped. We might be able to hold Sagmyn for a time while we train our men, but to what end? I need men, weapons, and supplies. I need more copper. I need a lot of things."

Ban's mouth quirked into a small smile as he turned to their board, removing most of Emrael's pieces and arranging the board so that Emrael was in a dire situation—almost certain to lose. He had left the Arbiter and the Commander to Emrael, however—the most powerful pieces. Enough to win a game by themselves, if played correctly. "What would your next moves be, should you find yourself in this situation in the game?"

Emrael gave his brother a flat glare. "I know what you're doing, Ban. But this isn't as simple as pieces on a board. When I issue orders, people die. Thousands have already died, between taking the city and liberating the Wells."

Ban shook his head. "If we do nothing, everyone dies, Em. You and I could likely flee to Ordena with Mother. Nobody else has that option, though. All of the men who followed you, fought for you, and many innocents besides will die or worse at Corrande's hand. All of our paths lead to bloodshed." He looked Emrael in the eyes and gestured to the board again. "What's your move?"

Emrael glared at his brother but made his move. They played for a solid half an hour in silence, making moves one after the other. Emrael did the only thing he could do—launched an all-out attack. Twenty moves later, the board was nearly even, Emrael having won back more pieces than he had lost. Ban sat back suddenly, a full smile baring his bright white teeth. "If anyone can do it, it's you, Em. Use the pieces you've got, and make your move."

Emrael leaned back, closed his eyes, and took a deep breath. "Glory take you, Ban, you're right. If anyone will join our cause, it's the Iraeans. We need to show them we can win against the Provinces, and need to have something to offer in return for joining us. Land, copper, and a cause. I wonder what's left of Trylla . . ." He trailed off, running one finger along his map of Iraea until it rested on a drawing of a ruined city. "Think they have usable wells and roads, still? Reviving the ancient capital could be just the thing."

Ban shrugged. "I'd imagine so. It's only been fifty years or so, and the Watchers can't have destroyed much of the critical infrastructure, which will be mostly masonry. Repairs will be needed, but it'd be better than starting from scratch."

Emrael clicked his tongue as he pondered. "Right. It might work. But first, we deal with Barros."

Ban looked from the map, his eyes wide in surprise. "You'd attack Elle's father?"

Emrael's face twisted in a snarl as his father's green eyes flashed vividly in his mind. Anger surged through him, trying in vain to smother the overwhelming sorrow that lurked in his core. When he spoke, emotion roughed his voice. "Barros is more rotten than you might think, Ban. When Father and I were ambushed at that bandit stronghold in Iraea, it was on Governor Barros's personal orders. He's not our ally and never will be."

Ban sucked a breath in between his teeth. "Elle won't like it."

"Elle won't like what?" a voice called from the foyer, just before they heard the door shut. Emrael shot a warning glance at Ban just before Elle swept into the room where they were playing.

"Ah . . . Emrael's drinking," Ban said, gesturing at Emrael's empty tankard and the empty pitcher to one side of the table. "I told him he needs to keep his wits about him."

Elle gave him a suspicious glare, which she soon turned on

Emrael. "Yes, well. If you're busy drinking yourself into a stupor, I can make other plans."

Elle had her own suite of rooms, but had taken to staying in Emrael's quarters over the last few months. She had even commandeered the vast majority of his closets. He didn't need the space anyway; he only owned two pairs of boots and five sets of cotton shirts and wool uniforms in Ire Legion green, and it still felt odd having so many clothes.

Emrael stood quickly to embrace her and give her a quick kiss on the cheek. "No, no. We're done here, Ban finally took a game from me. I'm coming."

Elle smiled predatorily. "That's what I thought."

She blushed a bit when her eyes flicked to her lifelong friend, Ban. Her gaze hardened quickly, however, as she took in Ban's tankard. "Ban, I expected this from Emrael, but it looks like you've had your share as well, eh? Don't forget that I'm still waiting on dozens of refrigeration Craftings and Crafted winches for the Merchants' Guild. They've been breathing down my neck for weeks."

Ban leaned back in his chair, wiping his hands across his face. "Glory, Elle, we're working as fast as we can. No harm in a drink or two in the evenings."

"Besides," Emrael chimed in, "he's supposed to be making more Observers for me, not wasting his beautiful brain on common contraptions for the merchants. They can wait until Ban's Crafting students finish them."

Elle glared at them both again, but soon laughed. "Fine. I can't think anymore about merchants or Craftings or ledgers or budgets tonight. I need a hot bath and a soft bed."

"The Citadel water heaters have charged *infusori* coils again, then?"

She flashed a smile. "Not yet. We'll have coils enough for that within a month or so, but Ban made me a Crafting that will heat one bathtub."

Emrael glared at his brother. "Seriously? You don't have time for the Observers or Crafted crossbows I need, but you can make her a *bath warmer*?"

His brother, the smug bastard, shrugged and said simply, "Look, you put her in charge. I just follow orders."

"Idiot," Emrael mumbled, but only halfheartedly. He knew that such a small Crafting would not have taken Ban much time, and Elle had shouldered much of the stress of running their commandeered province.

Elle didn't look one bit abashed. She looked pointedly at Emrael, arching an eyebrow. "I'm going for that bath and bed. Now or never."

It was Emrael's turn to blush as Ban laughed.

"I'll take care of all this," Ban said with a smile, gesturing at the remains of their meal. "Go."

Emrael gave his brother a brief hug before following Elle out of the room.

2

The next morning, Emrael settled into the massive feather bed, staring at the wood-beamed ceiling of his room. The first rays of the morning sun only dimly lit the spacious quarters, but he had been awake for hours. Every time he shut his eyes, his mind replayed his torture at the hand of his father, whom the Malithii had enslaved and controlled with a mindbinder. He could hardly get a few hours of rest now before he woke up shaking, covered in sweat.

At least he was comfortable. He would have been happy in a room like the small utilitarian one he and Ban had once shared in a remote wing near the kitchens, but had to admit that he enjoyed the luxury.

He idly traced the thin scars that entwined his chest with one hand while the other mimed the same pattern on the soft, bare skin of Elle's back. She lay next to him, still sleeping. Her hair smelled of the expensive floral perfume she liked to wear. She stirred at his touch, turned her head to murmur, "Mmmm. You need to prepare for your meeting with the Merchants' Guild. I promised you'd speak with them today."

Emrael leaned over to finish the bit of Iraean whisky left in his glass from the night before, savoring its warmth and hint of wood-smoke flavor. He had never been much for strong spirits before they had taken the Citadel, largely because he hadn't been able to afford them. Now, he had a collection pilfered from the Master's quarters, and good thing. The liquor was the only way he got any sleep anymore. He poured himself more whisky from the decanter and shook his head, trying to clear his mind.

"I could use a morning off, Elle. I need to prepare my plans for the war council this afternoon, and I'm just . . . tired."

She turned to smirk at him. "You don't get to be tired, *Lord Ire*. You've conquered a province, and now the men and women that keep the province running need to see your face, hear your voice."

"I thought that's what you were for," he grumbled.

She threw a pillow at him. "I'm not being paid properly, and it's not like you've appointed me an official position. I can only do so much in your stead, Em. You're the conqueror, and they know it."

He nodded, biting at his cheek as he thought. He'd been so consumed by the battles for the Wells in the mountains and now by his plans to escalate the war further that he hadn't properly considered the governance of the province he already controlled. "You're right, of course. I'll name you my official steward."

Elle looked surprised. "Not your mother? She's far more experienced, Emrael."

He laughed, sitting up finally. "You want me to hand a province over to an Ordenan? An Ordenan Councilor for that matter? No, it has to be you, Elle. You can do it. And I trust you more than anyone but Ban."

Her smile as she leaned in to kiss him made what he had to tell her even harder. As Elle slipped one leg over his during their long kiss, he put his hands on her shoulders to hold her at a distance so they could talk before things could get more heated. "Before you decide, however, you should know something. I intend to take the war to the Provinces. We can't sit here and hope to be able to hold Sagmyn with the men we've got. We'll be slaughtered."

She stared at him, her bright blue eyes calm and unforgiving. She was more than smart enough to know what he was implying, but evidently meant to make him say it.

"That includes your father, Elle. He's put his Legion between us and helping Whitehall, and I can't bargain from a position of weakness. I have to put him on his heels."

She sat back farther, shifting herself off of him, pulling the sheet up to cover her body.

Emrael sat in nervous silence for a moment. "Do you still want the stewardship?"

Elle shrugged, the muscles in her slender shoulders outlined beneath her soft skin. "I will take the stewardship on one condition. You let me talk to my father before the fighting begins."

Emrael frowned and shook his head. "He won't parley with us, Elle. We've already tried several times. Our last messenger never returned. I'm going to have to do something to get his attention to even get a meeting."

She pursed her lips, clearly unhappy but understanding the situation. "Fine. But I'm coming with you for as long as it takes to negotiate with my father. And the first chance possible, I'll take the lead. Afterward, I'll be your steward."

Emrael sighed with relief. "I can make that work. I'll go over it in detail in the war council tonight, but I will arrange for you to accompany the main component of our forces."

He looked her up and down, a small smile returning to his lips. "Do we still have time . . . ?"

Elle ignored him, climbing out of bed. She threw his pants at him, hard, but smiled mischievously. "Get dressed, *Lord Ire*. I'm going to put you to work today. And while you deal with the merchants, I'm going to inspect the prisoners you've taken. We might be fighting a war, but that's no excuse for us to act like barbarians. We won't have any chance at peaceful resolution if we mistreat our prisoners."

Elle stared daggers at Emrael as he and Jaina entered the Masters' dining hall that evening. That could only mean one thing: she had found out what had happened to the Malithii prisoner. She had received detailed reports after each battle and must have asked after that particular captive.

The rest of his de facto council—his mother, Voran, Ban, and Halrec—sat around the table once more, looking bored.

Emrael addressed Elle without looking at her as he strode to his chair at the head of the table, booted heels snapping sharply on the stone floors. "Just say it, Elle."

"What did you do with the Malithii priest?"

"We questioned him."

Her face tightened with anger. "Questioned? You mean tortured?"

"Yes." Emrael kept a straight face, though sorrow weighed heavy in his chest when he saw the contempt in her eyes.

"That's barbaric, Emrael!"

He pulled his chair out, sat, and scooted up to the table before looking her in the eye. One hand traced the scars in his face as he spoke. "I'm familiar with the process, Elle."

She shook her head sadly. "Why fight if we are no different from them?"

He locked eyes with her and responded, his voice now hard as anger quickly replaced sorrow. "Because either we kill them, or they kill us, Elle. It's that simple. We have to *win*, or we *die*, and everyone we love dies. I don't know whether you've noticed, but your father and Corrande can field nearly three times our current numbers. Not to mention the Malithii; who knows what they've managed to sneak into the Provinces. We need all the information we can get. However we can get it."

Everyone else at the table watched, uncomfortable expressions on their faces. All except Maira. She smiled icily as she looked from one to the other. "Are you quite done, children? We have business to discuss. Voran, I believe you have some news?"

Voran coughed, shuffling a few papers in his hand. "Yes, well. We've received a steady stream of new recruits in the past weeks, mostly deserters from the Barros Legion. All are of Iraean descent, and all have come for the land bounty that Emrael has promised."

"A square league for every two years served is enough to attract even current Legionmen, just as we thought," Halrec interjected happily.

Toravin chuckled. "Now we just have to capture land to give them."

"We'll have it and more," Emrael said, meeting Ban's eye briefly. "Go on, Voran."

Voran eyed them with raised eyebrows for a moment before continuing. "The most recent recruits from Barros have reported further fortifications around Lidran and major inflows of Legionmen to the area. Nearly the entire Legion has been mobilized. Even the southern Lords Holder are rumored to be joining the governor. Barros now has nearly thirty thousand soldiers in Lidran or otherwise within a day's ride of the West Pass."

"Absent Gods," Emrael cursed. "Can he spare that many and still run his province?"

Halrec nodded. "He can, but won't have mobilized that many men for nothing, however. The cost is enormous."

Jaina was still staring at Voran. "How are you verifying that your deserters are of Iraean descent? Even if they are, couldn't they be here to spy for Barros or Corrande?"

Voran threw his hands in the air. "Four months ago, this 'Legion' of ours didn't exist. Any of our men could be here for any purpose. I've appointed Captains I trust, and we spread newcomers between squads. It's all I can do for now."

"The men who have joined us have proven themselves in battle against the Sagmynans and will have the chance to do so again soon against Barros and the Watchers," Emrael said dismissively, leaning back in his chair. "What do you advise we do first, Voran?"

The stout, greying man grunted, a frown wrinkling his square face. "I don't see what we *can* do besides fortify the defenses in the west and east passes, and any other route these bastards can use to attack us. Then we train the men as they ought to be trained and pray to the Holy Departed that we aren't attacked before we can establish solid relations with the Ordenans."

"You'd leave Dorae to fight the Watchers alone? He has fewer men than we do, and faces the entire might of the Watchers and the Corrande Legion. You told me yourself just days ago that Dorae won't last the summer without our help."

Voran looked to Halrec and Toravin before responding. "Aye. Whitehall will have to fend for itself, just as we will. It's our best chance at survival."

Emrael sighed with frustration. "What happened to fighting for Iraean freedom? You led Dorae's revolt, for Glory's sake! Don't we owe something to our men that left family in Whitehall? We can't leave them to be slaughtered. We'll have mutiny as soon as word of their fate reaches Myntar."

Voran pursed his lips but didn't respond. The room was painfully quiet.

Emrael pressed him further, though he now stared at his mother as well. "Do you think we can count on the Ordenans for anything more than the Imperators they've already sent? Will Barros choose us over Corrande if we hide here, like turtles in a shell?"

Silence. Even from Elle, though she looked as though she wanted to kill someone. Probably him.

Emrael leaned forward, staring intensely at each of his trusted companions in turn. "We can't bargain from a position of weakness with the Ordenans, or with the Provinces. A defensive strategy will end with all of our heads on pikes. We're making the first move."

Ban, Halrec, Toravin, and Jaina all nodded at that. Elle still didn't look convinced, and neither did Voran. Maira still surveyed the room with a calm smile as Emrael spoke.

"Governor Barros is our first problem. We'll feint toward Lidran, then take Gadford to secure the bridge to Whitehall. Hopefully this also incentivizes him to meet with us. Please prepare our supplies and mobilize the Legion. We march the day after tomorrow."

Elle's expression turned indignant in a flash. "We don't have *infusori* nor food stores gathered to support a military campaign with only a day's notice, Emrael. We just opened the Wells, our logisticians will need more time to arrange resources."

He locked gazes with her. In just a few short months, she had taken over all of the ledgers for the province and knew the status of all of the merchants, trade activity, and military movements. Even his mother had started deferring to her, though that was in large part because the Sagmynan Merchants' Guild refused to take directives from an Ordenan. She was being difficult, but he knew he needed her to support his plan if he was to succeed—now and in the future.

He softened his voice as much as he could. "We don't have any choice, Elle. If your father takes the pass, we're doomed. If he blocks our passage at Gadford, we're doomed. I've played it a million ways in my head, and this is the scenario in which all sides suffer the fewest casualties. I don't want to spill Barros blood any more than you do, but I don't have a better option."

Elle finally broke off her glare to bite one lip and sway her head from side to side as she spoke quietly. "I'm going to have to use a large portion of the copper left in the treasury, and the Merchants' Guild may revolt, but I can gather supplies to support the men we have for perhaps a one-month campaign."

Emrael smiled at her gratefully, then looked to Jaina, Toravin, and Halrec. "We leave the day after tomorrow, then. Gather twenty-five thousand of our men, or as many as we can manage and still guard the Sagmyn borders and the port at Ladeska. The main force will fortify the pass until Elle can arrange for supplies enough for them to move on Gadford. Hal, make sure you have at least one hundred squads outfitted for raiding. Jaina, you and the Imperators will be with us as well. Any that my mother doesn't need here, of course. Tor, you'll command the main party."

He turned to Voran. "I want you and my mother to support Elle here in Myntar. If we lose Sagmyn Province, we're fucked."

Voran stayed silent, jaw clenched, but Maira soon spoke. "Voran and I will stay to help Elle strengthen our position here. Won't we, Voran dear?"

Voran's countenance softened visibly as he shifted his attention to the raven-haired Ordenan woman. "Aye," he said finally. "Plenty of work to be done here. We haven't seen the last of Sagmynans rebels, mark my words."

"Thank you, Commander Loire," Emrael said with a brief smile.

Just as Emrael was about to call an end to the meeting, Elle spoke. "I'm coming with you, at least to Gadford. I should be there to dissuade you and my father both from unnecessary violence. He'll talk to me."

Emrael considered. "I think that's a wonderful idea, as long as you stay clear of any fighting and return here to govern when negotiations are finished. You should ride with Toravin's forces. But remember Elle, your father is our enemy of his own choice, not mine. He has ignored all of our offers of parley and now gathers his Legion at our doorstep. He's given us no choice."

He looked to the rest of the room. "Let's get to work. Ban, see to the engineers. I want every Crafted crossbow available for the raiding party."

The night before he and his Legion were due to ride for the Barros Province, Emrael made his way through the silent, dark halls of the Citadel to his rooms. The sun was closer to rising than it was to having set; he had again stayed in Ban's rooms playing game after game of Reign the way they used to when they had attended the Citadel as students. Elle had decided to sleep in her own rooms after the war council the day before, so all he had to look forward to in his bed were his ever-present nightmares.

He was reluctant to leave Ban, who would be staying behind to focus on his Crafting projects. He would be well protected here with the greater part of their Legion, their mother, and half of her Imperators besides. Still, Emrael worried about being separated from his brother.

A figure appeared suddenly in a dimly lit side hallway. Emrael jumped into a defensive stance as his tired, sluggish mind reacted to the threat. The person put their hands up in a comforting gesture and stepped into the meager *infusori* light of the main hallway when they saw his reaction. It was his mother.

She chuckled quietly, though her eyes and smile were warm. "Emrael. I didn't mean to startle you." She stepped forward and embraced him, pulling him tightly to her. The hug caught him off guard. His mother was not typically so . . . loving. He could count on one hand the number of times she had hugged him. After a tense moment of discomfort, however, he relaxed and rested his head on hers.

The familiar scent of cinnamon and roses sent his mind to the past, and for a brief sweet moment, he was safe. Calm. His mother had been demanding with her children, even severe at times. He had found himself at odds with her more than once, to be sure. But for all her severity and stern manner, he had always felt safe with her—even more than with his father, who had been a renowned Citadel-trained Master of War and Commander First of the Barros Legion. Perhaps on some level, he had always known that she was more than a simple healer.

Then the hug was over, and his mother glided back down the darker hallway. "Come, my son. I could not sleep, and have been looking for you. I need to speak with you before you leave."

He wiped at his eyes discreetly as he followed her to her rooms, which were of course well-lit with multiple *infusori* coils. She was not the type to go without what she deemed to be simple necessities, and he had yet to meet anyone who dared tell her no. Even his father had ceded nine out of ten arguments to her . . . in private, of course.

When they had settled in her sitting room, she with a glass of white wine and he with a cup of peach brandy, his mother reached over to trace a finger along one of the complex scars that covered his hand. "I have never failed to Heal such a simple wound, you know. I wonder why these are still visible."

She fixed him with a serious stare. This was her way of asking him what had really happened to him in the Citadel after he had been taken captive. She couldn't—or wouldn't—ask him outright.

He stared back, a lump in his throat. "Ah . . . He . . . They used a copper knife," he responded finally, shaking his head slightly. "There was some sort of binder that left me paralyzed. I don't know why they did it, or why the scars didn't heal. But I don't mind them terribly."

She tilted her head sideways slightly and raised the corner of her mouth in a smile that said she knew he was keeping something from her. "I heard from my Imperators that you took unnecessary risks in the battles for the Wells."

Emrael chuckled. "Jaina told you, you mean."

She smiled as she squinted at him. "You are learning my tricks."

Emrael took a sip of his brandy. "Well, you're not exactly subtle."

Maira frowned at him. "What do you mean?"

"*Voran, dear . . .*" he mimicked.

She smiled and threw a small paperweight from her side table at him, which he caught easily. Soon her eyes grew sad, and the smile melted. "I only wish to see you safe, Emrael."

He grunted. "Jaina has already berated me. And I'll tell you the same I told her. I fight with my men. It's who I am, and it's how I'll keep their loyalty. And if I die—I die as myself. Not some useless shadow on a throne."

His mother nodded grudgingly, though a concerned frown still wrinkled her face. "I understand."

Emrael raised a quizzical eyebrow, not wanting to ruin the moment with a fight as they would have done three years ago. Another life, really. This was the first time he could remember his mother talking to him as an equal. An equal she liked. It was a nice change.

"Thank you," he managed finally, then took a large sip of brandy before going quiet.

"No doubt you have learned some things about me by now," she said finally, breaking the awkward silence.

He laughed a harsh, deep laugh. "I guess you could say that. Councilor."

Her eyes flashed, and for the first time he fully considered that his mother might be a very, very dangerous person. She smiled as she responded, but her eyes still glowed with a hint of *infusori*— and anger.

"That . . . was not my plan, and happened rather suddenly. But yes. I should have told you." She leaned forward. "But what you may not yet appreciate is that I am more than just my job, my title. We have a family in Ordena, Emrael."

Emrael shrugged. "A sister, right? You said you hardly knew each other. Barely even mentioned her other than that time Ban asked."

Maira had the grace to look embarrassed. "Well . . ."

Emrael laughed harshly again. "If you have something to tell me, just tell me, Mother. I think we've had our fill of secrets."

Her eyes flashed again, and he could feel the old anger rising up in him in response.

"I have one sister and two brothers who still live," his mother said evenly. "I love them and their children deeply."

Emrael stared at her for a long moment, speechless. "Children? Why haven't you told us any of this? Why haven't we met them?" he asked incredulously. "They were our only family in the world, and you chose to keep them to yourself? Honestly, Mother, why would you do that?"

His mother hung her head. "I have given up much for the Order, Emrael, and I was forced to keep my life in Ordena completely separate from my life in the Provinces. As if it never happened. I hope you can trust me when I say that it was necessary. I can share no more." Her voice was tired and full of emotion.

Questions coursed through his head. He knew that she owed loyalty to Ordena as a leader on their Council of Imperators, but given all that had transpired, why was she still keeping secrets? And why keep family in Ordena a secret from him, of all things?

He reined in his frustration as he stared at the hilt of his father's sword, which hung from his belt, calming himself with a deep breath. She wasn't the only one with secrets, these days.

"Why are you telling me this now?" he asked.

She looked back up at him and smiled. "Timan Tinoas is my eldest brother's son. Your cousin. He's five years your elder, and one of the finest Battle-Mages the Order has to offer. He is one of the

Imperators that accompanied me, and I want him to stay by your side. You will need someone you can trust, and I am confident that you can trust him completely."

Emrael nodded slowly. He had met Timan several times during his training sessions with the Imperators. The man fought like a devil, and had a dark, dry wit that Emrael enjoyed.

"I know him. He knows that we are kin?"

She nodded. "None of the others do save Jaina, however. It would be best to keep it as quiet as possible."

"You arranged for him to be here, didn't you?"

She nodded again with a small smile that gave him another lump in his throat. His mother could be infuriating, but she cared and sacrificed for him in her own way. "Thank you, Mother."

"Elle will be wondering where you are, dear," she said after an awkward moment of silence, standing.

He blushed and stood quickly to hide it as best he could. "She's . . . ah. In her own rooms tonight."

His mother laughed her warm laugh again. "I saw her reaction in your council meeting. Give her time. Do what you need to in Iraea, and we'll take care of things here in Myntar. I'm with you to the end, Emrael. You and Ban above all."

He gave her another hug and a quick kiss on the top of the head, and was almost to the door when she said quietly, "He would be proud, you know. You are everything he hoped for, everything he wished he could have been. I wish he could be here to see you. And Ban."

Emrael stopped with one hand on the doorframe. Silence filled the room as he bowed his head, still turned away from her. Tears flowed unbidden down his cheeks, and he couldn't have spoken a word if he had wanted to.

Finally, he wiped his face and turned to meet his mother's eyes. Hers were red, puffy, and tear-streaked just as his undoubtedly were.

"He knows," Emrael choked out, too ashamed to tell her the truth. That his father, her husband, had been a Malithii captive for years, and had been forced to torture his own sons. That Emrael had been the one to kill him—to consume his very life source—before he knew the truth. How could he tell his family that he had killed his own father? Better for everyone if some secrets lived on.

His mother looked to the sword at Emrael's hip—the rune-etched sword of the Ire Mage kings, which Janrael had been wearing when he disappeared. She met his gaze again, a sad question in her eyes, but still didn't ask. Just as she hadn't asked for the past several months. She understood painful secrets all too well.

Emrael looked away from her pleading eyes, steeling his resolve to protect her from the pain he held inside. Not knowing would be better than what he felt. Anything was better than this.

"He knows," he rasped again before stepping into the darkness of the stone hallway.

3

Crimson rays of light crowned the eastern mountains as the sun emerged from the hidden reaches of the sky. Hundreds of Emrael's men had blackened their armor to avoid reflecting the light as they waited in the trees just off the Barros Kingroad, and Emrael was glad they had.

Emrael had scouts hidden near the road, waiting for the Barros Legion supply wagons coming from the capital city of Naeran to supply the forces that had gathered in Lidran. Toravin had received word from contacts he had throughout the Stemwood Forest—likely brigands, but Emrael hadn't pried—that a large supply train would be arriving at the city today. It was the perfect opportunity to put Governor Barros on his heels, so they had led a raiding party of one thousand men down from their camp in the West Pass four days ago, using trails deep in the forest to keep their movements hidden. Halrec led five hundred who waited up ahead and on the other side of the road to attack the enemy vanguard, while Emrael led five hundred of his own who lay in wait to attack the rear flank. Toravin had stayed with the main force in the pass to continue preparations for their upcoming assault on Gadford.

A series of quiet, short whistles echoed through the trees as his scouts signaled that the supply wagons were approaching. A muted shuffle rolled through the forest as five hundred armored men drew their weapons and readied their shields.

Emrael motioned to the Captains Third who led his five companies, and Jaina and Timan took up positions on either side of Emrael as his raiding party crept quietly toward the road. The soft, dark loam of the forest floor soaked up any sound his men's booted feet would have otherwise made. Still, he hardly dared breathe as he listened for the next whistles, which would indicate that the wagons and Barros Legionmen guarding them had passed enough for them to attack the rear flank.

He leaned on a tree, bare sword in one hand and teardrop-shaped wooden shield in the other, waiting tensely for the signal. He shifted his armor, then perked up when he heard shouts and the clash of weapons from the east where Halrec and his men were, but still no signal from his scouts. More shouts of confusion, more weapons clanging on steel, more screams. Still no whistles. Had he missed them?

Jaina silently approached to lay a hand on his shoulder. "Wait. My Imperators are among the scouts, they will give the signal when the time is right."

Still, something didn't feel right to Emrael. He couldn't let Halrec fight the entire supply party himself.

"Fallen take it," he growled, shaking her off and lurching into a jog, knowing his men would follow. He shouted anyway, "Forward! Double ranks, shields ready!"

As he and his Legionmen marched through the trees in a rough rank, shields up, he caught sight of his scouts. They looked back at him, panic and confusion on their faces. One of Jaina's Imperators who had been a sentry waved frantically from his position near the road, shielding the motion behind a large bush. Emrael stopped, and slowly his men stopped with him, maintaining a ragged double line.

He saw immediately why his scouts hadn't signaled for an attack. The Barrosian supply party wasn't riding all together, but had split into two large groups of wagons, with what looked to be at least three hundred Barros Legionmen guarding each. Maybe as many as five hundred, making this now an even battle instead of an ambush that would have ended in a lopsided victory. Halrec and Toravin must not have seen the separation and attacked the forward party, which had given the rear party time to prepare for battle. Barros Legionmen from the rear supply party marched up the road in a formation of five across, crossbows, shields, and spears at the ready. They hadn't quite reached the section of road where Emrael's half-battalion waited, and now Emrael's thin, ragged ranks were exposed on the side of the road just in front of them.

"Five ranks, on me!" Emrael shouted. "Five ranks, behind me! Five ranks!"

As his men began to shift into formation, crossbow bolts flew at them. Emrael's men had shields at the ready, so most *thunked* harmlessly into the hardened wood, but a few quarrels blew clear through shields in a spray of splinters to rend the flesh of the men behind. Blood spattered, men screamed.

"Fallen bind me, they have Crafted weapons," Emrael muttered to no one in particular. He crouched behind his shield, praying he wouldn't be hit by a bolt launched from an *infusori*-Crafted weapon. Hopefully his helmet did enough to conceal the white hair that would have made him an instant target.

He turned to Jaina, who held no shield but crouched next to him where Timan had locked his shield with Emrael's. "Jaina, take companies four and five, flank on the right. Hit them hard, but only after I've engaged them head-on. Go!"

He gave her a gentle shove, which only earned him a threatening glare. She stepped closer to him, closed her hand around his hand that held his sword, and sent a small pulse of *infusori* coursing through him. "Remember what we practiced. Push *infusori* just as you swing."

Emrael responded without taking his eyes from the approaching line of Barros Legionmen. "I've got it, Jaina. Go, quickly."

Jaina ran, crouched, bellowing at the two companies on the right side of Emrael's battle line. "Companies four and five, on me. Into the trees, four and five!"

Emrael was relieved to see the two hundred men follow Jaina quickly, still in orderly ranks. They maneuvered well for units that had only been drilling together for a few months.

An arrow or bolt slammed into his shield, but thankfully wasn't *infusori*-enhanced, so it simply stuck there, quivering.

His remaining three hundred men had gathered into a wall five shields deep that spanned the entirety of the dirt road and the cleared space to either side. They were now evenly matched with the Barros Legionmen guarding the wagons. He needed to move fast to avoid losing men to Crafted crossbows, and to keep the Barrosians' attention while Jaina maneuvered a flank through the trees.

"Sir! Lord Ire sir, we've a place for you here." One of the Captains

Third leading a company shouted, trying to get Emrael to move back in the formation with the rest of the officers. He ignored the man. This was his fight.

He dropped his sword-bearing hand to his side for a moment, touching the gold coil he had fastened to his belt, drawing on its energy. The scars not covered by clothing and armor began to glow as the power coursed through him.

"Fast trot, shields up!" Emrael shouted from his position in the front rank, and began to jog with his shield mates, all of whom made sure to keep their overlapped shields touching as they moved.

Timan, his long dark hair tied back from his face, stood to his right, his bared copper-alloy sword sparkling in the morning light. He winked at Emrael even as they jogged, and Emrael grinned. He still didn't know how to react to meeting a cousin he hadn't known existed, but he liked Timan, and knew from training with the Imperators that he was skilled with a blade.

As they drew within ten paces, Emrael released a wordless shout, full of battle rage, panic, and bloodlust. His men screamed their fear and rage with him. The Barros Legionmen had stopped loosing arrows and bolts and now stood fast, waiting for the charge behind their own overlapped shields.

They slammed into the enemy shield wall, planting their feet and pushing as they made contact. The Barros soldiers recoiled but held firm. Emrael's men in the second rank with spears thrust through openings between shields, over the top, or underneath as the front ranks of each side struggled to gain an advantage. Emrael and those in the front rank danced to avoid similar attempts from the Barros ranks, stabbing around shields with swords and shorter blades of their own. Men all around him screamed and grunted as steel met flesh.

Ducking his head behind his shield to avoid a spear from his left, Emrael thrust his sword over the right side of his shield, not bothering to aim for the opposing warrior's exposed face or neck. Instead, he released a burst of *infusori* as his weapon made contact. Raw power coursed through his sword and into the enemy Legionman, throwing him violently to the ground.

Emrael lunged, piercing steel mail to impale the downed man. He twisted his blade in his enemy's gut, then wrenched it free. He and Timan immediately took advantage of the gap in the enemy shield wall, stabbing the Barros Legionmen to either side of the fallen man who thrashed and screamed. Blood slicked the packed dirt of the road. Emrael struck home again, driving his sword into the neck of the enemy to his left in a spray of blood. Timan had killed the man on the other side, and together they created a sizable gap in the Barros ranks.

Before the stunned Iraeans could press the advantage and break through, men from the enemy reserves rushed forward with shields extended. Emrael stumbled as a shield slammed into him from the side. Timan was there in a flash, knocking the shield-bearer back with an *infusori*-bolstered kick, then sweeping beneath the shield with his blade to chop at the stumbling man's unprotected legs. The Barrosian went down with a cry, knocking his comrades back momentarily as well.

Emrael and Timan scrambled back to the safety of their own men as the well-trained Barros formation retreated several steps but solidified their shield wall once again.

Their attack had the intended effect, however, and slowly the Ire forces pushed the Barros Legionmen back toward the wagons, stepping over their dead and wounded foes. Spears and swords gored those that still clung to their weapons.

"Keep pushing!" Emrael screamed, knowing that once the Barros line hit the wagons, it would be a slaughter in their favor. But they shouldn't need to wait that long.

A chorus of shouts emanated from the right side of the road as Jaina's two hundred warriors burst from the trees, slamming into the Barros Legionmen from the flank. The Barrosian line broke, Legionmen and wagon teams alike throwing down their weapons and begging for mercy.

"Let them live!" Emrael shouted after a time, waving to his men.

He knew that the battle rage could be irresistible, and indeed he saw more than one of his men slash savagely at Barrosians who had cast down their weapons. Emrael held on to his shield and sword as he sprinted along his own line, ramming his shield into any of his men who still threatened the surrendering Barros Legionmen. Timan still followed him like a shadow.

"Let them live, Fallen take you," he shouted again, facing his own men. "Strip them, tie them to the wagons, and let's move!"

Some few of the Barros Legionmen had raced for the safety of the woods instead of surrender, but Jaina and her men had pursued them. Emrael climbed to stand on the seat of a wagon as his men secured the prisoners. From his vantage, he could see that Halrec had successfully subdued the lead wagon train as well. By some miracle, their attack had gone nearly according to plan.

When the prisoners that could walk had been lashed to the wagon train to march alongside, the two Iraean groups gathered on the road. Emrael walked toward his old friend with a fierce grin on his face.

"*Lord* Ire," Halrec said with a wry smile as they clasped hands. His right arm, shoulder, and face were covered in blood that didn't appear to be his. Apparently, he hadn't hesitated to fight against his old Legion. "We've secured all that surrendered. A handful escaped and rode toward Lidran."

Emrael nodded, but before he responded, the men behind him began beating their shields with their weapons. Soon, the whole war party drummed their exhilaration at having lived through another battle. His men were quickly becoming seasoned veterans.

"Just like we always dreamed, eh, Halrec?"

"Yeah . . . almost," Halrec replied, his face wrinkling with sadness as he stared at the dozens of corpses in Barros Legion uniforms littering the sides of the road. "Almost."

"We do what we must." Emrael surveyed the dozens of dead and grievously wounded men that would have been his friends and allies just a few short years ago. The sickly sweet smell of blood and the putrid scent of punctured innards permeated the air. "The Provinces started this war, and now we all must pay the price."

Gadford, stone-walled like most large, old towns in the Provinces, was built around the Barrosian side of the massive Whitehall Bridge. The town could easily hold ten thousand people, if not more, but Emrael doubted whether half that many lived there now. Most were likely the Legionmen stationed there and their families, besides. The War of Unification and subsequent castigation of the Iraeans shut down most of the trade that had flowed across the river, and now Gadford was principally a Barrosian military outpost.

"You sure you want to do this?" Toravin asked Emrael and Halrec one more time as they marched toward the gate at the head of what they hoped looked like a Barros supply party. Emrael and Halrec had met Toravin and the main portion of their army several leagues from the town, and had left Elle and the bulk of the men in the woods more than a league away while they led a smaller force in an attempt to impersonate the supply party they had just captured.

Halrec, who rode the only horse not hitched to a wagon, grimaced as he nodded. "Em's right, it's worth the risk. If we don't take Gadford quickly, Barros will hit us hard from behind and we'll be done for."

"Imbeciles," Jaina grumbled from where she marched to the other side of Emrael but didn't attempt to argue again. She had tried to convince them that going to the gate themselves was foolhardy, but Emrael wouldn't hear of it. He wouldn't ask his men to take a risk he wouldn't, not if we wanted to keep their loyalty. Halrec and Toravin had agreed with him on that point and had volunteered as well. They knew that their hold on the hearts of their newly formed Legionmen was tenuous.

They had unloaded most of the goods from the wagons, leaving just enough to disguise what now occupied them—Jaina's Imperators, with Toravin's best crossbowmen, lying beneath canvas sheets draped over the few supplies left in place.

Another five hundred men formed up around the wagons, dressed in uniforms and armor taken from the supply party they had ambushed the previous day. He put the men with the newest and least blood-smeared armor near the front of the party. It was a gamble, but was a chance to take the town quickly and with minimal losses. They had to try.

Halrec, dressed in his old Barros Captain Second armor, led the column. Emrael and Toravin marched right behind him, helmets on to conceal their faces. None of them carried shields, leaving them hung on the wagons so as to not arouse suspicion.

Emrael began to sweat as they neared the gates. Even if the garrison here was stripped nearly bare, they would easily slaughter him and his men outside the gate if they discovered their ruse.

Halrec showed none of Emrael's nerves as he rode his horse

calmly to the gate and called to the squad of Barros Legionmen perched on the ramparts three paces or so above the ground. They all held crossbows at the ready. "Oi! Open the gates. We have supplies from Lidran!"

The Barros men above the gate all turned to one wearing the uniform of a sergeant, who leaned farther over the wall to peer at Halrec, face wrinkled as he peered down at them. "And who in the Departed are you? We've had supply wagons not three days ago, and we've only ten companies left here. We got orders to keep the gates closed, ain't expecting anybody 'til next week!"

Emrael tensed, ready to spring their backup plan, charging the gate using a wagon as a battering ram. Halrec, however, put on his most arrogant officer's expression. "Open the damn gates, Sergeant. The Subcommander gave me the orders himself, I've got them right here."

He pulled papers from his saddlebag and waved them at the sergeant, who chewed on his lip for a moment before waving to his men. Plans changed for Legionmen such as him often, and he was trained to follow whatever officers like Halrec ordered, not to think for himself. Emrael's plan depended on it.

"All right, all right. We'll be down in a Fallen minute," the Barros sergeant grumbled. "I'll fetch men to unload the wagons."

Five men remained on top of the wall, crossbows relaxed.

Emrael edged back to the squad escorting the second wagon. "Crossbows still on the wall. Take your squad to deal with them as soon as you're inside the gates. *Quietly,* understand?"

The sergeant leading the squad, an Iraean he recognized but could not name, nodded his acknowledgement and passed the orders to his men.

The gate opened and Halrec dismounted to lead his horse through the gate. Emrael, Toravin, and a squad of their men preceded the first wagon into the small square on the other side.

The Barros Legion sergeant had evidently accepted their ruse completely, because eighty or so Barros Legionmen trotted into the square ready to unload goods from wagons into smaller handcarts. Most weren't even armed.

Still, Emrael waited until he had fifty men inside the gates. They didn't have enough men in serviceable Barros armor to continue the ruse beyond the first fifty, so the game was almost up. He pounded on the side of the first wagon three times with his fist, and he could hear the wagon drivers behind him doing the same.

At the signal, his men leapt to grab their shields, creating a ring of overlapped shields around the wagons in the space of two breaths. Dozens of Ire crossbowmen took positions behind the shields, and hundreds more of his Legionmen streamed through the gates. The plan was going far better than he had dared hope.

One of his men assigned to take the wall screamed as he took a quarrel to the leg, but within moments the Barros crossbowmen had been disarmed.

Caught by surprise, the bulk of the Barros Legionmen in the square were slow to raise the alarm, though a few now shouted as they ran into the town. Most hefted their weapons, but their eyes darted this way and that as they realized that they were badly out-numbered and unprepared for the battle that the Ire Legion had brought to their town.

Their plan hinged on attacking with overwhelming force before the Barros Legionmen could organize a defense. If he had to face the entirety of the Gadford garrison before the bulk of his army reached the city, he would be fighting two Barrosians for every man he had managed to get through the gate, or worse. This needed to end now.

He drew deeply on the *infusori* coil in a pouch on his belt and felt battle rage surging within him as he did. The scars on his arms glowed, and he knew his eyes would be blazing blue. As none of the enemy appeared to have a crossbow ready to fire, he let his shield hang at his side and pulled off his helmet so the Barrosians would know who they faced.

"Throw down your weapons and live," he shouted, half-expecting the Barrosians to laugh and lunge at him with the spears they carried. To his surprise, the Barrosians complied, dropping their weapons and kneeling, their hands behind their heads.

An idea came to him as he stared in near disbelief at the Barros men who had surrendered. He turned to his men. "Strip and secure them, but keep them close. I'll need them for what comes next."

To their credit, the Barros Legion did not give up the city easily even after he had breached their walls. Emrael hadn't expected them to, as they still had numbers nearly equal to his own. His men had been lucky to secure half the town while the Barros Legion was still rousing itself, but now they had fought to a stalemate.

He met with Toravin and Halrec in the main square as their men reported back to them periodically. Halrec gestured to the open gates. "We need to secure these gates while we wait for our reinforcements, then move on the main garrison quickly. They still have enough men to overwhelm us once they've recovered their wits."

Emrael nodded, but waited for a nod from Toravin before replying. "You're not going to like it, Hal, but there might a better way to end this without any more of our men dying."

Halrec's expression turned sour. "The prisoners?"

Emrael nodded. "I know it's not the honorable thing to do. But our honor is not worth our men's lives."

Halrec didn't respond, his lips pursed as he stared back at Emrael.

Toravin looked between them with an eyebrow raised, one hand on the hilt of his scabbarded sword. "Are we doing this or not?"

Emrael nodded, eyes still locked on Halrec. "Yes. Get the prisoners ready. Send someone to tell Jaina and her Imperators to stay out of sight. The Barrosians won't cooperate if they see the Ordenans with us."

A company of their men escorted fifty of the captive Barros Legionmen down the main avenue that led to the bridge. The Barrosians had been stripped naked and marched with their heads down, looking altogether dejected after a half-day of humiliation and exposure to the late summer sun. Toravin and Emrael marched side by side, shadowed by Jaina and Timan. Halrec had elected to stay behind to coordinate their own defenses.

The Ire Legionmen had cleared the town all the way to the bridge district, which included the Barros garrison, but even still they watched the two- and three-story brick and wood buildings carefully. Crossbows could wreak havoc on a column of soldiers marching in close formation.

The company arrived at their front line, where a wall of Iraeans with large shields held formation some hundred or so paces from where the Barrosians had erected a hasty barrier, tipping wagons and stacking wooden crates to block the road. Emrael's men reported that all other entrances to the bridge district had been similarly blockaded.

He couldn't see well past the barricade, but his scouts had braved enemy crossbow quarrels to climb onto rooftops. They estimated the remaining enemy forces at around eight hundred men.

He waved Toravin forward. "Tie the prisoners to poles—wagon shafts, whatever you can find. We'll march our line right up to them, using their own men to shield us."

Toravin quirked a small smile. "Then what?"

"Then I talk to them."

When all was arranged, Emrael and several squads marched toward the barrier just behind the line of prisoners. As expected, the Barros Legionmen didn't shoot.

When they stopped several paces from the barrier, he heard shouting from the other side. A wagon groaned, then moved to reveal two Barrosian officers, a Captain Second and a Captain Third. They both glared at Emrael, who still wore no helmet and held significant amounts of *infusori* that caused his hair to glow a faint blue, even in the full sunlight.

The Captain Second surveyed his naked, captured men. He spat, then addressed Emrael. "What do you want, you Iraean devil bastard?"

Emrael smiled. "I want to return your men to you, Captain."

Both officers' faces wrinkled in confusion. The Captain Second tipped his head forward as if trying to hear Emrael better. "You what?"

"I want to return your men to you."

The Captain Second hesitated, clearly hearing the mirth in Emrael's tone, but not knowing where it was going. "All right then, send them on through."

Emrael smiled wider. "Oh, we will, we will. But I have a price, of course. Surrender your weapons and exit the city. When you are outside the gates, we will send every one of these men we've captured to you, unharmed. You'll be free to join your Legion Commanders in Lidran."

The Captain Second scoffed. "You want me to hand you the city *and* give you our weapons? I think we'll take our chances. Reinforcements will be here within the day."

Emrael shrugged. "Mine will be here much sooner, Captain. Gadford will be mine, whether I have to spill your blood for it or not."

The Captain Second spat. "I'm no coward, neither are my men."

Emrael sighed. "Captain. I have over three hundred prisoners taken from your ranks and from the supply party we captured this morning. Each of them is being prepared to march in front of our shield wall, as these here currently are. Further fighting is not in the best interest of your men."

The Captain's lips pulled back in a snarl as he surveyed the prisoners Emrael had paraded in front of him. With a command this small, many of them were likely his friends, or at least close acquaintances. He was young enough that he had likely not seen much bloodshed in his years in the Barros Legion, if any at all. Despite the recent conflict in Whitehall—or maybe because of it—the Barros Legion had stayed on their side of the Whitehall Bridge, and otherwise hadn't seen real battle for many years.

"Wait!" the Captain shouted as Emrael turned to leave the parley. "Just wait." He looked to his Captain Third, who looked even more lost.

This was Emrael's best opportunity. It wouldn't be easy to dig eight companies out of a defensive position. He strode to the front line, drew his sword, and cut the ropes tying one of the Barros captives with a flourish.

"I'll give you this man as a token of good faith. Order your men to throw down their weapons and exit the city via the west river gate. We will make no move to stop you, nor harm you. Leave within the hour, and all our captives will join you. At the hour, I'll order an attack with your men strapped to our shields."

Emrael didn't wait for a response. He kicked the now-freed captive gently in the rump to get him started stumbling toward the Barros lines, then strode back the way he had come.

"Gather them all," Emrael told one of his men guarding the prisoners. "Keep the captives in plain sight until they surrender."

4

Emrael stood atop the low wall that surrounded Gadford, just beside the west river gate with Timan, Jaina, and a squad of Ire Legionmen, watching as unarmed Barros Legionmen filed out of the city.

He kept his face stoic, trying not to betray his incredulity that his plan had worked. He had thought they'd fight to the bitter end.

He spotted the Captain Second as he passed through the gates—the last man out, as an officer should be—and called out to him. "Captain!"

The Captain looked up, expression dejected and fearful.

Emrael raised his hands to show he meant no harm. "We will release the captives to you shortly, but I'd like you to take a message to Governor Barros. Tell him I won't let him sit this war out. He's got to choose a side. I don't want to continue fighting the Barrosians, but I will conquer you if I must. Tell him I want to talk, and I'll wait right here. His daughter Arielle is with me."

The Captain nodded, eyes full of shame. "I'll tell him. Holy Departed preserve me."

Emrael handed a sealed letter for Governor Barros to the Captain, then signaled to the men guarding the captive Barros Legionmen in the square below. They cut the ropes that bound each one, and the still-naked captives stumbled through the gate after their comrades.

As the Barrosians disappeared into the forest to trudge the ten or so leagues to Lidran, Emrael pulled the Captain Second leading his scouts, Dorvan, aside. "I need you to send a few messengers, men that can get through to our camp in the pass, even if Barros has men trying to stop them."

Dorvan just nodded. He knew his business. Like Toravin, he had spent many years in the woods on the Iraean and Barrosian side of the river, trafficking less-than-legal goods, evading the Legion and Watchers.

"Tell Voran that we've managed to piss Governor Barros off, and he should fortify the pass as much as he's able. Barros might try something sneaky like we've just done."

Dorvan nodded again.

"I also need you to get someone across the bridge to Whitehall. Tell Dorae that we have weapons and men to help him in his fight with the Watchers. Get a full report from him and tell him I'll be there within a week."

"Yes, Lord Ire. Anything else?"

Emrael spat and gestured toward the forest to the south. "Make sure those Barrosian bastards don't sneak up on us. I want to know when they leave Lidran, and how many they bring. Coward though he is, Barros can't let a move like this go unanswered."

The next morning, Emrael waved a hand and smiled at Elle as she passed through the south gate. She had been left with the bulk of their twenty-five thousand mobilized men in case the subterfuge hadn't gone according to plan.

She smiled briefly, then resumed her conversation with the tall, muscular woman in the armor of a Captain Second next to her, presumably the one leading the battalion assigned to accompany Elle herself. The officer still wore a Sagmynan uniform. Interesting that Toravin had trusted such a large command to a Sagmynan, and one that hadn't adopted the Ire Legion green at that.

He marched down the stairs to the courtyard, Jaina and Timan still following him like shadows. He wouldn't be surprised if Jaina had someone watching him as he slept, too.

Elle and the Sagmynan officer—his officer now, he reminded himself—seemed to be finishing their conversation, so he decided to wait politely. He idly reached into the pouch he kept hooked to his belt and drew *infusori* from the coil to the point that his scars and eyes glowed, then poured the energy back into it, over and over. The exercise had become something of an anxiety crutch for him.

Elle noticed his impatient fidgeting and rolled her eyes. "Em, this is Captain Second Sylar. Toravin put her in charge of the battalion assigned to me. Sylar, this is Emrael Ire."

Emrael extended his hand to the Captain Second, and she grasped it with a firm hand. "Honored, Lord Ire."

Emrael cocked his head to one side. "When did you join us, Sylar?"

Sylar squinted, wary. "Ah, just after you took the city, sir. I was there when you executed the governor. I joined soon after."

Emrael quirked his mouth to one side. "Why?"

"Why what, sir?"

"Why did you join us instead of the rest of the Sagmynans that held the Wells and harbor? If more of you had stayed with them, you might have starved us out of the city."

Sylar shifted uncomfortably, then said in a quiet voice, "I saw them, Lord Ire. I saw the monsters they created at the Citadel. Governor Sagmyn deserved what he got."

Emrael clapped her on the shoulder. "Good answer."

Sylar's expression turned mischievous, a slight smirk on her lips. "The land bounty and steady pay didn't hurt either, Lord Ire."

He laughed. "That's why we did it, Sylar. Please call me Emrael. Welcome to Gadford, we're glad to have you. The barracks on the other side of town is likely full by now, but we can commandeer empty buildings as needed. Report to Halrec—Subcommander Syrtsan. He'll have your orders and accommodations ready for your men. Then join us in the command building. Any of the sentries will be able to direct you."

Captain Second Sylar saluted before turning to lead her horse down the avenue toward the barracks.

"Your plan is going well, then," Elle asked once the officer had departed.

"Yes," he replied carefully.

Her lips twisted in a frown as she took in the aftermath of the morning's battle. "How many died?"

Emrael took a deep breath. "Too many. Nearly fifty of our men."

"And Barros men?" she asked coolly.

"Two hundred or so."

"What did you do with them?"

Emrael grimaced. "The Ire Legion dead are being buried just

outside the city. The Barros dead are being buried right beside them. I'm not a monster, Elle. I'm just doing what I must."

Angry now, he turned to walk toward the barracks, Jaina and Timan at his side. The clop of hooves told him that Elle followed close behind.

Toravin waited for them in the conference hall of the barracks command building, maps laid out on the large table.

"Good, you're here. Finally," he said as they entered. He shifted several painted wood figures sitting on top of the maps at various places between Lidran and Gadford. "Our scouts say Barros is marching this way with twenty battalions. We're roughly even in number. I doubt he attacks with us behind these walls."

"He won't attack as long as I'm here," Elle said confidently, taking a chair at the head of the table. "He's reasonable; he'll talk first. Even to Emrael."

Emrael rasped a sardonic laugh. "Have one of our squads fly a white flag at the north gate, but recall the scouts and put more men on the walls just in case. I don't want any surprises."

That evening, Emrael, Elle, Jaina, Toravin, and Halrec all stood on the platform above the north gate, watching as twenty thousand Barros Legionmen filled the clear area around Gadford. They stayed several hundred paces away from the walls, out of bowshot even for *infusori*-powered crossbows, and immediately began digging fortifications.

"How sure are we that they don't intend to attack?" Halrec asked, eyeing the fortifications. "Could they mean to besiege us?"

Toravin surveyed the Barrosians with a skeptical frown on his face. "They can't be that dumb. The only access to the bridge is within these walls—we can resupply from Iraea anytime we need. A siege would be pointless."

Halrec spat. "The Barrosian Commander and senior officers are not idiots. Best assume they know something we don't. They might even try to attack the pass to get at the Sagmyn Province while these hold us here."

Emrael nodded. "I've already sent a message to Voran. The pass should be secure for now."

Halrec and Toravin left to see to the town's defenses, leaving Emrael with Jaina, Elle, and Timan.

Jaina pointed. "Here they come."

A party of twenty or so men rode toward the north gate from the Barros camp, white flag flown. Emrael shouted to the Captain Third in charge of the gate, a lanky Iraean with a full red-brown beard. "Ready your men! Two squads to ride out with me!"

Horns blew and fully armored Ire Legionmen with shields, pikes, and crossbows rushed to fill the square. More crowded the walls to either side of the platform above the gate. He wasn't about to let Governor Barros use their peace party as a ploy to hold the gates open for an assault as Emrael had done to Gadford's garrison just days ago.

Elle grabbed Emrael's arm as her father and his men approached. "Let me do the talking, Em. If you want any chance at peace after taking this town, keep quiet."

"Hmm," he grunted.

Jaina growled as Governor Barros's party reined in fifty paces from the gate and planted their white flag. "They have a Malithii priest with them," she said softly. "The man next to the governor in the strange helmet. Be wary."

Emrael, Jaina, and Elle descended from the platform and took positions in the middle of two squads who accompanied them through the gates. They reined in a short distance from the Barrosian envoy, Elle in the lead, Emrael and Jaina flanking. Timan hung back with the Ire Legionmen.

Elle was the first to speak. "Father," she said simply.

Governor Barros, a massively fat man atop a very large draft horse, glared at Emrael before directing his anger at his daughter. "Arielle," he said, shaking his head, visibly emotional. "You sweet fool, what have you done?"

Elle lifted her chin, defiant. "What I must, Father. I'm fighting against undeniable evil, as should you."

The Barros Legion officers shifted in their saddles, grumbling here and there. Governor Barros's eyes bulged, incredulous. "What are you talking about, Elle? You've attacked us! *Me!* You've killed your countrymen, all for the sake of this miscreant." He gestured toward Emrael, disdain clear on his face.

Emrael could hold his tongue no longer. He pointed at the Malithii, who sat calmly astride his horse in full armor. "What do you know of that man next to you, Governor?"

"I know he didn't kill hundreds of my men attacking my supply party. I know he didn't raise a rabble army and execute the Governor of Sagmyn. I know he didn't brainwash my child!"

He was screaming by the end of his rant, spittle flying from his swollen, bearded lips. Emrael nudged his horse closer. Jaina followed close at his heels.

When Emrael was within just a few paces of Governor Barros, he calmly peeled off his gloves, then the bracers that covered his arms. Last, he removed his helmet and hooked it on the pommel of his saddle. He pulled up his sleeves to point to his scars, tracing where they curved and slashed across his hands, arms, and face. "I think you know very little, Governor. These foreigners attacked the Citadel, killed thousands while they held it. They enslaved my brother and other Crafters. They carved their runes into my flesh. They turned captives into mindless monsters, worse than dead. What do you know about that?"

The governor's eyes flicked toward the Malithii.

Emrael leaned forward. "Or perhaps you do know what kind of man sits next to you. Maybe he's taken something dear to you, as they did to me? I'll kill this one for you. I'll kill them all if you'll join me."

Emrael stared into Governor Barros's eyes, intense, earnest. Governor Barros chewed his cheek, sweating.

Elle moved her horse forward. "Emrael, enough."

As if startled out of a trance, Governor Barros blinked at the sound of his daughter's voice. "Join you? *Join you?*" he sneered, incredulous. "You're going to the hangman's noose, boy!"

Elle began to say something, but Emrael lost his temper. "The Sagmyn Province is mine. I have twenty thousand Iraeans and as many Sagmynans that have joined me. The Ordenans are with me, and soon I will have the entirety of the Iraean Kingdom. This is your last chance. I can protect you from the Watchers, the Corrandes, and their dark priests."

Governor Barros laughed, shaking his head. "Your grip on Sagmyn is tenuous, boy, and the Ordenans don't have forces to spare from their war over the Aerwyn Ocean. The Iraean Lords hate you as much as they hate the Corrandes—maybe more. You'll be dead within the year. Assuming we don't dig you out of this town and kill you right now."

Emrael smiled, anger coursing through him. "You'll do no such thing. We both know you're a coward. There will be no middle ground, Governor. Either you join us in fighting Corrande, or we will bury you. You have until tomorrow at dawn to give your answer."

He spat at the smirking Malithii priest as he turned his horse and trotted back through Gadford's gates.

The moon cast a blue sheen on the surface of the Stem River, making it look like a torrent of *infusori*. Thousands of stars twinkled from horizon to horizon, reminding Emrael how little he knew about the world. How strange to think that he didn't even know the true nature of the moon and stars.

He walked the wall around Gadford alone, surveying the campfires of the Barrosians that surrounded the town. His eyes were drawn to the circle of fires and blue glow of *infusori* coils that surrounded a sprawling tent that undoubtedly belonged to Governor Barros. That smug Malithii bastard wouldn't be far from the governor.

Elle was furious with him, and the way he had handled the treatise with her father. She still hadn't spoken to him. She'd really be upset at what he planned to do next.

He reached a dark section of wall near the river. They didn't have sufficient coils or torches to light every stretch of wall, which was just as well. The bright light of the moon would reveal anyone trying to cross the clearing, and his men's eyes would have been blinded by lights on the wall anyhow. Toravin had wisely made sure their men guarding the wall were stationed well away from any torch or lighting coil.

Timan and the other Imperators waited for him at the bend where the wall turned to parallel the river. All were dressed in black, with no metal showing that would reflect light and give away their positions in the darkness.

Timan had been the one to suggest a night raid on the Malithii priest and any other Malithii that might be with him. Emrael had been quick to agree. If they could kill the priest, who was almost certainly extorting Barros in some fashion, the governor might be more likely to join Emrael. It was his last, best shot at resolving the conflict with Barros without any more of his men—or Barros men—being killed.

"Where's Jaina?" Emrael asked.

Timan shrugged. "I did not tell her. I could send for her . . . I do not think she would approve of this raid, however."

Emrael grunted a laugh. "You're right. Leave her to sleep in peace. Let's get this done."

The Ire Legionmen watching this section of the wall had been more than happy to take a few coins to make sure that everyone knew to expect the raiding party back within the next few hours. The last thing he needed was to be shot by his own men upon their return. Just in case, Timan was leaving an Imperator on the wall to wait for them.

When everything had been arranged, he and the Imperators knelt to grab the edge of the wall and dropped to the ground a few paces below. They landed lightly and ran along the riverbank, skirting the fires and the sentries the Barrosians had undoubtedly posted.

They crept through the woods behind the Barros camp until they could see the tents, including the tent that they thought to be the governor's. Legionmen with crossbows and short pikes formed a perimeter around the camp but were easy to avoid, as most stood within the circles of light cast by the numerous campfires or by *infusori* coils hanging from posts around the largest tents. They were blind to the night, confident that their enemy would stay safe behind the walls of Gadford. Who would do something as stupid as raiding an army of twenty thousand men, after all?

Timan and his Imperators fanned out, and the occasional rustle in the brush told Emrael that they were dealing with sentries posted farther from the tents. No cries escaped the lips of any of the Barros guards. These Imperators were as good as Jaina and Timan claimed.

Anxiety roiling through his chest, Emrael crept forward until he could see the people moving around in the camp. Almost immediately, he spotted the Malithii priest. He sat talking quietly beside a fire with two more men in the traditional robes of the Malithii, in front of a modest tent situated at the edge of the camp, several hundred paces to the side of the governor's and thus well outside the extra security. In fact, Emrael couldn't see a single guard posted near their tent. Excellent.

He found a good place to observe his target, a small depression in the soil surrounded by thick undergrowth. Shortly, the Malithii extinguished their fire and retired to their tent. He considered finding Timan and his Imperators before attacking the tent, but decided that he'd be better able to avoid detection alone.

I can handle three at once, if I surprise them. If not . . .

Crickets played their quiet nocturnal orchestra as he crept from his hiding spot to stalk to the back side of the tent. He pulled *infusori* from a coil in his belt pouch, wishing he knew how to keep his eyes and scars from glowing. He'd have to ask Jaina about a potential mitigation, though as far as he could tell, other mages only had to deal with the irises of their eyes glowing when they held large amounts of *infusori*.

A quick slash of his dagger opened the rear wall of the canvas tent. He pushed a small amount of *infusori* into a dull coil as he tossed it inside, just before he darted in himself, blade at the ready.

None of three bundles of blankets moved as he stepped in. The glowing *infusori* coil lay on the ground, casting long, disorienting shadows. Something felt wrong.

He stooped to plunge his dagger into the nearest pile of blankets. Empty. Panic surged through him.

Had he walked right into another trap?

He snatched up the coil he had thrown and pulled the *infusori* back into himself until he was once again shrouded in darkness. A few quick steps carried him through the canvas flap he had created at the back of the tent and into the moonlit night. All was quiet.

Senses on high alert, he stalked quickly but quietly back through the forest. Just as he began to think he would escape undetected, an odd hissing in the air made him jump. Cold metal slapped his back as he tucked and dove to roll over one shoulder. *Infusori* ripped through him, but he was able to rebuff the attack before it could harm him.

He sprinted immediately upon regaining his feet, but another hiss and a copper cable coiled itself around his leg. His pants began to smoke as the Malithii on the other end sent a surge of *infusori* through the weapon.

Rather than combat the surge of energy, Emrael drank it in, reconverting the heat into pure *infusori* without needing to think about what he did—it just came naturally in the unthinking chaos of a struggle to the death. He could feel the Malithii priest on the other end of the copper cable, a ball of fear and fury. A source of *infusori*.

The Malithii who had thought to trap him now gasped and whimpered as Emrael overwhelmed his will and drank the *infusori* that was his life source. Shouts from the trees on either side of Emrael told him that others—the other Malithii, Barros guards, or perhaps Timan and his Imperators—were converging on him. He drew his sword as he depleted the Malithii's life source and shook himself free of the copper-cable weapon.

For the first time, he could feel the difference between multiple types of *infusori* energy pulsing within him—the pure, clean, cold *infusori* pulled from the coil; the complex, chaotic energy stolen from the Malithii priest; the warm, familiar pulse of his own *infusori*, his life energy.

Two Malithii—including the one who had accompanied Governor Barros, he thought—emerged from the trees at a run, copper-cable weapons in hand. Emrael, full of *infusori* and feeling immortal, stood his ground, sword in hand. The Malithii slowed, then stopped a safe distance from Emrael. They glanced at each other, neither willing to be the first to attack.

Men shouted in the woods, most seeming to come from the direction of the Barros camp. Timan and several of his Imperators emerged from the trees to either side of Emrael. Without hesitation and in beautifully coordinated silence, the Imperators surrounded and attacked the Malithii. Emrael stayed where he was, watched as an Imperator he didn't know by name was struck in the neck by a Malithii cable and immediately convulsed, dropped to the ground. Timan lunged, stabbing the Malithii through the heart. Both the Malithii and the fallen Imperator lay still on the ground.

Four Imperators circled the last Malithii as Timan tended to his fallen comrade. The shouts from the Barros camp drew nearer.

The Malithii priest raised his voice to address Emrael, ignoring the Imperators that surrounded him. "It would be better for you to join us, Brother Ire. Better by far. The Prophet has arrived, and with him the hordes of the Hidden Kingdoms."

The *infusori* within Emrael screamed to be released. He walked purposefully through the circle of Imperators to raise his sword in challenge. The Malithii shrugged slightly before lashing out with an impossibly quick strike of his cable weapon. *Infusori* cracked in the air as Emrael dodged, just enough that the cable snapped to the side of his face. He countered with an upward swing of his blade that caught the Malithii's forearm. He felt the crunch of metal cutting through bone.

The Malithii wasted no time in striking with his own sword despite having just taken a crippling wound in his other arm. Emrael was forced to throw himself backward and to the side, rolling over one shoulder to avoid the attack. As he regained his feet, an Imperator thrust his sword into the Malithii's back and twisted the blade viciously as he withdrew. The Malithii choked on a scream as blood and viscera leaked from his opened sternum. He died clawing at the open wound.

All dozen or so of the Imperators who had joined him and Timan had gathered around them. They bounced nervously as Barros Legionmen with torches drew near enough that they could see them clearly through the thick forest. Timan and one other, a woman, carried the downed Imperator between them.

"Oram is dead," Timan said quietly as he drew near. A spike of guilt seared Emrael, and he moved to take the Imperator's body from Timan. His cousin refused, however, waving Emrael back.

"We should go, quickly, before the Barros men find us. My mages will stall them while we escape," Timan said curtly, already motioning to his Imperators.

5

Emrael, Timan, and the Imperators retreated at a fast jog. Timan and the Mage-Healer with curly black hair and dark skin carried the dead Imperator without showing any signs of tiring. Men shouted and horses crashed through the dense forest somewhere behind them, but they managed to stay ahead of any pursuit.

When they reached the river just short of where the clearing around Gadford began, Timan called a halt. "Kemme, Noro: take the lead. Orris will be waiting where we climbed down. Tell him we need rope to pull Oram up."

The Imperators filed out until only Emrael remained. He was happy enough to take the rear, as there had been no sound or sign of pursuit for the last half a league or so. While he waited, he reached into his pouch to push most of the *infusori* he still held into the gold coils he carried there. For the first time in the hours since he had consumed the life source of the Malithii priest, he felt like himself. Rage and anxiety well beyond what was normal even for a night such as this bled from him in an instant. Perhaps there was something to Jaina's warnings against consuming the life source of other human beings, especially twisted men like the followers of the Fallen.

As the last Imperators reached the wall, he moved to join them. Before he stepped past the last tree at the edge of the clearing, however, his legs were swept out from under him. He hit the turf and rolled instinctively, coming to his feet in a crouch, belt knife in hand. He looked frantically from side to side, straining his peripheral vision in the darkness to see who had attacked him.

Too late, he felt a surge of *infusori* building behind him. Something hit his arm, and his dagger flew from numb fingers. He tried to duck again as he turned, but his attacker tackled him from behind, snaked an arm around his neck, and pulled tight.

Surprise at not being stabbed to death quickly gave way to panic as the blood flow to his brain ceased. His head throbbed, his vision grew bright at the periphery. He twisted and clawed at the face of his attacker, to no avail. He opened himself to the attacker's *infusori*, tried to ingest it and thus snuff out the other's life, but found himself blocked.

"Did you think I would not know, Emrael?" Jaina's voice murmured into his ear.

Shock warred with relief as he realized he hadn't been attacked by a Malithii priest, but Jaina didn't release her hold. He tapped her arm in submission the way he had during training sessions at the Citadel, but still she held her choke.

"You think you are so strong that a Malithii could not kill you? Think again, boy."

His vision began to darken, and his weight began to sag against her arm as he lost consciousness. Jaina eased the pressure just a bit, and he gulped in air as his vision returned slowly.

"You got one of my Imperators killed, Emrael. Consider this a free lesson—you are nowhere near good enough to take risks like you did tonight."

She threw him to the ground, kicked him in the ribs, and jogged off to pull herself over the wall effortlessly.

Emrael waited on horseback one hundred paces from the south gate as the sun rose over the mountains that separated the Barros Province from the Sagmyn Province. Elle, Timan, Halrec, Toravin, and six Imperators flanked him, all on horseback. The gate behind them stood open, with Iraean Legionmen blocking the entrance with a shield wall three men deep. Jaina was conspicuously absent—she had refused to accompany him after the midnight raid that had resulted in Oram's death.

Governor Barros and ten men of his own walked their horses slowly from their camp to the south. The governor had deep, dark bags beneath his eyes, and the officers in his group glared at Emrael, faces pinched with stress. They stopped their horses and sat, silent. Emrael was content to wait.

Finally, Governor Barros spoke, his voice as haggard as his face. "You fool. You have no idea what you've done." He sounded dejected more than angry.

Emrael exchanged a glance with Elle, who had concern written all over her face. She nodded.

He looked back to Governor Barros. "I'm sorry to have attacked your camp, Governor. But I'm sure you are aware, I hurt none of your men. I've done nothing but rid you of the Malithii. You are better off without them, whatever you choose."

Governor Barros coughed out a laugh, shaking his head. "You idiot. I have no idea how you've done what you've done, capturing a province, convincing these men to join you, when you clearly know so little. Do you really think that those three are the only ones, boy? They and the Watchers are as thick as flies on a carcass in my province. You have only kicked an anthill. *My* anthill."

Elle urged her horse forward a few steps. "Father, let us help. Emrael and the Ordenans can fight them. We can win."

"You can't beat them, my dear girl," Governor Barros replied, tears in his eyes. "You will be dead within the season, as will I if Corrande and his foreigner priests think I had anything to do with this. I'm begging you, Arielle, abandon this foolishness and let me protect you. You'll find nothing but death and despair on the path this boy treads."

Elle shook her head, tears wetting her cheeks. "I can't, Father. Emrael may not be perfect, but what we are doing is right. We can't roll over to Corrande and his Malithii dogs. I've seen what they do to people."

Governor Barros nodded as if he had expected her answer. He said no more, simply turned to leave.

"Governor," Emrael shouted. "There will be no peace, this time. If you do not join us, you are against us."

Governor Barros didn't turn around, didn't even acknowledge that Emrael had spoken.

Jaina waited in the officers' dining hall of Gadford's Legion command building. Oram lay on the table, wrapped in heavy canvas so only his face showed. The canvas had been painted with the personal marks of the other Imperators, and with a large symbol representing the Silent Sisters—the same two hollow circles intersected by a black circle that each Imperator had inked on their skin.

The body had begun to stink despite the preparations they had performed, a regular procedure when fighting in the Dark Lands. Jaina wanted to make sure Emrael and the others were reminded of the cost of their folly.

Heavy footsteps in the adjoining lobby announced their return.

Emrael stepped into the room and blinked, obviously taken aback by the sight of Oram's body on the table. His nose wrinkled in distaste until he saw Jaina staring at him. The boy had learned to kill, to send men to their deaths, but was unused to dealing with the consequences on a personal level. It was time that changed.

Toravin, Elle, Halrec, and Timan—the insubordinate son of a bitch—filed in. They shuffled their way to seats around the table, clearly uncomfortable.

Emrael shifted in his seat so he could see Jaina over the body. "Why have you called us here, Jaina? Is this really necessary?" he asked, nodding at Oram's body.

Jaina set her jaw. "Yes, I do think it necessary, Emrael."

"Look, I'm sorry for the loss of your Imperator, Jaina. I certainly didn't mean for him to die, but his death may have prevented the deaths of thousands of our men."

Jaina stared at Emrael in disbelief for a moment, then laughed. "Emrael Ire, I mourn the loss of Oram, yes. But my anger is not for him—it is for your stupidity in trying to solve every problem yourself. This body on the table could just as easily have been yours. Should you perish, our entire cause will crumble, and tens of thousands that follow you will die, or worse. You do not have the luxury of only considering yourself any longer. This war, this movement, depends on you staying alive."

Emrael stared at Oram for a moment, a frown on his face, forehead furrowed. When he looked up, however, his eyes now glowed with anger and more than a hint of *infusori*. "While I can, and when I must, I will fight with my men. I have more to gain by earning their respect than will be lost if I die. Alive or dead, I must be seen as a hero. And if I die, one of you can lead the armies in my place."

"And yet, you didn't think to use—or even consult—any of us. We have risked just as much as you have, with considerably less to gain. We cannot be effective if we are kept in the dark."

Emrael clenched his jaw, but soon took a deep breath and looked around the room at everyone gathered. Despite the tension, everyone met his gaze. Good. "You're right, Jaina. You deserved to know, and to help. All of you. I'll not act alone again if I can help it."

She favored her understudy with a small smile before looking around the table. "You convinced Governor Barros to stand down, then? Join us, perhaps?"

Emrael grimaced. "Not exactly. He's scared, weak, and won't risk Corrande and the Malithii turning on him." He stopped, cast a worried glance at Elle. Her expression hadn't changed from the pinched, angry look she had worn the entire time. Interesting.

It was difficult to stop herself from smirking, but she did. Just barely. "Whoever could have anticipated such a reaction? What do you plan now?"

Emrael's eyes narrowed as he grew angry again. She liked that the boy had fire, even if it was excessive at times. "Same as we have planned, Jaina. We fight. Barros was never going to join us. Now he knows we'll retaliate if he moves against us. He'll sit this out just as his father did the War of Unification. We raise our army in Iraea, and we crush Corrande."

Elle rapped her fingernails on the tabletop loudly and shook her head. "No. I don't think my father can sit out this time. I think Corrande has a stronger hold on him than we know, and I think you are foolish to underestimate him."

Jaina hid a small smile. She could see why Maira liked the girl, especially when she stood up to Emrael.

Emrael clenched his jaw as he thought, as he often did. "We'll just have to make sure the road between Sagmyn and Gadford is secure, then. The Iraean Lords Holder that control the southern bank should be able to keep Barros's Legionmen out of the province without too much trouble. They are still the key to victory, not Barros."

This was the opening Jaina had been waiting for. "You are so sure that the Lords Holder of Iraea will stand up to Barros if he tries to land thousands of troops in deserted stretches of the riverbank?" She laughed to drive her point home.

"She's right," Toravin said, looking first at her then to Emrael. "Lord Holder Syrtsan and Lord Holder Raebren won't stop him, not as things stand. They are almost part of the Barros Province, these days. You will need to do something drastic to convince them."

"Then we do something drastic to convince them, Tor." Emrael pounded a fist on the table and shied away slightly when Oram's body shifted. "If the Lords Holder won't defend their land, I'll deal with them too." He looked at Halrec, as the Lord Holder Syrtsan, who controlled a large stretch of the river, was his estranged uncle. Halrec raised his eyebrows and quirked a small shrug but said nothing.

Emrael turned back to Elle, his expression plaintive now. "Perhaps you can still attempt to convince your father, or even the Lords Holder?"

"It's worth a try," she conceded after a pause, though she did not sound confident. "I do know several of the Lords Holder's heirs. I'll try."

Jaina lifted her chin slightly, staring Emrael in the eye. "You'll be lucky to hold even the Sagmyn Province with the troops you have, and now you must hold Gadford as well. You cannot know what the Iraeans will do. You may consider approaching my people."

Emrael grimaced. "At what cost, Jaina? We have a bare handful of Imperators—"

"Fifty Imperators is *not* a 'bare handful.' The Citadel would still belong to the Malithii if not for them, and I cannot imagine what your mother had to promise the Council to get that many. There are fewer than a thousand active Imperators, Emrael."

He frowned in thought. "Be that as it may, they won't win a war for us. We need soldiers, an army. Why would Ordena help us? What would it cost?"

Jaina tried not to show her nerves. She hadn't dared send a request to her Order for a larger force without talking to Emrael first. It was best to approach the idea carefully, get him used to it before pushing harder. "They—we—hate the Malithii more than even you do, Emrael. When they learn the extent to which the Malithii are involved here in the Provinces, they will send help. They will do it for their faith, and for the coin. Though . . . they will likely want a trade agreement as well. Land for a trading settlement, perhaps."

Timan nodded. It was no secret among Ordenans that the Order and the Imperial Army both wanted a foothold in the Provinces and anywhere else they could manage it.

A glare was Emrael's only reply for a prolonged, awkward moment. Then finally, "No land, and I don't have money enough to bribe them." He pointed a finger at her. "No Ordenan military in Iraea or Sagmyn without my permission. Or Barros. Not yet. Corrande is fair game if you can convince them to attack, but I'll not have those bastards laying claim to our land."

Jaina breathed deep, full of frustration even as she tried to keep her face still. "Emrael, you're hoarding land you don't even hold yet. I can negotiate for you, secure the most powerful empire in the world as your ally, and you'd not have to give them anything but a promise of a small share of future spoils."

His grey eyes never blinked. "I'll not negotiate from a position of weakness. We are not fighting one empire just to become the puppet of another."

She held the stare for a long moment, but Emrael finally turned to address the rest of those gathered. "Now, how many men can we take to Whitehall? And somebody get this fucking body out of here."

6

Emrael led ten thousand of his men across the bridge to For-angerr, the small town on the Iraean foot of the bridge, only a few miles west of Whitehall. Only one battalion was mounted, while the other nine were infantry. Some men had been outfit-ted with traditional Iraean gear: teardrop shields, long spears, and heavy swords. Others had the circular shields from the Sagmyn or Barros Legion, or square shields stolen from the Barros Legion, along with the shorter swords and spears favored in the southern Provinces.

He had left another ten thousand to hold Gadford and sent five thousand back to reinforce the pass between the Sagmyn and Bar-ros provinces. He would have liked to take more with him for the coming campaign in Iraea, but he could not risk losing any of the territory he already held.

His friends rode at his side, or close behind. Jaina, Timan, Elle, Halrec, and Toravin—all in armor save Elle. As they left the bridge behind and turned east on the road that led to Whitehall, Emrael noticed groups of tents pitched in the woods to the north of the road, away from the river. Single tents and small clusters soon became canvas-and-sackcloth villages.

Emrael turned to Toravin. "What in Glory's name is this?"

"The cost of war, Ire." Toravin's lips twisted into his ever-ready sardonic smile. "The Watchers have attacked Whitehall several times, or hadn't you heard? Many of the inhabitants of the upper city have fled rather than risk being caught in the fighting. The Barros Legion has stopped the *riffraff* from crossing to their side of the river, so they stay here. Nowhere else to go."

Emrael had read Dorae's letters detailing the retaliatory attacks from the Watchers, but busy as he had been with problems of his own, hadn't fully understood the dire nature of the situation for the inhabitants of Whitehall. "Don't they have anywhere safer to go here in Iraea? They'll starve or freeze this winter if they stay here."

Toravin actually laughed. "You think the nobles are going to invite these lot to their Holdings? They've already got more people than they can support on their lands, what with the reparation taxes and the Provincial order outlawing clearing any more land. They're not risking the Provinces' displeasure to help these."

"Even now that the Watchers have been thrown out of the Norta Holding? None have moved to help Dorae?"

"They've been thrown out of Whitehall, Ire. The Watchers and Corrande garrisons have been bolstered elsewhere. Whitehall could be flanked, and Absent Gods know that won't go well for us. *If* any other Iraean Lords Holder are going to join us, it'll be after we show them we can win more than one city."

Emrael was quiet for a long moment. Unbidden, the memory of his father's eyes, his intense green-eyed stare, flashed in his mind. Janrael had always wanted to do something about the Iraeans' sub-jugation to the Provinces, and now Emrael had the chance to act where his father had not.

Elle and Halrec were also looking around at all of the displaced citizens, concern and outrage on their faces. Jaina and Timan saw them, scanned them for possible threats, but no emotion showed on their faces.

He turned back to Toravin. "We've got to move quickly, then. If we push the Watchers out of another Holding, the Lord Holder may be forced to join us whether he wants to or not. Hopefully the others follow suit. But we're doing something for these people, Tor, and soon. They can't live like this. We will help them, and they can help us."

Toravin nodded and smiled, a broad true smile that bared all of his teeth. "Aye. That's a plan I'd fight for. The Lords Holder won't welcome a fight on their land, however. Some might even side with the Watchers."

Whitehall looked more like one of the abandoned ruins from the War of Unification than a living city. Emrael could hardly believe that this was the same place he had left just a few short months before. Entire swaths had been burned to nothing, and pathetic tent villages had been erected in the cleared ashes and wreckage.

The city was still obviously in Dorae's control, however, with hundreds of armored Norta men visible all along the stone ramparts of the walls that guarded the mountain pass to Corrande, and around Whitehall itself. The gate that barred the pass had been reinforced many times over with heavy timbers and steel sheets. Huge blocks of granite had been piled behind the gate doors so they could no longer be forced open. Large stones and cauldrons perched on the walls above the gates, ready to crush or scald those below. They had obviously seen heavy fighting, and recently, judging by the bandages visible on many of the soldiers.

Not all was going poorly in the city, however. Many buildings were being reconstructed, and everyone Emrael saw looked relatively clean and well-fed. Fully charged *infusori* coils blazed blue at every guard post and at the corner of every major avenue. He had never seen such an opulent lighting display, not even in Sagmyn, famous for the wealth of the merchants who made their homes there. Surely Dorae would be better off selling that *infusori* to fund his defense efforts.

Dorae's soldiers met them at the low half-wall that surrounded the city proper. They watched Emrael and his ten thousand with flat stares, and were somewhat curt when they spoke at all but allowed them into the city and to Whitehall without issue.

The Lord of Whitehall himself met them in the square in front of the keep, a coterie of soldiers and various advisors close behind him. Many looked to be either drunk, hungover, or both.

"Welcome!" Dorae shouted, boisterous and with the customary wild look in his eyes. More grey streaked his dark, shoulder-length hair than the last time Emrael had seen him. He looked tired, but strong. Hard. "I only have room for about a hundred of you scoundrels in the keep, the rest will have to arrange their own lodging." He swept his hand grandly, gesturing at the war-ravaged city. "Luckily, we have plenty of vacancies at the moment. Can't imagine why."

Emrael exchanged a carefully amused look with Toravin while Dorae cackled. The man took some getting used to.

"We'll set our men up somewhere close to the keep, if that's all right, and Halrec will coordinate with your commanders. Our Ire Legionmen can help rebuild while we're here, and we'll put two of our battalions on the wall at any given time. It looks like you could use the help."

Dorae stopped smiling and tilted his head to look at Emrael sideways. "*Ire* men, are they now? I seem to remember most of those men coming from my Hold lands. Most of the weapons and armor, too."

"Why do you think we came back to help you?" Emrael asked, expression serious. He stepped close to the Lord of Whitehall. "I will remember what you've done and will pay you back with interest. But this war is far from over, and bigger than Whitehall. Bigger than me. We have much to discuss."

Dorae breathed deep and nodded, his crooked smile back in an instant. "Yes. Full of plans, you are. I suppose I'll just have to be satisfied with my lot, and grateful you've come to help us in our lonely war. Come, get inside. My steward will see to your horses and take your things to a room. Then we'll hear this plan of yours."

He turned to one of the soldiers in his coterie. "Tald, arrange for Lord Ire's men to be housed and fed, please."

As they made their way through the keep, Emrael noticed that the entire building was lit by fully filled *infusori* coils.

"Dorae, I noticed that you have coils lighting much of the city. Why spend so much for lighting when you could use the *infusori* to buy food, weapons?"

Dorae gestured wildly at the city behind him. "Nobody to trade with after Barros and Lord Holder Syrtsan blockaded the river, Ire. The people need light. I have light. So I give them light."

When they had handed their things to the waiting servants, Dorae led them to a room with a table for about a dozen.

Emrael, Elle, Jaina, Toravin, and Halrec all took seats on one side, Dorae and his advisors on the other. While introductions were made, servants brought food. Pheasants and sage hens, paired with potatoes, leeks, and a dark stout ale.

Dorae smirked at Emrael. "Not a meal befitting the esteemed company, but it's what we have left. More than we have left, really. Most of the city is eating nothing but stored oats and barley. The other Holdings have refused to trade, as have Corrande and Barros, obviously."

Elle perked up at talk of trade. "Tell me, my Lord Norta. Do you have seafaring ships?"

Dorae's brows drew down; the corners of his mouth twitched upward. "Yes . . . but I don't have nearly enough to risk your father's blockade, Lady Barros."

Elle exchanged a look with Jaina and continued after the Ordenan woman nodded. "And if we can provide safe passage, or even have other merchant ships dock here? Can you trade copper or *infusori* for food?"

Dorae grew quiet, serious. Emrael thought his eyes might have shone with unshed tears, but that could have just been his imagination. "Girl, I can flood you with *infusori*. We can't use the *infusori* fast enough, the Wells are practically shut down. We can't trade it; merchants want nothing to do with the war here. We don't have the Craftings to use it, none that will help us in our war, leastwise. My people are going to starve come winter."

He looked from Emrael, to Jaina, back to Elle. "Can you really guarantee safe passage with your father? The ships we sailed didn't even make it out of the river."

"The Ordenan navy may be able to help," Jaina interjected. "I can send for an emissary. It would be a small thing to protect your trading ships. Your captains will have to make it to the sound themselves, but Ordena has a significant interest in protecting free trade in open waters."

She paused before adding, "The Ordenans, they may require payment, however. *Infusori* stores should suffice, but they may want an agreement for *infusori* trade well into the future."

Emrael chuckled and shook his head as he leaned back in his chair. "There's always an 'agreement' with you Ordenans. Let me guess, something like half of Whitehall's *infusori* trade in perpetuity?"

Jaina shrugged, unperturbed. "Perhaps. I do not speak for the Ordenan Empire."

"Fine, have the Ordenans come and we'll negotiate a deal. Dorae, don't agree to anything without me or Halrec here, you understand?"

"Yes, my lord," Dorae said, offering a mocking bow from his chair.

Emrael flushed, but didn't apologize. "We will be well served to negotiate together."

"Aye, makes fair sense, though I won't wait for you if it means I can feed my people. Now, tell me about your plan to get these Watcher bastards off my back."

Emrael stood to pace the room, finally stopping beside a map of Iraea that had been laid out on one end of the table. He leaned over Jaina's shoulder, then thought better of it as she subtly feinted toward his groin with her elbow. Chuckling, he instead went to the empty foot of the table and pulled the map toward him.

He planted a finger on the Tarelle lands to the north of the Norta Holding. Tarelle and Norta were two of three Holdings that shared a border with Corrande, drawn directly down the spine of the northern Duskan mountain range. The third Holding, Paellar, occupied the northernmost portion of the border with the Corrande Province, and was the tightest in Corrande's pocket.

"How many Watchers are in Larreburgh?"

"Probably a battalion or two, but you'll have to pass Durran, and Raeic, and they'll have a battalion each. And they can have more in Larreburgh with only a few days of warning. They'd have five thousand Watchers waiting for us, and Tarelle men besides."

"I don't mean to give them that much warning," Emrael said. "We'll have to cover the distance between here and Larreburgh more quickly than word can be sent ahead, then fight at the end of the trip. That means only the fittest and best outfitted come. I'll take five thousand of our best and leave the rest here to bolster your defenses under Halrec's command. I need Toravin to guide our scouts and make sure that we only have to fight two thousand once we get there, not five."

He didn't say it, but he was sure Dorae didn't miss the other reason he was leaving Halrec to command the men from Emrael's Legion instead of Toravin. Toravin had never given him any reason to doubt his loyalty, but he had left Voran in Sagmyn for the same reason. Both had a much longer history with Dorae than they did with him, and if either one decided to split from Emrael's cause, a significant number of the Iraean men in the Ire Legion were likely to go with them. He liked Dorae well enough but wasn't about to give him an opportunity to commandeer his followers. The man was unpredictable at best.

He needed time to solidify his power and reputation before he could trust any of them fully. Halrec was one he could trust, though they didn't always see eye to eye. And of course Elle, and Ban. Always Ban. Jaina and his mother . . . he trusted them to a point, but knew that the Ordenan Empire had its hooks in them. Time would tell.

Dorae scratched his nose. "You take risks, Emrael. Risks that even I would not agree to, if I had any choice. Absent Gods know I hate Tarelle as much as anyone. He's a rat like his father before him. The Tarelles and Paellars joined the Corrandes to oppose your grandfather in the War of Unification, and the current Lord Holder Tarelle sent men to support my father when Toravin and I raised our first rebellion. I'd happily gut the man. But are you certain the risk is justified? We need allies, not more enemies."

"If we sit here in Whitehall, they will do the same as they have always done. We don't have the resources or time to fight a war of attrition, not with Corrande and his Watchers knocking on your doorstep, to say nothing of Barros. Taking Tarelle will show the others they can't ignore us and wait for the Watchers to deal with us."

Dorae wagged his head back and forth, lips pursed. "Could work. Could get us killed. Like I said, we don't have much choice, do we? We unite Iraea or we die."

All eyes in the room turned to Emrael. Elle bit her lip. Halrec smiled only on one side of his face. Emrael knew that meant he felt deeply uncomfortable. Jaina showed no emotion.

Emrael placed his hands on the table and leaned down to look over the map that showed the seven Holdings of Iraea: Norta, Tarelle, Paellar, Ire, Raebren, Syrtsan, and Bayr. This map showed the Ire Holding, which was his by blood right, as a shattered shell of what it had been before the War of Unification, half-consumed by the vulturous Lords Holder that shared its borders, the remnant ruled by a steward appointed by the United Provinces.

The Iraean Lords Holder likely had little affection for him or his family. Less for Dorae after he overthrew his father. But they had to try. He raised his head. "If we summon the Lords for a Council, will they come?"

Dorae flashed his wicked grin once more. "If you tweak their pricks by capturing Tarelle? Probably."

Emrael matched his grin. "Good." He turned to the side of the table where his friends sat. "Toravin, have five battalions of our fittest companies ready to march in three days. We will travel light and fast. Jaina, please assign half of the Imperators in pairs to some of the companies staying here. We'll take Timan and the other half north with us."

He waited for Toravin and Jaina to nod before turning to Halrec. "Hal, the command of the remaining five thousand is yours—under Dorae's direction, of course. When we have Larreburgh, you'll escort a group of engineers to reinforce the defenses there and will take command of the city."

They all nodded their assent, though Dorae's manic grin ruined the moment somewhat.

There was a plan, and it might even work. It had to work. He could feel time working against him, could *feel* the seconds winding down before the Malithii played their hand again, bringing their soulbound and *sanja'ahn* to complicate an already precarious situation.

After the meeting, Emrael and the others were shown to their rooms by Dorae's steward Domran, a short, hefty man with thick grey hair cut into a bowl that hung past his ears. The steward's key ring jingled merrily as he chatted, telling them all about the years he had served the Norta family, and how Dorae, impulsive though he was, treated the Whitehall staff far more kindly than his father had. A solid indication that he had made a good ally.

Jaina was the first to be shown a room, then Halrec. Toravin had stayed behind to catch up with Dorae, so only Elle and Emrael were left, though one of Jaina's Imperators assigned to guard him followed at a respectful distance.

In between the steward's comments about each part of the keep they passed, Emrael tried to make conversation with Elle. Things had been odd, distant between them since they had quarreled in

Myntar. She had not seemed very happy to see him when she arrived in Gadford, and certainly hadn't been affectionate since.

"What do you think of the plan?" he asked tentatively.

Elle turned her head to meet his eyes briefly, her blond curls swirling about her head and neck. "I think it's likely one of the best options left to you. You're doing it again, though, you know."

"Doing what?"

"Trying to do it all yourself. Keeping secrets, even from your friends."

Emrael was quiet as he processed what she said. "You're right. But I don't think I'm wrong to do it with most of them."

She shook her head. "It's not as simple as right and wrong. Your allies will react better to your propositions if they feel that they were a part of planning them. Or better, if they actually *are* a part of your planning. Otherwise, you've reduced everyone around you to servants taking orders. You don't have nearly the strength or status needed for that to work long-term."

He grunted his grudging acceptance. After a brief silence, he asked, "What do you think of the Iraean Lords Holder?"

Elle glanced at him sideways. "What do you have to offer that Corrande and the Watchers don't?"

"Well . . . I can free them from Corrande's reparation taxes, for one. If we are successful, there will be a lot more land and trade to go around, too. I mean, isn't it obvious? They've lived under the Watchers for ages but they must remember what it was like to be a free kingdom."

Elle nodded. "Make sure they know what you plan to offer them, even if it's obvious to you. Have you given thought to what your tax rate would be, should you be made a governor . . . or a king? *How* exactly is your offer any better than Corrande's? You must give them a reason to support you, to believe not only that you can win, but that you will make their lives better when you do. And to Lords—to most people—that usually means money. Or power."

"I'm not a complete idiot," he said defensively. "I have a plan."

"You need to have more than a plan if you want to convince the Lords of Iraea. People don't take kindly to being conquered." She looked at him pointedly as she uttered that last sentence. "We've got Sagmyn under control—barely. And only because your mother has ties to Ordena that have given us a trade partner. The Merchants' Guild there is placated for now, but we are far from having won the people's hearts."

"Dispersing Sagmynan Legionmen into existing Iraean squads helped too," Emrael pointed out.

Abruptly, they both realized that the steward had fallen silent, and was undoubtedly filing away everything he had heard for gossip tomorrow. Domran glanced back at them and started when he saw Emrael and Elle both looking at him. "Don't worry, Lord, Lady. Not a word from old Dom. Not that I heard anything, mind you."

Emrael didn't believe that for a minute but didn't press further.

Old Dom stopped at a room with large double doors of polished wood. "Here you are, Lord, Lady. Lord Norta prepared a lovely suite for the two of you."

Emrael looked at Elle, keeping his face still to hide the uncertainty roiling in his chest. "Come in to talk?"

Elle stared back, biting one lip, considering.

Emrael's stomach dropped.

Dom obviously didn't catch the mood, bustling through the now-open door to show them the grand suite. Sofas occupied a sitting room, and beyond waited a massive four-post bed. "This is the best room in the keep, save for Lord Norta's rooms, of course. He had them reserved just for the two of you."

Emrael looked at Elle again, eyebrows raised in a silent question. She had a hard gleam in her eye, but blushed and faltered, giving him some hope that things might return to normal between them. She didn't take long to disabuse him of the notion, however.

"Master Domran, Lord Dorae must be confused. I'd like a suite of my own, if you would be so kind."

Emrael smiled, trying to hide his disappointment. "I don't need anything half this grand. You stay here, Elle. I'll room somewhere else."

He turned to leave with the steward, whose chin had nearly disappeared into his jowls as he grimaced with horrific embarrassment, but Elle stopped him.

"Wait," she said suddenly. "We should talk, just a moment."

Emrael turned back to the steward. "You can go, Dom. Thank

you kindly for your help. I'll find a room down near where Halrec is staying. There were plenty of empty rooms in that wing."

Domran's face brightened. "Why yes, that's splendid. I'll have a room readied just for you, Lord Ire. The room just this side of Lord Syrtsan's. You won't want for anything, I swear it."

Emrael thanked him and finally managed to push him out the door. When he turned back, he found Elle sitting on one of the sofas, waiting for him with a small smile on her lips.

"I had a steward just like him, back in Naeran," she said sadly.

Emrael approached slowly, dropped his sword belt in the corner, and took a seat on the opposite end of the same sofa. "Elle . . . I know you're upset about how I handled things with your father . . ."

Elle pursed her lips, then scooted closer to lay a hand on his knee. "I . . . just don't think you understand how you affect those around you. The secrecy, the cruelty . . . If you don't work to win the hearts of those who have supported you, you'll fail just as surely as if Corrande and the Malithii defeat you."

Emrael looked at the ceiling and rubbed his hand across his stubbled face as he thought. "You're right, of course. You're almost always right. I'm trying, Elle. I don't know that I'll ever be what you seem to think I should be, but I'll keep trying."

She laughed and smiled sadly, settling back on the sofa. "You are doing well, when you're assigning responsibilities you don't care for, and when it's someone you trust. Do you think Toravin and Dorae won't catch on to you leaving your old friends to watch them? Do you think I don't feel the same about your mother in Myntar? You want us to share your fate without sharing in the decisions."

They sat in silence for a time, shoulder to shoulder. Finally, Emrael spoke, still staring at the ceiling. "I'm not leaving my mother in Myntar to watch you. You're there to watch her. And Voran. I trust you, Elle."

Elle shook her head, an slight tremor in her voice. "You barely let me negotiate with my own father, Em. I could have convinced him, given time."

"You tried diplomacy and it didn't work. Waiting would have meant more deaths and fewer options here in Iraea. I was wrong to lose my temper and to override you so quickly, Elle, but I can't answer to you for every decision."

She pressed her lips together and looked away as tears finally spilled from her eyes to wet her freckled cheeks.

When she stayed quiet, he clasped her hand gently. She turned her face up to look him in the eyes sadly. "Elle . . ." He leaned down to kiss her, but she turned her head. He planted a soft, brief kiss on her cheekbone.

She pushed back from him gently and looked at the floor. "I think I need some time to think, Em. We both need to focus on more important things. You obviously have your plans set here, and I need to stabilize the Sagmyn Province or we will have another war on our hands there too."

"Elle," he protested. "I want you to stay. My mother can handle herself a while longer. We can fight a war and still be human."

"I hope so," she said quietly, finally meeting his gaze. "I just need some time. I think you need to take some time to find yourself as well. It won't be long."

"I understand," he said, trying to keep his voice steady. He wasn't going to beg her to stay. "Thank you for being . . . my friend. My ally."

A tear rolled down Elle's cheek, but she was silent.

He took another deep breath, stood, and cleared his throat. "Right. Let's talk business, then. You'll need to travel quickly and in a small party that knows the backroads to the West Pass. I'll have Toravin arrange for the best to get you to Myntar safely."

She frowned at him. "I've already arranged it."

He risked a smile. "Great. Now for those plans you wanted to know about. I need Ban here as soon as possible, and I need all of the Crafters and equipment you can spare. Hire an Ordenan cruiser to transport them. Allocate as many resources to the Ladeskan shipbuilders as you can, and to buying any vessels the Ordenans will sell us. We need to open trade with the Free Cities and Ithans—"

"Emrael," she cut him off. "I know. I've already got shipbuilders working, and your mother has already sent a messenger to Ordena asking for further trade agreements to be negotiated. And don't worry, I won't let them take advantage of us. I can do this. This is one of those times you need to trust me. I will see this through."

"Thank you." He squeezed her hand one last time, and after an awkward pause, left to find his room.

7

Two nights later, Emrael sat around a small table playing cards with Jaina, Halrec, Toravin, and Dorae. Elle and two Imperators had left earlier that morning, accompanied by a squad of men who Toravin swore could get her into the Sagmyn Province without running into any Barros men.

Watching Dorae lay down a card, Emrael took a swig of the dark brown ale in his mug, savoring the rich nutty flavor. "Tell me about the attacks so far. Has Corrande been using his own Legion? Watchers?"

Dorae sipped his wine before responding. "Watchers, mostly. I think he wants to save his own troops as long as he can. He must not trust the High Sentinel all that much. Especially now that you killed the Commander First of the Watchers who was in his pocket, eh?"

"Have your men seen any Malithii or soulbound?" Emrael asked.

Frowning, Dorae shook his head and set his cards facedown on the table. "You say they dress in black robes? We haven't had any reports of such things. Just Watchers, though they've been enough trouble. More than once, I thought the city was lost."

Toravin clapped Dorae on the shoulder. "Trust me, you'd know about it if your men had encountered any of the foreigners. The bastards are mean, and their soulbound are enough to unnerve a man. Keep coming at you, even if they're dying."

Emrael met Jaina's eyes. "Why wouldn't the Malithii join the fight? Could we have killed them all?"

"I do not know," she answered pensively. "It is possible that the Malithii and *alai'ahn* we faced at the Citadel were the majority of the forces they managed to get into the Provinces, and the rest are being used to influence important people, like the ones who were with Governor Barros. The *alai* we found were all ancient, I do not believe the Malithii have discovered how to replicate them. We must be very wary of the *mentai*, however. Whichever Malithii discovered their making could still be using them."

A few more hands were played with only occasional comments until Halrec asked, "Em, what will you do if our capture of Larreburgh doesn't convince the other Lords Holder to join us?"

Instead of answering directly, Emrael asked Dorae, "Tell me, Dorae. What do the Lords Holder pay to the Provinces right now?"

The Lord of Whitehall grimaced. "Half. Half of their tax revenue on top of having half of their lands taken from them to be managed by the United Provinces. Each must host—and pay for—the Watcher garrisons in their Holdings, besides. And none of them do anything but complain where their overlords can't hear."

"And if I offer them a better arrangement in return for their support? What might they do if offered half the tax rate and their lands back?"

He ducked his head to look at Emrael from under his brows. "Crown you king, maybe?"

Emrael met his stare without blinking. "And you, Dorae? Would you give me your ring? I've heard your people have coveted the southern reaches of the Tarelle Holding for some time . . ."

Dorae's eyes gleamed, but he was quiet for longer than Emrael would have liked. "If you can deliver on Larreburgh? Aye, I reckon I would give you my ring. I'm in with you up to my tits already, aren't I?"

Emrael grinned. "Send for the Lords of Iraea, then. After we take Tarelle's Holding, they won't have a choice but to answer. Distribute a proclamation that any who join us will be given land, and copper. A new class of nobility will earn their place in our kingdom. That should get their attention."

Everyone's heads whipped around as bells clanged first a good distance away from the keep, then around the keep itself.

Whitehall was under attack.

By the time they had pulled on armor and weapons and reconvened in the entry hall, the Ire Legion companies and their assigned pairs of Imperators had formed up in the square outside. Pride swelled within Emrael at seeing his men muster so quickly and form such tight, orderly ranks. The Provincial Legions couldn't have done it better, and most of these men had been tradesmen a year earlier.

Pendants were set up in the middle of the square, where Halrec, Toravin, Dorae, and Dorae's senior staff set up with two companies to protect them. They would receive and relay messages, coordinating the battle from Whitehall Keep, where most of the city could be seen.

The gate blocking the mountain road to the Corrande Province had been set ablaze, and Watchers were on the other side working to knock it down. Most likely with some sort of siege engine, judging by the periodic thunderous impact. The Norta guardsmen on the walls above the canyon gate rained boulders and cauldrons of flaming pitch down on the attackers but seemed not to have deterred the attackers much. Several bodies already littered the ramparts, riddled with arrows.

Emrael and Jaina had been assigned to their own company to be held in reserve, so for a time they sat with Dorae and Halrec and watched as their men and Norta guardsmen marched to meet the army on the other side of the gate. Emrael grew more and more anxious to join the fighting, especially when Corrande's forces broke down the gate. They couldn't see the ensuing battle from their vantage, but they could hear the din from most of a league away.

From where he sat near the command tent, Emrael could see the blue flash of *infusori* periodically, but it was impossible to tell whether the Imperators were the source or whether Malithii had finally attacked with Corrande's forces.

The blue flashes grew closer and closer to the Whitehall square, and finally a messenger arrived at the command table, one arm wrapped in a bloody bandage. "Lords," he said breathlessly, "we're holding them near the gates, Lords, but there are more coming down the pass. They . . . they have monsters with them, Lords."

Emrael habitually drew in as much *infusori* as he could hold before pushing it back into his coils, and continually checked his satchel to ensure he had access to more. The Wells up the canyon were much too far away for him to access their power directly. He'd be limited to whatever he could carry, and it looked as if he and Jaina would be needed before much longer.

The highway on the Whitehall side of the gate was surrounded on both sides by a high barricade for several hundred paces, creating a killing ground intended to stop the invading forces. Soon, however, the fighting had progressed into the streets of the city below. Messengers returning from the battle to report grew more and more frantic. Many stopped reporting entirely as the fighting continued.

It was time. Emrael could wait no longer. He turned to the Captain Third leading their company and barked, "Ready the men! We march in five minutes. Lead with two ranks of shields and spears, crossbows right behind."

He shouldered in next to Halrec to inspect the map, small figures marking the approximate location of both enemy and their own forces. "What's our best route to the pass? We need to retake the gate or we'll be overrun."

"Here," Halrec said immediately, pointing to a medium-sized avenue that traversed the industrial district between Whitehall and the gate at the pass. "Dorae, is this avenue as straight as the map shows? It looks like the streets branching off it are all small, mostly blocked service alleys. You should have minimal chances of encountering resistance until you hit the highway. We have two companies holding the avenue here, with no reported engagements."

Dorae nodded, then continued scanning the rest of the map as he spoke. More messengers had arrived, and Dorae's senior officers were rearranging the models on the map. "Aye, it's a straight shot. If you get caught in there against a larger force, you've no way out but straight back up the hill, though. It's dangerous."

Emrael straightened, adjusting his sword belt. "Do we know how many are coming down the pass?"

"Scouts can't get close, but it's at least two battalions. We've got an equal number heading west and south to meet them head-on on the highway before they can disperse."

"You'll need mages to fight the Malithii that will be with the soulbound your men saw. Jaina, what do you say we take another Imperator pair and their company with us down Halrec's avenue, try to flank them?"

He waited for her nod, and they marched back to where their company waited together. Jaina sent a man running over to where another pair of Imperators—one was Timan, the other a woman with a wide, angular face—waited with their company of Ire Legionmen.

"Broulea," Jaina supplied, as if reading his thoughts. "Decent Healer."

When the two companies had formed up, Jaina and Emrael took positions with the crossbows, just behind the double rank of shield-bearing spearmen. As they marched downhill, fewer and fewer *infusori* coils lit the intersections. Soon they marched in darkness, save for the scant light of the waning moon that managed to sneak through the gaps between slate-tiled rooftops. Light rain drummed their armor as they marched, slicking the cobbled streets.

Now that they were down in the city among the jumble of stone and wood buildings, the din of battle had been damped to near silence. The quiet made Emrael nervous.

A shout sounded in the darkness, and Emrael's Captain Second called out with the appropriate response to identify themselves to the two companies holding the avenue. After a brief conversation and clearing sections of the hasty barricades that had been erected, they were through and continued on undisturbed.

As they drew close to the main highway, there was still no sign of fighting other than the faint sound of weapons clashing and the distant pulsing orange glow of fire somewhere nearer the gate.

Emrael and Jaina pushed through the ranks of shields to climb the barricade blocking the highway, peering to either side. It looked like there was fighting on the main highway farther into the city— likely the battalions Dorae had sent to stop the enemy reported by the scouts. Toward the pass, near the fires raging at the gate, Emrael saw a mass of men in Watcher blue pour into the city via streets like the one they had just come down. The Watchers must have broken through at least one of the Iraean companies blockading the avenues, and could be threatening Whitehall Keep itself before long. Several companies had been held in reserve, but only a few Imperators remained at the keep. Everyone would be slaughtered if the Watchers and Malithii overwhelmed the defenses.

"Jaina," he said, pointing. "Looks like they've broken through. If they've sent Malithii, I would bet they are there."

She came to stand at his shoulder. "Let us hit them from behind and hope our men near the keep can pressure from above."

They sent a runner dashing back the way they had come to report their plan to Dorae and Halrec at the command station, and relayed the orders back to their men. Emrael, Jaina, Timan, and Broulea lined up behind the double shield line once more, and their two hundred men marched up the main highway, which had been lit with both *infusori* coils and bonfires. Before long, the Watchers noticed them, and perhaps a hundred of them began to form shielded ranks of their own at the rear of their force. Thankfully, no *infusori*-Crafted crossbows were loosed—they must have all been deployed farther up the avenue, where hopefully his friends had managed to stall the Watcher advance.

When he and his men were just short of the Watcher line, he ordered a halt. He couldn't see any Malithii, but that didn't mean they weren't there, somewhere. The flickering orange light of the fires set by the attackers made it difficult to see much beyond the first few ranks of enemy soldiers.

The Watchers made no move to advance toward them, but Emrael couldn't tell whether Iraeans were holding them on the uphill slope, as the warehouses of the industrial district obscured his view. He'd just have to take a gamble. It would go worse for them if they allowed their enemy to organize further.

"Slow advance, shields together!" he called out, wishing he was in the front shield line. The battle rage and *infusori* in him clamored to be released.

The front lines crashed together, and Emrael's men pushed forward, their double shield wall too much for the single line of Watchers. Emrael and the third line of soldiers stepped over and stabbed fallen Watchers as their formation shuffled forward, corralling the Watchers into the side street.

As they pushed into the avenue, Emrael was about to call for another push to break the Watchers when he caught a flicker of motion to his right. The length of highway between here and the gate to the pass lay in partial darkness, the *infusori* coils that had lit the way torn down and cast to the ground. He pulled back from the battle line to peer up toward the pass.

"Glory take us," he breathed as his eyes adjusted to the darkness and he saw the shapes moving only a few hundred paces away. While the figures there were hardly more than shadows in the poor light, they moved with the unmistakable shambling gait of soulbound.

"Shield line to the right!" Emrael screamed to be heard over the deafening clash of weapons and cries of dying men. "Second Company to the right, form a wedge! Soulbound up the canyon! Imperators on me! First Company hold the avenue! Second form a wedge!"

After a brief period of confusion, the two companies split, forming a half-square two rows deep. Luckily, the Watchers in the side street seemed to be engaged in a tough uphill battle against a significant number of Iraean soldiers and hadn't yet rallied to make a push back downhill at Emrael's meager force.

Emrael, Jaina, and the other two Imperators picked up shields from fallen soldiers behind them so they could join the front rank in the formation to the right.

The soulbound, grey skin sagging, hair missing but for wisps that had not yet rotted away, approached with their fluid, mindless shuffle that turned into an aggressive trot as they came near. There were only a hundred or so of the beasts. These wore scattered armor and bore various weapons that were in relatively good shape compared to most he had seen.

The soulbound didn't slow as they slammed into the Iraean shield line.

Emrael crouched and held his shield at an angle as a soulbound crashed into him. He drove up and forward with his legs at the moment of impact, using the soulbound's momentum to lift it off its feet to land behind him, trusting the rank behind him to finish it off.

He was nearly knocked off his feet as a second slavering soulbound slammed into his shield before he could set himself again. As Emrael stumbled, the soulbound tried to hack at him with its sword. In short order, the top of his shield had been hacked to kindling, and he had only narrowly escaped having his head split.

Emrael deflected the next attack and thrust his sword through the soulbound's neck with a viper-quick thrust. The monster continued to hack wildly despite the killing stroke, however, and

Emrael was forced to parry again before chopping at one of the soulbound's knees and kicking it backward to bleed to death.

He could tell by the desperate grunts next to him that his comrades were in trouble. He slashed sideways into the exposed midsection of the large soulbound to his right. His blade sliced through the soulbound only to lodge in its spine. He still had to raise his splintered shield as it managed an awkward downward swing with its own sword despite being gravely wounded.

The soulbound's blow knocked Emrael's shield into his helmeted head, wrenching his shoulder nearly out of its socket and knocking him on his ass. Just barely, he managed to keep his grip on his sword, which he wrenched out of the soulbound's spine with a pop. The grey monster fell, abruptly unable to use its legs. Its guts hung from the terrible wound in its abdomen, but still it swung its sword feebly. Scrambling to his feet, he pinned the sword arm of the soulbound under one booted foot and stabbed the thing through the chest. He sent a burst of *infusori* through his weapon and into the monster with the thrust. The soulbound arced its back, eyes wide, then sank to the ground, motionless, as if the *infusori* had burned out whatever dark power the Malithii had instilled in the creature via the binder used to create it.

Glory, why didn't Jaina show me that?

Fighting the urge to vomit from exhaustion, he scuttled backward as quickly as he could, shouting "Cover!" and hoping there was a reserve soldier behind him to take his place. His lungs were on fire, his shoulder ached, and he needed to catch his breath. He nearly laughed in relief when one of his men from the second line stepped up to secure the shield wall. He shook the splintered shield from his arm as he surveyed the battle scene.

The Watchers they had attacked had surrendered to five companies of Iraeans—they looked like Dorae's men—that had been fighting from up the hill. Dorae's men were recovering their wounded, collecting weapons, and securing prisoners from among the defeated Watchers.

Emrael's men who had attacked the Watchers from the rear now moved to bolster the ranks fighting the soulbound. Most of the monsters had been killed, but it had cost them dearly. Perhaps half of the two hundred men he and Jaina had brought with them were dead or wounded, including Broulea, who lay motionless in a pool of blood behind the line of men that still fought the last of the *alai'ahn*.

Nearly a league up the highway in the pass beyond the gate, Emrael could see more shapes milling in the darkness. Hundreds, if not thousands. This must have been just an advance party.

He searched his ranks frantically until he found Jaina, who still fought ferociously where the remaining twenty or so of the first group of soulbound still attacked his men with blind, unthinking rage. He drew his long knife in his left hand and ran to her aid. They had to kill these last soulbound and get into better position before whoever—or whatever—lurked in the pass made it to them.

As he reached her and the knot of men still engaged with the soulbound, he planted a kick directly in the chest of one of the enraged monsters, then stabbed another in the back and fried it with a burst of *infusori*. A steady stream of his men followed him to encircle the monsters. In short order, all of the soulbound lay decapitated or in heaps of bloody twitching meat—a gruesome necessity with the beasts, which hardly acknowledged killing blows.

Emrael began shouting immediately, panting between sentences. "Get into the avenue, now! Form up at the top of that hill, shield wall all the way across, as deep as we have men. Send a messenger to tell Dorae and Halrec that we need men on the main highway. All of them. We're about to have more of these soulbound bastards on us."

Within ten minutes, Emrael, Jaina, and Timan stood at the top of a small hill behind a shield line four ranks deep that blocked the entire avenue that connected to the main highway about two hundred paces downhill.

The sound of hundreds of boots running accompanied by guttural grunts soon echoed from the highway. The soulbound and their Malithii masters came into sight at the mouth of the avenue. Some soulbound continued full speed down the highway, but many spotted Emrael and his forces in formation on top of the small hill and turned aside to attack.

The beasts ran up the incline to slam into Iraean shields with a resounding crash. The Iraeans were ready for the assault, but the sheer force exerted by the soulbound, unconcerned about personal safety as they were, knocked many of the shield-bearers back, disrupting the line. Blades flashed, men and beasts roared with rage and pain. Blood ran, and the Iraean ranks held.

Despite the battle raging just paces in front of him, Emrael's attention was still on the highway at the bottom of the hill. More and more soulbound packed the avenue, and Malithii now peppered their rear ranks, copper-cable weapons lashing at the backs of the already-seething soulbound.

Emrael's men still held, though most of the second rank was now at the front, covering for fallen comrades. The soulbound screamed as the Malithii behind them whipped them into a frenzy. The unnatural beasts swung their weapons wildly, chopping through shields and men alike.

Another ten minutes and his men would be overrun . . . if they didn't break and run first. Emrael was about to force his way to the front rank of the shield wall to fight alongside them when he realized that the flood of soulbound pouring into the avenue from the main highway had stopped. He and his men still faced too many, but there was a clear portion of street from which he could attack—if he could get there. If he could kill the Malithii directing the crazed beasts, he might disorient the soulbound enough to give his men a chance.

He tapped Jaina and Timan on the shoulder, then tapped the sergeant who led the squad assigned to protect him. The thirteen of them ditched their shields to climb onto the roof of a single-story building to one side of the avenue, climbing from there to the roof of a taller warehouse. They ran across the rooftops, jumping the space between tightly packed warehouses until they were well behind the attacking soulbound and their Malithii masters. So far, none seemed to have noticed them.

Emrael and the others lowered themselves from the rooftop and charged from behind. He put his sword through the back of one of the Malithii before they knew what was happening, his comrades to either side of him cutting down their chosen targets at nearly the same moment.

Then the fight turned ugly.

At least five more Malithii—that Emrael could see—turned to face them after their wounded friends screamed in pain. A dozen soulbound heard the commotion as well and broke away from the main battle to face the new threat.

Emrael jerked his sword free and lunged at the nearest priest, pressuring him so he could not bring his copper-cable weapon to bear.

A burst of *infusori* through his sword as it came into contact with the Malithii's blade sent the black-robed priest reeling. Emrael turned to the next foe, a soulbound already swinging its axe.

He parried and darted beneath the grey man's attack to slide his blade through its ribs, pulsing a flare of *infusori* through the beast as he did, frying the binder's hold on it. Two more soulbound died to his blade, and just like that he was in the clear, no enemies immediately near him. None living, anyway. Three Malithii lay motionless at Jaina's feet, two more at Timan's. The dozen soulbound who had turned their way were dead as well, but so were most of the Iraeans that had accompanied the mages across the rooftops. Only three of the original ten still stood.

Hundreds of soulbound still seethed twenty paces away, hacking at the Iraeans still holding them back. From the look of things, the shield wall was near the breaking point.

He locked eyes with Jaina, who nodded as she drew in *infusori* from a coil in her belt pouch until her eyes glowed. Emrael and Timan did the same, exhausting their stores and casting the dull gold coils aside as they ran to engage the remaining soulbound from behind.

They managed to kill several of the mindless beasts with pulses of *infusori* as their blades met rotten flesh, but soon dozens had turned to meet them. Without shields to effectively fight in cramped quarters against larger numbers, they were forced to flee back toward the highway.

As they reached the dark, now-abandoned highway, they slowed and turned to face the soulbound they had momentarily outrun. But the mindless beasts had lost interest, and turned back to the clamor of the battle raging behind them.

"Shit," Emrael cursed as he saw the Iraean shield wall buckle then collapse, letting the boiling mass of soulbound through. The beasts barely paid any attention to the Legionmen who now huddled against the sides of buildings in small clumps of locked shields, hurtling toward their objective in an enraged state. Emrael didn't completely understand how the binders that created and controlled the soulbound worked, but the Malithii must have given an order to attack the Whitehall Keep before he, Jaina, and Timan had killed them. The crazed soulbound seemingly remained compelled to comply, despite the change in circumstances.

Emrael's breath came in ragged pants, but he forced himself to run after the hundreds of soulbound. They might not have enough men left there to defeat the hundreds of beasts that had just broken through. Before he had gone far, a hand on the neck of his armored vest pulled him up short. He looked back to see Jaina's blood-streaked face smiling at him.

"Listen," she said, pointing to her ear.

Emrael did, then smiled with relief. A low rumble quickly turned into a thunderous avalanche of hooves. As he watched, several hundred of his cavalry burst through the mass of soulbound in a long wedge formation, chopping down their unnatural foes as they charged. His grin grew wider when he saw Halrec leading them.

Emrael, Jaina, Timan, and the three survivors from their squad of Legionmen scrambled to huddle against a building as the wave of cavalry swept through and onto the highway, where they reined in. The survivors from the shield wall already followed the mounted soldiers, finishing off soulbound injured in the charge and doing what they could for their own wounded.

Halrec approached and pulled off his helmet to reveal a broad smile. "We came just in the nick of time, eh?"

Emrael smiled back at his friend and joked, "We had them well in hand, just another few minutes and Jaina would have killed every last one."

Halrec gave Jaina an appraising look. "That, I believe."

Nearly every inch of her was soaked in blood. She and Timan had already begun collecting the binders from the arms of the dead and dying soulbound, chopping off their wrists as callously as if they were trimming trees.

They shared a look, mirrored frowns of disgust on their faces. Halrec shrugged, then turned his horse. "I need to see to my men. You weren't the only ones pinned down; we need to keep going."

Emrael nodded and waved him on. "Go, I'll take the queen of death over there to see what we can do about sealing the gates at the canyon. If they bring more soulbound before we can, we're in for a very bad day."

After Halrec had gone, he rounded up one company to march with them to the gate and sent the rest of the Legionmen back to the keep to care for their wounded and rest. He then pulled Jaina and Timan away from their gruesome butchering of soulbound and led them up the highway toward the pass, their men collecting glowing *infusori* coils from sconces lining the highway as they passed. They held their weapons at the ready and trod as quietly as possible for fear that there could be more Malithii and soulbound coming down the pass.

When they reached the gates that had been bashed in by the soulbound, Emrael told the Captain Third leading the company of Ire Legionmen with them to wait several hundred paces back. He didn't want to hurt any of his own men, and his skill with *infusori* was anything but predictable. Emrael and the two Imperators climbed the stone stairs to the keep that perched above the wall on the river side of the gate—the keep that had been occupied only months before by a garrison of Watchers. It appeared deserted, no Watchers, Malithii, or soulbound in sight. No living Iraeans, either.

After a quick inspection to ensure none of their men remained, they went back down to the roadway. Neither Jaina nor Timan had any skill with stonebreaking, so they stood clear and kept an eye on the pass while Emrael inspected the stonework that supported the keep.

He drew the *infusori* from every single coil they had gathered until his eyes glowed fiercely. He turned to see Timan staring at him, mouth agape.

"What?" Emrael asked, worried Timan had spotted more soulbound or Malithii.

Timan shook his head, then looked to Jaina. "He really doesn't know?"

Jaina just shrugged, so Timan turned back to Emrael. "There are very few Imperators—or mages of any kind—that could hold as much *infusori* as you have in you right now. And you are not shaking, not even sweating as far as I can tell. You are nowhere near your limit."

Emrael thought about it for a moment. He had certainly held more *infusori* before. He matched Jaina's shrug. "I think my mother can too, and Jaina said she knows others who can draw as much. Besides, I might be able to hold a lot, but I can't do much more than break stone and light small fires yet. I am nearly useless outside of those two tricks."

"Worse than useless at times," Jaina murmured.

Timan just shook his head again and muttered to himself as Emrael turned to the wall and pushed as much energy as he could through the stone of the keep's foundation, breaking the bonds that held it together. It turned to dust with a sharp crack.

"Run!" he shouted, heeding his own advice. After such an outlay of *infusori* on top of having fought a series of battles in the middle of the night, his feet felt leaden as he tried to run faster than the stone above him could fall. Jaina steadied him when he stumbled, and they ran shoulder to shoulder.

Before they managed to get more than a few hundred paces away, a deafening groan echoed through the canyon as the rock split, spilling the keep and a portion of the mountainside into the opening, blocking the pass from Corrande to Whitehall for good—or as near as made no difference.

A wave of dust and debris flowed over them, and they covered their faces with their arms, ducking for whatever cover they could find.

When the dust had settled enough for them to see—and breathe—Timan turned back to look at the destruction Emrael had wrought. "Silent Sisters save us," he breathed.

Emrael fell to his knees, retching from exhaustion. "They won't," he rasped between heaves of his stomach.

8

Late that night, nearly dawn the next day, the city had been secured. Everyone who still lived made their way to their quarters or to the healers' tents that had been erected in the square in front of the keep.

Emrael and the others who ranked a room in Whitehall Keep stumbled up the front steps, stripped in the grand foyer, and handed their armor to Ire Legion and Norta servants. Now in just smallclothes soiled with sour sweat, blood, and dirt, they trudged in exhausted silence to the enormous bathhouse. Steaming hot water poured from dozens of shower heads on one side of the men's bath chambers, and spigots filled as many large copper tubs on the other. Unlike the Citadel, Dorae's keep had plenty of *infusori* to power his Craftings that heated water for his bathing chambers.

Afraid he wouldn't stay awake in a bath, Emrael trudged over to an unoccupied shower. He stripped and scrubbed the filth from himself, finding various minor but painful cuts and bruises along the way. When he was done, a waiting servant handed him a clean bathrobe and he trudged the empty stone-walled corridors of Whitehall with Jaina, Timan, and Halrec.

They had issued the appropriate orders to delay the assault on Larreburgh by a day, just enough to give their uninjured men time to recover before the campaign. Emrael couldn't allow the Watchers' assault here to derail his plans—it might even enhance the element of surprise.

He tapped Jaina on the arm as they walked back to their rooms. "Why hadn't Dorae and his men seen Malithii and soulbound until now? And why did they only bring those few hundred? Another hundred or two of those bastards and we would have been overrun."

She shrugged one shoulder. "The Mindless are not created easily, Emrael. Each takes months to transform, and each requires an ancient soulbinder. Each of the soulbinders my Imperators recovered here is of the same design we find in the Dark Nations. Truthfully, I am surprised they had as many as they did. And that they used them here, and now."

"So that might have been all the soulbound they had? We may not have to worry about them, at least not for a few months?"

Jaina's short dark hair swayed as she shook her head. "I did not say that. I do not think they knew we would be here. They would have crushed Whitehall's defenses with the numbers they brought tonight if not for our ten thousand men, and they would not have sent their *alai'ahn* if they had foreseen defeat. They are too smart to expend these cheaply."

Halrec grunted his dismay. "How many soulbound could they conceivably send against us? Even with well-trained troops, it takes at least two men to take one of those things down. If they have more of these soulbinders, and people to use them on . . ."

Timan was the one to answer this time. "We have seen armies of soulbound in the tens of thousands before, in the Westlands. But it is rare. Very rare. I cannot believe they've landed that many *alai* on this continent. If they have, you're doomed," he said in a flat, matter-of-fact tone.

Emrael chuckled darkly. "As if being outnumbered by the Fallen-cursed Watchers wasn't enough. We need to unite the Irae-ans, all of them, and quickly. And maybe we do need to strike a deal with the Ordenans after all," he said, watching Jaina carefully from the corner of his eye.

She frowned. "The Ordenan Imperial Army is hard-pressed just to keep the war on the far side of the Aerwyn Ocean. If there may be tens of thousands of *alai'ahn* to fight here, the Councils will want more resources than you presently have to give, Emrael."

Emrael pursed his lips and shared a serious glance with Halrec. "We'll just have to acquire more assets, then."

They walked on in silence after that, too tired to discuss the bleak outlook further. All found their rooms to sleep as much as they could before the following day, when they'd have their hands full assessing their casualties and preparing five battalions to as-sault Larreburgh.

Emrael locked and chained the door to his room. Moving in the slow trance of exhaustion, he shed his robe, pulled all the *infusori* from the gold coil lamp to plunge the room into darkness, and collapsed on the bed.

Just as he was drifting off to sleep, however, there was a whisper of cloth rubbing against cloth nearby. His eyes snapped open, straining to see in the darkness. It could have just been his imagination, but even in his exhausted state, he knew he couldn't afford to take chances.

He could see very little in the shadow-drenched room, even once his eyes adjusted. Heavy curtains over small square windows blocked out nearly every bit of the late-night moon.

He moved one hand slowly toward the dagger he kept under his mattress while reaching with his other hand for the dull gold coil on the table next to the bed. When his fingers found the cold metal, he pushed some *infusori* into the gold and sat up, dagger and glowing coil at the ready.

He froze as he saw that he was not, in fact, alone. A Malithii priest sat calmly in an armchair in the far corner of his room, a tall man with tattoos that covered every inch of skin that Emrael could see. According to Jaina, a priest with this many of their religious markings would be someone of considerable status.

The priest had a small crossbow loaded and trained directly on Emrael's chest. He showed large white teeth in a smile and made placating motions with his free hand.

"Calm, dear Ire boy," the priest said soothingly. "Calm. I have not come here to harm you. My master simply wishes to speak. That is all. Just speak with you."

Emrael tensed, ready to spring, but the priest lifted his eyebrows and waggled the crossbow in his direction. "No, please. None of that. I told you once. I'll swear on my life and hope of a Glorious rebirth. We mean no harm. Drop the knife."

The priest waggled the crossbow again, and Emrael slowly set the dagger down next to him.

"Better," the priest said, resting the crossbow in the crook of his arm but still keeping a cautious eye on him. Then, he bowed formally, still seated. "I am Savian, the Prophet of Glory," he said in a deep, resonant voice.

Emrael stared for a moment, expecting the priest to continue. Savian just sat, as if expecting Emrael to recognize his name. "And what do you want from me, Savian? Why don't I already have a crossbow bolt in my chest?"

Savian chuckled, a deep, genuine laugh. "Oh my dear boy, you do not understand at all. My master has never wished to kill you. This," he said, nodding at the weapon, "is just insurance."

Fear began to turn to a smoldering anger in Emrael's chest despite the obvious danger. "Say what you've got to say and begone, then."

Savian drew back a bit, as if offended. "Dear boy, I am here to help you, to bring you warning. I will prove myself to you." He leaned forward slightly, an excited gleam in his eye. "Did you know the southern Lords Holder of Barros are ready to revolt against their governor? Hmmm? Ah, I thought not. They would answer your call more readily than these stubborn Iraeans, oh yes they will. I have made sure of it."

It wouldn't surprise Emrael if the southern Lords Holder of Barros were on the verge of revolt. They were ever threatening the governor in a bid to return to the old ways, when the provinces had been independent kingdoms and the Lords Holder had enjoyed much freer rein over their Holdings.

"Why are you telling me this? You and your priests are the ones who caused this entire war. You forced my own father to carve me with a knife, for Mercy's sake. Why would I possibly trust you?" This man must have been insane, lying, or both. But then again, why would he be here, in the heart of Whitehall, talking to Emrael when he could easily have killed him already?

The Prophet licked his lips and hunched in on himself as if suddenly in pain. His eyes widened abruptly and he straightened, with a large smile plastered on his face once more. "My master tests you, Son of Glory. You should be done with the Ordenan devils and their wiles." His gaze locked on the book Emrael had taken from the Ravan temple, which sat on his nightstand. His smile became a snarl. "They pervert the gifts of the holy God of Glory."

Emrael sat up, suddenly curious even as he watched the priest— Prophet, he supposed, whatever that meant. "You know of this book?" he asked cautiously. "What is it?"

Savian looked at him in surprise, then narrowed his eyes. "Surely you know by now?"

When Emrael only shook his head slightly, the Prophet continued, speaking more slowly than before. "Perhaps it is best you find out for yourself, young master?"

Savian framed that last as a question, which struck Emrael as odd. Just what was this book? He'd have to make time to explore it further—if Jaina and this odd Prophet were so interested in it, it likely held something of value.

"Okay . . . I'll keep that in mind," Emrael said, trying not to offend the man who could put a bolt through his chest with the twitch of a finger. How had this man entered the keep plainly dressed as a Malithii priest and armed with a crossbow?

"Is that all you came for, Savian?"

Savian laughed again, louder this time. Emrael hoped that someone in the rooms next to his—Halrec was in one—would hear the odd laugh, clearly deeper than Emrael's voice, and come running to his rescue. Alas, the keep remained silent.

"No, my dear Ire. My master wishes to speak with you directly. Do not be afraid," he said, now reaching slowly toward Emrael, the crossbow in his other hand still aimed at his chest. "I don't have any of my beautiful mindbinders, no need to worry. Just a touch, and I'll be gone."

Emrael could see no sure way to knock the weapon aside without risking being shot, and so prepared himself to consume Savian's *infusori*, Jaina's warnings be damned.

As soon as Emrael felt Savian's long fingers touch him, he pulled with all the might of his considerable will, intending to snuff out the priest's life instantly. He recoiled in shock when he found that Savian's life source didn't budge, not a bit. His efforts were as futile as if he had tried to push over Whitehall Keep with his bare hands.

He had just enough time for that shock to register before every muscle in his body spasmed, his back arcing backward to the point of agony. His vision spun, then turned dark, an experience similar to that of being pulled into the visions of the book.

Angular, glowing runes soon broke the darkness that filled his vision. The script glowed blue just as it had in the Ravan temple, and as in the temple, it seemed to have been inscribed into the walls of a structure. Unlike the temple, however, the script seemed to fill nearly every inch of the four triangular interior walls. Even still, the structure was large enough that the majority of the interior lay obscured in deep shadow.

A light flickered in the dim room. He peered at it, then recoiled as bright blue light burst from a huge, bald figure seated in a large stone chair—a throne, almost—near the far wall. The same runic script that covered the walls glowed fiercely on the figure's skin. Emrael grew uneasy when he realized that the markings were very similar, possibly identical, to the scars that had been carved into his own skin.

"Come, Son of Glory," the figure said in an impossibly deep voice that seemed to set every fiber of Emrael's being aquiver. "Come. Attend me."

Emrael's mind did not seem to work correctly. Positive emotions flooded him—adoration, longing, loyalty toward this Being—and he wanted to obey. But something in the core of him resisted. Sweat beaded on his face from the effort, but he stood still despite the powerful urge to go to the immense Being. He was no pawn.

"COME," the Being roared. Fear clenched in Emrael's chest now, an avalanche of cold that drowned all thought.

His legs began to move of their own accord. But something inside him resisted still, and he stopped again, angry more than scared now. His emotions were obviously affected by whatever this Being was doing, whoever this Being was. But the anger was his. He owned it, enveloped himself in it, shielding himself from the artificial emotions that tried to control him.

The Being surged to its feet, obviously irate. It—he—stalked over to Emrael and loomed over him, studying him with an unblinking stare. His eyes were pure black. Emrael didn't know whether this was an ethereal vision or whether he had actually been transported physically somehow, but either way, panic started to worm its way through his shell of anger. He didn't look away from the Being's gaze, though, and held tightly to his rage—his anchor in a sea of dread.

Abruptly, the Being smiled, revealing perfectly white teeth behind plump grey lips. "Good," he purred, pacing closer. "Very good."

Emrael was now frozen in place, helpless as the Being laid a hand on each of Emrael's shoulders and stared into his eyes. The emotions flooding Emrael faded suddenly, leaving him weak and alone with his defiant anger—and the constant vibrating power that seemed to have settled in his soul when the Being had awoken.

"At last, a Child with promise. My Sisters have ever been silent since abandoning me to this world. Old and worn as I am, I am stuck in this place of Power. We will yet see that they share my fate, my Son."

Emrael shot up from where he had been fast asleep atop his bed, heart racing, eyes scanning the room frantically. He was alone.

Where had Savian gone? Could it have all been an exhausted dream, an illusion?

The sun shone through the small gaps in the heavy curtains that covered his windows. His room was empty, no sign that anyone had been there. But his memory was clear, both of the odd visit from the Prophet and the vision that followed. He could still feel the Being's vibrant power coursing through him, like a parasite wriggling its way through his soul.

Oh Absent Gods, did I really just talk to the Fallen? It was him, it had to be. Either that or I have lost my mind.

He sat on the edge of his bed, blankets in a tangle, trying to process what had just happened to him. Why had the Fallen called him his "Son"? Nothing about it made sense, but he was sure it wasn't a good thing.

He crossed the room to unlock the door and to take a swig from the flask of brandy he had left on the table next to the entryway. He stared at the flask a moment, then drained it with three more quick gulps.

His hands were shaking. Could it have been just soldier's madness come to haunt him after the fight yesterday? No. He could still feel the power of the Fallen's voice reverberating through him, as if he were still deep in the vision. He thought it might drive him mad if it lasted much longer.

A knock sounded at the door. "Shit," Emrael muttered, scrambling to find his clothes. He was supposed to have met Jaina back in the courtyard at the seventh hour, and from what he could tell by the light streaming through his window, he was late. The door handle turned and whoever was outside pushed on the door.

"Just a moment," he croaked, tripping as he scrambled to pull his pants on. He managed to cover himself just as Jaina's face peeked into the room.

"You are late," she said, frowning in disapproval. "You are sleeping while your officers muster on your orders? I thought better of you, Emrael."

Emrael felt a flush of shame, but scrambled to fasten his pants as he beckoned her into his room. "Come in and shut the door, Jaina."

She looked him up and down, eyebrow raised as she stared at him fumbling with his pants. "Perhaps I should be flattered?"

"No . . . no, Jaina. Gods, not that . . ."

She surprised him by entering and closing the door while he mumbled, eyes locked to his. She smiled wickedly and approached, eyeing him up and down. He drew back. "Jaina, I don't think . . ."

Awkwardly, he backed all the way to his bed and stumbled backward to sit, still staring at her in disbelief. She doubled over and began laughing so hard that tears dripped from the corners of her eyes. "Silent Sisters, your face! You thought I—"

She trailed off, unable to speak for laughing so hard.

Emrael drew a deep breath and set his jaw, finally securing the last of the buttons on his pants. "Very funny. Would you listen for one Fallen minute?"

Finally, she calmed and stared at him expectantly. Emrael hesitated, weighing what he could tell her safely about the visit from the Prophet of the Fallen. Jaina was . . . Jaina. She had proven herself loyal many times, but at the end of the day she was Ordenan. Her true loyalties undoubtedly lay with her Order. How well did he *really* know her?

Still, if he couldn't trust her, now was the time to know it. And if anyone could help, it was her. And so he told her every detail of the visit from the Prophet of the Fallen, Savian, and the vision of the Fallen himself. Her laughter faded quickly.

Closing his eyes, he dipped his head, focusing on feeling his internal *infusori*, then met her eyes as he placed a hand on his bare chest for visual effect. "I can feel him, Jaina. It's like my life source is still vibrating. His power was unbelievable, and he called me his son. If he can affect me, affect anyone like that without even using a mindbinder, we have a major problem. If the Fallen himself is real and involved in this war, we're fucked."

Jaina considered him for a long time, stone-faced. A flash of suspicion marred her expression, and she began running her hands along his arms, then his head and neck. "If that Malithii was here, he could have left you with a mindbinder or worse."

"The Malithii priest seemed to want to help me, as odd as that sounds. I don't think I have a mindbinder on me. Whatever the Fallen did is *inside* me." He thumped his chest for emphasis, though he allowed her to continue. His skin tingled as she used minute amounts of *infusori* to scan his body for malicious Craftings.

After a time, she sat back, apparently satisfied that the Malithii priest—prophet, whatever—hadn't put a mindbinder of any sort on him. "Be careful about who learns this, Emrael. Some in my Order would kill you without remorse if they knew that the Fallen had touched you, even through a dream or vision. I would like to meld to feel this. May I?"

He nodded, and she gently placed her hands on either side of his head. His skin pebbled as her *infusori* senses coursed through him, her consciousness examining his. Memories and emotions flickered through his mind as she perused his inner being. The reverberation he had felt since his encounter with the Fallen swelled for a moment, then he felt an even deeper connection form, something different from what she had normally done in their training sessions. Momentarily, their emotions, their thoughts, their very beings melded. For the first time in ages, maybe ever, he felt like someone understood him. The constant struggle with the memory of his torture, his father's death, the prospect of facing overwhelming odds against the Malithii, Iraeans, Corrande, Barros, Elle, everything. And he felt her in return. He was astonished at the depth of the loyalty and fondness she felt for him. He had never stopped to consider that she seemed to have nobody else in her life, no purpose beside that of her Order—except for him, now. As their connection lingered, he felt some of the pain, some of the anxiety of the Fallen's influence bleed from him.

She released him and sank to the bed beside him, drawing in a shaky breath. "That was . . . significant," she said finally, a slight rasp to her voice. "I had never thought the Fallen One's residuals would feel so . . . pure. Chaotic, overwhelming, but pure. I suppose we should have known that he had awoken, but to know it for certain is . . ."

She shook herself, then leaned into him, shoulder to shoulder. "I have taken as much of the Fallen's effects onto myself as I can handle, and the rest should subside in time. Just . . . just be careful. Tell no one but those you trust with your life. And for Mercy's sake, let me post an Imperator at your door. The Fallen and his Malithii obviously have a particular interest in you. Which means that I do as well."

He hung his head, tears falling from his eyes. He had not expected so profound a reaction to their connection. He hadn't felt much emotion other than anger since the battle for the Citadel, just . . . empty. The torture and death of his father had numbed him, hardened him. He still hadn't told anyone the truth of what had happened there, not even Ban. Especially not Ban.

Something about knowing that Jaina understood, had *felt* what he felt . . . he felt human again. Almost.

"It was really the Fallen then? You believe me?"

Jaina gripped the back of his head, turned his tear-filled gaze to meet hers. "I believe you. I don't know how the Fallen could possibly affect you without being here himself. But I believe you. What I just felt could not have come from anything—anyone—else."

Her eyes grew unfocused for a moment as she thought, then she nodded to herself. "I am with you, Emrael. If you are with me, we will fight him together."

He nodded, and put an arm around her shoulders as he would have done with Ban. "Together, then."

Finally, he didn't feel alone.

9

Back in her room after the encounter with Emrael, Jaina collapsed on her bed, unable to contain the sobs that racked her. She muffled the cries in her pillow as she forced her mind to make sense of what she was feeling.

She had known he was changed by whatever had happened to him inside the Citadel, though he still would not speak of it to her, or to anyone that she knew of. What could have hurt him to that degree? She had known pain. She had watched as her beloved Welitan had turned into an *alai'ahn* before her very eyes, sobbed as he was dragged away to be *euthanized* by their fellow Imperators. The ache she felt in Emrael rivaled what she had harbored for so long after her husband's death. Could torture have wounded his soul so deeply? She did not think so.

Further, the immensity of the Fallen's touch was . . . not what she had expected. And oddly benevolent, though Jaina was almost certain that the Fallen's imparted energy had been trying to change or shape Emrael's own life source in some way. She could feel the small portion she had taken upon herself doing the same to her. Her consciousness—her very being—vibrated inside of her, molding her in some way.

It terrified her that she didn't understand what it was doing to her—to them—or why. She screamed into her pillow as she brought her full force of will to bear, finally subduing her emotions. She took a deep breath and half-stumbled over to her washbasin, where she splashed her face with cold water and scrubbed away the snot and tears.

As she toweled herself dry, the metal disk on her writing desk began to vibrate with a constant rhythm for a minute or so. One of the Ordenan Council of Imperators' representatives here in the Provinces had recently come to the city and delivered the beacon

Crafting to her, with instructions to meet at a nearby Order safe-house when summoned.

Useful as the device was, she couldn't help but think about Banron Ire's Observers. They transmitted actual voices, whereas the best Crafters in mighty Ordena had only managed this pulsating disk. Remarkable.

Buckling on her sword and various hidden daggers, she stopped to consume the *infusori* from the lighting coils in the hall just outside her room. She filled herself with the glorious power until her eyes were just shy of glowing visibly, which would immediately give her powered-up state away. She checked herself in her small mirror, then set off for the Ordenan safehouse near Whitehall's docks.

To anyone but those who knew, the stone-block building and surrounding fenced yard looked like any other merchant's yard in the district. Even the warehouse workers and wagoneers were legitimate. This was in fact a merchant's yard, likely operated by someone with few or no connections to Ordena. Certainly not to the Order of Imperators or the Ordenan Councils.

Her trepidation returned as she crossed the yard and entered the office. She had no idea why, after months of uninterrupted clandestine operation and encrypted reports, the Order was contacting her now, and in such an open manner. She was following Maira's instructions, for Mercy's sake! A member of the Council of Imperators!

As she entered the merchant's office, a short, portly man with only a fringe of hair ringing his head looked up from a large desk. Recognition widened his eyes immediately, and he beckoned her toward the back of the building. She didn't like that they had given her description to low-level operatives, but followed.

She stopped at the door to a small office, shocked. At the desk inside sat her dead husband's best friend, Jeric. Grey now streaked the temples of his sleek shoulder-length hair, and the tan skin of his face and hands had creased gently, but he had the same big-toothed grin she had seen so often when they had been assigned to the same squad in the Dark Lands. She met his smile, but the old ache of sorrow that constantly chewed at her suddenly amplified. She couldn't see Jeric without being reminded of that day they had recovered Welitan together.

"Jer," she blurted, unable to find any other words. "What are you doing here? I thought you were training recruits at the Academy. Are you who the Council sent to negotiate with Emrael? How did you arrive so quickly?"

Jeric was a good Imperator—better than good—and handy in a fight. However, he would not have been her first choice to negotiate a trade deal.

He threw his hands up in an exaggerated shrug. "No, I only learned about your request when I landed in Naeran. The Councils will likely be months still in replying. They will take their time assessing what they can commit to the Provinces . . . and their price, of course."

Her old friend leaned forward in his seat, his gaze intense. "Jaina, I am here for you. They pulled me into an emergency meeting—pulled me out of a class, for Mercy's sake. Next thing I knew, I was on a cruiser headed here, to talk to you. You've made some people on the Councils very angry. Or very excited, I cannot tell which. Probably both, knowing you."

She showed her teeth in a smile she didn't feel. Something was very wrong if a Councilor had sent for her without going through Maira first. Chain of command mattered a great deal in the Order. "I am only doing what they sent me here to do, what Maira Ire herself ordered me to do. I was told that I take my orders directly from her."

He squinted at her in amusement, licking his front teeth. "Never were one for small talk, were you, Jaina? That is just as well, I do not have much time, my ship leaves this evening. The Council is concerned about the Ire boy. They would not say so right out, but I do not think they trust Maira to rein him in, and they fear you have lost control. No more soldiers are coming—I am surprised they have not recalled the Imperators already here. They want you to return to the island."

Jaina threw her head back and laughed. "Sisters, Jer, you have no idea. Control Emrael?" She laughed again. "I tried that, at first. I thought I would have him in the palm of my hand to deliver to the Council by now. You have not met him, have not seen what he can do. None of you have. If they want to send someone else to try to put a leash on him, they are welcome to. I cannot wait to see them try. But for now, I am the Order's best chance at maintaining some sort of relationship with him. I am staying."

Jeric was taken aback. "You will defy orders? You were on track to be on the Council someday. If you do this . . ."

She stared at him, unamused. "I am obeying *orders*. From a Councilor, same as you. I need your help, Jer, not threats. I am too busy to be getting involved in games between Councilors."

"Glory, Jaina. What am I supposed to do? I may be here for the Councils, but I'm still your friend first and foremost. Tell me what's going on, tell me how I can help."

Her mind flashed back to her conversation with Emrael earlier that day, his communion with the Fallen. The residual energy left in the boy—energy she had taken upon herself to share, for Mercy only knew what reason.

Tempted as she was to trust one of her oldest friends with what she had experienced, she knew that even he would not understand. None of the Ordenans would, not unless they had seen the truth for themselves as she had. Ordenans, and particularly the Council of Imperators, thought in stark terms. Either someone was guilty, or they were not. They would likely kill Emrael, and her, if they knew even half of the truth.

She held his gaze with her own. "We have fought dozens of Malithii and *alai'ahn* by the thousand already, and I suspect that is only the beginning. I need more Imperators, and soldiers who know how to fight the Westlanders. Stay here with me. Help me."

"That is not how it works and you know it. You don't negotiate with the Order. I can't just decide to stay here. They would almost certainly execute me as a defector. They will have you killed too if you don't come with me. Please, Jaina."

"No, they won't, Jeric. They know that Emrael is their best chance to gain a foothold in the Provinces, and they have wanted that for decades. And what if Ire really is one of the chosen the Malithii have raved about for centuries, what if the Fallen really is awake, Jer? What then? We are just supposed to lead him on a leash to a duel with a god? Do you really think that is how this will work?"

Jeric sat silent, chin resting on his hand, one finger tapping his cheek as if in thought. His other hand, however, drifted toward his belt. Jaina just now noticed the glint of copper—one of the Malithii's copper-cable weapons. Imperators often took them from vanquished Malithii priests and used them in situations intended to be nonlethal. She had seen them used on rogue Imperators, had used them herself more than once.

Jaina kicked the table with a burst of *infusori* to bolster the blow. Jeric was knocked backward; his head slammed into the wall, stunning him momentarily. Jaina kicked the table again, flipping it on top of her former friend. She jumped the table to pin him with her knees as she elbowed him in the face one, two, three times in rapid succession. Blood dripped from his nose and his eye began to swell immediately, but he was still conscious. Mostly.

"What in Mercy's name were you thinking? Trying to detain *me*? You thought that you could subdue *me*?"

"Forgot . . . how fast you are. Damn," he groaned.

"Why, Jer? I am still following orders. The Council's orders. This is not how things are done."

Jeric was a bit more lucid now. He shook his head slightly, wincing as he did. "They really will kill you," he grunted. "I heard them talking. You know the Council members often take matters into their own hands when fighting among themselves. My patron thinks you have let Ire get too powerful, taught him things he should not know. Someone in your party must be passing him information."

"Who?"

Jeric shook his head and spoke quickly. "I do not know, I swear. I only know that if I take you back now, they will reprimand and replace you, but you'll be safe. I made sure of it. I'm trying to save you, Jaina."

"I have unfinished business here, Jeric Alloda. My place is with Emrael. Which Councilor threatened me?"

When he didn't answer, she gripped his throat in one hand. Weakened and dazed as he was, he would not stand a chance against her in a match of wills. She could devour his life source if she wished, could mold him to her will, and he knew it.

He jerked his head as far away as he could. "Glory, Jaina. It was Yaris. He wants you gone and one of his favorites in charge here. He's likely moving against Maira as well."

"Did he pay you?"

Jeric was again slow to answer, but the silence was answer enough.

"Sisters damn you, Jer," she said quietly. "This is so much larger than your petty Council politics. I'm acting on Councilor Maira's orders, and Jer . . ."

She paused, considering how much to tell him. At this point, he and his patron were as good as sworn enemies anyway. She might as well try one last gambit to win her old friend over.

"I think it might be even more than that," she said finally. "I think . . . I think the Fallen is awake. I think he's behind everything that's happening here in the Provinces. And the Ire boy might just be our best chance at surviving him."

Her old friend shook his head. "I always knew you didn't take the Book of Ages seriously, but this? The Fallen God, awake? A backwoods Provincial boy, our best hope to defeat a god, when we have the might of the Silent Sisters and their Councils behind us? Please reconsider, Jaina. You know what they are capable of."

Jaina loomed over him. "I ought to kill you for this. But for days past, for the love I had for you, and that Welitan had for you . . . you will be gone by nightfall, do you understand?"

He nodded, and she stood. She stared him in the eye as he gained his feet and said again, "Sisters damn you, Jeric. You, of all people."

Propping himself up on one arm, he wiped some of the blood from his mouth and chin. "Whether I was wise to come here or not, I am your friend. I am doing this for you, not them. I will give you the money, if that appeases you. Please, Jaina. Come with me."

She smiled at him, but inside felt cold as ice. "Be gone by nightfall."

Emrael stood shoulder to shoulder with Jaina in a hastily erected tent in the woods just a few miles from Larreburgh. Two Captains First from the Ire Legion, Garrus and Worren, stood on the other side of the small table, inspecting the large map of the surrounding area by the light of two dimmed *infusori* coils. Timan had planted himself near the door of the tent, one hand resting on the hilt of his sheathed sword. Crickets chirped in the cool evening air, barely audible over the sounds of the Ire Legion camp around them.

Toravin was still out leading a host of scouts, where he would stay through the attack. It was imperative that word didn't reach any of the nearby Watcher garrisons until after they secured Larreburgh, and that Emrael's forces receive word early if any approached.

Three thousand Ire men had been left with Halrec after two thousand had died or been injured in the fight to defend Whitehall. Halrec would follow with a small force and a group of Ire Legion engineers within two days, but five battalions were what Emrael had to work with against a walled town garrisoned by nearly an equal number of Watchers and Tarelle guardsmen.

Emrael and his five thousand had reached their current position outside the city in just under a week, encountering only a few Watcher patrols, which they had killed or captured. They had taken most of a day to rest the men and scout the enemy defenses.

"Are we going to send a messenger to Lord Holder Tarelle?" Worren Duraec, an Iraean with grey peppering the sides of his short-cropped hair, looked to Emrael. "They must have had some word of our army, but their gates stayed open during daylight hours. They don't seem to be preparing for fight."

Worren had been a Watcher Captain before joining Dorae and Toravin's Whitehall rebellion several years ago. Like Toravin, he had then turned brigand until the call for men to assault the Citadel in Myntar went out from Whitehall. He had quickly proven himself one of Emrael's best officers, ferocious and clever as a wolf. He and a single battalion of Ire men had taken half of Myntar nearly by themselves, according to Toravin. Toravin and Halrec seemed to take his advice as pure truth, which was all Emrael needed to trust him as well. For the most part.

Emrael made a clicking sound with his tongue before responding. "He already rebuffed Dorae's attempts to communicate. Do you think sending a messenger now would do any good?"

The other Captain First, Garrus Imarin, a dependable Sagmynan with far more experience in engineering and administrative matters than fighting, answered stoutly. "No, Lord Ire."

Emrael nodded. "Then we don't give him any more warning. We don't approach as supplicants. We take the city with four of our five battalions, each entering at a different point. We'll attack the Watcher barracks, two outposts, and the Watcher command building"—he paused to point them out on the map—"but we leave Tarelle's men alone unless they join the fight."

"Quite a risk," Timan murmured. "The Watchers reportedly have three thousand men here, Tarelle has nearly that many. Why risk letting Tarelle decide the outcome of the battle when we could incapacitate them all with a surprise assault?"

Emrael acknowledged the question with an approving smile. "I don't just need to win here, Timan. I need Tarelle's men to join us afterward. We may be forced to fight them, but we will keep Tarelle's men out of the fighting for as long as we can. Besides, I'm hoping we can neutralize the Lord Holder without much of a fight if we quickly eliminate the Watcher forces."

Timan just shrugged, but Worren nodded in approval, as did Jaina.

He pointed at his serious Sagmynan Captain. "Your battalion will hold back from the initial assault, Garrus. The squads assigned to secure the walls will signal when we have engaged the Watchers. Go straight for Tarelle's palace, don't stop for anything. Take the Lord Holder and his family prisoner and secure the palace. Do not engage the Watchers until we've all arrived."

Garrus's eyes crinkled with concern, but he saluted with little hesitation. Emrael watched the Sagmynan for a moment, trying to gauge the man. He held no illusions that he loved him. But thus far, he had obeyed without complaint, and the Sagmynans listened when he talked. Emrael suspected that the unassuming Captain First was likely the key to keeping the Sagmynans in his Legion loyal.

"Jaina will have her Stonebreakers and their support teams ready in blacked-out gear at the first hour past midnight. Each of you will wait on the Imperators assigned to you before getting close to the walls. You know your objectives once they get you in. I'll see you at the Lord Holder's palace."

The thick timber-and-steel gates of Larreburgh stood tightly shut as Emrael and his battalion trotted up the tree-lined cobblestone highway in full view of the Watchers lining the city walls, though the defenders could likely only see an indistinguishable mass of men in the near darkness. Faint blue light from the waning moon concealed as much as it revealed, and the fires burning in large metal braziers atop the battlements and at regular intervals just outside the walls served only to light the ground in the immediate vicinity of the city. They marched in darkness, revealing nothing to the fire-blind guards atop the walls.

Jaina rode at his side, having opted to grant Timan command of one of the four battalions attacking other parts of the city. At about six hundred paces, just out of range of even *infusori*-powered crossbows, Emrael jammed on his helmet and dismounted his horse. He unlatched his small round shield from where he had tied it to his saddle and lashed it to his left arm.

The other officers followed suit, dismounting to don their gear and join their men, who all marched afoot with shields at the ready. A rudimentary siege engine had been constructed by his engineers, a great wheeled contraption with a steel-sheeted roof to shield the men who pushed it.

Emrael jogged back to find to his assault team. Each of the four battalions attacking the city had one hundred men among them dressed all in black even down to their boots, carrying small shields also painted black. They had even rubbed their faces and hands with charcoal to blend into the shadows of the night. Three Imperators accompanied each blacked company, one Stonebreaker and two more to guard him while he worked. All had satchels full of glowing *infusori* coils. They were the true assault plan—the siege engine and assault on the gates would be largely for show.

Satisfied that the company would not give themselves away approaching the city walls, he gave them their orders, and they filed quietly into the trees.

He stalked forward, making a show of giving his orders. "Engine at the ready!" he shouted as he approached the front ranks. "Crossbows and shields at two hundred paces."

The jingle of equipment and the muttered curses of anxious soldiers marching to battle disturbed the silence of the night.

Panicked shouts echoed and horns wailed atop Larreburgh's walls in answer. Watchers in blue streamed onto the ramparts, their shadows dancing in the light of the braziers. Fire arrows were lit in the braziers as Emrael and his men drew within bow range of the wall, and no doubt buckets of pitch were waiting for the siege engine above the gate.

Emrael called for a halt, and his men huddled behind overlapped shields. Just a year ago, most of these men had been farmers and tradesmen, or had been his enemies. Now they fought side by side, veterans of more battles than most career soldiers in the Provinces.

He and Jaina walked out from behind their line of shields. Emrael held a white flag above his head to signal that he wanted to parley, and Jaina carried a large *infusori* coil lamp fitted atop a wooden pole to ensure that the defenders of Larreburgh could see it clearly. Two soldiers accompanied each with oversized shields at the ready should the men of Larreburgh decide to ignore the white flag.

When they were close enough, some one hundred paces from both their lines and the wall, Emrael stopped to shout, "I am Emrael Ire. I would speak with your Lord Holder."

His demand was met with silence for a long moment. Just as he thought arrows would be loosed at them, someone in Watcher blue shuffled to the front of the group of men crowding the wall above the gate to shout back. "We know who you are, Ire. Lord Holder Tarelle honors the Unification Accord, unlike you swine at Whitehall. Crawl back the way you came. You'll have your battle soon enough."

Emrael chuckled darkly. "I thought you might feel that way," he yelled through the firelit darkness. "Does no one from the Lord Holder's guard wish to avoid bloodshed? All we ask is that you open the gates and stand aside. Our quarrel is with Corrande, not our fellow Iraeans. Any who wish to join me are welcome."

Many of the men atop the wall—those not garbed in Watcher blue—turned to mutter to each other, then stared at the Watchers.

Reaching into his satchel full of charged coils, he drew *infusori* until his eyes, hair, and scars were glowing blue. He wanted his enemies to know who—and what—was coming for them. "Men of Larreburgh! Any man found fighting with the Watchers will be treated as one. Any who stands aside or aids us will be allowed to join our ranks when we have taken the city. Choose wisely."

With that, they trotted back to their line, their men with shields covering their retreat. Much to his relief, no arrows flew at them as they rejoined their battalion. When they were out of immediate danger, Emrael pushed most of the *infusori* he held back into the coils so that he no longer glowed. Intimidation was all well and good, but he didn't intend to get shot tonight.

"Engine forward!" he bellowed as he walked among the nine hundred men still with him, not looking to the north to where the Imperator Stonebreaker was hopefully already doing his work. "Crossbowmen prepare to loose! Shields and pikes at the ready! On my command."

They went to stand behind the ranks of shields and crossbowmen who took aim at the men on the walls. The siege engine rumbled forward, propelled by forty of their burliest men who huddled beneath the engine's low metal roof. An equal number shuffled along to either side, large shields and spears ready to defend their engine-pushing friends. All had been offered triple pay for a year to risk themselves in the assault on the gate.

Just before the siege engine reached the gate, Emrael screamed, "Loose!" Hundreds of crossbow strings snapped, sending bolts streaming through the darkness to rain down on the defenders above the gate.

The sharp front wedge of the siege engine collided with the gate with a resounding crash of splitting timber and tearing steel. The men pushing the engine hauled backward and prepared for another charge as a continuous stream of arrows, crossbow bolts, and throwing spears were hurled at them. The vast majority of them hit the steel roof with a clang or lodged into the shields of the men skirting the engine, but here and there a scream of pain erupted where one snuck through or a Watcher's *infusori*-Crafted crossbow sent a bolt clean through a wooden shield. Not for the first time, Emrael made a mental note to talk to Ban and the Legion engineers about a design for shields that could protect against such attacks, and still be light enough to carry and fight with.

His men continued to reload and loose crossbows of their own. Some of them were even the *infusori*-Crafted variety, either stolen from vanquished Watchers or part of the batch Ban and his Crafters at the Citadel had built. Even at this distance, many struck home.

Bolt-ridden bodies littered the firelit ground in front of the gate and walls, and most wore Watcher blue. They wouldn't win the battle this way, but they were keeping the defenders at bay.

As the retreating siege engine revealed the gate, Emrael was surprised by the amount of damage done with just one collision. He hadn't put much faith in a siege engine built so hastily by his engineers, who had carted the steel portions of the contraption in wagons that had slowed them down considerably, but he would have to reward them. It might only take another few blows to break the gate open. This assault was looking like it would go even better than he had hoped.

Emrael was peripherally aware of his men—half of them— leaving the battlefield squad by squad to slink through the woods toward where the Imperators and the first company had disappeared earlier.

The engine smashed into the gate a second time, and one side hung askew, secured by a single hinge. He hadn't planned to charge the gate this early, but he wasn't opposed to taking advantage of fortuitous circumstances.

Just as he opened his mouth to order his men ready for the charge, however, the Watchers above poured several large cauldrons of pitch onto the siege engine. He watched in horror as several Watchers loosed fire arrows immediately, engulfing the siege engine in flames. Though the contraption had been designed to protect the men from just this eventuality, several of his men ran screaming from beneath the inferno. The Watchers shot mercilessly, loosing more bolts and arrows into the fleeing men, who had dropped their shields to escape the fire. The siege engine and the bodies of many of the men who had manned it now lay abandoned in front of the gate.

Emrael took a few involuntary steps forward, his heart aching for the men who had just been burned alive for him, on his orders. Jaina took one look at his face and immediately wrapped an arm around his waist, pulling him back from the front line of shields. "You *will not* risk yourself, Emrael. Let your soldiers do their jobs."

Emrael grunted at her, then took up an *infusori*-Crafted crossbow that had been dropped by one of the wounded. Not all of

Larreburgh's defenders had aimed at the siege engine—more and more bolts flew their way now that the engine had been destroyed. Training the crossbow on a Watcher atop the wall, he squeezed the trigger with a smooth, practiced motion and watched as his bolt raced through the darkness to take the Watcher in the chest.

He reloaded the crossbow and loosed again, and again, exhausting a full quiver of twenty or so bolts. Nearly every bolt took a Watcher in the chest, and soon they began to look for cover.

He ditched his crossbow for a shield and moved back out of harm's way, ordering the men around him to do the same. At that point, their efforts didn't matter anymore. Thousands of Emrael's men had already entered the city via gaps created in the city wall by his Imperator Stonebreakers. Pillars of smoke and tall pyres of flame licked the sky in various spots in the city. As he watched, several of his squads, all clad in black, stormed the walls on either side of the gate. In just moments, they had control of the wall, the Watchers defending it either dead or taken captive.

Emrael ordered the men that remained with him forward, and one of the Imperators on the wall shouted down, "A thousand paces to the north, Meran brought down an entire section of the wall. Turned it to sand mostly, men on horse should be able to get through. We have the walls but there's fighting near the Watcher headquarters."

The plan had worked. His captains and sergeants began shouting orders at their men, and all but a few squads designated to recover their wounded trotted after Emrael.

When they reached the opening, Emrael couldn't help but be impressed. The five-pace-wide gap in the wall was a perfectly uniform rectangle. The sections of the wall still standing on either side ended abruptly in smooth-cut stone, finer than any stonemason could have done.

"Absent Gods," Emrael whispered, running his hands along the smooth stone as his men filed past him. He might be able to wield significant amounts of *infusori*, but he couldn't imagine replicating this level of precision. When he used *infusori* to break stone, it was nearly always a haphazard, destructive affair.

Jaina clapped him on the back. "You have much to learn, Emrael."

She chuckled as she joined the Ire Legionmen filing through the gap and into the brick-walled storehouse that stood on the other side of the wall.

"Well, maybe I need to be training with your Imperators more instead of the exercises you make me do every day," he grumbled as they made their way through the broken-down doors of the storehouse to where his men had formed ranks in the square on the other side.

Jaina smacked his helmet. "My *exercises* are responsible for your gains in strength and control, Emrael. They are what you need to stay alive. The skill work can come later."

He chuckled. "Fine, fine. Let's get this over with."

Five hundred strong, they marched down a wide stone-paved avenue that led to the square where the Lord Holder's palace sat, passing several empty intersections along the way. They saw very few people about, and those they did see scurried out of the way of the marching soldiers. The citizens of Larreburgh were wisely locked up in their homes, but Emrael had expected more resistance than this from the Watchers, even after they had taken the walls.

Just as he thought they might march straight to the Lord Holder's palace without a fight, the ringing of swords on metal, the thump of wooden shields, and the screams of wounded men reached his ear.

"Fast march," he called out. They picked up the pace, trotting toward the sounds of battle until they arrived at a large square ringed with merchants' stalls, a large fountain in the middle. Roughly five hundred men in the drab green of the Ire Legion fought an equal number of well-organized Watchers. As he watched, the Watcher shield-bearers shifted and retracted a step, all at the same time. A volley of *infusori*-enhanced crossbow bolts immediately whistled between their opened shield wall to tear through the front ranks of Iraeans. Shields burst apart before the power of the Watchers' crossbows, clouds of blood misted into the air, and men fell thrashing, screaming.

"Shields locked, flank left!" Emrael roared to be heard over the death screams of the wounded. His men locked shields and moved to flank the Watchers at a deliberate march. Just before they reached the side of the Watchers' square formation, Emrael shouted again. "Charge! Three ranks! Hold three ranks!"

His men shouted as they ran, surging forward to slam into the waiting Watchers. They pushed the Watchers back several steps, as the Watchers were only two men deep on the sides, having committed the majority of their men to the front ranks.

"Push! For Glory's sake, push or we die!" Emrael shouted again. If they gave the Watchers space to maneuver their crossbowmen behind the shields, they'd suffer the same fate as the poor Iraean companies who had just been decimated to their right.

His men thrust spears over shields and jabbed short swords under them. Blood pooled on the cobblestones as soldiers fell on both sides of the shield wall. Emrael had the numbers, however, and inch by inch they pushed the Watchers into a tighter formation.

A command was shouted behind the Watcher lines, unintelligible over the deafening sounds of battle, though Emrael stood near the front of his battle line. The Watchers pulled back suddenly, shifting their shields out of the way for a volley of crossbow bolts, but his men were ready. The Ire Legion pushed forward immediately, jamming the Watchers' shields and knocking them off balance.

"Push!" he shouted again as they shoved the Watcher line back farther. The Watchers were giving ground and losing men quickly, at least here on the flank, but still they held. Damn, but they were disciplined. He needed to break through somewhere; this stalemate was costing him dearly in time and lives.

He growled in frustration as he watched the front ranks of Watchers to their right contract again, shifting so their crossbowmen could decimate the Ire men fighting on that side of the square yet again. Whatever Captain was in charge of that contingent hadn't figured out how to counter the tactic yet.

He slapped Jaina's shoulder to get her attention, then pointed to the Ire Legionmen to the right, who were inching backward, close to breaking ranks after being hit with *infusori*-Crafted crossbow volleys twice in the space of a few minutes. She nodded, and Emrael tapped three of the squad leaders waiting in reserve. "You three squads on me, shields up, two ranks. We're going to take command of the men on the right flank."

Emrael found the Captain Second nearest him and transferred

command to him, telling him to hold the line and press forward as they had been until they saw him break through on the right flank, at which point he was to send his reserve to the rear flank and push the line as hard as possible.

The three squads jogged out from behind their ranks into the empty space between them and the formation of Ire men to the right. Emrael made sure to move at an angle relative to the Watcher formation. A few crossbow bolts still thumped into the shields of their small group, but thank Mercy they were far enough away and held their shields at such an angle that none pierced through.

The ranks of the other Iraean formation opened quickly to let them through. Emrael strode to the nearest man with the metal rivets of a Captain he could find—a Captain Third—and seized him by his chest plate, pulling him close to shout, "Who in Glory's name is in charge here?"

The Captain's eyes widened in outrage momentarily, but the blood drained from his face as he realized who shouted at him.

He pointed mutely at a man a hundred paces away who wore the armor of a Captain Second. Emrael vaguely recognized him as a Sagmynan, but didn't know much more about him. The Captain appeared to be arguing with an Imperator rather than commanding his men despite the battle raging just a dozen paces from them. The Imperator looked ready to do murder.

"Absent Gods damn him," Emrael growled, already running toward the Captain Second. The man noticed Emrael just as he reached him. Emrael didn't hesitate a moment, grabbing him roughly by his chest plate and shoving him toward the back ranks. "You're relieved of your command, Captain."

Emrael pointed his finger at the Imperator, who now had a smug smile on his face. "You, Mage! You now command these men. Jaina and I are going to lead our thirty in a wedge straight up the middle of your battle line, you follow damn quick on our heels with the entire reserve, understand? Press them so they can't shoot at us."

The Imperator's smile vanished and he saluted sharply. "Yes, Lord Ire."

Emrael strapped his shield to his arm and formed up with his three squads, him at the point, and Jaina to his right, where he'd be most vulnerable when they attacked. The battle raged much as it had, Watchers and the Ire Legion locked in a desperate struggle. Eventually, one side would become exhausted and fall.

He rapped his sword against his shield three times, and his thirty men responded with their own rattle of steel on wood. They were ready. His hand tightened around his sword hilt as he shouted, "Move! Make way!"

With tired, jerky motions, the exhausted men just in front of them pulled back from the fight, forming a shield-lined gap just wide enough for the wedge to fit through. The Watchers at the front lurched forward into the sudden gap, breaking their line slightly.

"For Ire and glory!" Emrael bellowed as he launched into a sprint.

As he hit the first line of Watcher shields with his own, he kept his legs under him and pushed with all his might, unleashing a burst of *infusori* to fuel his effort. Two Watchers who had met his charge with overlapped shields were thrown from their feet, tumbling back into the second line so hard that a few of them stumbled as well.

Emrael did not slow. He hit the second line of Watcher shields like a battering ram, throwing another blue-clad enemy soldier to the ground. He darted into the opening in their shield wall, already arcing a fluid strike of his sword into the Watcher to his right, opening a gruesome gash in his side as he passed through.

And then he was among the Watcher reserves, most of whom held crossbows. They hesitated, unable to shoot their weapons for fear of hitting their comrades.

Taking advantage of their confusion, he thrust into the throat of one, then the unarmored armpit of the next. Emrael kept his shield to his left and trusted Jaina to watch his back. Shouts of dismay surrounded him as he flowed from one Watcher to the next, striking farther into the heart of the unprepared Watcher reserves.

Finally he slowed, tired and aware that his men would not be able to keep up if he pushed too far into the enemy ranks. He struck at the man nearest him, but this one, an officer, was ready for him. The Watcher officer parried and slid to the side, lunging quickly at Emrael with a long dagger he held in his other hand. Emrael, slowed by exhaustion, brought his shield up too slowly.

The man's blade carved a line of agony across his forehead before Emrael managed to knock the man away with his shield.

Blood sheeted down Emrael's face, nearly blinding his left eye. He blocked again with his shield as the officer lunged, then feinted with his sword and brought the shield up to catch the man under the chin with the steel rim. Bone and teeth crunched at the impact and the Watcher fell to one knee. Emrael pulsed *infusori* through his blade as he followed quickly with a finishing thrust. His sword punched through steel plate and leather armor with a satisfying crunch.

Though the fight with the officer had taken only a moment, a shiver ran down his back as he realized that dozens of Watchers now surrounded him and he couldn't see Jaina or his own men anywhere.

Panic spurred him to a frenzy. He kicked a nearby shield-bearing Watcher to the ground, then whipped his sword in a brutal arc, dipping low as he did, slashing three nearby crossbowmen across the lower torso. Coils of innards flopped to the ground, and the men fell screaming their death throes. Their comrades drew back and formed a haphazard shield wall here in the midst of their formation, with fear plain on their faces as Emrael bashed his shield with his sword and roared at them.

"Fight, you Watcher bastards! Fight and die!"

Then Jaina caught up to him, and the survivors of his three squads. They overlapped their shields with his, pulling him into a protective formation whether he wanted it or not. He didn't. He wanted to cut his way through the enemy, to feel their blood spray his face, run down his sword and over his hand, slick the stones beneath his boots. Even his own exhaustion and his own blood oozing down his face did nothing to deter him. With *infusori* and battle joy storming through him, he was death incarnate.

Good sense finally prevailed over his instincts, and he snuck a glance behind him. He was relieved to see that the opening he had created in the enemy shield wall had turned the battle into a full rout. Watchers all around him threw down their shields and ran before the tide of Ire Legionmen, a flood of blue uniforms flee- ing before a wave of green. Knots of blue-clad men were caught between the converging sides of his men and threw down their weapons in surrender, screaming their pleas for mercy.

As the battle rage began to drain from Emrael, weariness took its place. He pulled back behind the front lines and tossed his shield and helmet to the ground. He cleaned and sheathed his sword, then motioned to a squad leader who waited with the few reserves who had not chased the fleeing Watchers.

"Send officers out to ensure the men grant quarter. We'll not slaughter any who surrender."

The sergeant saluted, relayed the message to his squad, and all left at a sprint to shout the orders.

Jaina found Emrael in the aftermath of the battle and gripped his head between her hands to inspect his wound. Judging by the amount of blood still running down his face, he must have had quite the gash. She called for a Mage-Healer, but he put a hand on her arm to stop her. "Leave it. There are men that need their Healing far worse than I. I can make do with just a bandage for now. It'll do the Legion good to see that I fight alongside them."

"I don't think they'll mistake you for an aristocrat," she said, looking him up and down.

Blood soaked his leather and plate armor and the clothing underneath. His boots squelched when he stepped. He shrugged. "We need to get to the main square. Who knows what the other groups have run into. Everything hinges on us neutralizing the Watchers and taking Tarelle's palace quickly."

He sat briefly while Jaina took a bandage wrap from one of their men and wound it around his head for him. Once he had sat a moment and had some water from his canteen, he started to feel bone-weary. All too soon, however, she clapped him on the shoulder and offered her hand to help him up. He took it and lurched to his feet, already shouting orders.

In a few short minutes, hundreds of captive Watchers had been secured, the wounded were being cared for, and he was at the head of eight hundred or so of the Ire Legion who could still march to the city center. With luck, his four other such groups had succeeded similarly and would be converging on the Watcher headquarters as well.

As they drew near the Lord Holder's square, the sounds of men shouting were clear, but were not accompanied by the clamor of weapons, shields, and screams that Emrael would have expected. He grew more and more curious until they finally reached the point where the avenue exited into the main square.

Five or so of his squads formed a shield wall at the entrance to the square, blocking any unwanted forces from entering. They moved aside as soon as they recognized their fellow Ire Legionmen.

Two full battalions of Ire men lined up across the entire breadth of the square, facing a formation of Watchers of perhaps half their strength twenty paces away. Now that Emrael had arrived with what remained of his battalion, the Watchers were outnumbered drastically. He recognized Timan and Worren leading these two battalions, but where was that fourth battalion, and Garrus with the reserves? He might not need them even if this came to a fight, but they might have helped him intimidate the Watchers into surrender.

The Ire Legionmen guarding the avenue recognized Emrael after he pulled his helmet off. They cheered, "Ire! Ire! Ire!"

The men following Emrael took up the cheer, and soon those gathered in the square echoed it as well, slamming shields and spear butts against the cobblestones of the great square to accentuate the thunderous chanting.

He strode straight to where the two forces faced each other, thousands of men at his back and Jaina at his side. A year ago, he had been a destitute outcast, and now his own Legion cheered his name.

The Ire shield wall parted as he pushed through. He put his helmet back on and held his shield at the ready, aware that just one crossbow bolt could end him. Jaina, Timan, and a full squad of Imperators flanked him to either side.

He strode to the center of the clear space between the two forces and raised his sword in the air. The chanting from his men stopped so he could be heard. "I want to speak with your commanders," he called into the sudden silence. "I prefer to avoid further bloodshed."

A ripple shimmered through the ranks of Watchers, who stared death in the face. They knew as well as Emrael did that either they could surrender now, or they could fight, lose, and the survivors would surrender afterward.

He waited a moment to let them comprehend what was happening, then shouted again, addressing the soldiers—those who would do the fighting, the dying. "You don't need to die. My quarrel is not with you, but with your commanders. Turn over your commander and senior staff, and any of you who wish may join my Legion. You will receive pay and a land bounty like any other Ire Legionman. All others will be granted quarter and treated fairly."

An immediate murmur rose among the men in blue, and more shifting of shields. The Watchers were professional soldiers, well trained and equipped. Most had likely only seen real fighting along the Ithan frontier, however, and even then only small skirmishes with mercenaries who wanted nothing to do with the military might of the Provinces. Most of them were used to bullying Iraeans and others who never stood a chance against them in battle. They had never stared at men ready and able to slaughter them as they did now.

The murmur among the Watchers grew louder, and Emrael saw movement in the back ranks near the command building, where the senior officers likely still hid while sending their men out to die. Abruptly, the Watcher shield wall opened and three men in blue officer dress uniforms were tossed from among the ranks into the courtyard. None of the three were armed or even armored, and their clothes were mussed from the abrupt manhandling.

Emrael dragged his sword point lightly on the cobblestones as he strode toward the men. They panicked, kicking and scrabbling at the shield wall to be let back in, but the Watchers held firm, even shoving the officers with their shields. He waited until the three faced him—well, him and the twelve Imperators at his back. Fear was clear in their eyes. They knew their fate.

"Take them," Emrael said calmly to the Imperators, belying the fury he felt at the sight of these men who had oppressed the Iraean people at the point of a sword for decades. "There will be a trial, and the Lord Holder will have his say."

He was now close enough to look the Watcher soldiers still holding their shield wall in the eye. He called out to them. "The rest of you, put down your weapons and shields. You will not be harmed."

The Watchers hesitated, but first a few men in the front rank threw down their shields and swords, then all of them seemed to follow at once. Emrael smiled amid the metallic thunder of shields and swords hitting the cobblestones.

Larreburgh belonged to him.

Early the next morning, Emrael, Jaina, and their entourage of Ire Legion officers and Imperators exited the Lord Holder Garan Tarelle's palace just as the sun peeked over the Duskan Mountains. The red-gold light revealed a large gibbet that had been erected overnight in the middle of the square.

They'd only managed about an hour of sleep after the city had been secured and his wound had finally been tended to. Jaina and her Imperators had insisted on checking Tarelle and everyone of any importance for mindbinders before resting but hadn't found any. Her theory was that whichever Malithii priest had discovered that Craft had not shared the knowledge with the others and must be using them only for matters of great importance. Not for the first time, he got the sense that this war with the Malithii and Corrande was larger in scope than he dared imagine. Absent Gods help him.

Emrael's eyes were bloodshot and grainy, as were Jaina's. His muscles were stiff and his head pulsed with pain, especially the stitched-up wound on his forehead. The city and his Legion needed today's events more than any of them needed sleep, however.

The Ire Legion filled the large square with tidy ranks, including those that had defected from the Watchers and Tarelle's guard the night before. The new recruits had been assigned to Ire Legion squads, and he wanted them lined up with their units for the events of the day. Today would separate them from their old loyalties for good.

The vast majority of the Watchers in the city—nearly fifteen hundred of them—had surrendered, and most of those who had remained at the Watcher command building rather than join the battle in the city were native Iraeans, pressed into service and quick to join Emrael's Legion when they learned who had taken the city. They had already shed their Watcher blues and donned their civilian clothes. A substantial number of Lord Holder Tarelle's men had joined Emrael when given the chance as well, something the Lord Holder had not been happy about. Emrael now had close to seven thousand men under his command in Larreburgh despite the losses in the attack.

Some five hundred or so Watchers who had surrendered but had not joined Emrael—native Corrandians, for the most part, judging by the scorn in their eyes and the pale hair prominent among their people—had been stripped of their blues as well, but these sat near the gibbet with elbows bound behind their backs, guarded by an equal number of flat-eyed Ire Legionmen. So long as they didn't fight or try to escape, Emrael and his men would honor the quarter they had granted. But he wanted them to see today's proceedings up close.

Townsfolk milled about the square as well. Emrael's soldiers had posted a notice at every square that there would be an announcement at sunrise in front of the Lord Holder's palace, and that the townsfolk would not be harmed.

Emrael climbed the platform next to the gibbet just as Lord Holder Tarelle was escorted from his palace by Timan and a squad of Emrael's men. The Imperator flashed a wicked grin at Emrael as he shepherded the nervous Lord Holder along.

Next came the three Watcher senior officers, guarded by another squad. The show was about to start. He raised an *infusori*-Crafted speaking cone and addressed the gathered crowd.

"People of Larreburgh—my fellow Iraeans. My name is Emrael Ire, son of Janrael Ire, and grandson of the late King Konrael Ire. The blood of your fellow free Iraeans and Sagmynans has freed you from the tyranny of Corrande and the Watchers."

A few scattered cheers rose in the crowd. Many of his men stood proud but stone-faced, likely remembering their fallen comrades. Emrael himself had helped cart the bodies of their dead inside the captured Watcher compound for hours last night. This attack had been necessary to show their strength and coerce another Lord Holder into joining them, but it had been costly. Nearly a thousand of his men had been killed, and even a resounding victory was little consolation when your brother, or cousin, or friend had just died next to you, screaming and crying with a sword in his gut.

But, they had killed or captured nearly four times as many Watchers as their losses, and bolstered their numbers with new recruits besides. For the first time, Emrael felt real hope that his insane plan to conquer Iraea might actually work.

He lifted the speaking Crafting back to his mouth. "Lord Holder Tarelle has decided to join Lord Holder Norta and me in repelling the Watchers and reclaiming our once-great kingdom."

More cheers rose, and the Legionmen battered their shields with drawn swords just as they had the night before.

"Those that have wronged us will pay for their crimes, starting today."

At that, the three Watcher officers were forced onto the platform beneath the gibbet. A low roar erupted from the gathered townsfolk when a noose was fitted around each of their necks. The Watchers had notoriously been quick to deal harshly with any Iraeans that fell afoul of Provincial Law—a legal code that did little to protect the conquered Iraeans, particularly any who could not pay what the Corrandes and Watchers demanded as a retributory tax for a war that had ended nearly half a century ago. These three officers would have sent hundreds of Iraeans to the gallows in their time commanding the Watcher forces in the Tarelle Holding.

The townsfolk, most in humble garb, pressed forward. His men let them come. The roar of the crowd grew louder and louder as they realized it was safe to openly oppose the Watchers for the first time in decades.

One of the Watcher officers began to sob and cry for mercy. Justice didn't feel very just when you were the one about to swing.

Emrael turned back to the roaring crowd and raised his voice. "How many of our people have suffered at the hands of these men? How deaf have they been to your cries?"

He motioned sharply, and his men pushed the Watcher officers from the platform to dangle by their necks. Their feet kicked, their bodies jerked, and Emrael could faintly hear them rasping as they strangled. Jaina, of all people, stared at him with a worried look on her face as he watched them die. Soon, the Watchers swung lifeless from the gallows and were cut down unceremoniously.

A collective gasp and not a few angry murmurs erupted from the townsfolk—and even some from his own men—when the next captive was led from the Lord Holder's palace to the gallows. A sweating, nervous old man in the elaborate robes of a Sentinel priest was forced up to the platform. Even the Legionmen who had just hanged the officers without hesitation now grimaced, eyes downcast as they fitted the noose around the Sentinel's neck.

Emrael raised the speaking cone again, glaring at his men and the muttering crowds as the Sentinel priest stood below the gibbet. "You would spare this man, after hanging the Watchers that follow his orders? This man is the one hoarding the money stolen from you. This man is the one fueling the Provinces' hatred of us and our heritage. You fear him because you think he speaks for the Gods? There are no Gods, or they've abandoned us to our fate. Our ancestors knew this, and I know this. It's time you learned it."

He strode to the gallows and shoved the shrieking priest off himself, then watched him dangle and squirm at the end of the rope.

"Our bondage has ended!" Emrael shouted, no longer bothering with the Crafted cone. "Men and women are needed to fight, to defend our land once more! My Legion will be taking volunteers for the rest of the day here in the square. Any who can fight or support our army will be well rewarded with gold and land in our captured territories. Iraea will soon be ours again!"

A cheer rose from the crowd, both his men and most of the townsfolk, though a noticeable portion of the townspeople—those in the brighter garb of merchants, especially—drifted away quietly, likely trying to leave town as quickly as they could. Just as well that they did—Emrael wanted word of what had happened here to spread far and wide.

He now had Whitehall and Larreburgh firmly within his control, and soon it would be time to bind the rest of the Lords of Iraea to him. They couldn't afford to ignore him, now.

10

Elle sat up in her chair as a woman in the uniform of an Ordenan naval officer walked into the back of the Hearing Hall of the Sagmynan palace. She beckoned to Captain Sylar, whom Elle had promoted to Captain First and taken as the leader of her personal guard, and was thus responsible for security at today's public hearings. She pointed at the Ordenan officer and murmured, "Bring her to me straightaway and close the hearings for the day."

She had only returned to the city two weeks ago, but Maira had been very quick to turn these and most other administrative duties over to her. It was not exactly what she had imagined governing a province would feel like, but she still enjoyed herself, despite boring hearings like this one.

A relatively minor merchant from the Lower Guild, which represented the business interests of the lower tiers of Myntar, was twenty minutes into petitioning for more *infusori*-cooled storage for himself and his fellow Lower merchants, who had been edged out of the premier cooled storage facilities by the Upper Guild. Elle had already arranged for as much of the *infusori* stores coming from the Wells as possible to be going to the merchants in equal shares, but they were understandably impatient.

The man ceased his droning speech when Elle held up a hand and cleared her throat.

"Good merchant, I understand your plight. I've committed our current *infusori* production to the highest-priority facilities for operation of the province, but you can rest assured that as our production increases, those on the list our clerks have established will receive their due. You can find our clerks in audience chamber three, just down the hall to your left. Thank you, and I'm afraid that petitions are over for the day."

Captain Sylar escorted the Ordenan to the front. Elle was only vaguely aware of the dismayed grumbles echoing through the large hall as everyone was ushered to the doors. She could placate them later. The Ordenans were her top priority.

"Do you have word from your Councils?" Elle asked without preamble as the officer drew near. The Ordenan, a tall dark-haired woman with olive skin, looked affronted for a moment. Elle was too eager for her answer to care.

"Yes, Lady Barros," the Ordenan replied. "I have news. The Councils have agreed. We will patrol the Provincial coast with three ships and sink any Provincial warships that interfere with your province. We will carry your cargo to Ordena and to the Ithans for sixty percent of the profits from each shipment we carry. We require a minimum of twenty such shipments per month."

Elle grimaced, though it had been her idea to offer half of the profits of each shipment. They needed the Ordenans in a bad way until they could build more ships to make up for the lack of land trade routes now that the Provinces were at war and the Ithans had gone silent. She wanted to find a way to get her trade caravans through the Great Rift as well but hadn't been able to get any response from the Free Cities as of yet. Sagmynan trade was dead without the Ordenans, and trade was the lifeblood of the province, of the city of Myntar in particular.

Ordenan pirates, she thought.

Out loud, she said, "Sixty percent is acceptable, though I will limit the terms to one year at that rate. I assume you've prepared at least one ship for immediate voyage, or you wouldn't be here."

The Ordenan officer nodded. "And three more behind us, all headed for Dun-Suun, then to the Ithan territories. Your produce and Craftings will fetch a good price there. More ships will arrive soon after the papers are signed."

When papers had been signed and arrangements had been made for the Upper Guild merchants to load their wares the next day in Ladeska, Elle made her way across the courtyard and to the old Masters' dining hall in the Citadel, where Voran, Ban, and Maira waited for her.

"Sorry I'm late," she said, taking an empty chair next to Ban, who smiled and touched her arm in greeting. She smiled back and turned to the other two. "I wouldn't be surprised if Maira already knows, but the Ordenans have agreed to sink all Provincial warships that sail past our border, and to carry our cargo. They agreed to do it for sixty percent of the profits of each shipment. Twenty ships per month at a minimum."

Voran frowned thoughtfully. He likely only cared that the Ordenans were going to protect them from a sea invasion. Maira smiled and nodded, though she didn't say anything. Elle wondered whether she was happier about the protection for the province they now ran or that the Ordenans had gained a *very* profitable trade foothold. Holy Departed, but the woman was difficult to read.

"I've already signed the agreement for one year, and arranged the first shipment with three more to follow quickly. This buys us some time to build a few of our own ships, both military and trading. The merchants will likely try to do the same, but not nearly enough to sustain past levels of trade. I still can't believe that Governor Sagmyn let his province become so dependent on the Barrosian navy and Ithan traders. How quickly can you build us the beginnings of a fleet if I can guarantee the funding, Voran?"

Voran grimaced, thinking. "I've only five hundred or so shipwrights. I can have five simple fighting vessels and crews for them by the end of the summer, and as many cargo ships in about the same time. They won't be Ordenan cruisers by any stretch of the imagination, but they'll reach the Ithan Empire. If you've got the copper to pay for the lumber and labor?"

"You'll have your money." She turned to Ban. "Do you have designs ready for propulsion, and that naval weapon you were telling me about at dinner last night?"

Ban's eyes lit up with pure excitement. Funny how he could look so much like his elder brother but have such a different heart and mind. "Well, yes and no," he said quickly. "This version of the weapon is really just a giant crossbow, so perhaps not very practical to mount more than one or two on a midsized ship. But they should be ready before the ships are. The propulsion engines . . . that's quite a difficult request, as it turns out. We know what the primary mechanism looks like . . . more or less, even though Mother claims not to know anything about the design. But not only do I have to build a motor to operate in a marine environment, I'll have to figure out how to store enough *infusori* to power an entire ship. We just don't have the technology—"

"Can you do it or not, kid?" Voran cut in. Maira pressed her lips together, annoyed. Elle seethed. Voran often irritated her, but never more than when he was harsh with Ban.

Ban's eyebrows drew down. "Ah, no. Best not to plan on it. I don't have the resources the Ordenans do, and they aren't exactly handing over their schematics. The Master Crafters of the Citadel never managed to make a motor or the supercoils needed to retain *infusori* long enough to power it on a sea voyage. And the charging apparatus . . . we just don't have the Crafters or Crafting knowledge that Ordena does."

Elle put a protective hand on his arm and locked eyes with Voran. "You may have to do without even the weapons for now, though the Masters left at the Citadel can build from Ban's designs. Emrael needs him in Iraea. He leaves the day after tomorrow on an Ordenan cruiser."

She felt a pang of sorrow, or perhaps guilt at mention of Emrael. She didn't regret what she had said—she still didn't know how she felt about him, and it was only fair that neither of them expected things that the other wasn't ready for. Besides, they both had much more pressing matters at hand. They were the Provinces' best hope at earning freedom from Corrande and his Malithii coconspirators, after all. They would have to sort out any feelings—or lack thereof—in due time.

Turning her attention back to the conversation at hand, she could tell that Ban's impending departure was news to Voran, who was not pleased.

"Great," he grumbled. "Sending our best Crafter to twiddle his thumbs in Iraea while Emrael plays king. We should be sending him fighting men, not Crafters and trinkets!"

Maira finally spoke. "Come now, Voran. He must build there, just as we are here, or any military conquest will be for naught. We now have the trade support we need from the Ordenans. Let Ban join Emrael. It will be good for them both, I think."

Voran didn't look happy, but he didn't argue further.

He continued his progress update. Elle tried to pay attention, but her thoughts kept wandering to the Merchants' Guilds, and the grief she was about to catch from the Lower Guild over allowing the Upper Guild sole access to the first Ordenan shipments, never mind that the Lower Guild would never have been able to arrange to fill a ship that quickly. It was simple logistics.

Two of Voran's Legionmen saluted he as he left the meeting with Maira and the two children. He still didn't like the Barros girl having so much influence, but Maira insisted, and he wasn't about to cross that woman.

He saluted in return and stalked down a hallway that led to a small gate connected to the city by way of a steep, narrow stone staircase. The blue glow of *infusori* coils banished all of the evening shadows from the Citadel halls and courtyard, a luxury he had insisted on in the name of security. They had taken this city with blood and fire, after all. There were bound to be those that would try to exact revenge sooner or later. Already they had put down several small uprisings in the city, and his officers had reported similar in the smaller cities and towns that dotted the Sagmyn Valley. He and his officers who had taken residence in the Citadel deserved proper lighting. The pampered merchants in the city would get their *infusori* soon enough.

The Legionmen at the small service gate gave him odd looks— the Commander First of their makeshift Legion would surely use the front entrance, and should likely have an escort—but none said a word as he strode through the gate and down one of the long, narrow stairways that led to the third tier, where his associates waited. He was not a man to be questioned.

After ducking into a side street to wrap himself in an inconspicuous grey cloak, he walked the wide, opulent stone-paved streets of the upper tiers, wondering at the circumstances that had led to him being here in Myntar, playing errand boy for the Ire family. Though he had served with and respected Janrael Ire, he didn't feel much loyalty toward the man's spoiled child, lording about like his noble blood made him better than everyone else. Voran Loire's respect could only be earned.

The amount of copper these black-robed priests had given him back before Dorae had overthrown the previous Lord Holder Norta had been more than enough to get him to listen, however. Curiously, they had paid him to help Dorae win Whitehall, and to help the Ire boy assault Myntar. How had they known the boy's plans before Ire himself had made them? And why would they pay him to fight against them?

Nothing the tattooed foreigners did made any sense at all, but they always accompanied each request with enough copper to buy a mansion in any city in the civilized world. He didn't claim to understand it, but for that kind of money, he didn't need to. Even now that he and his men fought and killed these priests and their allies, they still continued to contact him and pay in good, cold copper for information and small favors here and there. Nothing that would endanger his men, of course. The whole business made him more than a bit uncomfortable, but Absent Gods, the copper. He was nearly as rich as a Lord Holder, now.

His nerves jumped as he passed through the Copper Square, full of massive buildings of stone, steel, and glass construction that housed the offices of Upper Guild merchants and lawyers and the like. He gripped the hilt of his sword as he turned onto the lane where he had been directed, wary of the dim lighting. Perhaps he should have brought an escort after all.

He arrived at the address he had been given and checked it against the instructions he had been delivered one more time to be sure:

8th street, 3rd Tier, #7. The receptionist will be expecting you.

Nothing about the brick building he ducked into was unique or conspicuous in any way. There were thousands like it in the third tier of Myntar. Most wealthy merchants kept not just offices near the Copper Square, but secure storehouses for their most valuable goods destined to leave by the west gate.

Every message he had received—always a ciphered note slipped under his door, or into his clean laundry, or into goods delivered from the city—directed him to a new place. Always in the so-called Copper Tier, though, where most of the city's heavy traffic flowed, presumably making it easier for the priests to sneak in and out of the city undetected. Emrael had placed a very generous bounty of one hundred copper rounds on each Malithii head as soon as he had control of the province, so they must be paying much more than that to whomever they had recruited as their hosts here in the city.

He entered a nondescript wooden door to find a thin, grey-haired attendant behind an expansive, gleaming walnut desk. She looked at him over her spectacles, not the slightest bit perturbed by his arrival well after normal business hours, nor at the sword that hung at his hip. "Yes?"

"I was told you would be expecting me."

The woman smiled. "Ah yes, Mr. Jenneth said his associates would be expecting company this evening. Just down the hall behind me, last door on the left."

Voran flashed a perfunctory smile and nodded his thanks, taking note of the paintings, copper fixtures, and brightly glowing *infusori* coils that lined the wide hallway. These people had money and weren't afraid to flaunt it. How the hell had they obtained charged coils for lighting, with the Barros girl rationing the supply?

He gripped his sword hilt tightly as he opened the last door on the left to find an unoccupied room containing a table set with a dozen chairs. Uneasy, he took a seat, slipping a sheathed dagger under one thigh as he did. He hadn't lived through as many fights as he had by being easy to kill.

Before long, he started to fidget, wondering if he should just leave and be done with these Malithii. He already had enough money to be comfortable for the rest of his life, and could do without the stress of keeping his subterfuge from the Ires. They'd have his head inside the hour if they knew he was even talking to the dark priests, let alone taking their coin. Besides, he stood to profit handsomely should Emrael manage to achieve his aim of reclaiming Iraea, and Mercy forsake him if that didn't seem more likely every day. He had no need to take further risks.

A click of the door was all the warning he had before two Malithii priests entered, accompanied by a middle-aged man in a grey three-piece suit with copper buttons. Mr. Jenneth, must be. These priests always had some rich coin-hoarder or another facilitating these meetings.

The banker—or whatever he was—smiled broadly and offered

his hand as they entered. "Voran, I presume. Jenneth Kyn, proprietor of the Kyn Company."

"*Commander First* Voran Loire, Mr. Jenneth," Voran replied with emphasis, gripping the man's hand firmly but not standing, as he didn't want to reveal the dagger under his leg.

The Malithii ignored Jenneth completely. Both had their light brown eyes fixed on Voran, and each had the same half-smile on his lips.

"Commander," the one on the left chimed in his sharp, singsong accent. The unfamiliar features and extensive, nearly identical tattoos made it difficult for Voran to tell the Malithii he met with apart, but thought that this priest was one he'd seen at least once before. His tattoos covered most of his neck and head, nearly to where his hairline would be if not for the smooth-shaven head, but the face was unmarked. "We have another task for you, and more copper. Much more copper."

More copper was good, but almost certainly more dangerous. "Is that right? Well, as long as your request does not put my current position with the Ires in jeopardy, I'll listen."

The Malithii's smile widened. "You were able to explain allowing young Ire to be captured in the Citadel, were you not? Our copper pays for your ingenuity. If what we asked were easy, we would not pay so handsomely."

A pang of guilt lanced through Voran. The Malithii had paid him well for that one, but he still lost sleep over the Iraeans killed when Emrael had led the sortie into the Citadel. They were far from the first men he had lost. Being paid to allow them to die, though . . . no amount of rationalization had banished his nightmares these past months.

"Yes well," he grumbled. "Just tell me how much, and what you want."

Jenneth shifted uncomfortably in his seat to the side, but the Malithii smiled broadly, leaning forward to put his elbows on the table. "We have two tasks for you. First, your scouts will not venture past the Great Rift for any reason, nor within fifty leagues of any Rift crossing."

"I may be able to arrange that," Voran hedged. His scouts rarely went that far anyway, and he had no plans to increase his scouts' range, whatever the Barros girl wanted. He wasn't about to tell these priests that, though. If they were willing to pay a noble's ransom for something he already planned, he wouldn't object.

"Good, we thought you might. Attend closely, Commander, for the second task is the most important. On the first day of the seventh month, you will return to this location. You will allow some few of my associates into the Citadel dungeons via the secret passage," he said, laying his hand on the silent priest's arm. "You will arrange for Arielle Barros and Maira Ire to be alone where we can reach them that evening."

Voran flinched, slipping one hand to grip at the dagger beneath his leg. He'd seen these bastards fight and didn't think he'd best two of them, but he'd try if it came to it.

He shook his head. "No. I'll limit my scouts and hide whatever you're doing on the other side of the Rift, but I won't let you have Maira. She is off the table."

The Malithii's smile evaporated. "Tsk tsk tsk, Commander. We have had such a profitable friendship thus far. It would be a shame to ruin it so soon. What would Maira say if she knew you were working with us? If she knew the extent to which you had compromised her sons?"

Voran began to sweat. His mouth twisted in a sardonic snarl. "She'd have your guts in a pile on the floor before you said a single word."

The priest spread his hands wide. "Perhaps, perhaps not. But consider that Mr. Jenneth here can attest to all we've discussed here today, and we have other associates who can document our past transactions."

The tattooed bastard fixed Voran with a long stare. "We can avoid any unpleasantness if you'll only assist us, Commander. I'll even remove Maira Ire from the arrangement since she is meaningful to you. Just lead us to the Barros girl. Are we not reasonable?"

He sat in silence, still gripping the dagger under his leg, staring at each of the dark priests in turn. Could he kill them quickly enough to not alert whatever retinue they had undoubtedly brought with them?

The Malithii's eyes lit up after a time. "Ah! I almost forgot.

I think this will help. The prize for this task is fifty thousand copper rounds. Ten thousand now, to ease your mind. The rest will be guaranteed by a contract kept in Mr. Jenneth's possession."

The black-robed priest knocked on the door, and a manservant entered the room to place a small wooden chest on the table. The servant, burly though he was, labored to lift the chest to the table. The priest opened the chest with a flick of his hand, revealing heaps of bright copper coins.

Voran's eyes widened, and this time he was silent due to shock. How did these men have access to such funds? He could buy a minor kingdom in the Ithan Empire for that, or a major Holding in most of the Provinces. He might even be able to acquire a Lord Holdership in Iraea, should he play his cards right with whoever won the war there.

He licked his lips. "The first day of the seventh month, you say? Only the Barros girl?"

11

"You hanged a Sentinel priest?" Halrec almost shouted at Emrael. They sat in the Lord Holder Tarelle's private dining room with Jaina, Toravin, and the Lord Holder himself, almost a week after the capture of the city.

Halrec turned to the rest of the table. "And you sat there and watched? Are you all mad?"

"I . . . I had no choice," said Tarelle. "You stormed my walls and started a war right in my streets. What did you *expect* me to do?"

"But you didn't fight us, either, did you? You left the Watchers to their slaughter," Toravin murmured, feeling at a tooth with his tongue.

Tarelle fell quiet.

"And the priest?" Halrec asked again. "What the Fallen hell were you thinking, Em?"

Emrael bared his teeth in a smile he didn't feel. "Tell me, Halrec, why should he have been spared? If anything, I should round them up and hang every one. Every Watcher injustice can be laid directly at their feet as well. They write the orders, pass the judgements, and reap the benefits of the Watchers' thefts."

"That old man had nothing to do with the Watchers, Em! They have answered only to the High Sentinel and Corrande himself since the War of Unification, and you know it. He was no more than a clerk taking orders. You killed him to make a point."

Emrael stepped up to plant a finger in Halrec's chest. "Precisely! To make the point that they are complicit. Corrande, his priests, and his Watchers are a plague that we will eradicate, or we will all die just like our grandfathers did. Have you forgotten the soul-bound and Corrande's pet Malithii already? That's what this war is about, that's what they've brought to our continent. They are all a part of it."

Halrec slapped Emrael's hand away. "Even still, we can fight and win this war without resorting to thoughtless executions. You think the people who saw that will follow you? Many Iraeans now believe in the Faceless Gods—some of the Lords Holder probably do too! The old ways of ancestor worship are just that—old. You've likely just offended as many as you've encouraged."

Emrael's anger surged and he pulled *infusori* from his life source until his eyes glowed faintly. When he spoke, his voice was quiet. "Any who balk at the demise of their oppressors would not have joined us anyway, and now word will spread among those that are willing to fight the Provinces and everything they stand for. That dead priest is a symbol, a declaration that this is more than a war between Lords. It is a war for the people, to restore Iraean freedom and their way of life."

"Are you going to bring back mage worship too, then? Seems convenient."

"If you think I'm only after my own glory, why are you here, Halrec?"

Halrec opened his mouth to reply but was interrupted by Timan throwing the door open.

The Imperator looked appraisingly at Emrael and Halrec, who stood toe-to-toe, clearly arguing while the others around the table watched with varying degrees of discomfort.

"Norta sent word that the Lords Holder have agreed to a Council of Lords. The tenth day of the third week of summer—three weeks from tomorrow. In Whitehall."

Emrael breathed deeply, finally looking away from Halrec. "Good. We'll march the day after tomorrow."

Timan nodded, took another look at everyone in the room, then stepped back out into the hall.

Emrael called to him. "Timan. Come in, take a seat. You should hear this too."

The Imperator shrugged and walked back in to take a seat next to Jaina.

Halrec stalked over to a chair on the other side of the table from Emrael, where he glared but stayed quiet.

Emrael met his glare, but when he spoke, it was with a hint of pleading. "Hal, we found a good portion of the Watchers' reparation takings in his mansion. The bastard was living like a king on the backs of Iraeans who are nearly starving."

After a moment, Halrec nodded grudgingly. "Just think about what you're doing, how it looks, Em. You can't let your anger lead you around by the nose anymore."

A sardonic smile twisted Emrael's lips. "Not only did the old man deserve it, but his death served an additional purpose. Now that Lord Holder Tarelle here was party to hanging a Sentinel, one step removed from the High Sentinel himself? His fate is tied to ours for good, whether he likes it or not. Isn't that right, Tarelle?"

Tarelle's face went pale. He knew the only greeting he'd receive from Corrande now was his own noose, or maybe a knife to the gut.

Toravin and Jaina had stayed quiet through the entire argument. They had known his plan from the beginning—hanging the priest had been Toravin's idea, in fact. "Now. We need to get those walls fixed as soon as possible. Toravin will leave a full company of his best scouts to patrol every known route the Watchers might take, and he's hired a few men to spy on the surrounding Holdings. Tor, how quickly will your men be able to get word to Halrec if they learn something?"

Toravin chewed on his lower lip as he considered. "You'll know at least a day before any army can reach you, even if they come out of the Tarelle Gap. Worst case, my men will have to send word with merchants or travel through the woods themselves if the Watchers set up blockades. Word should get to you before the Watchers are at your doorstep in any event. Unless they do what we did, and strike quickly." He chuckled. "They have some Iraean boys in their ranks that know the back roads almost as well as my men do. Nothing is certain in war."

Emrael nodded his thanks. "You'll want to set a good watch regardless, Hal. I'll leave some Imperators with you as well, in case any of those Malithii and their soulbound turn up. You can build your army by offering land to those who join you, same as I'll be doing in the west."

Halrec sighed, but nodded again. "I can hold Larreburgh with three thousand for now, as long as they can't bring down the walls like you did. You had better get those Lords Holder on your side quick, though, or we're dead as dirt."

"I'll charm them right out of their boots. One way or another," Emrael laughed, which finally put a small smile on Halrec's face.

He stared his oldest friend in the eyes. "I know you don't always agree with my tactics. But I need you. You're the only one I trust to defend this Holding, Hal. Everything I'm about to do depends on you keeping Corrande at bay."

Halrec nodded. "I'll do my best, Em."

"So will I, Hal. I swear it."

Ten days later, Emrael sat next to Toravin on the steps outside Whitehall Keep, watching their Captains Third and Second drill nearly five thousand new recruits down in the main square. These recruits were the latest to answer Emrael's proclamation promising land and gold. They were untrained, poorly outfitted folk, barely able to keep up. For now.

"Sorry lot, aren't they?" Toravin commented idly.

Emrael grunted. "When we're staring at a horde of Watchers, Corrande Legionmen, and soulbound, you'll be glad for them. We'll turn them into soldiers yet."

Toravin turned to look Emrael in the eye. "Lot of the poor bastards are going to die."

"I know," Emrael said quietly. "We're about to get a lot of people killed, Tor. I don't like it, but I don't have a better option. The real question is this: Is it worth the cost?"

Toravin was quiet for a time, then spat. "Aye, I reckon it is. Better dead than forced to live half a life under those Watcher bastards. You and I are risking our lives for freedom, it's not so hard to understand why they would as well. Just be sure they're cut in on the winnings, eh?"

Emrael nodded. "Everyone that joins us will have a place here, Tor. Every one. I mean to see us all free and prosperous, not just the nobility."

Toravin looked him in the eye, a solemn expression on his face. "Give us a reason to believe that, and we'll fight to the death for you, Ire."

The city rang with the sound of smiths hammering out spear blades. Carpenters were already turning out various sizes of wooden shields, finished spears, and crossbow bolts by the thousands. Nearly every loom in the city wove green wool for Ire Legion uniforms. Their Legion engineers, equipped with designs Ban had provided, had organized workshops that turned out hundreds of *infusori*-Crafted crossbows daily.

These farmers-turned-soldiers wouldn't be an even match for seasoned Legionmen anytime soon, but with a few months of drilling they'd hold a shield wall passably well. A crossbow turned a farmer into a deadly soldier in remarkably little time.

Some of the newcomers had even asked to learn magecraft, including many of the former Citadel students Emrael had freed in Whitehall earlier that year. Those that had passed an initial test now trained with Timan and four other Imperators day and night. Most of the Imperators wouldn't deign to teach *A Me'trae*, "the Art," to heathens, but Timan and a few others apparently didn't adhere as carefully to whatever exclusionary religious beliefs the others held. Or perhaps they believed in Emrael's cause enough to risk it. Whatever the reason, he was grateful. If he could train a group of mages loyal to him . . . well, that might just win him a war. Maybe more.

However, he had a long way to go before his Legion would be able to truly challenge Corrande, Barros, and the Malithii. Between the Watchers and the two Provincial Legions, his enemies could likely field a hundred and fifty thousand trained soldiers. If the Malithii had more soulbound under their control, Emrael and his followers faced long odds indeed.

He only had fifty thousand or so in his Ire Legion, and most of those were tied up holding the Sagmyn Province, Gadford across the river in Barros territory, and now Larreburgh. He had left many of his seasoned veterans with Halrec in Larreburgh, which would likely be square in Corrande's sights. Emrael was left with five thousand Legionmen of varying levels of experience, plus five thousand raw recruits here in Whitehall.

Dorae had another ten or fifteen thousand at his disposal, but many of them were just as green and poorly equipped as Emrael's.

Probably worse, as the man didn't have the same advantage of having appropriated much of the Sagmyn Legion and their equipment.

He looked across the city, past the small lake shimmering at the head of the Stem River, at the far bank in the distance. Barros land. Thank the Absent Gods Barros hadn't attacked Gadford yet. He'd have to do something about Barros, and soon; he needed to be able to move supplies and men between Sagmyn and Iraea freely.

But first, he needed the Lords of Iraea. None of them had shown their faces yet, even though the scheduled Council of Lords was only a few days away. He worried that they would ignore Dorae's summons despite centuries of tradition, and despite his demonstrated willingness to conquer them one by one. Worse, they could be outside Whitehall somewhere, plotting against him. If the Lords of Iraea attacked Whitehall instead of joining him, his war with Corrande would be over before it began. And they might, after he had taken Larreburgh by force—he might have done so, in their place.

"Do you think they'll come?" Emrael asked Toravin finally.

Toravin grunted, shifting a bit as if he could find a softer spot on the stone steps of the keep. "Who?"

"The Lords Holder."

Toravin chuckled. "Aye, one or two at least. Raebren fought with Ire, back in the war. Syrtsan too, though not the current Lord Holder. Bayr—nobody knows what those stodgy bastards are up to, ever. Marol and Paellar . . . I wouldn't hold your breath. Though Glory knows Iraeans love their tradition. Even the assholes who've sold their dignity to the Watchers. Whoever comes, you'll not convince them easily. Our path is not the prudent one."

"Fallen take the bastards if they accept comfortable bondage over bloody peace. I'll give that to them too, if I must."

For all his bravado, the declaration did little to make him feel less anxious. Anything other than winning over some of the Lords Holder was likely a death sentence for him and his followers. He needed them, and was afraid he wouldn't be up to the task of convincing them that the benefits of joining him would be worth the risk.

A rider in the green-and-black coat of a Norta guardsman trotted into the square, heading toward him and Toravin. When he reached them, he vaulted from the saddle and saluted.

"Sirs . . . a party is at the harbor. One of them claims to be Lord Ire's brother, sirs."

Emrael jumped up immediately. "Where are they? You let them in, right?"

"Yes, Lord Ire. They're headed up the main avenue just now."

Emrael smiled what felt like his first true smile in weeks as he caught sight of the small mounted party. A big wagon trailed them, accompanied by more than a dozen studious-looking men and women—the Crafters from the Citadel he had asked Elle to send, he hoped—and three squads of his Legionmen as an escort, most of them in old Sagmyn Legion uniforms.

He shouted to his brother and ran down the stairs to meet him in the square. "Welcome to Iraea, Ban! Did the Ordenans manage to get you here without any trouble?"

Ban jumped down from his horse and they met with a fierce hug.

"Barros's ships didn't even come within firing range of the Ordenans. Mother convinced them to send us here on a cruiser."

Emrael patted his brother's back and squeezed his shoulders as he held him at arm's length. "Gods, you've put on some muscle!"

Ducking his head sheepishly, Ban smiled at the compliment. "I've been training with the Imperators you left at the Citadel."

Emrael's smile faltered before he was able to smooth his face. "I wish you didn't have to learn to fight, Ban, but it's a good idea. You'll keep training with me and the Imperators here. Have they taught you any of their *A Me'trae*?"

"Some." His brother fished a small wood block out of his pocket and held it in his hand, palm up. This close, Emrael could feel a small pulse of *infusori* emanate from his brother as the block exploded in a shower of wood chips and dust.

Emrael smiled, mildly impressed, but his jaw dropped when he saw what was inside the pile of wood dust—a toy soldier. He snatched it from Ban's hand, marveling at the detail of the wooden figurine. It even had a little sword in its hand.

He stared at his brother in shock for a moment. "Ban . . . that's incredible! That level of precision . . ."

Ban's face reddened despite his smile. "Once I learned to use the *infusori* directly, I just started using it however I could. I don't have nearly the capacity you do, but detail comes naturally, I suppose. I hardly need to use any tools when Crafting anymore."

"I can imagine," Emrael marveled. "When we get settled, I want you to show me more. I'll have a workshop set up for you. But first, you should give everyone a report on things in Sagmyn. I'll call Dorae and the others together."

When they had entered Whitehall Keep and messengers had been tasked with gathering the others in a private room, Emrael showed Ban to lodging quarters across from his own. The rooms weren't anything extravagant—he had turned such accommodations down when Dorae had offered—but they were certainly better than what he and his brother had shared at the Citadel.

"Hey Em, do you think we could just move a bed into your room and share, like we used to? I think I'd like that, at least for a while. Unless you have other . . . plans?"

"No, I don't have other 'plans.'" His brother must have learned that Elle had ended things with him, then. "The castle steward might shout at me a bit for moving this bed, but I'm 'Lord Ire' now. They'll get over it."

They each grabbed one end of the bed and lugged it out of the room. As they were carrying it through the hallway, Toravin popped around a nearby corner. "What in Glory's name are you two doing? We have servants for that kind of thing, you know."

Emrael bared his teeth at Toravin as he rested the wooden bed frame on his shoulder to try to kick the door to his room open. "Maybe I'm just used to *being* the servant, Tor. I'm not waiting around for some poor bloke to do my work for me." He cursed at the door as he tried again and failed to catch the door latch with the toe of his boot.

Toravin folded his arms and lounged against the wall. "Okay then."

"Tor?"

"Hmm?"

"Get your ass over here and open this door."

Toravin chuckled and took his time sauntering over to hold the door. He grunted a laugh again as he watched them situate the second bed in Emrael's room, shifting the nightstand and a work-table out of the way to make it fit. "You know you could get a bigger room? Adjoining rooms, even, if you like?"

Emrael and Ban sat down next to each other on the bed, sweat-ing. The damn thing was heavier than it looked. "We used to share a room half this size at the Citadel. We're fine here."

Toravin pursed his lips and raised his hands in exaggerated ac-ceptance. "Fine by me. I'll take the fancy rooms if you don't want them. Speaking of fancy, the first Lord Holder has just arrived. Lord Syrtsan and his entourage are being settled as we speak. He says Bayr and Raebren are on their way as well. Looks like you'll have your Council after all."

Ban looked back and forth between Toravin and Emrael. "What's all this?"

"I've called a Council of Lords of Iraea, Ban. Well, Dorae did. I'm not a Lord Holder—not yet."

Toravin sucked at his teeth. "Speaking of. Dorae sent me to take you to a tailor—says we can't let the other Lords Holder see you looking like a peasant."

Emrael looked down at his clothes—they were plain but in fine condition. Maybe a bit worn and sweat-stained from wearing ar-mor over them. He gestured at Toravin, who wore fine clothes that looked like they cost a great deal, when they weren't on the road. "I don't see why it matters, Tor. You can wear frippery if you like, but this suits me fine. Clothes don't make a man."

Toravin smirked at him. "Clothes matter to nobility, Ire. Real nobility, that is."

Emrael glared. "What would you know about nobility?"

Toravin just shrugged. "I'm only trying to help. Take my word or don't, but how you look will matter."

"Fine, but nothing too extravagant. I won't be dressed up like a show horse at a fair." He reached into his pocket to draw out an en-velope sealed with wax and handed it to the man. "Can you make sure this gets to Lord Bayr when he arrives?"

Toravin's eyes narrowed as he turned the letter over in his hands. "Why Bayr? What are you up to, Ire?"

He looked Toravin in the eyes, serious now. "I'm setting the stage. Make sure Bayr gets that letter. Nobody else sees it. Bring me his answer discreetly, please."

Five days later, all of the Lords of Iraea had arrived at Whitehall—even the Provinces-appointed steward of the Ire Holding had come, which Emrael hadn't expected.

The night before the Council of Lords, Emrael chose to dine in a small, private room. Everything that could be done to prepare had been, and he needed some time to think.

The table had six chairs, but only three were occupied. Ban sat to his right, Jaina to his left. The empty seats reminded him of how few people he truly trusted, how thin he was stretched. Loneliness was inherent in the life of the ambitious, he supposed.

He did have a few capable friends to help him manage the territories they had captured, but most were otherwise occupied. Halrec commanded the Ire Legion in Larreburgh. Elle and his mother governed Sagmyn in his stead. Dorae and Toravin were busy hosting the newly arrived Lords Holder, who had no doubt only answered Dorae's invitation to voice their complaints. Or maybe to get a firsthand look at Emrael's Legion. The Council tomorrow would set the stage for everything he hoped to accomplish in the coming months and years, would determine whether they stood a chance against Corrande and his Malithii allies.

The table had been set with roast ducks, platters of seared vegetables, summer-ripe stone fruits from the orchards outside Whitehall, and soft brown bread with a large wedge of cheese. Only ravaged duck carcasses and scattered bits of food remained. Emrael hadn't thought he would be able to eat much due to his nerves, but he had been very mistaken.

Now they sat quietly, drinks in hand. Jaina had her customary glass of red Sagmynan wine, which she swirled and stared at in mute contemplation. Ban clutched a steel mug of amber ale in one hand while scribbling occasionally in a leather-bound notebook.

Emrael had asked for a bottle of whatever spirit the steward of the keep liked best and had been rewarded with a bottle of oak-barrel-aged peach brandy, apparently a favorite in these parts.

Having drunk nearly half the bottle by himself, he had to agree with them. Particularly when paired with the rich duck, the clean, fruity brandy seemed to just slide down his throat. And he had found that if he held a bit of *infusori,* he could drink what should have been an incapacitating amount of liquor and still function. Mostly.

Earlier in the evening, he had told Ban about the Prophet's visit and the vision of the Fallen that came after. He had been fretting incessantly since about the ease with which Savian had infiltrated the keep, and something occurred to him in his half-drunken trance. He turned to Jaina. "You can feel mindbinders, right?"

Jaina's eyes were full of disapproval. She didn't like it when he drank, and the night before the Council of Lords at that. Still, she said nothing of it, only nodded in answer to his question.

"Hmm," he said, squinting as he thought. He pointed at his brother. "Can you show him how it works? The mechanics of how you feel it, or whatever?"

Ban's eyes lit up as he looked up from his notebook. "Yes, yes show me. I've been practicing with your mages . . . Imperators, rather. You can show me."

Jaina flashed her characteristic sardonic smirk. "I'm babysitting two of you now, am I?" She put her hands on the table, now staring hard at each of them in turn. "Some of the things I'm teaching you would get me expelled from my Order, if they knew. I'll show you, but I want your word—both of you—that you'll keep it between us."

Ban nodded. Emrael smiled and said simply, "Our secrets are safe with each other, don't you think?"

She gave him a mock glare but soon smiled. She pushed away from the table to stalk over to Ban, clasping his outstretched hand. Both closed their eyes, faces suddenly slack. After a moment, Jaina opened her eyes, which now glowed with a muted blue fire.

"Good. A *mentai,* it feels like this. I will only place it on you briefly." She reached into her pocket with her free hand to procure a small bracelet that she then placed on Ban's wrist. Ban froze, eyes wide, for the fraction of a moment it took Jaina to undo the clasp. He drew in a sharp breath immediately, pulling away in a panic, breathing heavily.

Ban jumped when Emrael put a hand on his shoulder. Fear and

anger lit his brother's eyes, but after a moment, he relaxed. "Sorry, I . . . I just didn't expect that. It felt just like . . ." He trailed off, and looked away, embarrassed. "I'm fine. I . . . I know what they feel like." He drew in a deep breath and looked at Jaina. "I'll feel the same through anyone else who is wearing one?"

She nodded. "More or less. There are some that affect the victim less, like the one Yerdon wore. Those are much harder to feel but exude the same energy. You won't miss it, I think. It is not the sort of thing one forgets."

Ban drew another deep breath. "I think you're right. I'll get to work right now." He stood and exited the room with a squeeze on the arm for Emrael. He'd be locked up in their room working on a design for hours now that he had a new project.

When the door had closed behind his brother, Emrael paced back to his chair, where his bottle of peach brandy waited. Jaina gave him another disapproving glare as he filled his glass again but took her chair next to his without comment.

After a long but comfortable silence, Emrael said, "I need someone to take a message to the southern Barros Lords Holder."

Jaina sipped her wine and stayed silent, content to stare at him until he said more.

He frowned at her. "I need an Imperator or two that you trust. I'll send a few of Toravin's best men that know the Barros Province with them. I think we can turn them against Governor Barros. They'll at least keep him off our backs and might even deliver the province to us if we play it correctly."

Setting down her glass, she looked at him. "What do you know, and how? You seem confident that these Lords Holder will listen. Why?"

Emrael's pulse quickened. "Savian, when he was here . . . he said something about them," he said finally. "I didn't think much of it until just now. He was out of his mind, Jaina, but I don't think he was lying about this."

Jaina threw her head back and laughed. "You have let liquor rot your brain. You really think to trust a servant of the Fallen? Silent Sisters, Emrael, I thought you were nearly cured of your idiocy."

"I don't trust him, Jaina. But he wasn't lying about that. I could feel it."

"Oh? You don't think there are mages good enough to trick the likes of you? You are like an ignorant child still, and there is no such ability to detect truths. Your strength in *A Me'trae* does not make you skilled." She snapped her fingers and sat up slightly, eyes locked on his intently now. "But suppose he was not lying, what then? Might there be some other motive, some other scheme, even if his words were true?"

"Well . . ." Emrael drew out the word, thinking. "He could have an ulterior motive, I suppose, but it's not like I'm doing anything we wouldn't have done anyway. I'm not committing resources, I'm merely proposing an alliance. We need Barros off our backs. You know it as well as I do."

She raised one eyebrow at him, frowning speculatively. "Yes, perhaps your plan is not so bad. But you cannot trust that Malithii priest, Emrael. If he wants you to ally with the southern Barros Holders, I am suspicious as to why."

Emrael sloshed brandy on his wrist as he set his glass on the table a little too hard. "What am I supposed to do, Jaina? I'd have done the same without what he said. I'm out of options. I want your Imperators to accompany our messengers to make sure we aren't walking into some Malithii scheme, but tell me clearly: What danger do you see that I don't?"

Silence filled the air, not at all comfortable now. Jaina didn't seem to be bothered by Emrael's stare, however. "Fine. I will send Imarra and Daoro with your men. They will get your message to the Lords Holder safely. But be wary, Emrael Ire."

Early the next morning, Emrael flexed his shoulders as he entered Whitehall's main hall, testing the stretch of his new shirt and coat. Ban and Jaina walked on either side of him, with Toravin just behind. He had to admit he looked good, especially after a shave and cutting his hair short again. Who knew that wool could feel so soft and light?

He sat in the middle of a large table that had been placed on the dais of Whitehall's main hall, facing the room. Ban and Dorae sat to either side, and the ever-sweating Lord Holder Tarelle sat next to Dorae. Dorae and Ban wore fine wool as he did, but Tarelle wore a shimmering cloth Emrael did not know the name of. Jaina and Toravin sat behind Emrael and to one side.

On the other side of the table, five men were just settling into their seats. Lord Delin Paellar, a skinny fellow with a pointed black and white goatee, ruled the lands north of Tarelle and was closely tied to Corrande. Emrael was honestly surprised that the man had answered Dorae's call for a Council of Lords, though Paellar had shown up with over three thousand armed men to ensure his safety. Some of the three thousand were almost certainly Watcher spies.

Baric Raebren, a stocky old man with only wisps of snow-white hair left on his sun-spotted scalp, was lord of the river lands to the west of the Norta Holding. He was the only Lord Holder on the other side of the table who had fought against the United Provinces with Emrael's grandfather in the War of Unification.

Lord Callan Syrtsan looked quite like his nephew, Halrec, except for his perpetual frown and deep wrinkles in his long face. Callan had ruled the Syrtsan Holding under heavy Watcher scrutiny since his father had been killed in the War of Unification, fighting to keep Iraea a free kingdom.

Tall, muscular Davis Bayr was Lord of a Holding so small between Syrtsan and Ire lands that some minor lords in other Holdings actually held more land. Emrael was willing to bet that nobody brought that up to his face, though. Bayr commanded more than twenty thousand soldiers famous for their prowess in battle, or had before the Provinces put an end to Iraean Lords Holder keeping standing armies. The Lords Holder of Iraea were supposed to limit their armed guards to five thousand, but Toravin was certain that Bayr had trained and outfitted many times that amount among the populace of his small but prosperous Holding.

And finally, fidgeting with his sleeves near the end of the table farthest from Emrael, sat a bulky, hard-looking man with iron-grey hair. Emrael knew little about Lord Marol except that he was the son of a lord in the Ire Holding whom the Watchers promoted to Lord Holder when he turned against Emrael's grandfather in the War of Unification. The man was a rat, Corrande's lackey. He stood directly in the way of Emrael regaining his ancestral Holding.

Various lesser nobles and other people Emrael didn't care about today sat some distance away in chairs scattered about the hall to witness the meeting, all people that the Lords of Iraea had brought with them or functionaries from Dorae's staff. Each Lord Holder had brought soldiers too, thousands of them altogether, but left them camped far enough from the city that he and Dorae didn't feel threatened—though they had sent scouting parties to keep watch. All inconsequential, compared to Emrael's plans. He only had eyes for the four Lords across from him.

He looked to each in turn, then gestured to Marol. "I called for the Lords of Iraea, and you bring him? Wearing my family's ring?"

Marol shifted in his seat, face angry, but Lord Syrtsan spoke first in a calm, measured voice. "He is a Lord Holder by the grace of the Provinces. Which is more than can be said of you. Your family lost the War of Unification, and have paid the just price for it. Lord Marol has also paid for your family's failures, paid for the Ire Holding while you and your family hid in the Barros Province with my brother and nephew. Who, I hear, is holding the Tarelle lands for you?"

Emrael leaned forward in his chair, hands in fists on top of the table. "Not everyone had the choice to stay and live, Callan," he said quietly. "And we are here, now, fighting for our freedom. And yours. Which of you can say the same?"

Lord Raebren laughed then, a raspy chortling sound. "Boy, you've got failed rebels and a coward who was too stupid to see you coming for allies. You have an army that wouldn't hold up against a single Provincial Legion, much less the Watchers. You aren't fighting for freedom. You're hanging yourselves and don't know it yet."

Emrael's anger was tempered by respect for the old man as he responded. "Lord Raebren, we started with a ragtag army of Iraeans, but now control the Sagmyn Province and two Holdings in Iraea. I can call upon as many men as any governor. Thousands more join me every week, and I have the support of the Ordenans through my mother." He gestured to Jaina to illustrate his point. "I'm offering you a chance at victory, and freedom. With the Lords of Iraea behind me, we can have all the Provinces. Maybe more."

Raebren grunted and grumbled, sipping his cup of wine as he considered. For some reason, the old man frowned at Toravin repeatedly before he turned to look at a striking young dark-haired woman who had Raebren's same high cheekbones and pointed nose. There was clearly a connection there.

Paellar smirked and waved his hand. "Corrande and his Watchers will kill you by the end of the summer, boy. And if he doesn't, the winter will starve you and your rabble."

Emrael smiled viciously. "I hear the warehouses in your port cities are fat with salt fish and grain, Paellar. We won't go hungry."

He motioned silently in Tarelle's direction to drive his point home.

Lord Bayr fixed Emrael with a hard stare. "So what is it you want, Ire? Why would we join you when we stand to profit from your demise? Lord Corrande has offered us much if we help him defeat your little . . . movement. I don't imagine you called us here just to threaten us?"

Emrael straightened, looked over at Ban and Dorae, then addressed the four Lords Holder sitting across from him. "No, Lord Bayr, I didn't. I called you here because it's time that Iraea becomes its own kingdom again. Not a conquered territory at Corrande's beck and call."

Whether these men were willing cooperators with Corrande and the Watchers or had accepted a lesser place in the world under duress, they all paid the Unification tax. They were all subject to the whims of a Provincial governor not their own, and they knew it.

"My fight is not with you, but with Corrande," he continued before the silence invited any of them to respond. "I want fighting men, I want my ancestral lands returned to me, and I want your allegiance. In return, I will give you a share in the whole of the Provinces. Lands, copper, kingdoms. Even you, Lord Marol. I will take my lands, but you will have others. Any who join me willingly will rule Iraea again, and more."

He swept his gaze across the room. Raebren's watery eyes gleamed with fiery ambition, as did Bayr's eyes. Dorae smiled. Syrtsan sat quiet as a stone, as did Lord Marol. Paellar looked as if he had eaten bad fish.

"I want you to see what Corrande will bring to your lands if you side with him," Emrael announced after a tense moment of quiet. At his signal, one of his men waiting at the main door slipped out. Moments later, a squad of his men entered, carrying two large canvas-wrapped bundles gingerly between them. The men dropped the bundles on the floor between the table and those sitting in the rest of the hall, then cut away the cloth on one end, revealing the rotting heads of a Malithii priest and one of the slain soulbound. The lesser nobility seated near the bodies covered their noses against the smell; several of them closest to the rotting corpses began to retch. The Lords of Iraea, however, inspected the bodies calmly.

Circling the table, Emrael nudged the dead Malithii. The flesh had decayed, but the tattoos that covered nearly its entire head were clearly evident. "The world is changing, whether you like it or not. You can no longer pay your taxes, kneel to the Watchers, and expect to live in peace. Corrande has allied with Malithii priests, dark mages against whom the Ordenans wage their holy war in the Westlands. They have brought their evils with them, have made Provincial citizens into these soulbound monsters. They'll do the same to your people, if they haven't already. Corrande will let these Malithii into Iraea, and will turn our people into these monsters to fight for them. Pawns, slaves in his war against the Ordenans. Unite with us, or die as their slaves. Only I can free you from their grasp."

Lord Raebren nodded openly. Bayr frowned at the corpses, but his expression was otherwise unreadable. Paellar, however, looked sick. Rumor said that Paellar was cooperating fully with Corrande, which meant that he had likely met the Malithii and their soulbound monsters.

Syrtsan sat stone-faced and unreadable, as did Marol. Emrael walked back around the table to take his seat, motioning for his men to remove the corpses as he did. Just as he sat, Lord Raebren started coughing and did not stop. When Emrael saw the man slump onto the table, spittle beginning to gather at the corners of his mouth, he stood and shouted, "A Healer, Jaina, quickly!"

He couldn't risk losing a lord who had seemed on the brink of supporting him. He dashed around the table to help Lord Syrtsan ease Raebren to the floor.

The beautiful young woman sitting in the front row of observers rushed forward, unstoppered a small vial, and shouldered Emrael aside with a glare.

He stepped back, surprised, but she had already forgotten him as she knelt to pin Lord Raebren down forcibly. She gripped his jaw to force his mouth open and poured a few drops carefully into the old man's mouth as he shook and coughed feebly. Within moments, he had calmed and the coughing subsided.

An Imperator Mage-Healer rushed into the room on Jaina's heels, but the Raebren woman—presumably the Lord Holder's relative—waved them away as well. Emrael stepped forward again to touch the woman on the shoulder. "My lady, that man is a Healer, a mage from Ordena. He can help."

She drew herself up to her full height to stand nearly nose to nose with Emrael. He was only of average height, and she was tall for a woman. "I'll not have any of those devils touch my father. We have a healer of our own here with us."

Emrael raised his hands in surrender and took a step backward. "Father?"

The young woman glared at him, but Toravin was the one to answer. "Aye, she's his daughter, from a late second marriage. You'll have to forgive her, Saravellin doesn't much like the Ordenans. Doesn't like many people, far as I can tell." He breathed deep and said quietly, "She's a relative. Was a relative."

As far as Emrael had known, Toravin was just a soldier turned smuggler after Dorae's rebellion had failed. "I didn't take you for nobility, Toravin."

Toravin's expression turned wry as he continued staring at Saravellin. "Is there still a bounty on my head in Raebren Holding, Sar?"

Saravellin looked up from tending to her father, who now seemed to be recovering and was being loaded on a litter to be helped to his rooms to rest. "Aye. I doubled it recently when you resurfaced. Five hundred copper rounds, Iraean. Though most of my men would kill you for free. The Watchers blamed my father when you deserted them for Dorae's rebellion, you know, and we have been paying for it while you hid away. Thousands of copper rounds paid to keep them and their Sentinel priests from exacting their vengeance on our people."

Toravin nodded sadly, very unlike him. "Right, then. I'm not nobility, not anymore, Emrael. I'm just a soldier, now."

Emrael's gaze lingered on Saravellin for a long moment before he turned to the rest of the Lords Holder. "I think it's best if we adjourn for now, given Lord Raebren's condition. I'll host you for a dinner tonight, Raebren's health permitting."

The Lords of Iraea reconvened that night in Dorae's private dining room. This time, only the Lords Holder were in the room, save Saravellin, who accompanied her father.

Emrael drummed his fingers as he stared at the Lords Holder. The meeting had not gone well thus far—Paellar and Syrtsan had even suggested that Emrael didn't deserve to be a part of the Council of Lords, but Dorae and Lord Raebren had put a stop to that nearly as soon as it was voiced. They were firmly behind him, it seemed, though Emrael was not stupid enough to think that Raebren's support could be considered loyalty. He was Lord over the small Holding right next to Whitehall, an easy target. Whatever his reasons, Emrael would use any such leverage he could.

Tarelle was well in hand, of course. He remained quiet the whole time, sweating.

Emrael pointed at the map laid on the table again, spreading his hands in mock defeat. "Lords, send your own scouts if you do not believe me. The Watchers and Corrande Legion have mobilized, with their Malithii priests and soulbound monsters in tow."

Syrtsan grumbled, not for the first time. "If we join them, they will not harm us. They are coming for you."

"Do you really believe that they'll treat you well while they're here, Callan? The Watchers will treat Iraeans like dogs, as they always have. War is here, whether you like it or not."

"A war you brought us," Syrtsan retorted.

Emrael slammed his fist on the table, making the weights holding the map to the table jump. "This war is not my doing, but I'll not back down from it now. This is your chance to join me peacefully and earn your place in the new Iraean Kingdom. I am asking for your rings."

The seven Lords of Iraea still wore signet rings representing their ancestral Holdings. The ritual of giving the rings had named every Iraean king since the kingdom had formed from the ashes of the Ravan Empire millennia before. Lords Holder withholding rings had also set the stage for several civil wars. Monarchy was not a certain thing in Iraea, and had passed from house to house throughout the kingdom's thousand-year history.

Dorae did not hesitate to pull his ring from his finger and toss it to the table. It rolled and came to rest atop the map of the Provinces that Emrael had used to illustrate the coming war. A glance from Emrael goaded Tarelle into setting his ring on the table as well, though he placed it just in front of himself.

Raebren grunted as he fumbled with his ring, trying to remove it with shaking hands and failing. The episode that morning had rendered him feeble, though his mind still seemed sharp. His daughter took his hands in hers and leaned down to murmur in his ear, staring at Emrael all the while. He wondered if he might have an enemy in the heir to the Raebren Holding. The old man soon grumbled his displeasure at whatever she said and finally tore the ring from his finger and awkwardly tossed it onto the table.

"We fight," he said haltingly, still waving his daughter off. "Raebren will ride with Ire."

"Baric! You cannot," Syrtsan protested. "It will mean death and destruction for your people, just like the last time! Corrande will raze your Holding to the ground!"

Raebren met the stare of the younger Lord Holder, fire in his eyes. "We ride with Ire."

Putting a hand on her father's arm, Saravellin joined him in glaring at Syrtsan, though she chewed her lip in unconscious worry. "Trade ships—even our own vessels—are not reaching our river ports, Lord Syrtsan. Would you know anything about that? You and your people have been silent for weeks."

Syrtsan shifted in his chair and looked away from the Raebrens. "Yes, well, times are hard for all of us. The damned Ordenans have crowded our seas like wolves. They sank a ship right off the coast of Duurn! I don't know what you want me to do about that."

"Exactly my father's point, Callan. You can't—or won't—do anything about it. If the Ordenans are the true cause of trade stoppage, Corrande can't stop them either. The traders traveling from Duurn seem well supplied, however."

"Maybe you should be trading with Barros as we are, then! I can't run your Holding for you, now can I?"

They glared at each other for a long, uncomfortable moment.

Emrael studied the room while the neighboring Lords Holder feuded. He now had the Norta, Tarelle, and Raebren rings on the table in front of him. Which left Bayr, Syrtsan, Paellar, and Lord Marol, the Corrande-appointed steward of the vast Ire Holding. Raebren's men and supplies would be a very welcome addition to their campaign, but Emrael knew that without the others, Syrtsan in particular, their chances at victory would be slim. They could not fight on so many fronts at once and hope to survive.

Sensing that this was likely his last opportunity to convince the remaining Lords Holder, Emrael broke the tense silence. "Welcome, Lord Raebren. Your willing aid will not be forgotten. Will the rest of you join us or hide like cowards while we fight?"

Paellar smirked, and in response Emrael locked eyes with him, drawing *infusori* from the high-grade coil he always kept in a special pouch that hung on his belt. Eyes and scars glowing, Emrael stared until Paellar looked away, an angry set to his jaw.

Emrael scanned the rest of the room, settling his gaze on Bayr, who licked his teeth and twisted his ring as he considered. After a moment, the big man nodded to Emrael, but kept his ring.

Emrael let the silence drag on until Syrtsan spoke up. "You know, boy," he said, face now scrunched with anger, "if it were anyone but you, I might send my swords to join you. I want to be rid of those Watcher bastards as much as anyone, but I can't support a boy who doesn't even belong at this table. Let alone make him my king."

Throwing his arms wide, Emrael laughed. "What makes any of you fit to sit at this table, Lord Syrtsan? Is it your blood? I have the blood of the Mage Kings in my veins. Is it power? I have more soldiers at my command than any province has had since the Unification. The Ordenans will strike deals with me that you couldn't even begin to negotiate, under Corrande's thumb as you are."

Lord Syrtsan still shook his head. "Loyalty, boy. History. That's what you don't have. I don't trust Corrande, but I don't trust you either."

Emrael grunted a mirthless laugh. "I can't change how or where I was born, but I am who I am. And know this. If you are not with me, after you leave this keep, you will be against me. My fight is with Corrande, but I will show no mercy to those here who oppose me."

Syrtsan shrugged. "I will not make you my king."

Paellar sneered. "Nor will I. Your rabble army does not scare us. Nor do your petty displays of mage trickery."

"So be it," Emrael said, trying not to show his disappointment. Dorae had warned him that Syrtsan would not join him. He had built close ties with both Barros and Corrande, positioned as he was on the Iraean side of the Stem River Bay. Lord Syrtsan was practically Barrosian by this point, and apparently held no fondness for Emrael or the Ire family.

Emrael turned to Lord Marol. Once again, he knew the answer before he asked, but he had to try. Any territory and men he could win without spilling blood would be a major victory. "And you, Lord Marol? Corrande and these men let you wear my ring, but I'll give you this one chance to give me what is mine. Will you pledge loyalty to me as the rightful Lord of Ire? I will compensate you well."

Lord Marol seemed taken aback, but soon guffawed. "Hand the Holding over to a rebel fool?"

"To the rightful heir of the Ire Holding, Marol."

Marol leaned forward to place his fists on the table, his round face scrunched in a sneer. "Never. *I* am the rightful lord of the Ire Holding. Even if I were foolish enough to turn my back on Corrande, the lesser Lords of Ire would not follow you. You are nothing, boy! And you call us here and ask for our lands, and to be king! These idiots who have given you their rings will be sorry."

Emrael smiled. "I'll ask the Lords of the Ire Holding myself, when the time comes."

Marol's face turned white, then red again. "We'll be ready for you."

"I know."

He slowly gathered up the rings of the men who had pledged themselves to him.

"Those who gave me your ring, please stay a moment. The rest of you, get out. You and your men are safe here until nightfall tomorrow. After that, you are my enemies—until and unless you become my allies. Stand against me at your own peril."

When Bayr, Paellar, Syrtsan, and Marol had left, Saravellin addressed Emrael directly for the first time. "You just made very powerful enemies, Ire. Are you certain you know what you're doing?"

Emrael smiled his best smile at her. "No, I'm not certain, Saravellin. But they've just made themselves a powerful enemy as well. I mean to show them the error of their ways sooner rather than later."

Before they adjourned, Emrael gave his orders to each of his new vassals. They were to stop paying taxes to the Watchers, and arm more fighting men and women with the money instead. He gave each of them instructions for the Crafters he planned to send with them, two each to train locals in how to make *infusori*-Crafted crossbows and other basic contraptions.

"I'll send you each further details by tomorrow evening. I'll thank you to keep them to yourselves," Emrael said. "Make no mistake, this will be a bloody war. But I mean to win it, and win quickly."

That drew solemn nods, and even a clap on the back from Raebren as they left the dining chamber. Even Saravellin nodded to him as she left, though grudgingly.

Once they were alone, Dorae let out an explosive breath of relief. "Glory and Absent Gods, but I didn't think we'd even get one! We might have a chance, now, with Raebren. I hoped we'd get Bayr to give his ring, though."

Emrael smiled. "I offered him a deal, and asked him to keep his ring if Syrtsan withheld his. He'll be more valuable if the others don't see him coming. We'll see soon enough whether he follows through."

Dorae laughed and shrugged, then wordlessly skipped out of the room humming a folk song about farmers' daughters. Mad bastard.

Emrael left soon after and found Toravin lounging in the main hall, where the large table was still set with food for a larger meal that had been provided hours ago for the lesser lords who had come with the Lords Holder. His friend picked at a platter of bread, olives, and cheeses and drank from a tankard of ale at his elbow. Several other minor lords and ladies still lingered at the table as well, most of them quite drunk.

Leaning in close, Emrael spoke quietly, ensuring that nobody could hear. "Send five hundred of our good men with our best Iraean officer, one who knows the territory. Worren, probably. Tomorrow before sunrise. Find some Paellar colors for the men and set them to attacking Watcher garrisons and patrols on the border of Paellar, nearest the Ire Holding. Steal weapons and copper but move quickly. Make it look like Paellar has joined us. Maybe we can get the Watchers to do some of our work for us in Paellar, eh? At least keep them off our back for a while?"

Toravin nodded as if Emrael had commented on something as tame as the weather. "Aye, I reckon we can. Worth a shot. And we get richer no matter the outcome," he said with a laugh.

"We'll need everything they can steal," Emrael agreed. "Have them hit one or two of their nearest outposts, then I want them to meet us in the ruins of Trylla as quickly as possible. Can they attack a few garrisons and then cover that distance in four weeks?"

Toravin nodded and frowned thoughtfully. "Trylla? Does that mean what I think it means?"

Emrael shrugged. "It just might."

His friend grinned. "We should be able to fortify Trylla before the Watchers even know we're there. Most of their garrisons are well north or south, and they have no reason to patrol the area regularly, especially if they are focused on retaking Larreburgh. Worren's raids should ensure that."

"That's what I'm counting on."

Toravin guffawed and drained the rest of his tankard, which was nearly full. "I could drink five more and still have a better memory than you."

Emrael rolled his eyes but clapped him on the shoulder. "Good. Remember, be quick about it, and tell Worren not to take unnecessary risks. Just rattle the Watchers a bit, put Paellar on his heels, and join us quickly with whatever they can get their hands on. I'll have more work for them in Trylla."

As Emrael turned to leave the hall, Toravin caught his sleeve and stood, his expression uncharacteristically serious. "Whatever your plan, we'd better be about it quickly. If Lord Raebren dies, Saravellin inherits his seat. She's not likely to support you like he does. Like I do, though the Fallen only knows why."

"I'll move quickly," Emrael promised. "And I'll deal with Raebren. Just get those Watchers good and mad while we head for the ruins. We need to keep their attention on Larreburgh."

12

The next morning, Emrael and Ban were alone in a loading yard to the rear of the keep.

"Okay, Ban, show me what you've got," Emrael said, genuinely happy for the first time in days. "Glory, it's good to have you here."

Ban stood next to an enormous wagon that had been freighted with him from the Citadel. The thing looked like an ordinary enclosed wagon, but this had sides that folded out to reveal a mobile Crafting laboratory, complete with rows of secured drawers, smelters, casting dyes, *infusori* coils, transfer mechanisms, the whole lot.

Rather than respond, Ban held up one finger, then pulled one of the sides down and began rifling through the drawers.

"Shit, what do you even need me for?" Emrael asked, eyeing the various tools. "You've got all the supplies you need already."

"Who said I need you?" Ban retorted. They both laughed while Ban hopped up into the wagon to start pulling things out of drawers and cubbies where they had been stored.

"Take a look at this," his brother said, holding out a leather vest that was thicker and heavier than it should have been. The inside had been lined with fine linen, and copper strips had been sewn into the vest at various points.

"What is it?"

"Put it on, touching your skin."

Emrael pulled his shirt off, revealing the deep-carved scars and hard, lean muscles beneath his naturally tan skin.

"You haven't been eating enough, Em."

Emrael just shrugged. "I haven't had a lot of time to sit around getting fat, Ban. That time will come, I hope. But there's a lot of blood between us and peace."

Ban nodded, his eyebrows drawn down in a serious expression. "That's why I made this. Put it on," he ordered again, already digging around in more drawers for charged *infusori* coils. He tossed them down to Emrael, who pulled the armored vest on and fastened it.

Emrael shrugged his shoulders and worked his arms. "It's a bit heavy, Ban. What does it do?"

"Just draw the *infusori* from the coils and push it into the vest, Em."

Emrael chuckled and did as he said. He gasped when the *infusori* sank into the vest just as it would into a coil. "What . . . what did you do? How did you do that? There aren't any gold coils in this, I'm sure of it!"

Just as he always had when he did something he was proud of, Ban smiled, his mouth slightly lopsided. "It'll take five standard coils of *infusori* and I think I can improve the design considerably if I build the right equipment. This is just an early prototype. Em, coils as we know them are incredibly inefficient—all I've done is shrink the geometry needed to retain rather than emit *infusori*, and then extend the length into small cables I've sewn into that vest. It's like you're wearing five coils' worth, but with only the equivalent of a coil or two of gold in the vest."

Emrael shook his head, amazed. "Glory and Absent Gods, Ban, you are a genius. You'll have all the copper I can lay my hands on and more."

He practiced drawing *infusori* from the vest and pushing it back for a moment. "Can I keep this in the meantime? I think I can fit it under my armor."

Ban shook his head. "No, that's the only one I have and need it for my work. I'll have a new one built right into an armored vest for you as soon as I can. You like the idea, though?"

"I love the idea," Emrael said, smiling and slapping Ban's leg. "Now, I have a few other things I want you to make. First, you told me about the network of Observers you set up for Elle in the Sagmyn Province. Can you do that here so I can talk to Halrec in Larreburgh, and Mother in Myntar? Maybe more?"

"Perhaps, but it wouldn't be practical. To be reliable, there would have to be a fully powered transmitter every few hundred leagues, and that's just not possible given the terrain we'll cover here in Iraea."

"Still, that's something. If I can give one to each Imperator in my army and communicate over even just a few leagues, I'll have a significant advantage. How many can you make in a week?"

"A week!" Ban exclaimed. "I'd be hard-pressed to make a single one in a week, and I'm the only one who can make them at present. I can go set up my workshop right now, though."

Emrael shook his head. "You'll have to do it with whatever you can load into your mobile workshop here, and you'll have to teach some of the other Crafters the trick. I have other plans for us. We're going to take back the Ire Holding. Tomorrow."

"Tomorrow? So soon?"

"We need to move fast, Ban. But we'll finally have a home of our own, and you'll have everything you need to make your Crafts. You and your Crafters are the fulcrum of our strategy. I hope you know that. If we win this war, it'll be because of you and your inventions."

Ban nodded and hopped down from the wagon. Emrael cupped the back of his head affectionately with one hand. "Leave Dorae a Crafter or two but bring the best with us. You have a lot of work ahead of you."

Emrael ducked into a small room located in a distant, sparsely lighted hallway of Whitehall Keep. Within the musty stone-walled room, he found a group quite a bit smaller than he had expected.

Jaina waited with a dozen Imperators, seated on benches facing the door, all unarmored but carrying their copper-colored weapons. Not actually copper at all, he had discovered, but rather a superconductive steel alloy that only the Ordenans knew how to forge. He wondered if any of the Imperators here with them knew the secret to making it.

Timan and a few others he recognized were among them.

"Where are the others?" he asked.

The Imperators exchanged quick glances, then looked to Jaina. She pursed her lips, then shrugged. "Loyalties among the Imperators are . . . complex, Emrael. Those here are those loyal to Maira's faction within the Council of Mages in Ordena. The others . . . they can be trusted, but how far? There are some that owe loyalty to those on the Council that oppose Maira's goals. Best to keep some plans to us, for now."

Emrael chewed on his lip, considering. He didn't know much of Ordenan politics—nobody did, Ordenans being a remarkably closed society as they were—but this surprised him. He had assumed that the Imperators who came with his mother would have been loyal to her and Jaina. If he couldn't trust them, there could be major problems.

"Does that mean that we might have more to fear from them, Jaina? If Barros offers your Councils a better deal, for example, or if one of your Councilors decides to move against my mother, will we be caught in the middle?"

Jaina looked back at him calmly. "Perhaps."

He couldn't help but laugh. He was about to start a war for Iraea at the same time as he was fighting the entire Provincial military, and now he had to worry about his own allies stabbing him in the back.

"You Ordenans don't make for very good allies, do you? Can't we just send the others back to Ordena?"

Jaina shook her head. "No, we cannot send them back. The Council might rescind the authorization for any of the Imperators to be here, even your mother and me. All would have to return or be declared *foradan*, outlaws to be hunted like rats. So, you see, it is not simple. We must keep them, but not trust them too far."

"And you're certain I can trust these here?" He gestured to the Imperators seated in front of him, several of whom had the gall to look offended.

Timan laughed. "As much as you can trust anyone, Ire. We here were handpicked by your mother herself."

Not for the first time, Emrael was impressed with how quickly his mother had risen to prominence back in her native Ordena. She had only been there for the three years Emrael and Ban had been at the Citadel, after all. It seemed very quick for an outsider to ascend to power in a governing body. He had some questions for the next time he saw her.

After an agreeing nod from Jaina, he addressed the room once more. "Fair enough. I need two volunteers to escort my squads carrying messages to the Lords Holder of the Barros Province. The four Holders in the south are ready to revolt against the Lord Governor, and I am going to offer an alliance if they'll keep Barros off our ass. I need another two of you to stay here with Dorae, and two more to go to Halrec in Larreburgh."

"Where will the rest go?" one of the Imperator Healers, Cailla, asked. Several others nodded at the question.

"The others will be with me," Emrael said. "We're going to Trylla, where we'll build a settlement. From there, we'll fight a war to reclaim the Ire Holding and eventually the entire Iraean Kingdom. It will be fast, ruthless, and I'll need every one of you."

The Imperators nodded, and Emrael looked to Jaina. "We have three Healers, correct?"

She nodded.

"I'd like to send one to Halrec and keep two with us. I'll leave the rest of the assignments to you. I'll have the sealed letters ready for the Barros Lords Holder in the morning. They are to leave immediately."

"Can I leave Tarelle here with you, then?" Emrael asked Dorae as they sat together in the Lord Holder's private study. Shelves of books filled the room, a large writing desk perched near the single window, and a few cushioned chairs for reading sat in a crescent about the large stone fireplace. Timan, ever present, sat near the door and kept to himself.

Dorae pursed his lips as he thought about it. "I suppose, but if he is working with Corrande and the Malithii, he'll be easier for them to reach here. I don't know what good it'll do them now that you hold Larreburgh, but he might be able to stir up trouble. He still has his family lands in the west of his Holding, and a personal guard he could call on. He didn't retain his Holding by being a brainless lump, you know. Watch him carefully."

Emrael clicked his tongue in annoyance. "Fine, I'll cart him along with me. But I swear to the Absent Gods, if he causes any trouble, I'm hanging him."

Dorae laughed and lounged back in his chair. "Fine by me, but I won't save you if his Holding goes up in flames. I've got more than I can handle just keeping the Fallen-damned Watchers at bay. Half the city is in ruins, Absent Gods only know where I'm going to find the coin to pay for repairs and supplies for the city. Ships have stopped sailing up the river, and I suspect Syrtsan is as much to blame as Barros."

Emrael nodded slowly. "Raebren obviously believes the same. The Ordenans will likely want to make a deal with us, but I don't know what kind of volume they'll be able to move or for what price. I'll deal with Syrtsan, Barros, and the rest of them in time."

"Bayr?" Dorae asked.

Emrael kept a straight face. "We'll see about Bayr. We'll see. I offered him Syrtsan lands if he joins us."

Dorae smiled and lifted his eyebrows, incredulous. "How did you know Syrtsan wouldn't give you his ring?"

Emrael shook his head. "I didn't, not for certain. The offer was for Ire lands if Syrtsan allied himself with us. But you and Toravin said that Bayr covets the Syrtsan ports more than anything else. We'll only know for sure if he shows up in Trylla."

"What if he runs to the Watchers, has them waiting for you at Trylla?"

"I haven't told him where to meet us yet. I'm not an idiot. I told him to be ready to travel, and that I'll send him word shortly."

Dorae stroked his chin, face serious but eyes gleaming mischievously. "Clever, Emrael. Very clever. Seems as though you've thought of everything."

"I'm trying," Emrael said, pouring himself more brandy to hide how pleased he was at the compliment. "There's one more thing. As I said before, Halrec is going to need your help."

He passed him a letter sealed with wax stamped with his family's ancient crest that was carved into the butt of the pommel of his sword, a shaggy red mountain stag surrounded by angular runes.

"I sent Halrec an offer. He will be the new Lord Holder of the Tarelle Holding if he can keep it intact, but that won't happen unless you keep supplies flowing to him, and men. He'll be fighting on two fronts. Maybe more."

Picking up his mug of dark ale, Dorae took a sip before responding. "I have problems of my own, remember?"

Emrael smiled. "Yes, but you have more men, more supplies,

and I'll make sure trade resumes up the Stem. And if Larreburgh falls, you're next. All the same, there's something in it for you. That letter grants you half of Tarelle's fertile lands west of the Burned Hills . . . *if* we hold the Tarelle Holding with your help. Make sure Halrec has the men and supplies he needs, Dorae."

Dorae licked his teeth, nodding. "That'll work."

13

Darmon Corrande rode his mottled grey-and-black stallion along the nearly empty center boulevard of Surra, the large trading city on the coast of the Grey Sea, right at the edge of the Rift. Positioned as it was, it was the primary entry point for goods from the northern portions of the Ithan Empire into his province. His father's province, he supposed. Though it didn't feel much like it belonged to either of them, now.

Surra was a city unlike any other he had seen, and he had seen a fair few. Most of the buildings were of stone—the buildings that mattered, at least. There was plenty of tarred timber and red mud brick down in the rougher parts of town, the slums near the docks in particular.

Stone buildings weren't distinctive in and of themselves, of course. But every stone in the city had been quarried from the coarse black granite found in the cliffs at the northern point of the Great Rift where it met the sea. Dull black streets, black buildings, and all too often, a cloud-darkened sky to match. Though it was quite beautiful in sunlight, Surra was often depressing and ominous.

Black suited his mood that day, and certainly fit his companions well. A black-robed Malithii priest rode to either side of him, an "honor guard" that felt more like a prison detail.

They arrived at their destination, a worksite in the hills above the city where the Malithii were building a huge pyramid of the same black stone as the city center, though the stones used here were huge blocks as tall as a man. Darmon and his two Malithii guards stopped their horses on a bluff overlooking the enormous project.

Thousands of manacled slaves, either Provincial prisoners or men the Malithii had captured in the Ithan Kingdoms, toiled at the building site below. They dragged thousands of black stone blocks, hauled them up to the top of the structure via large chains, pulleys, and elevators to scaffolds where stonemasons laid them in place. His blood ran cold when he spied giant figures among the throngs of slaves, half again as tall as the captives they patrolled. Malithii masters directed the slaves, but these giant *sanja'ahn* kept them in line just with their fearsome presence. Darmon had seen one of the monsters tear a defiant slave in half with its bare hands once, weeks ago at an encampment of captives near Brugg, the capital. Seeing that was enough to quell most thoughts of fighting back against these oppressors, though Darmon figured the Malithii only had perhaps two hundred of the giants at their command.

The pyramid was very impressive, but Darmon didn't understand it one bit. Why had he and his father been dragged out of their capital, away from the looming war with Emrael Ire, just to see this? Why was the Prophet so obsessed with this pyramid, out here in the hills near the Rift?

One of his Malithii keepers gestured toward the structure and grunted, "Come," and kicked his horse down the hill toward the unfinished pyramid. The second Malithii stared at Darmon and clucked at him until he moved.

To his surprise, when they arrived, the Malithii dismounted and went inside. Darmon didn't see any alternative—he certainly wasn't going to try to escape now, not with those damned *sanja'ahn* on the loose.

The inside of the structure had its own crews of workmen, but all of the workers here were Malithii priests in their dark robes. Standing on ladders and scaffolds, they worked at the walls with hammer and chisel, while others hammered copper into the chiseled-out spaces, creating a giant interconnected mural of angular script.

Darmon and his guards wove their way through the bustle to the center of the floor, where rare noon sun made a square of light as it passed through the unfinished peak of the pyramid. There waited his father, Bortisse, and Savian, the self-proclaimed Prophet of the Fallen God of Glory. There was a time when Darmon would have scoffed at such a claim, but that was a time before he had seen the *sanja'ahn* giants, the pens of humans enslaved and turned into raving soulbound beasts, and before he had seen his father cowed by Savian and his mage-priests. He didn't know what he believed anymore.

Just a year ago, Darmon wouldn't have fathomed fearing anything more than he feared his father, but now he only felt pity and contempt when he looked at the man. His father had changed these last few months. His tall, strong frame was now stooped, his eyes perpetually haunted. Once, Darmon would have been glad to see the man suffer. But not like this.

As he drew closer to the two men, he could hear Savian speaking loudly through the din. "It will be magnificent, dear Bortisse! You will see! Our master will be most pleased, most pleased."

His father just nodded despondently.

His curiosity piqued, Darmon stayed quiet, hoping to hear more, but Savian turned to greet them.

"Ah! The boy is here, good good." He rubbed his hands together and giggled gleefully. Such an odd man to have completely subdued his father, to have cast a blanket of fear on their entire province. "I have a treat for you both, I do."

Darmon watched curiously as his father glanced at him, grimaced as his eyes touched on Darmon's pinned sleeve where his sword hand should have been, then looked away. He would have suspected that Savian had used one of those awful mindbinders on his father, but it didn't make sense. The elder Corrande was fully lucid and had brief flashes where Darmon could see the old anger behind his eyes. Savian must have done something else, something worse.

Besides, just the other day Darmon had overheard Savian complaining that he hadn't had time in months to make more mindbinders. Likely he wanted to use them to control people close to Emrael Ire. Everything Savian did seemed to focus on that damn Ire bastard. And yet, Ire seemed to be giving this lunatic a fight, where his father had simply capitulated and ceded control of the Watchers and his own Corrande Legion. Darmon could not understand.

Savian shouted, and three of his fellow priests scurried toward one wall where the shadows were deepest, carrying armfuls of Crafted metal parts, which they began to assemble into a box nearly as tall as a man. Darmon didn't have the faintest idea what it would do, but he recognized it as an *infusori* Crafting, equal to or more impressive than anything he had seen at the Citadel. Copper wires, coils of gold, and bars of silver intertwined in an impossibly complex configuration.

As the setup neared completion, Savian shouted "Silence!" and all work in the pyramid ceased immediately. Every single Malithii priest in the structure bowed immediately, hands to their faces. Even the throngs of slaves outside quieted quickly. A jitter of anxiety coursed through Darmon.

The priests that had set up the contraption now beckoned to others of their ilk, who dragged two struggling Ithan slaves toward their machine. The prisoners were pinned on their backs as the waiting priests connected a series of cables to the arms and legs of the poor men. When the cables were attached, the priests flipped a switch, and the two prisoners fell silent, backs arced so severely that only their feet, heads, and hands touched the ground. The priests stepped back, bowing to the ground and staying there. The machine began to *whiz* and *burr* as several parts glowed with *infusori* drawn from the captives. Darmon had never seen its like. Why had they not simply used *infusori* from charged coils?

After a moment, light flickered above the assembled contraption, then coalesced into a solid, crisp image of a man, taller even than the *sanja'ahn*, and perfectly muscled. Angular marks covered his ashen skin, scars that glowed with a light that ebbed and flowed.

The figure opened its eyes, and Darmon took an unconscious step backward as the walls of the pyramid began to glow faintly where the copper had been laid in an angular script.

"Yes," the figure boomed in a deep voice that was not loud, but somehow reverberated through every fiber of Darmon's being. "Yes, this will do nicely. When will the full schema be complete, Savian?"

Savian stepped forward, rapture lighting his face. "Soon, Master, soon. Our army of Servants is growing. The structure is almost complete, and the . . . device will follow soon after."

"Hmmm," the giant figure crooned. "I am not pleased with the delay, Savian, for my arrival is paramount. All that I have planned will be for naught without this."

"Yes, Glory," Savian said, cringing and lowering further to the floor. He began whimpering as if in pain.

The image of the figure turned, scanning those present, regarding them as if seeing stones lying on the ground. He turned back to the Prophet and waved a hand. "Rise. The work with the Ire boy. It progresses?"

"Ye-yes, Master," Savian stammered, shaking.

"He grows strong, cunning," Glory rumbled. "You have done well."

Savian wept tears of joy, his teeth bared in an ecstatic grin.

Glory's eyes now glowed fiercely, as did the angular script in his skin. "But not fast enough! I can feel my time approaching, Savian. You must hurry. Push him harder, ever harder."

"It is not so easy, God Glory. The Ordenans still wage war on our shores. They have weapons, and ships, that we cannot match. They delay our plans."

Glory, or the image of him, growled with rage. "The children of my Sisters have ever been a thorn in my side. I will give you what you need to defeat them."

At that, the image of Glory disappeared. The contraption hummed and whirred, then grew quiet. The bodies of the captives used to fuel the Crafting were now shriveled, deflated corpses that looked as if they had dried in the sun for months.

Darmon looked around him, half in shock. The Malithii priests remained cowered on the ground or on scaffolds where they had been when the image of the Fallen God had appeared. Darmon no longer doubted that the Fallen was real, not after what he had just seen.

Savian turned to the rest of them, now completely composed despite the tears still wetting his face. "You heard our master. We must press harder. I cannot spare my *sanya'oin,* but we can use Servants. Bortisse! Send your Watchers to hound him. Hurt him, bring me those he loves. Lord Holder Paellar and Lord Holder Marol will welcome you. Go, send your best."

An idea ignited in Darmon's mind. "I'll go," he said forcefully, eyes darting to the dead husks that had been living humans just a moment before. "Let me lead them."

His father considered him quietly with dull eyes, but Savian crooned, "Ahh, yes. The boy wishes to exact his revenge. Perfect. Just remember, Ire is not to be killed. He belongs to our master, and none other."

Darmon forced a confident smile. "Of course."

14

Mist from the mountain lake wrapped Whitehall in a shroud of wet quiet as Emrael's forces gathered in the square below the keep. Ten thousand soldiers and nearly an equal number of civilians who had answered his recent call for settlers. Carpenters, blacksmiths, stonemasons, farmers, millers, and tradespeople of all kinds had loaded their critical belongings into large wagons contracted for the voyage. Emrael wasn't just going to the Ire Holding to fight, he was going to build. He had offered land and passage to any who came with them, and these people wanted to be a part of it.

Emrael kicked his horse to a walk to do a quick route around the raucous gathering in the early-morning light. The last preparations seemed to be wrapping up. Ducks and chickens squawked in their crates, hogs had been penned in wagons, and cattle would follow after the main party, driven by drovers when the path was clear.

His Ire Legion, five thousand trained and five thousand raw recruits, formed the front and rear ranks. He stopped in front of them and a ripple of pride made his skin tingle with goosebumps. His Legion was outfitted with every sort of armor imaginable, and many of their uniforms only matched in the sense that they were all dyed some shade of green. But every spear stood at the perfect angle, each fresh-made wood and leather shield was grounded properly, ready to raise in an instant. His officers were doing good work, in large part thanks to Toravin's efforts.

"Soldiers of the Ire Legion!" he shouted. "We ride today to reclaim our homeland."

His men whooped at that, and he paused for their show of bravado. "We ride not just to battle, but to build a new home. To rebuild Trylla, a new Ire Holding, and a new Iraea. Land, copper, and freedom from the oppression of the Provinces will be our prize. My gain will be your gain. I swear it."

His Legion cheered as he joined the small group at the head of the column where Ban and his Crafters, Jaina and her Imperators, and Toravin rode with the senior officers.

"Lead the way, Toravin."

A little over two weeks later, Emrael trotted his horse forward as Toravin came into view on the horizon. The scouts had said they should arrive at the ruined city of Trylla sometime today. Emrael had pushed hard, hoping to give them time to set up a defensible fort near Trylla before Marol and the Watchers found out they were there.

Twenty leagues or so outside of Whitehall, however, the road to Trylla had turned from a nicely cobbled highway into a series of meandering dirt roads carved through the hills and small mountains that rippled across the Iraean landscape. The last few days, they'd had to send crews to clear trees from the road ahead of the wagons. There were still large portions of their wagon train days behind, but Emrael had assigned protection details and insisted that the main force continue onward as quickly as possible to secure the city.

As Emrael rode ahead of the column, accompanied by Ban, Jaina, and Timan, he noticed hundreds of huge vine-covered lumps amid the verdant forest undergrowth. As he peered through a gap between trees, he recognized a peaked roof on a particularly large stone-walled structure. They must have reached the outskirts, where smaller homes and shops would have been decades ago, before the Watchers razed the city.

When he reached Toravin, his rangy Iraean friend gave him a mocking salute. "Scouts say we're about ten leagues from the city center. There's a small village built among the ruins. A priest who follows the old ways, sounds like. The locals seem to revere him as some sort of shaman or something." He smirked as he said that last, making Emrael suspect that he knew more than he was going to tell.

Jaina scoffed. "It is almost unheard of for a person to learn *A Me'trae* without training." She glanced at Emrael. He had used *infusori* for the first time without guidance, though he had been around *infusori* Crafting for quite some time by that point. He had likely been unknowingly exposed to his mother's mage abilities during his childhood, as well.

Emrael raised an eyebrow at her, not convinced that it was as impossible as she claimed. Though he'd never met anyone who practiced the old Iraean ways of worshipping ancient mages and magecraft, he'd heard enough tales about them to suspect that there was some truth there.

Something Toravin said registered in his mind. "Tor, did you say ten leagues? We're on the outskirts now. This place is twenty leagues wide? That's half again as big as Myntar!"

Toravin shrugged. "Guess so. Always heard it was big, back before the Watchers burned it down."

"Why has nobody moved back?" Timan asked, looking around. "If there was a city of this size here, there must have been a reason. Resources, fertile soil, good growing conditions. Water and a navigable river to be sure."

Toravin looked at him askance and muttered something about Ordenans before responding. "Aye, it has all of that and more. It was the home of some of the most powerful mages throughout Iraean history. Some say the contraptions they built here in centuries past rivaled even what the Ordenans have. But now," he said, gesturing about at the mind-numbing amount of wreckage. "Fucking Watchers come back here every year and kill anyone they find. Been doing it for near on fifty years, now. Only ones that'll live here now are the followers of the old ways. The mage worshippers hide in the woods when the Watchers come, then rebuild their little village each and every year. You'll see."

They rode through leagues of burned-out, vine-choked buildings in near silence, save for the occasional ring of their horses' hooves striking the cobbled road where the stones showed through dirt. There were piles of rubble and small plants and grass growing on the roads, but few trees due to the depth of the ancient roadways, making the highways and avenues into beautiful carpets of green running through the husks of buildings and trees that grew among the ruined houses and larger buildings that Emrael could only guess the previous use of. Warehouses? Meeting halls? Restaurants? Mansions? It was hard to tell after fifty years of destruction and disrepair.

The statues were clear enough, though—dozens and dozens of stone-and-metal statues, all with green eyes. Copper, he realized. They must be statues of mages. Incredible that nobody had pilfered the copper over all these years. Worship of the Descended—mages regarded as demigods, from what he understood—must still have been strong in these parts.

He felt profound sadness and a deep, smoldering anger at the loss of what this city must have been. All for Provincial ambition, and the Sentinels' empty worship of the Holy Departed.

As they drew near the city center, Emrael smelled smoke. They entered a huge clearing, likely once a massive city square. Now, there were nearly a hundred green-timber log houses built near the center, each with a trail of white smoke curling from a chimney.

Two large men with long hair and long beards met them a hundred paces from the settlement, wicked-looking spiked axes in hand. "Who are you? What is your purpose here in the Holy City?"

Emrael looked to Toravin, who slid out of his saddle and approached the men. "We are here for the same reason you are, brother: to see the City of the Descended rise again. This man behind me and to my right is of Ire blood."

The men looked at each other, shocked, then back to Toravin. "Truly?"

Toravin nodded, and the two men conferred briefly before one sprinted back to the settlement, disappearing into the largest building near the center of the odd log town. They didn't have to wait long before there was a considerable amount of shouting, and an old man dressed in what looked to be a bearskin emerged from the large building.

The old man shouted something incomprehensible at this distance, and people stopped what they were doing to follow him out of the enclosure.

By the time the old man and his group reached Emrael, the main column of Ire Legion soldiers had reached the square and had begun to line up in square formations a few hundred paces behind him. If the villagers were intimidated, however, they didn't show it.

The old man in the bearskin had a fringe of wispy white hair and a long white beard. He walked with purpose, only stopping when he was an arm's length away. "I am Raemus, the Eldest Voice for the Ancestors and their Descended. Which of you claims to be of Ire blood?" in a gravelly voice.

Emrael stepped forward. "I am." He motioned Ban forward. "My name is Emrael Ire, and this is my brother, Banron Ire."

The old man stepped forward suddenly and grabbed at Emrael's hand. Emrael flinched reactively, but caught himself and stepped forward instead, clasping the old man's hand. Timan shifted uncomfortably, but Emrael signaled for him to stand down.

The old man looked him in the eyes, and Emrael nearly gasped when his eyes began to glow softly. He felt the man's *infusori* senses probing at him weakly, and despite his misgivings about opening himself to a strange tribal leader in the middle of a ruined forest city, he met the probe with his own *infusori* senses. Nervous shifting behind him told him that Jaina and Timan were more surprised than he was.

Emrael sensed that the man was waiting for something, so he pulled all of the *infusori* from a coil he held in a pouch on his belt. He held the pulsing power ready, knowing the man would be able to feel it.

Rather than be cowed or even impressed, however, the man grunted in unimpressed frustration. "No no," he grumbled, then poked at Emrael's chest with one finger as he probed at him with his *infusori* senses once more. "I want to see what's inside."

Jaina took a step forward but was careful not to touch either of them. "Don't, Emrael. It is dangerous, even with an untrained mage like him."

Emrael ignored her and lowered his defenses. He felt a sincerity from the man, odd though he was. The old man melded his *infusori* senses with Emrael's, and asked simply, "Are you of Ire blood?"

"I am," Emrael said.

"You have a father?"

"Janrael Ire. Dead," he said, his voice catching.

The old man blinked, then turned, still holding Emrael's hand. "The Mage Kings have returned!" he roared, raising his hands in the air. The villagers behind him emitted a collective gasp, then followed their leader in raising their hands to the sky. They began chanting a kind of harsh, guttural song.

Emrael, confused and embarrassed, glanced at his companions with wide eyes. Toravin was having a hard time keeping from laughing out loud, and Jaina looked angry with him. Ban looked as confused as Emrael felt.

Emrael tried to get the shaman's attention and failed. Finally, he pulled his hand free, which got the old man to turn to him finally. "Why are you singing?" he asked.

It was the old man's turn to look confused, and slightly annoyed. "We are celebrating, Lord King. We serve the Descended and have awaited your return all these decades. We stand ready to expel the god-worshippers and their Watcher minions." He swept his had grandly at his gathering of perhaps two hundred people, including women and children. "We will follow you to great glory."

"Okay . . . great," Emrael said. "You can start by helping us find food and shelter for twenty thousand people."

Emrael stood atop a large stone building that had kept its sturdy stone roof through the decades of Watcher abuse, observing his men as they built a new wall around the inner city—part of it, at least. A large avenue followed the River Lys that split the city roughly north and south, about two leagues from the huge center square where Raemus and his people had built their village.

Emrael had chosen the avenue as the site for the wall so that he could leave the stone bridges that still spanned the wide river in place. Any army attacking from the north would only have the very limited space of the avenue next to the river from which to mount their assault, and that only if they made it across the bridges. It would become a perfect killing ground for Emrael and his Legion.

Thousands of his Legionmen had been put to work tearing down fallen buildings to create a space for the masons to fill. His thousand or so civilian masons had accomplished more than he thought they could have in the two weeks they had been there. They laid stones from the torn-down buildings to form a wall in every gap, using the buildings still standing to create a patchwork wall that Emrael judged would function nearly as well as a solid wall, for his purposes. With the limited number of men he would be able to leave here, it would be difficult to defend properly, but it would give them a chance. It was almost time to begin his campaign in truth.

Though he had left the majority of the ruined city outside his new wall, a two-league radius gave him and his people more than enough room to create their new home. Already his carpenters and other craftsmen had restored drinking wells and had repaired hundreds of buildings to be livable, though sparsely appointed for now. He still needed to find defensible farmland nearby for long-term food production, but things were progressing nicely.

For a moment, he indulged himself in a mental fantasy of a thriving city, people filling the buildings and streets within the newly constructed wall. A lot of work, and a lot of blood, stood between him and that day. If it ever came.

He turned to Garrus, the Captain First in charge of the construction of the wall. A practical man, perfect for overseeing the construction of the city's defenses. He'd do a damn fine job of it, too.

"Excellent work, Captain. Keep them at it."

Garrus smiled, as excited as Emrael had ever seen him. "The men work hard, knowing they'll own a good part of what they fight for, or build. We'll have it as tall as the walls of Myntar someday, eh, Lord Ire?"

Emrael smiled back. "That we will, Captain, and we'll have you to thank for it. I've got to get back, Toravin is expecting me. Report on your progress tomorrow, I want to hear your thoughts on how we can rebuild and protect the river docks. We'll want access, of course, but can't just leave it out in the open. And my brother will need help soon with his plans for a sewer system. We can't keep letting the men shit in whatever vacant building they happen upon."

"Sir!" Garrus said with a perfect salute, but he had a wry smile on his face. Emrael liked the man. He had fought well at Larreburgh, for certain.

When Emrael arrived back at what had become their headquarters, the largest intact building on the huge central square, Toravin was waiting in the room Emrael had made into an office of sorts. He only had a small travel desk and single wooden chair, but it was better than nothing. His friend lounged in that chair, his feet resting on the table.

Toravin didn't stand as Emrael strode into the room. "Don't hurry on my account, Ire."

Emrael waved him off. "Get over it. I was out looking at the walls. I think we can hold it with a thousand men, assuming we aren't attacked in force. That leaves us nine thousand to work with under normal circumstances."

"Aye, these outposts you want outside the city, we'll need at least a company or two for those once they're complete. And horses. Men will need to stay behind to keep order here in the city as well, and we'll need some to escort our supply parties."

Emrael nodded. "Eight thousand and some change to fight with, then. Worren should be back soon with his five hundred. And Bayr should show up before too long." He smiled conspiratorially.

Toravin raised his eyebrows at him. "And then what? We just build here until someone attacks us?"

"We're taking the Syrtsan Holding."

Toravin sat up suddenly. "Syrtsan! Are you mad? He didn't join you, but he's hardly your enemy, Emrael. You might still convince him to join you."

Emrael shook his head. "Syrtsan will sit out the entire war if he can, playing both sides, but he'll attack if he sees gain in it. My grandfather lost his war because of weak political bastards like him, and I'll not repeat his mistake." He began pacing the room as he spoke. "I can't fight a war against Marol and Paellar with Syrtsan behind me. If we're attacked from the south, we're dead. Besides, I gave the Lords Holder fair warning. Right to their face, Tor."

Toravin grimaced, lounging back in the chair again. "Aye . . ."

"We need more men, Tor, many more, if we're to challenge the Watchers and their pet Lords Holder. We need another victory, something to show people we're the winning horse. When we do, men will join us for the land grants, the pay, and the glory. You watch. We'll have more recruits than we know what to do with after Syrtsan falls, or surrenders. We'll get more men from Bayr and Raebren after a victory, too." He leaned forward, grinning wickedly as he tapped his finger hard on the wood desktop. "And it's the last thing any of them will expect. Syrtsan will fall within the month."

Toravin frowned and dragged both hands down his face while

letting out a loud groan, then started laughing. "You mad bastard. You mad fucking bastard. It might even work."

Emrael shrugged. "That's the idea."

"What are our next steps, then?"

"We wait for Raebren and Bayr to arrive. And Worren with his men. In the meantime, we have a city to build. We have people willing to farm, and I need you to find some land for them."

"There are plenty of farms in the area, Ire. We can just buy the food we need."

"We will buy every bit of food that is for sale, but for how long will that suffice? We'll need stores for winter, and so will the farmers. They haven't planted enough to feed an entire city popping up in these ruins from nothing. We need contingencies. We need arable land for the settlers loyal to us to plant and sow, and we need it yesterday. Find it. Nearer to the city the better so we can defend them. Maybe the area next to the river south of the city. Livestock can likely be raised in some of the remote portions of the city itself."

Toravin shrugged. "What would I know about farming, Ire? I'm a soldier, not a clerk."

Emrael pursed his lips. "Pass the order to Garrus then, he'll get it done right. Just make sure they end up somewhere close enough that they can make it back here when the Watchers attack."

"*When* the Watchers attack?"

"They must know we're here by now. It won't be long before we've got a fight on our hands. I'd say a month, two if we're lucky."

"Aye," Toravin agreed. "We'll handle it. We've got some good men who'll fight hard. You've given them something to fight for, a better future for their families."

Emrael found a good spot to lean up against the wall and resolved to get a few more chairs in here as soon as he could. He fixed Toravin with a stare, trying to come up with a good way to say what was on his mind. "I can understand why most of them are here. Freedom, money, land. It's enough to attract most people. But why are *you* here, Tor? Since I met you, you've never once asked for anything from me. Why did you follow Dorae in the first place, years ago? Did you want the Raebren Holding for yourself?"

Toravin grew quiet and put his feet on the desk once more. After a long, tense moment, he laughed softly. "No, I don't suppose I did. I fought for Dorae because I was a fool. I believed in ideals like freedom, and I'd seen too much cruelty, too much injustice. I just wanted to do something good to right my wrongs in the blue uniform, you know? I never meant to hurt Lord Raebren or any Iraean—I was trying to help them."

"And now? Why are you here? Why are you helping me?"

Toravin was quiet again for a long time. "Because," he said slowly, emotion thickening his voice a bit, "I finally found someone as stupid as I am." He barked a laugh, a rough sound that belied the awkward smile on his face. "When we met, you took a spear for that innkeeper's wife. Any fool who knows how to use a sword would have fought to save himself. You, though, put yourself between those monsters and an innocent woman and child you didn't know, when you could no longer defend yourself. You may be an ass and a fool, but that kind of . . . nobility? It's rare, in my experience. I'd fight with you even if you didn't have a chance at becoming king."

Emrael bit his cheek, embarrassed and unsure how to take the compliment, but moved by Toravin's loyalty. "Thank you, Tor. I won't forget it. When this is over, you'll have a Holding of your own if you want it."

Toravin reassumed his wry smile. "Me, a Lord Holder? We'll see. We have a war to win, first."

The next morning, Emrael, Ban, and Jaina got their breakfast from one of the large mess tents with everyone else. It wasn't quite the culinary experience Emrael would have preferred, but truth be told there was no other food, and Emrael didn't have time to secure his own stores and cook for himself.

As they sat on the steps of their building eating hard pork sausage and bread, the Tryllan shaman, Raemus, approached Emrael.

"Lord King," he intoned. "I have something to show you."

Emrael, who had a very long day of inspections and planning ahead of him, said, "Can it wait until tomorrow?"

Raemus frowned. "Sooner is better, I think. It is a thing for the Descended only."

Emrael put a chunk of sausage in his mouth, then wiped the grease on his pants. "Can it be quick? I have many appointments to keep today."

Raemus snorted, still frowning. "It will take as long as you want it to take. My duty is only to take you there."

Emrael looked to Jaina, then to Ban, and back to the shaman. "I suppose we can spare a few moments now."

Raemus looked at Jaina and opened his mouth. "It is for Ire blood—"

Emrael put a hand up to cut the shaman off. "She comes with me, Raemus."

The old man glared at both him and Jaina, but did not argue.

They followed Raemus to the north side of the square, where he apparently intended to lead them through the abandoned streets of Trylla. Timan saw them leaving and ran to catch up.

Raemus never slowed his stalk through the streets of the giant city, never paused to consider his path. They crossed the large stone bridges spanning the River Lys just outside the wall his engineers and masons were building around the inner city. Emrael grew a bit nervous as they ventured outside the wall and across the river, but figured that even if the man meant them harm, he had Jaina and Timan with him. They were just about the best protection anyone could ask for.

They continued for another league or so to the northeast, toward where the tallest peaks of the Burned Hills were visible in the distance. When they passed through an empty gateway of a stone wall that looked like it enclosed several blocks of the dilapidated city, Emrael became even more wary. If he were planning to lead someone into an ambush, he would do it in an enclosed space just like this.

A few hundred paces into the compound, Raemus turned abruptly in to a building that looked much like many others, a ruin with empty windows and doors that gaped like the eye sockets of a giant stone skull. However, this one had runic markings running all around the doorways, windows, and around the top edge of the building.

A dim foyer seemed to comprise the entirety of the interior of the building. Raemus stood at the far end near a stone wall. As they joined him, the shaman put a hand to the wall. A small burst of *infusori* surged from the shaman's hand, and the entire wall slid backward to reveal a huge set of descending stairs.

"Justice, Mercy, and Fallen Glory," Timan murmured. "What's something like that doing here?"

Jaina and Emrael exchanged glances but followed Raemus without comment. The shaman had descended the unlit stairs rapidly before the wall had even revealed half of the doorway.

They reached the bottom of the stairs, holding charged coils aloft because very little light from the building above reached the lower part of the stairs. They found the shaman standing in the dark, arms raised. "Behold," he intoned, "the Sanctuary of the Ancients! I, the Eldest Voice for our Mage Ancestors, bid you enter."

He made a dramatic gesture with his hands and slapped the wall, releasing another small burst of *infusori* as he did. Bright blue light sprang from copper wrought into an angular script that lined every wall.

It was nearly identical to the Ravan temple they had found in the woods above Ben's Crossing in the Barros Province. They stood in a large circular primary chamber, and through one of the several open doorways leading from the main room, he could see that at least one room held the same kind of odd bunks they had once slept on. One of the doorways led to a long hallway that looked to have numerous doorways sealed with stone.

Emrael moved toward the long hallway, expecting his friends to follow. The shaman had other ideas, however.

"Only the King and his blood kin may enter the inner chambers," Raemus roared. Timan put a hand to the hilt of his sword.

"They come with me, Raemus," Emrael said quietly. "It is the will of your king."

Raemus opened his mouth to speak, hesitated, then thought better of it. He stood back against the wall, his bearded face twisted with disapproval.

Continuing forward, Emrael put his hand to a stone door and pushed a trickle of *infusori* into it to actuate the locking mechanism he could feel within.

"You might be learning something after all," Jaina quipped from beside him.

Emrael flashed a soft smile, remembering a door just like this in the Ravan temple that he had reduced to rubble just half a year before. "Maybe I am," he said, stepping into the dimly lit room.

Ban hurried in behind him, attaching an *infusori* coil to a copper and silver apparatus that amplified the natural blue glow. Shelves full of ancient Craftings revealed themselves as the darkness retreated. One of the Craftings looked to be a thick metal gauntlet that reflected the light of the coil perfectly, its brightly burnished metal gleaming. None of the artifacts had been touched by dust or tarnish of any kind, and despite the edifice's obvious age, everything smelled . . . sterile.

Ban gasped as he touched one of the objects near him, a perfect sphere nearly a pace tall, seemingly carved of black basalt. "They're *Craftings*, Emrael!"

Jaina hurried into the room to slap Ban's hand away. "These can be dangerous, you blundering fool of a boy. I thought you had more sense than your brother, but it appears as though your idiocy is genetic." Her voice lilted slightly with the Ordenan accent that only became noticeable when she grew angry.

Emrael and Ban lifted their eyebrows at each other but hid their smiles from Jaina. Emrael pushed at his brother's shoulder. "Yeah, Ban. Be careful."

Jaina slapped Emrael in turn, and he backed away, chuckling.

Ban squared his shoulders to face Jaina, as if he were going to be in a physical fight with her. "I understand very well that strange Craftings may be dangerous, Jaina. But how are we supposed to learn about them if we don't investigate? There aren't markings or a catalogue of any sort. Or is there?"

He directed the question at Jaina but glanced at Raemus. Jaina shrugged to indicate that she didn't know. The old shaman shuffled his feet a bit and grumbled under his breath.

Emrael peered at the shaman, trying to gauge the man's behavior. Raemus called him a king, but had seemed less than happy since he had arrived to take over the city.

"Speak up, man. Do you know anything about these devices?"

The shaman grumbled some more before saying, "I don't know anything about what's in these rooms, but I do know of one book. Might say something useful."

"Lead on, then."

The shaman shuffled his way out of the room and down the long hallway. Emrael was surprised when they walked for nearly half an hour, passing hundreds of rooms like the one they had opened, each sealed by a closed stone door. He exchanged several disbelieving looks with his brother and Ordenan friends. Timan in particular seemed to be in awe, almost to the point of tears. Emrael was reminded that this place was holy in some way to Ordenans, a reminder of a past when the Ravan Empire had ruled these lands and filled them with wonders of *infusori* Crafting and magic. It likely meant something similar to Raemus and his followers, a shrine to the Mage Ancestors they revered. Emrael could not help but see it as another potential advantage in his war for his homeland. He didn't have the luxury of pure wonder.

Finally, they arrived at a door that looked similar to the others, save for perhaps a slightly more ornate script around the head of the door. Raemus opened the stone sealing the entrance with a pulse of *infusori* and stood to the side. He did not attempt to stop Jaina or Timan this time, but clenched his jaw as they walked in.

This room was much the same size as the others, lit by the same glowing copper script in the walls. Instead of row on row of shelving that contained various Craftings, however, this room had only one pedestal. Atop that pedestal sat an enormous book bound in some sort of stone, the bottom of which seemed to be carved into the pedestal itself.

"I think I know what this is," Emrael said, approaching the enormous volume. "Are these books in all temples, Jaina?"

Timan looked shocked and was the first to reply, looking back and forth between him and Jaina. "You've been in a temple before?"

Jaina brushed her fellow Imperator off to answer Emrael. "I cannot be sure that this will be the same as your other book, Emrael. Understand that if you open this tome, anything could happen."

Emrael had stopped using the Ravan book of visions currently in his possession because it only seemed to contain the same few visions he had already seen, replayed over and over. Who knew what new visions this book might hold, what knowledge?

He approached the pedestal and paused with his hand on the

cold stone cover. "I didn't get this far by being overly cautious, Jaina."

He opened the book and the same wash of light filled his vision, his mind. When it cleared, he was left looking at a familiar giant, bald, grey-skinned figure.

The Fallen God, glowing angular script burned onto every inch of his perfect body, faced a large group of much smaller humans dressed in rough linens and furs. Most of them held crude weapons—sharpened sticks and clubs, mostly—but a dozen or so people closest to the Fallen stood unarmed. The leader of the un-armed humans, a woman with long white hair, stood at the front of the group, pointing a finger at the God, speaking words Emrael could not understand. The white-haired woman was unarmed, but stepped forward boldly, eyes glowing blue with *infusori*.

The Fallen God of Glory stepped back, hands raised, head shak-ing back and forth. Emrael could not hear the words, but it was clear to him that the Fallen was pleading with the female mage in front of him. The mage, however, was determined. Her followers surrounded the Fallen, and she approached him resolutely.

Infusori flashed as the mage touched the Fallen with one hand. Though they stood still as statues, an internal war was evidenced by the roiling emotions and struggle plain on their faces. Could this woman really be a match for a god?

As the fight continued, one of the mage's unarmed followers stepped forward to lay her hand on her leader's shoulders, and the ones behind followed suit, touching the shoulders of the person in front of them until they formed a connected line, eyes all glowing furiously with *infusori*.

Still the struggle continued on the faces of the line of mages, but now the Fallen straightened. His face was no longer twisted with sorrow but set with a stony resolve of his own. He reached out one giant hand to encircle the white-haired mage's neck, releas-ing a burst of *infusori* that felt . . . complex. Emrael was far from a master of the *infusori* Art, but knew that each action—modifying stone, fiber, water, or pure *infusori* energy itself—required a dis-tinct method, or type of energy modification. This felt as if the Fallen had just used every *infusori* skill at once, and more besides that Emrael couldn't name.

Tears streaked the Fallen's cheeks as the entire line of mages collapsed, convulsing. Soon they were still, then stood to form a ring around the Fallen, facing outward. The surrounding crowd of humans armed with sticks and clubs backed away, not understanding what had just happened, why their mages had just turned their backs to the Fallen to face them instead.

The Fallen waved a hand and hung his head, tears now flowing freely down his face. The circle of mages swept outward, touching the humans on the wrist. Each human touched grew placid, vacant-eyed. They began wandering like cattle, weapons discarded or dragging on the ground.

The Fallen stalked toward a great black pyramid in the distance, his head hung low. The mages herded the now-vapid humans after him, like dogs driving a flock of sheep.

Emrael snapped from the vision and drew a deep breath like he had been underwater and just come up for air. "Fallen take me. It's just like the other one." He paused to catch his breath. "I saw the Fallen, he . . . Absent Gods, I don't know what he did. Touched a group of mages around the neck and they went from trying to kill him to following him like dogs."

Jaina approached the book quickly, turning the pages impatiently. "It does nothing, for me. Just pages filled with runes I cannot read." She shook her head in obvious frustration. "I *need* to see these visions, Emrael. Why does it work only for you?"

"I don't know, Jaina. I didn't do anything special. I just open it and see the vision in my head, clear as I'm seeing you now."

Jaina looked at Timan, who backed away, shaking his head, eyes wide. "No, Jaina. I do not wish to touch anything in this place. No."

Her stare was flat, a look she usually reserved for Emrael. "Don't be a coward."

Timan's brows drew down in anger. He stood straighter and approached the book, reaching down with a pause that was only barely noticeable. He opened the book, then looked up. "Nothing," he said, clearly relieved. "These things are better left to the Crafters, Jaina. I am just a Battle-Mage."

Jaina shoved him aside, though she did it with a wry smile. "Ban, your turn."

Ban walked to the book, opened it, and immediately stiffened, eyes wide. Jaina shared a long look with Emrael, and they waited in silence for the few short minutes it took Ban to recover his faculties, taking a deep breath as Emrael had done.

"Glory!" Ban cursed, out of breath. "Glory and the Holy Departed. It was just as Emrael said. I think . . . I think he Bound them, Jaina. They acted like the Fallen had used mindbinders, but he doesn't need the binders at all."

Jaina nodded somberly. "My people believe that the Fallen himself created every soulbinder in existence. It stands to reason that he also has the power to Bind without a Crafting."

"There were nearly a dozen mages fighting him, Jaina," Emrael said quietly. "And I don't think they posed a threat to the Fallen at all. If he's real . . . how can we ever hope to defeat him?"

Silence settled on the room like a heavy blanket. Finally, Jaina looked him in the eye. "I do not know, Emrael. I truly do not know."

Emrael sighed and turned to clasp his brother's shoulder. "Great. Well, my bet is on you and your Craftings, Ban. Have a look around at whatever Craftings you like, but be careful, okay? Maybe something the Ancients left behind will be useful for a change."

15

The tack of two hundred horses jingled in time with the clatter of their iron-shod hooves on the broken cobbles of Trylla's dirt-covered streets as Emrael and two companies of his mounted soldiers trotted through the streets of Trylla. Ten days had passed since Raemus had taken them to the temple in Trylla, ten days that Emrael, Toravin, and Timan had been scouting the villages and towns surrounding the giant abandoned city. They had covered a lot of ground quickly, looking for locations for outposts twenty leagues and farther to the north. Most were along the River Lys, which flowed first north to south and then east to west, effectively splitting the Iraean Kingdom diagonally.

He wanted plenty of warning should the Watchers move on Trylla, and eventually the forts he built would serve as supply stations for their campaign in the north. Just as soon as he dealt with Syrtsan.

Emrael arrived in the square and pulled his horse to a stop, surveying his people. The carpenters and masons had been busy—nearly every building facing the square that had retained structural integrity now had a fresh roof and oiled cloth across the windows and doors. He would have expected fewer tents in the main square as more of his people moved into the renovated buildings, but the opposite was true. There was hardly a clear lane left.

"Looks like we've had more arrivals," he commented to Timan. "I'll have to start holding court or some such to get to know them all. Isn't that what kings are supposed to do?"

The Imperator only grunted in return. Emrael smiled despite his cousin's apparent lack of enthusiasm. He had been fretting over his call for men to join them, afraid that nobody would support him despite the promise of significant lands and good pay. That fear had been unfounded. He had arrived in Trylla just over a month ago, and already another five thousand had arrived to take the Legion's land and coin bounty, and nearly as many craftsmen and farmers had answered his promise that any empty land farmed or buildings rebuilt and occupied here in Trylla could be kept.

Of course, Emrael had retained a number of buildings for himself, as had the Legion to house their operations, but nearly the entire city was open for the Iraean people to claim and rebuild. The word had spread quickly. Men and women from towns and villages in Holdings across southern Iraea had flocked to Trylla, and many had brought families with them. The sounds of carpentry, masonwork, and smithies echoed throughout the square and the surrounding blocks, where folk were already busy rebuilding their new homes.

Even some minor lords and their household guards had arrived to pledge themselves to Emrael, likely in hopes of increasing their fortunes and holdings in the new kingdom Emrael was forging in the heart of Iraea.

He dismissed his men before crossing the square to his residence, where he gave his horse to one of the groomers. It was still odd to him, handing off a horse for someone else to care for. It still felt wrong to not be doing the work himself.

He walked past the house where he, Ban, and Jaina stayed in separate suites to the small open courtyard that lay nestled between it and the surrounding buildings. The building that the Imperators had taken for themselves sat just behind Emrael's, and on the opposite corner of the block sat the huge stone building in which Ban and his Crafters had set up shop.

He desperately needed a bath, but decided to speak with Jaina first. At this time of day, he knew he'd find her in the courtyard, training her Imperators and their new understudies—the former Citadel students and various others who had asked to train with the mages and had passed the Ordenans' tests.

To his surprise, he found her sparring with Ban. Emrael lurked in the shadows of the alleyway by which he and Timan had entered and put a hand to his cousin's chest to stop him from entering the courtyard and giving them away.

As he watched, Jaina threw a punch that caught Ban in the ribs. His brother flinched, but still managed to duck out of range as she threw two more lightning-fast strikes that just missed his face. Ban

still favored his sore ribs but feinted with a jab before whipping his
rear leg at her body. His kick missed but forced her backward—
more than most managed against her. Emrael felt a burst of pride
for his brother, who had only been training seriously for a matter of
a few months. The kid was talented.

Within moments, however, Jaina had Ban on the ground, tapping
for mercy. Emrael stepped into the courtyard, a smile on his face.
"Nicely done, Ban!"

His brother smiled, still on hands and knees, sweat dripping
down his dust-covered face. "I'm learning the sword, too. Well . . .
I'm learning the stick. Jaina won't let me touch a blade yet."

"Nor should she. You'll get there. Just keep at it."

Jaina cleared her throat. He turned to raise an eyebrow at her.

"You look like shit," Jaina said, face passive except for her small
smirk. She wrinkled her nose as she took a few steps toward him.
"And smell worse."

Sweat ran down her forehead and shone on her bare arms,
but she wasn't the slightest bit out of breath despite likely having
sparred for hours.

Ban, on the other hand, stayed on his knees, chest heaving as
he struggled to catch his breath. His hair and shirt were soaked in
sweat. When he heaved himself to his feet a moment later, however,
a competitive fire twinkled in his eye. "Absent Gods, Emrael, now
I understand why you were so tired all the time at the Citadel. Jaina
is unstoppable."

"You didn't hit her once, did you?"

Ban shook his head, smile turning sour in embarrassment.

Emrael slapped his back playfully. "Don't get too down, it took
me months before I could land a strike on her, and I had been
training for years."

"Perhaps you'd like to land a strike now?" Jaina asked with a
raised eyebrow.

"Not just now, Jaina. I came here to ask you about our deal with
the Ordenans. Have they responded to our request for negotiation?"

She shook her head, sweat-darkened hair swinging about her
neck. "Nothing yet. They may not know where to find us, and will
be hesitant to send anyone important this far inland. We may need

to meet them near the Stem, or on the coast. I can get word to them, if you give me a location for a meeting."

Emrael nodded. "I think I can manage that. Let's talk later."

He had just turned to leave when something hit him in the ass, nearly knocking him off his feet. He whipped around in alarm only to find Jaina, Ban, and Timan laughing. She had kicked him. Many of the Imperators and their Iraean apprentices turned to watch.

Emrael looked up at the sky and sighed. "Jaina, I'm tired. I've been riding nonstop for days. Another time."

Her smile disappeared and she closed the distance between them in a few quick strides to punch him in the gut. Even through his leather and metal plate armor, it hurt.

"Do you think your enemies will wait until you are clean and well rested to kill you? We fight now, Emrael Ire."

She proceeded to punch him again in the midsection and followed it with a jab to the face that made his nose start to trickle blood. Emrael instinctively blocked a few strikes, and after a moment gained his bearings enough to fight back. He knew that she meant business when she sparred with him, especially now that they had access to Mage-Healers. If he didn't fight to win, she'd beat him half to death.

He surged forward with a growl, planted his shoulder in her gut, got his arms around her midsection, and drove her to the ground. He scrambled to keep his weight on top of her, then lashed out with his elbows. He landed clean blows to the head once, twice. She quickly jabbed a thumb at his eye and forced him to roll off her or be blinded.

Blood trickled down his face, but Jaina bled too—a rarity. His elbow had cut her over one eye, and blood streamed down to obscure her vision. She grinned, a fierce look given the blood covering her face. "Finally, you fight me in truth. Do not hold back."

He matched her smile with one of his own, and they stepped forward to trade blows at nearly the same moment. Emrael connected with two quick jabs, but Jaina's faster and more accurate punches drove him backward. This close, he could feel the *infusori* flowing through her, likely bolstering her strength as she burned whatever spare *infusori* energy she held within her.

Curiously, Jaina's hand darted out not to strike him, but to lightly touch his hand, which he now held out in front of him to feel and maintain his range. As soon as their hands connected, a jolt of *infusori* coursed through him, freezing his body and numbing his mind. She followed with a hard kick to his side, where his armor was only fine chain mail between leather and plate that covered the front and back. He heard the pop and felt the searing pain of ribs breaking under the force of her *infusori*-strengthened strike. He managed to roll his shoulder in front of his face just in time to avoid taking the following punch that would have knocked him unconscious.

The pain and anger welling within him gave him easy access to *infusori,* which he burned to give him strength to fight through the pain. Even still, he kept his left arm low now to protect his broken ribs. Another blow to that spot could cause the broken ribs to puncture his lungs, and he knew Jaina wasn't going to give up until he surrendered. She'd rather kill him.

Not today.

A straight kick to Jaina's stomach doubled her over briefly, sending her backward and making her pause her incessant attacks. He moved forward, punched with his right hand despite the pain screaming in his left side.

His punch landed, but his subsequent leg sweep went wide. Jaina recovered before he did and kicked his leg out from under him. He landed flat on his back with a crash of armor and a grunt as his breath left him. His side was agony. He was almost certainly bleeding internally.

He tried to roll to his feet, but Jaina stomped a foot on his throat. "Yield," she said thickly. Her jaw was swollen already, possibly dislocated or broken. A minor satisfaction, but paltry compared to the shame of defeat.

He tapped her leg three times with his hand, and rasped, "Yield."

When she took her foot from his neck, he coughed and spat blood. "Absent Gods, Jaina, were you trying to kill me?"

She leaned down to help him stand. The fire of battle rage still shone in her eyes, as he was sure it did in his, but her voice held unmistakable affection. "No, boy. Quite the opposite. Train as if your life depends on it. If we hold back now, we limit what we are capable of in battle. You will get my best, and I had better get yours."

Emrael grunted his acknowledgement but winced at the pain. "That's great, but I think you've broken my ribs. If you don't have a Mage-Healer close by, I'm going to be in real trouble."

He leaned heavily on his mentor as she called urgently, "Cailla! Now! Bring your coils and your pack. The boy needs Healing. Dairus, you can see to my wounds when we have the boy situated."

Jaina leaned closer to him as the willowy black-haired Healer approached. "Watch yourself with her, Emrael. Cailla is as good a Healer as I've known, and a good Imperator. But she is not loyal to your mother."

"I can handle myself."

She studied him briefly through her eye that wasn't blood-crusted. "Can you?" She touched his wrist again, and Emrael felt her project her emotions, warm, deep sincerity. Loyalty. It brought tears to his eyes. Or perhaps that was the broken ribs. Maybe both.

He gave her arm a squeeze before he followed a smiling Cailla toward his residence, holding his side carefully.

Before the sun rose the next morning, Emrael left his bed while most still slept. He twisted back and forth, testing his ribs. He was a bit sore, like he had gone through a particularly hard day of training, nothing more. Not like he had been coughing up blood.

Such Healing was a luxury, however, and not one they could afford indefinitely. They only had a few weeks' supply of charged *infusori* coils left. If Emrael didn't find a supply source closer than Whitehall soon, nobody would be Healed or be able to use any of Ban's Craftings.

The sky was just turning grey when he walked down the two flights of stairs and into the large main entry hall. He didn't have to wait long before Ban emerged from his rooms and skipped down the stairs to join him.

"You're late," Emrael said.

Ban gave him an unamused frown, face still swollen with sleep. "Why are we up so early, anyway? My Crafters won't be happy, most of them keep odd hours."

Emrael clapped his brother on the shoulder. "Our allies should be arriving today. If we're going to see your Craftings, it's going to have to be now."

They headed out to the mess tents in the main square. The camp cooks were already serving breakfast. The brothers stacked rashers of bacon and fried eggs on a thick slice of bread, filled their cups with fresh milk, and walked over to the Crafters' building.

"This is good," Ban mumbled around a mouthful of hot food as they walked. Emrael nodded and smiled, though inwardly he worried about whether he'd be able to keep his men this well supplied for long, especially on military campaigns. Maintaining a supply line in hostile territory was going to be an issue, and he couldn't very well commandeer the common people's produce and hope that they'd be loyal to him after the war. No, he'd have to be smart about supplies, and pay good copper for food where he was required to take it from the Iraean locals. Which meant he needed more copper.

"Okay, Ban, let's see what you've got."

"You were supposed to visit last night," his brother replied slyly. "We had everything all set up to demonstrate."

Emrael blushed, ducking his head as he fought an embarrassed smile. "Yeah well, I was a bit busy coughing up blood."

"Mmm. Still getting your ass kicked by Jaina. Sad, really."

Emrael punched his brother in the arm, hard.

"Owwww, you Fallen bastard. Fine, fine, I'll leave it alone."

They walked and ate in silence and soon arrived at the Crafting laboratory, where several Crafters waited for them. The halls of the large building were still dim in the early-morning light, but the rooms occupied by Crafters were well-lit with *infusori* coils. They reached a large room with equipment arranged on roughly built tables, *infusori* coils attached here and there, smoke and the acrid scent of molten metal already permeating the air despite the early hour. A middle-aged man with wild hair and disheveled clothing moved erratically from machine to machine, mumbling to himself.

"Geryl hasn't slept in a few days," Ban whispered as they stopped in the doorway. "He's mad as they come, but a genius with Craftings. Ran the Masters' laboratory at the Citadel, now keeps our manufacturing room running for us. He can cast and machine like nobody I've ever seen."

They continued, stopping briefly at several doorways to peer in at tired-looking men and women working on various devices.

"You'll want to see this one," Ban said, pulling him into a small workroom where a muscular young woman wearing spectacles sat at a workbench working with an *infusori*-powered welding tool that spat acrid smoke as she connected various spun wires and components to a cylindrical object about the size of two fists held together. Emrael was passingly familiar with common Crafting schemas, but hardly recognized a single component or design in the object.

The young woman didn't look up as they entered. Ban walked straight to the three large windows, tying back the oiled cloth to let air into the room, clearing the smoke somewhat. He moved to a large box near the back and after rummaging for a moment came back with a coil and lighting apparatus, which he set up on the young woman's workbench near where she worked, improving the lighting significantly. The girl grunted in satisfaction, but still didn't acknowledge their existence.

After some time, the girl grunted in satisfaction again as she made a connection, apparently the final one. She reached for a plate that covered the internal components and fastened it in place with a few quick spot welds. She stood and walked to a side shelf to open the lid of a steel case, where she placed the Crafting on a padded rack next to a dozen or so just like it. That done, she turned to look silently at Ban and Emrael, acknowledging their existence for the first time.

Glory. Emrael knew Crafters could be an eccentric bunch, but Ban had found some real treasures.

Ban gestured toward the woman with one hand. "Emrael, this is Darrain. Darrain, meet my brother Emrael . . . the one paying for our supplies."

"I know who he is, Ban," Darrain said curtly. "Do you want me to show him?"

Ban smiled rather than take offense. "Yes, please."

"Good. Come with me." Darrain took one of the Craftings from the case and walked quickly to a door that led outside. They walked for nearly ten minutes into a part of the city that hadn't been re-populated or touched in any way, until they came to a two-story building next to a pile of scorched, scattered rubble.

Emrael turned to Ban. "I'm going to like this one, aren't I?" he asked quietly.

"Stay back," Darrain barked.

Emrael took a few steps back, but Ban dragged him back farther, now with a worried look on his face. Darrain twisted her Crafting, pressed something with her thumb, then tossed it into the worn-out old building next to the pile of rubble. She immediately sprinted back to where Emrael and Ban stood, but didn't stop when she reached them. She kept running, not slowing down a whit. They took the cue and ran after her.

Emrael hadn't taken three steps when a wave of pure *infusori* energy washed over him from behind, knocking him from his feet to pitch forward on his stomach. An instant later, a deafening roar and a shower of detritus hit him. His mind flashed to nearly a year before, when a wagon had exploded similarly on the bridge between Lidran and Naeran.

He lay flat on the ground and put his hands over his head, only looking up when flying stones stopped hitting him. He raised his head to find Darrain and Ban several paces ahead of him, having taken cover behind a nearby stone wall. They both grinned at Emrael, who shook his head and spat a stream of curses as he stood and brushed the dirt off of himself. His ears rang as he stalked toward his brother, who skipped away laughing.

Emrael soon desisted and turned to Darrain. "Glory's burnt balls, Darrain, what the fuck was that?"

Darrain's grin turned to a cackle of laughter so strong she couldn't speak. Ban had to shout to be heard over her squeals of glee. "An exothermic hyper-release device. It holds a large amount of *infusori* energy and explodes on a timer. Darrain's done a great deal of dangerous work to make them potent and reliable."

Emrael stared hard at Darrain. "When did you first make these?"

Darrain's laughter cut short. "Why?" she asked, eyes narrowing.

Emrael kept his eyes locked on her. "Do our enemies have access to these?"

Darrain's face drooped. "They . . . I made some for them, before. I had to. But they already had a design, I just improved it. I had no choice."

Ban cut in quickly. "Em. Stop. You should understand that better than most."

Emrael nodded, breathing deep to calm himself. "We encountered something like this a week or so after the Watchers took the Citadel. I just want to know whether that would have been your device or of Malithii make."

Darrain quirked her mouth. "I had made similar devices for years at the Citadel, and my Master there had several of my early prototypes. He cooperated with the Watchers, so it could have been one of my early designs."

Emrael forced himself to stay calm. "Thank you, Darrain. We'll just have to hope it was one of yours, then. How many did you make for the Malithii while you were held captive?"

Ban answered. "They have maybe a dozen or two of these, isn't that right, Darrain?"

Darrain nodded, then dared a small smile. "And the schema they stole from me is incorrect. I made it incorrect on purpose. The only real design is here." She tapped her head with one finger, then said in a flat, emotionless voice, "If they build what is on the schema they took, it will explode as soon as it's primed."

Emrael blinked, surprised at the matter-of-fact tone from the seemingly harmless Crafter. "Right. Okay. So they have a dozen of them. How many do we have?"

Darrain shrugged. "Fifty? Get me more materials and *infusori* charges, and I can set underlings to making hundreds per week."

Emrael paced through the rubble-strewn street until he stood next to the building Darrain had just incinerated. What had been a two-story stone structure was now a pile of smoldering rubble. "I'll get you what you need. Could we attach them to crossbow bolts, or maybe ballistae, catapults, that kind of thing? I can't risk my Stonebreakers every time I need to breach a wall, and we're going to be breaching a lot of walls."

Ban was the one to answer. "Yes, easily. The projectile will need to be large and heavy to fly true with these attached, and will need to be actuated with pressure plates or accelerometers rather than timers. But we can do it."

"How soon?"

Ban scratched his head as he looked to Darrain, then brushed dust from his hair. "A few days?"

Emrael started walking. "Good. Let's get back and you can get started. I need them, and any other explosives you have, ready to move in two days. And I want you to train some engineers from my Legion on how to use them."

Back at the Crafter's workshop, Ban took Emrael to his personal workspace, a room on the second floor not unlike Darrain's on the ground floor. A Legion-style vest of armor lay on his table, but this one was a bit bulkier.

"I've been working on the vest for a while, Em. I think you're going to like the changes I've made."

Ban hefted the vest and handed it to Emrael. "Darrain's work with supercoil geometry for her explosive devices got me thinking: not only could we make coils with higher density, but they could have far lower loss—that is, it won't glow or hum. Even to a mage's *infusori* senses, it won't feel like much until you touch it, so it shouldn't give you away to any Malithii or even Imperators, I suppose. That vest should now hold as much as ten high-grade gold coils."

Emrael caught the vest and looked inside to find that where there had been inflexible copper strips, there were now several copper plates that on closer inspection were scaled to make them flexible. "Ten coils of *infusori* is amazing. I can't wear it without a padded shirt underneath, though, it'll rub my nipples clear off."

Ban laughed and pulled a shirt from a bundle on a nearby table. "I had a hell of a time doing it, but managed to extrude copper wire fine enough to be woven into a linen tunic. You should be able to wear one of these and maintain contact with the *infusori* storage in the vest just fine. Besides, once you start sweating enough, any old tunic should conduct just fine."

Shrugging out of his usual armor, Emrael put Ban's on. He was pleased to find that the vest was nearly a perfect fit, and not noticeably heavier than typical armor. "How did you do this, Ban? It should weigh as much as a side of beef with that much gold in it."

Ban shook his head. "I told you, this is the new design—Darrain and I worked on it together. Rather revolutionary, really. Darrain is quite a genius. Our new microcoil design holds the equivalent energy with less than a tenth the amount of gold. This invention alone will change the world of Crafting."

Emrael reached into the coils—microcoils, whatever—and found an ocean of pulsating energy waiting there. Ban was right, it must have been the equivalent of ten very good coils. But it didn't feel full, not even close. He pulled out the coils he always carried and sucked the *infusori* from them both as quickly and easily as he drew breath. He pushed them into the vest, which accepted the additional energy easily.

"What happens if I try to put too much in? Will it just stop holding additional *infusori* like a normal coil?"

Ban shrugged. "I don't know, haven't tried. Theoretically, it should work the same. It will simply bleed excess energy—it will get hot. So don't do that."

"And if I'm stabbed? It won't explode, will it?" he asked, still a bit traumatized by Darrain's demonstration. His ears still rang slightly.

Ban laughed. "No, Em, it's perfectly safe. The array is connected in parallel. If any of the microcoils are severed, it will simply render a small portion of the *infusori* energy inaccessible."

Emrael shook his head in wonder. "Absent Gods, Ban. You and your Crafters have already produced some amazing Craftings. These are going to do real good, you know. Think about a world with lossless *infusori* transportation, and without having to lug millions of pounds of gold all around the world!"

Ban smiled, obviously pleased but embarrassed at the compliment. "Thanks, Em."

"Can I get a vest like this for all of my mages? And don't forget, I need more of your Observers. I can't wait weeks for correspondence if we're going to move as quickly as we need to."

Ban shook his head, frowning at his brother now. "Emrael," he said in a flat tone. "I'm doing what I can, but these things take time. It will take weeks to make another vest, or any microcoils at all. The process is very intensive. And I have two Observers ready to test, but I don't know how long that will take, or how quickly I can make as many as you need. I'll have to pull Crafters off their projects to build the ones you want first. They won't like that."

Emrael plopped into a nearby wooden armchair. "I know, Ban.

You're doing well. Train more Crafters if you need to. I'm sure you can ask around, pull a few interested folk into your building here."

"This isn't a school, Emrael. Folk off the street can't do what we do."

Sitting forward, Emrael looked his brother in the eye. "Make it a Fallen-damned school, Ban. If you don't give us a technological advantage, and a big one at that, we die. People are looking at me to save them, but you and your Crafters will decide this war. And the next one, and the one after that. Remember, Corrande still has plenty of Crafters he abducted from the Citadel. And who knows what the Malithii are capable of."

He closed his eyes and rested his face in one hand. How much should he tell his brother? Was it fair to keep the Fallen's visit from him, any of it, when so much rested on his shoulders as well? Ban risked everything Emrael did, with less control. When he looked back up, his mood had turned somber.

"The Fallen is real, Ban. He's alive. I've seen him, talked to him." He rubbed his face with one hand, suddenly tired. "This is bigger than just a fight for the Ire lands, Iraea, or even the Provinces. It's going to be bad."

Ban looked at him sideways, between squinted eyelids. "You've . . . seen him? The vision books? I've seen them too, remember? You let me have your book after the one in the temple worked for me."

Emrael shook his head. "No, not just that. A Malithii priest, their Prophet, got to me in the Citadel . . . he touched me, and it was like I was transported to wherever the Fallen was. I could feel him, Ban. See him. He's unlike anything I ever imagined. We're fighting a real living god. You've seen the visions I have. I think he had something to do with *creating* humans in the first place. How do we fight that and win?"

Ban bit his lip, thinking. "I don't know, Emrael. One thing to consider, however, is that he wouldn't be fighting at all if he were all-powerful. He must have weaknesses, despite his power. He must need something from us. Where did you see him?"

"Inside some sort of giant stone structure. A pyramid, lit with glowing runic script in the walls similar to what's in the Ravan temples."

Ban nodded, again biting his lip as he thought. "I'll look through your book of visions some more and let you know what I find, but something is tickling my memory."

Just then, a soldier in Ire Legion forest-green clothing rushed down the hallway to stop at the door. "Lord Ire sir, Commander Toravin requests your presence. Lord Bayr and Lady Raebren have entered the city. They'll be here soon."

Emrael stood immediately. "You said *Lady* Raebren?"

The Legionman nodded. "Yes, sir. Lady Saravellin."

Emrael turned to Ban. "How do I look?"

"Like you took a bath in a stonemason's scrap heap."

Emrael tried to dust himself off as he turned back to the Legionman. "Thank you, Legionman. Lead the way, please."

Emrael waited for Lord Davis Bayr and Lady Saravellin Raebren on the stone stairs that descended from his residence to the square below. He had recently ordered those living in the square to find living arrangements elsewhere—either in buildings on which they did makeshift renovations themselves, or in tents located in one of the many smaller squares that dotted the city around the enormous central square.

The huge space in the center of the city was now a dedicated training ground and mess area on one side, with a small but growing market area on the other, where the blacksmiths, merchants, and other craftspeople now ran their trades out of fixed-up stone buildings and temporary canvas tents.

More people still arrived daily, some looking to join Emrael's Legion, merchants looking for trade opportunities, tradesmen and commoners looking to build a new life. Trylla was still far short of the hundreds of thousands of residents it had once held but was starting to feel like a living city once more.

Emrael had ordered the Legion to form up so Lord Bayr and Lady Raebren would have to approach through a wide lane left open between his battalions formed up in squares. He waited on the broad sweeping steps of his residence—some were calling it a palace, which he supposed it was—with Jaina, Toravin, Ban, Timan, Garrus, and Worren, who had just returned from his campaign in the Paellar Holding.

His Legion was nearly twenty thousand strong after only a few short months here in Trylla. More than half of them had joined him in that time, and though they were garbed in every style of armor and weaponry possible—some had none at all—they had come ready to fight. Just as they had done when assimilating the Sagmyn Legion into their own, Toravin had divided them into companies and squads led by veterans who had proven themselves in battle. While there were still a few discipline issues as happened in any army, and even some desertions, all in all it had worked rather well.

A ripple through the ranks near the south entrance to the square preceded Saravellin, who rode in with what looked to be a single battalion of soldiers in the distinctive teal Raebren uniforms. He tried to hide his dismay at Saravellin's small force, but Toravin made no such effort as he looked to Emrael with a frown and raised eyebrows. Emrael waved a hand at him. They would have words with the heir of Raebren.

Lord Bayr entered the square on Saravellin's heels, and he had also brought only one thousand soldiers. Emrael hadn't expected him to bring more, as he was only in Trylla to coordinate their next moves with Emrael.

Saravellin formed her battalion into a long column just in front of Emrael's residence where a space had been left clear—a much larger space than needed, as it turned out—and waited for Bayr to do the same before ascending the steps to join Emrael and his council. While Toravin and his Captains First dismissed the Legion, Emrael ushered the newcomers inside to a room that had been prepared with a long table, chairs, and food.

He stood at the door while everyone took their places. Jaina stepped close to him as she entered the room to whisper in his ear, "She's testing you. Press her."

He didn't need her to clarify who she meant.

Saravellin hadn't missed the interaction. She looked from Emrael to Jaina with a carefully neutral expression, but Emrael could see the tension at the corners of her eyes, could practically *feel* her processing the information, filing it away for future use. She seemed the type that didn't miss much.

When Toravin, Captain First Garrus, and Captain First Worren arrived and took their seats, Emrael closed the double doors to the large room and had just taken his place at the head of the table when there was a commotion at the door.

". . . Let me through!" a voice said just outside the door. It was Lord Tarelle. There were sounds of a quick scuffle, then a squeal of indignation. "Unhand me! I am a Lord Holder and should be in that room." The voice grew louder, obviously pitched for those in the room. "Ire! Lord Ire! I am one of the seven Lords of Iraea and demand to be treated as such!"

Emrael looked at Lord Bayr, whose face betrayed no emotion. Saravellin looked amused as she watched to see what he would do.

"I don't have time for this shit," Emrael grumbled, slapping one hand on the table as he got to his feet. He kicked the door open and strode past the mages and soldiers guarding the door. He stopped just inches from the shocked Lord Tarelle and the five armed men with him—all that he had been allowed to bring with him to Trylla.

"What do you want, Tarelle?"

"I . . . I should be a part of your plans. I deserve a seat at your table!"

Emrael looked from him to the five soldiers, who looked prepared for a fight. "And you thought these five would bolster your case? Scare me into letting you hear my plans?"

"No!" Tarelle's face sank. "No," he said again, more quietly this time. "I just want to help. Lord Ire, I've handed over my Holding to your men. I have been bullied into this coalition of yours. And I have not objected, until now. I can help, I can be an ally. I can raise more men from my Holding. I want to earn a place in your new kingdom."

Emrael stared at him for a moment, and the men backing him. They obviously felt some loyalty toward their Lord Holder despite his current severe disadvantage. That meant something.

Emrael pointed a finger in Tarelle's face. "I don't trust you. You had a chance to use your men to help us expel the Watchers, and you didn't. You stood aside, but you didn't help."

Emrael turned to reenter the room, but Tarelle surprised him by answering his rhetorical question.

"I will give you copper. And men," Tarelle said resolutely. "Your man, the Syrtsan outcast. He'll have little cooperation from the minor lords loyal to me, and there are many. I can give you copper from my personal estates, and I can give you five thousand good men that will not join you if not for me. Maybe more."

Emrael turned back to him. He had already promised part of Tarelle's lands to Dorae, and planned to give the rest to Halrec. That didn't mean Tarelle couldn't be useful, though, in the meantime. There would be other Holdings to grant, should he prove his worth. "How much money?"

"Twenty thousand copper rounds?" Tarelle was obviously in pain at offering so much, and with good reason. Twenty thousand copper rounds was a huge sum—likely more than half of the coin in his coffers.

Emrael tried not to show his surprise. "Twenty-five thousand."

Tarelle shuddered—rich men held tight to their coin—but acceded with a nod that bounced his jowls.

"Your five thousand men will report to me here, with the coin, within thirty days."

Tarelle's eyes opened in shock. "Y-you don't want them in my Holding? With Commander Syrtsan?"

"Nope," Emrael said with a certain amount of pleasure. Whether Tarelle was sincere or not, he obviously didn't like this idea. "I need them here; the coin too. Halrec will have to manage until I've taken the rest of the kingdom. Thirty days, Garan."

He turned his back to the man and strode back into the room, gesturing to his men to close the door behind him.

"Aren't you going to invite me in?" Tarelle shouted.

Emrael called over his shoulder without looking back, "Thirty days, Garan. Pay up, then you're in."

Emrael took his seat and looked around the room. He settled his gaze on Saravellin, his expression serious. "One thousand men?"

Saravellin smiled, no mirth in the expression. "My father is a conservative man, Lord Ire. Besides expelling the Watchers garrisoned in our Holding, he must contend with the possibility that the Norta Holding falls, allowing Corrande to reach our Holding undeterred. Syrtsan to our west is a risk as long as he withholds his support. Due to activity in our Holding during the most recent rebellion," she said with a glance at Toravin, "we have been sanctioned more heavily than others, and have limited military resources."

Emrael held her gaze until her smile faltered. "And what else can you offer, Lady Raebren? One thousand men hardly earns a place of honor in the new kingdom."

She didn't show fear or unease, but her expression was serious, now. "Due to our unfortunate position on the Stem between Whitehall and Duurn, Raebren has been forced to build superior ground transport assets to attract trade to our capital. I am prepared to provide a supply chain to Trylla, and for the war campaign . . . at a discounted price, of course."

Emrael laughed, both from relief and genuine humor. "I merit a discount, do I?"

Saravellin smiled again, and this time her eye gleamed as she shrugged. "A girl's got to eat."

Emrael couldn't help but match her smile, amused at her audacity. When he spoke, though, his words were hard as stone. "Wagons and supplies will be welcome. But this is not a trade bargain. This is a war."

She didn't look happy about it, but she nodded.

"Good. Now. Can you truly spare no more soldiers than one single battalion?"

Saravellin made an irritated clicking sound with her tongue. "We only have five thousand trained, and cannot spare more while Syrtsan, Corrande, and Barros remain threats on our borders."

Pressing the issue here and now would not help him retain his tenuous allies. "When can we expect your wagons and supplies to be available?"

"The first party is only a half-day behind us," she replied smugly. "Five hundred wagons with food, building materials, gear, and weapons. Your men out there in the courtyard with nothing but a spear will have real armor and shields. We have tents and bandages and a dozen trained healers as well."

Five hundred wagons of supplies was more than a token contribution. "Thank you," he said simply. "My clerks will arrange appropriate compensation."

Saravellin's smirk softened into a sincere smile, and she nodded in acknowledgement. "And when you neutralize the threats on our borders, my father will be happy to put more of his troops under your command. He has already issued a call for more conscripts."

"Right," Emrael said, standing. "About that. We'll be moving on the Syrtsan Holding."

He paused, expecting Saravellin to react to the news—Bayr, Toravin, Ban, Jaina, and his Captains First already knew. She simply furrowed her eyebrows and frowned thoughtfully. She understood his intent nearly immediately, it seemed.

"The campaign begins in two days. Our first target is Gnalius, the Syrtsan Well town on the border with Ire and Raebren. While we mobilize most of our twenty thousand men—plus Raebren's one thousand—to take Gnalius and draw Syrtsan and the Watchers in his Holding toward Gnalius, Lord Bayr will lead his ten thousand directly to Duurn. With any luck, the Bayr men will have taken Syrtsan's capital while we occupy their attention to the east. The Syrtsan Holding will be ours within weeks."

Duurn was Syrtsan's capital, a large port city on the Iraean side of the Stem River Sound. It was as far from Emrael's occupied land as anywhere in Iraea, and would be the last place they'd expect an assault even once they realized that Emrael had attacked Gnalius. If Emrael and those loyal to him could take his capital, they would fully neutralize Syrtsan quickly so they could focus on Lord Marol and the Watchers holding the Ire lands in the north. He was gambling a great deal on not only Lord Bayr's loyalty, but his military abilities.

Saravellin watched him sharply now, nodding to herself as he finished.

Lord Bayr cleared his throat loudly. "I want to take Arras. That is the prize I wish to keep, and I can take it easily with my ten thousand. Duurn is too large, too well defended."

Emrael had to clench his jaw to keep himself from saying something rash. "Lord Bayr, you'll have your prize. But not until Syrtsan is completely neutralized. Taking Arras first would only serve to alert Syrtsan to your presence and to spread our forces thin. Surely you agree?"

Bayr frowned, but acceded with a nod after a moment. "Aye. But capturing Duurn is not so easy as you make it sound."

Emrael smiled patiently. "By your own estimates, Lord Syrtsan has fifteen thousand of his own men and five thousand Watchers garrisoned at Duurn. He will be forced to field nearly every soldier to confront me when I move on Gnalius. Hopefully he knows nothing of your involvement?"

Bayr shook his head. "He knows nothing of our alliance."

"Good," Emrael replied. "You can have Arras and the entire western seaboard as we agreed, but take Duurn for me first. We cannot afford to let Syrtsan lure us into a prolonged siege. I figure we have a month, maybe two before Lord Marol and the Watchers in the north bring the fight to us. If we're still engaged in the Syrtsan Holding by that time, we'll have lost the war."

Lord Bayr sat silent, stroking his chin. Dorae had assured Emrael that Bayr was an ambitious man, ready to join them if offered a sufficient prize.

After a long silence, Emrael spoke. "When you take Duurn, you can keep it as well. Everything west of the Teneralle. But you have to take Duurn first and do it quickly."

He had just offered up the richest portion of the most valuable land in Iraea. Still, Bayr hesitated. Finally, the Lord Holder nodded. "I'll see it done."

Relieved, Emrael turned to the rest of the room. "Everyone who fights with us—and those who provide other skilled services," he said with a pointed look at Saravellin, "will be entitled to land or edifices equal in value to five copper rounds. They'll get five full rounds of credit for each year they fight. When we've secured the entire kingdom, they will be able to choose from lands my clerks deem eligible here in Trylla, in the Ire Holding, and in any Holdings we take by force. I encourage you to do the same for your people with any lands you acquire through me."

Saravellin and Bayr had surprised looks on their faces, and not in a good way. Toravin and his two Captains, however, nodded their approval. They knew that a tangible reward would not only attract more soldiers to their cause, but would motivate their forces to stick with them and fight hard. Five copper rounds was more than most would earn in a decade of simple work. Silver, gold, and iron were the coin of the commons.

Saravellin cleared her throat. "What recompense can Raebren expect for our contributions?"

Emrael pressed his tongue to the front of his teeth as he considered. "What do you want?"

"Surprise me," she said.

"Syrtsan lands along the Stem Sound?"

Saravellin's smile deepened to wrinkle the skin around her eyes as she squared her shoulders. "Perhaps. We will negotiate later. When my wagons arrive."

He nodded, grateful to avoid the question for now, and looked around the room. "Anything else?"

Lord Bayr grunted, gesturing at the two Ordenans in the room, who had sat quietly during the meeting. "Yes. What do these vultures want?"

Good question, Emrael thought to himself. He trusted Jaina and Timan more than he trusted most anyone. But he himself wondered what Ordena hoped to gain from their sudden involvement in the Provinces.

To Bayr, he said, "The Ordenans with me are our allies, and I trust them. I don't expect you to deal with the Ordenans except through me."

Bayr shrugged, apparently appeased.

He stared around the room, and all nodded their heads, though some with more vigor than others.

"One more thing," he said firmly. "No pillage, no rape, no more destruction than necessary to take our targets. Any lands and coin we take will come from the nobility, not the common folk. Our current enemies will soon be our allies and countrymen; we cannot afford to turn the people against us. I will hang anyone not treating the populace as such."

Most in the room nodded again, but the military leaders among them now had sour looks on their faces, Toravin included. Not because they wished to pillage their countrymen, but because enforcing such an edict was not a simple thing, nor popular among soldiers, and they knew it. Emrael didn't care—conquering a kingdom was never an easy proposition, but he was determined to do it right, and to do right by the people he would one day govern.

Emrael stood. "You'll have your orders by nightfall. Day after tomorrow at dawn, we march. Ban and Garrus will keep the remaining men to hold Trylla."

16

Darmon Corrande rode the last stretch of the road to Vahle, detachedly admiring the towering conifers, aspens, and various hardwoods that grew in the water-rich alpine clime of northern Iraea. A stream ran next to the road, trickling its way toward the river that would carry it northward to the sea.

While Porshim Holding was as dry as the Corrande Province, nearly the entirety of the Ire Holding he had traversed had been like this—trees and verdant fields occasionally interrupted by stark blue-grey stone protruding from the earth's surface. The Holding even *smelled* fertile. The air was full of rich, earthy scents and the resinous perfume of the various conifers. It was so different from the dry rolling grasslands of his own province on the other side of the Duskan mountain range. No wonder his grandfather had coveted this land and its bounty.

Dense forest sporadically gave way to more farms and villages with expansive swaths of green fields heavy with midsummer crops, and as they came around a bend in the road, he spied a large stone wall that could only be the city of Vahle. They had arrived at last.

He rode at the head of a long column of Watchers, Malithii, and the Malithii's various minions, but stopped at one side of the large square just inside the gate to watch as the army entered the city. There were several thousand of the disgusting soulbound, herded like sheep along the broad dirt highways. Perhaps more disconcerting even than those monsters were the men that willingly followed the dark priests.

Fighting men in dark garb and armor who spoke the same harshly musical tongue as the Malithii priests had begun arriving in the Corrande Province in recent months, and several thousand of them now followed Darmon and his Malithii keepers in impressively ordered ranks. Their curved-blade spears glittered in the sunlight as they marched through the large timber gate in perfect step.

A smattering of other soldiers followed: mercenaries from the Free Cities, Ithan clansmen, and horsemen from beyond the Ithan Empire who dressed in vests woven from a strange pale leather. The ferocious-looking warriors painted their faces red and white, and the red had deepened to crimson as their journey wore on. Darmon didn't think he wanted to know what kind of animal produced the pale leather they wore.

All told, their force numbered more than ten thousand. Added to the Watcher and Corrande forces his father already commanded here in the Iraean Province, he estimated upward of fifty thousand soldiers had been deployed to Iraea to fight Emrael Ire. Odd, that he should now find himself hoping that Ire had sufficient numbers to withstand his father's forces. As much as he might hope for a horrible death for the arrogant bastard who cut off his hand, he prayed it came after he freed the Provinces from Malithii oppression.

His gut roiled with dread, remembering the vision—or whatever it had been—of the Fallen God. He looked sideways at the two priests who were his constant shadow. How in the name of the Holy Departed had these bastards taken control so quickly?

They rode into the city, a large port where trade flowed between the Ire and Paellar provinces, and from Ordena in the west. Or had, when the Provinces had allowed Ordenan trade in Iraea.

Darmon and his escorts were quickly ushered to a small room in a large stone building that overlooked the harbor. He stared through the glass pane of the window, doing his best to ignore his escort. There were perhaps two dozen small fishing vessels sailing in and out of the harbor, but no larger ships. No merchants, no barges, no warships. Even here, the Ordenans ruled the sea.

He turned from the large window as the door to the small meeting room opened, and a short Malithii priest with a round, extensively tattooed face bustled into the room. The little priest had ink smudges on his pale hands. Several black-robed priests with far fewer tattoos followed, ledger books, pens, and ink at the ready. Even the dread Malithii empire was run by clerks, it appeared.

The small tattooed man's eyes flitted to Darmon's pinned sleeve where his right hand should have been, and pulled a pair of round-lensed spectacles from a pocket of his robes. "Lord Darmon Corrande, correct?" he asked in the best Provincial common tongue Darmon had heard from one of the Malithii, nearly without accent.

"Yes." Darmon took a seat across the table from the clerk and his assistants. His Malithii escorts took up positions near the door.

"So nice to see the local leadership joining the fight." The clerk priest shuffled through a few papers, then looked at Darmon over his spectacles. "Ah yes, here they are. Your orders. You are to take a battalion and occupy the town of Doriscter, fifty leagues north-west of Trylla, where our enemies have taken root. Take the town, fortify it, and await further orders. These two Faithful will stay assigned to you. Your men will be waiting for you just outside the city walls when we conclude this meeting. Your guides will show you to them. Good day to you."

Darmon knew he was in no position to argue, so he accepted his written orders with only a nod. He wasn't looking forward to leaving again without so much as a night to rest, but he wouldn't have slept well in this city anyhow. Not while these Malithii crawled about like flies on a fresh corpse.

His "guides" led him from the room and to a small gate to the south of the city. There, he was relieved to find a full battalion of Watchers waiting for him, all in pristine blue uniforms. He had been afraid he'd be stuck with those foreigners or a bunch of wild Ithans. Or worse, a horde of soulbound abominations and more Malithii priests. He would have been powerless.

Most of his thousand men were on foot with pikes or *infusori*-Crafted crossbows, but one company looked to be engineers, and another was mounted cavalry. A well-balanced force for taking and holding a small bit of territory. The Malithii clerk knew his business.

Their commanding officer, a Captain Second with a strong build and greying hair, saluted sharply from atop his horse when Darmon reined up in front of him. "Sir! We've been told that you'll have orders for us, sir. Best battalion in the territory, the Fifty-Third."

Darmon studied the man as he nodded his acknowledgement. The Captain Second was clearly Iraean, judging by the accent. That wasn't an oddity, of course; the Watchers recruited heavily from the local population. Downtrodden as the former kingdom was due to the trading restrictions and reparation taxes enforced by the Provinces, the recruiting efforts were very successful. Nearly half of the Watcher Legion was Iraean.

"Most of them Iraean boys, then?" Darmon asked.

"Aye, Lord Corrande. A few from around the Provinces, but the larger part are Iraeans. Loyal to a man, they are, sir. To a man. We aren't green, we've seen action against the Ordenans, outlaws, even on the Ithan frontier a time or two. We know our business."

Darmon nodded again. "I'm sure you do, Captain . . ."

"Vaslat, sir. Teuri Vaslat."

"Right, Captain Vaslat. Are your men ready to march?"

"Aye sir."

"Good. We're to hold the town of Doriscter to the south. Do you know it?"

"Aye, sir. Been there plenty. Shouldn't be any trouble, we keep a full company garrisoned there, the folks are used to us. We treat them right, and they treat us right, for the most part. Hard to say how they'll react to news of the Ire boy building his city in the ruins, but there won't be a fight to get into the town."

Captain Vaslat seemed a good man, a fighting man who had worked himself up through the ranks over decades of hard work. His weathered face showed his years of marching and riding in the saddle.

Darmon's mind started spinning, weighing the risks and rewards of trusting him so quickly. He didn't have much choice, though, he realized shortly. This was his best chance to talk to the man frankly without arousing the suspicion of the Malithii tailing him.

He nudged his horse forward and lowered his voice. "Captain . . . you know about the Malithii? The dark-robed bastards like the ones behind me?"

Captain Vaslat's face froze in a careful mask. "Yes, sir. I know of them. They are the ones who gave me my orders. Seem like a . . . foul lot, but we're loyal to the Provinces, sir. And . . . our allies."

Darmon locked eyes with the officer and lowered his voice further. "They are no allies of mine, or my father's, Captain. I'm afraid they have us in quite the stranglehold. I want you to send your scouts as far afield as you dare. Gather information from any contacts you have in the United Provincial Legion. I need to know everything I can about where these foreigners are and what they're planning. I need to know who else in the Watchers remains loyal to the Provinces, not to these Malithii. Report to me only when these two following me can't hear."

He forced himself to not look back at the Malithii priests shadowing him as he raised his voice again. "And make sure we know where every one of that Ire bastard's rebels are hiding."

Captain Vaslat nodded slowly, relief clear in his bearing. He saluted sharply. "We'll find them, Lord Corrande."

17

Countless stars painted the night sky in great streaks and clusters, shining bright in the absence of the moon like so many snowflakes frozen in the unknowable abyss. Not for the first time, Emrael wondered whether those twinkling points could really be the guardian spirits the Silent Sisters had set to watching this earth, as the Ordenans believed.

He breathed in the cool night air, smelling the damp loam and pines of the forest around him. The wind shifted to carry the smells of the high-walled city below him; just a hint of the dust, human sewage, horse droppings, and other less pleasant smells associated with civilization.

Despite its physical size, Gnalius didn't have nearly the population of Whitehall or even Lidran. It was primarily an *infusori* Well town now, with few other reasons for large numbers of people to live here at the southern tail of the Burned Hills mountain range. The soil was rocky and poorly suited to farming, the city sat nearly equidistant from both the Lys and Stem rivers, and no significant trade other than *infusori* flowed from here.

A wide stone-paved highway ran roughly north to south within a hundred paces of the city's north gate, a relic of its past importance but still well maintained. Gnalius was still the primary source of *infusori* for much of the southern and western reaches of the kingdom.

Like Lidran, Gadford, Whitehall, and so many ancient settlements built around *infusori* Wells and trade focal points, Gnalius had been heavily fortified. Enormous stone walls towered fifty paces or more overhead and looked to be at least twenty paces thick. Even an expert Stonebreaker mage like Yirram wouldn't be able to get through that. Not fast enough to be useful today, at any rate.

The ancient builders hadn't planned for the contraptions that

Ban and his cabal of Crafters and engineers had built, however. Darrain's current explosive projectiles probably wouldn't bring the wall down, but Emrael trusted that she could build something that would. Nothing was safe anymore.

He made a mental note to talk to Ban later about how to prepare to defend against a similar assault on his holdings. Ban had stayed behind in Trylla to help oversee the building of the defenses, and to keep working on the Observers Emrael had asked for.

Emrael turned to where Darrain waited with her group of engineers operating the ballista they had constructed just that day. "Is it ready? They'll fly true?"

Darrain shifted. It was hard to see her expression in the dark of the moonless night, but Emrael could tell she was uncomfortable with the question. "Yes . . . they should. It's hard to know with such an impromptu build, however."

"We can't delay the assault long enough for you to test it more than you already have. We'll just have to see how it goes."

Emrael issued orders to his runners, who relayed them to the officers who led the waiting attack parties.

Worren waited with his light infantry battalion on the left, one thousand men armed with grappling hooks. They were tasked with flanking the city and scaling the walls to the south once Emrael and the main force of eight battalions had engaged the gates to the north. Gnalius purportedly only held a garrison of two or three thousand soldiers, equally split between Watchers and Syrtsan men. The main force of eight thousand, led by Emrael himself, should be able to overwhelm them easily, but Worren's climbers would make sure they weren't bombarded with burning oil and crossbows from above for longer than was necessary.

The third force of two thousand men, a mix of cavalry and foot led by Toravin, was to stay in reserve to guard the engineers, supplies, and myriad other camp followers that had traveled with them from Trylla or joined their ranks on the march. Saravellin and her battalion were with the reserves, despite Saravellin's objections. Emrael wanted her under Toravin's watchful eye for now.

When he judged the runners had been given plenty of time to verify orders with Worren and the various Captains who led the men in his own primary assault force, Emrael rejoined Darrain just behind the giant ballista machines, an explosive Crafting secured near the tip of the several projectiles the Crafters had prepared. The explosion at the gate would serve as the signal for the main assault.

"Aim well," Emrael encouraged Darrain and her helpers. "You'll only have time to shoot this thing once, maybe twice. Try not to take down any of the wall if you can help it, we'll need it when the town is ours."

Darrain flashed him a flat glare. "Perhaps you'd like to do the calculations?"

Jaina laughed out loud from where she stood behind them. Emrael swallowed a hostile reply and waved her off. "Just know that lives depend on your mathematics today, Darrain. Many lives."

The Crafter's nose was already back in her notebook, her steel pen flashing in the muted light of a hooded *infusori* coil. The defenders of Gnalius must have known that an army was headed their way, but there was no point in showing them exactly where they were and what they were doing. Darrain occasionally called quietly to her Crafting assistants, who made minute adjustments to various parts of the ballista machines. Before long, Darrain looked up at Emrael. "Ready," she said.

Emrael looked behind him to where Jaina and Timan waited with him, ready to lead the Imperators into battle should they encounter any Malithii mages. After a nod from Jaina, Emrael called to Darrain. "Loose when ready."

Darrain tapped an engineer on the shoulder, and the wiry man pressed several actuators on the explosive Crafting attached to the projectile. When he called "Clear," Darrain pulled a small lever and the machine recoiled with a sharp snap and an immense flash of *infusori* from the coils that powered the ballista. The projectile, itself as large as a small tree, whistled through the night sky and hit the gate nearly five hundred paces away in the space of a breath.

There was an enormous thud, and an instant later the gate erupted in blue fire. A shock wave of energy followed the eruption, driving a hot, fierce wind across the flat empty ground that separated them from the city wall.

When the air cleared, Darrain had a grin on her dust-streaked face, and the others matched her. They were already working to load another projectile in the ballista.

The thick timber and steel gates had been reduced to smoldering scraps hanging from twisted hinges. If there had been any defenders near the gate, they had likely been disintegrated by the force of the explosion. Glory, what had he unleashed on the world?

He wasn't the only one awed at the destruction; Timan was growling a quiet string of curses under his breath. Maybe the Ordenans weren't so far ahead of them technologically after all.

Shouted orders emanated from the trees all around them, Emrael's captains and sergeants urging their men forward. Soon, the first two ranks of soldiers emerged, their oversized shields held in a solid line, edges overlapped. Most were adorned with metal scraps in anticipation of the Watchers' *infusori*-powered crossbow bolts. Those in rear ranks held more typical round wooden shields. They advanced at a fast walk, like a giant tortoise creeping across the clear space that surrounded the city walls. Bells began to ring throughout the city, and Emrael could see defenders rush to the tops of the walls.

"Do you want us to shoot more? Perhaps into the city?" Darrain asked with no hint of concern.

"Absent Gods, no, Darrain," Emrael replied. "We're not trying to turn the entire populace against us, we'll only fight until they surrender. Get ready to shoot at the gates again, but don't loose until I say so."

About a hundred paces from the smoldering remains of the large timber-and-steel gates, the large formation of Emrael's men stopped, tightening so no gaps showed, every other row lifting their shields above their heads. The defenders crowded atop the walls fired a storm of crossbow bolts and arrows, but most were rendered ineffective. Perfect.

The formation waited, letting the bolts and arrows rain down on them. For now, they were just a distraction while Worren and his thousand men scaled the walls from the south, which had hopefully been abandoned now that Emrael posed an obvious threat to the north.

Nearly half an hour ticked by, according to the watch Ban had gifted him. In the absence of further explosions, a large formation of Watchers and Syrtsan guardsmen had gathered in the smoldering breach where the gates had been. Likely, they had no clue what

could have done such a thing and therefore weren't able to anticipate a recurrence.

Fifty or so Watchers stood shoulder to shoulder to fill the gap,
and they had formed at least ten ranks of shield-bearing soldiers
behind them. Hundreds more milled about in the large plaza that
abutted the gate, ready to join their fellows.

"Shoot another into the gap," Emrael barked at the engineers. "Hit
the plaza just behind the gates."

Darrain adjusted a few wheels to aim her ballista and complied.
Another tree-sized projectile streaked through the gateless archway,
followed by a deafening blast of blue fire just inside the gates. Screams
echoed from behind the walls, the wails of the wounded rising into
the night sky with the smoke from the detritus in the square behind
the gate that was now ablaze.

Emrael had to remind himself that his brutal tactics would save
lives on both sides of the conflict, but especially the lives of those
who had sworn themselves to him. It pained him to be loosing such
carnage even on Watchers, however necessary it was.

The ranks of defenders who had lined up in the gap where the
gates had been, primarily Watchers, now shuffled nervously as
their comrades in the plaza behind them burned to death.

"Forward!" Emrael shouted, and his order echoed through the
ranks. His forces moved toward the city gates at a fast walk once
more, shields still up in a tight formation.

"Where is Worren?" Emrael asked no one in particular as he
scanned the tops of the walls. The Watchers on the walls, their
numbers growing by the minute, still shot bolts and arrows down
at his men at will, rending gaps in the Iraean formation despite
their best efforts to shield themselves. Even the best shield wall
would take some casualties from that many arrows and bolts. Worren
should have engaged the defenders on the walls by now.

Worse, he figured there must be close to a full battalion of
Watchers on the wall at this point. His scouts may have been mistaken about the size of the Watcher and Syrtsan garrisons here.
They might be fighting closer to five thousand, and them behind a
stout wall besides. He would need to take the gate quickly if he was
going to avoid his men being slaughtered.

His mind raced as he considered his options. He couldn't risk aiming one of Darrain's explosives at the top of the walls for fear of missing and hitting the city behind by accident. The civilian casualties would be horrendous. There was only one answer, really.

"Darrain. Put another of your explosives right where the gates were. Clear those ranks of Watchers for us. Loose as soon as you're ready."

The engineers scrambled to make the necessary adjustments, and within moments another projectile turned the waiting ranks of Watchers to flaming charnel.

"Forward, fast march! Charge the gates! Charge the gates!" Emrael shouted to the men waiting to run orders to the front. Soon, his battalions marched their shield formation to the now-empty entryway and filed into the city company by company. Each of the eight battalions had been assigned a portion of the city to secure and would soon move on their objectives. In the meantime, the Watchers on the wall continued to shoot arrows and quarrels at his men, inflicting casualties that he could ill afford.

"We're not doing any good out here," Emrael called to where Toravin waited nearby with the officers of his two mounted battalions. "You stay here with half of the reserves to keep the engineers clear of trouble. I'll take the other half and push the walls."

Toravin agreed, and together they assigned each company of the mounted battalion that would accompany Emrael to attack a different access point once inside the walls.

Rather than form a small shield wall of their own, Emrael elected to keep his battalion mounted. They trusted speed to protect them as much as their shields. Hitting a moving target was no easy task even for experienced archers and crossbowmen.

He allowed a company to form up in front of him and his guard, which earned an approving nod from Jaina. They started toward Gnalius at a walk, but when they were within range of the walls, they kicked their mounts to a fast canter, not slowing when several of their fellows or their mounts were felled by the few Watcher quarrels that found their marks.

And then they were through the gate tunnel and into the plaza beyond, where Darrain's Crafting had wreaked its havoc. Emrael followed the lead company toward the far end of the square, where ranks of Ire Legion soldiers still fought men in Watcher blue and Syrtsan grey-and-gold.

As they entered the city, each company of mounted Ire soldiers found an avenue clear of the enemy, each headed toward an access point that would allow them access to the walls. The city would be theirs before much longer. His objective now was to ensure that his Ire Legion took as few casualties as possible. To that end, he looked about the square for a place he and his guard could secure as a headquarters where they could effectively coordinate the battle without exposing themselves to unnecessary danger.

Screams erupted from the ranks of Ire men near him. He looked around frantically to find crossbow bolts protruding from the backs of the men fighting the Watchers and Syrtsan guardsmen still holding several of the primary avenues into the city. The Watchers atop the wall had braved returning to the sections of the wall near the smoldering gate and had now turned their attention to the interior of the city, where Emrael's men were exposed as they fought.

He gathered his guard and two other Captains Second waiting nearby with their squads, signaling them to follow him. He drew his sword from the sheath on his back and dashed to the stone tower built into the back side of Gnalius's wall next to the gate, where a large open doorway led to a spiraling staircase. The Watchers atop the wall were so preoccupied with the battle raging at the perimeter of the square that he and his guard reached it unharmed.

The tower stairwell was wide enough for three men to stand shoulder to shoulder and spiraled up the entire fifty-pace height of the city wall. The stairs were empty for the first twenty paces, and Emrael discovered why when he reached a landing halfway up the height of the tower. Watchers and Syrtsan guardsmen milled about, most pressing their way up the stairs with crossbows or longbows in hand. They didn't see Emrael, Jaina, and their companions until it was too late.

Emrael slipped his rune-etched blade expertly through the gaps in a Watcher's armor. A breath later, Jaina thrust her blade into the blue-clad soldier next to the first.

They twisted and jerked their swords back in nearly the same motion, then thrust again at Watchers who were only beginning to realize what was happening. Timan joined the fray, and suddenly the stairs were slick with dark rivulets of blood.

The rest of the defenders that had been pressing up the stairs cried out, some throwing their crossbows to the ground to draw swords and form a defensive line, some running faster up the stairs or out the doors that led from the enclosed portion of the tower. Most of those that had drawn swords and turned to face Emrael and his fellows were Syrtsan guardsmen, and several had shields.

"Throw down your weapons and you'll be spared!" Emrael shouted at the dozen or so Syrtsan men and the few Watchers that had stayed to fight. "The city is ours, and we have no wish to kill you. Stand down!"

A few of the Syrtsan men faltered, looking at their fellows as if to gauge whether surrender would be acceptable. The three Watchers left among them, however, shouted and charged at Emrael, shields forward and blades raised for powerful hacking strikes.

Emrael pulled in a measure of the *infusori* held in the armor Ban had made for him and met the first Watcher's shield with an *infusori*-fueled front kick. The kick pushed the rim of the shield back into the Watcher's face violently, crushing his nose and orbital bones in a spray of blood. Jaina and Timan similarly dispatched the Watchers to his sides.

The Syrtsan men looked at the blood-soaked Watchers still quivering their death throes on the ground, then at the Ire Legionmen now moving toward them in a wall of shields. They threw their weapons on the ground, crying for mercy.

Emrael ordered his soldiers to grant quarter, and their captives were quickly bound with strips of cloth cut from corpses and left with a squad assigned to watch the prisoners and hold the landing. He wasn't finished yet.

To his surprise, the stairwell was completely empty all the way up to the top landing. Large steel-banded timber doors on either side led out to the rampart on top of the wall. The doors were closed, the interior quiet, though still lit by a few *infusori* coils hanging in sconces. He could hear shouting and the distant sound of battle, but nothing close.

He called quietly for his soldiers to halt and stay clear of the doors and approached one motioning for Timan to do the same with the opposite door. Jaina stood in the stairwell with the rest of his men—hopefully a lot of them, though it was hard to tell since they were packed into the winding staircase.

"When we open the doors, keep clear while they shoot, then rush them with shields in a wedge," he called quietly to Jaina and Timan. "Put pikemen behind the shields. I'll go right, Timan left, Jaina holds the guardhouse."

She nodded and passed the word back, already forming two separate parties to rush out either door.

A moment later, Emrael and Timan nodded to each other and counted to three with their fingers. On three, they both jerked the doors open inward and hid themselves behind the thick timbers. Sure enough, the Watchers and Syrtsan defenders were waiting for them, and a thick wave of bolts and arrows *thunked* into the wooden doors and skittered through the enclosed landing.

Before the projectiles had even settled on the ground, Jaina commanded their men forward. They ran through the door, shields in tight formation, and were met with another volley from the waiting defenders. Emrael was still behind the door, but could hear the wet sound of crossbow bolts hitting flesh, could hear some of his men screaming in pain. He let two more ranks charge through the doors, then went himself.

He stumbled over one of his injured soldiers, lying on his side with two crossbow bolts jutting from one leg.

"Get the wounded inside!" he shouted, not slowing. The dozen or so of his men that had preceded him through the door were just ahead, pressing their shields against a wall of Syrtsan guardsmen with shields of their own. The two shield walls filled the width of the rampart with six men shoulder to shoulder, the waist-high parapets at the outside edges of the wall keeping the battle line from expanding.

Watchers behind the Syrtsan line handled long spears and crossbows, shooting or stabbing his men through whatever gaps presented themselves. His men were outnumbered at least two to one, and several lay wounded or already dead on the stone rampart. He needed to break that shield wall quickly, or he and his men would be stalemated while the rest of the defenders on the wall shot down on his army fighting below, inflicting horrible casualties that he could ill afford.

Strapping on a shield from one of his fallen men, he ran at a dead sprint, then leapt, using the short parapet to one side of the rampart to propel him up and over both ranks of shield-bearing soldiers. He slammed shield-first into a shocked Watcher, who didn't even try to raise his crossbow as Emrael's full weight crashed into him. The Watcher went down hard, head rebounding from the ground.

Crouching low, Emrael hoisted his shield above him as he lashed out in an arc, shearing through the back of the Syrtsan shield-bearers' legs. Half of their shield wall collapsed, hamstrung, and Emrael's men surged forward.

The defenders broke, running back toward the nearest guard-house, a few hundred paces farther down the city wall. Emrael and his men gave chase, cutting down those they could, shoving others to the ground with their shields as they passed.

Winded but in the throes of his battle rage, Emrael drew in more *infusori* from his armor until he glowed. He raced on, eventually outpacing his men to find himself at the heels of perhaps three squads' worth of Watchers and Syrtsan guardsmen. He shouted, "Surrender or die!"

To his surprise, many complied. One after the other they threw down their weapons and knelt, cowering. He left them there, chasing after those attempting to get into the door of the next guard-house farther along the wall. He kicked it open violently as they attempted to shut it behind themselves and immediately threw himself to the side when he saw several Watchers within with crossbows aimed directly at him. At that distance with *infusori*-strengthened weapons, the bolts would tear through his shield—and him—like they were made of paper.

The crossbows twanged as he jumped to the side, one bolt glancing off his shield at an angle. Another grazed his leg, scoring a long gash across the top of his right thigh. He rolled clear of the door and out of line of sight. Blood already seeped from the wound to cascade down his leg, but he couldn't tend to it without exposing himself.

Before the defenders could gather themselves and rush at him from inside the guardhouse, Emrael drew the rest of the considerable amount of *infusori* held in his armor and put his hand to the stone wall beside him. He projected his senses into the stone, feeling his way through the solid stone and the mortar joining it. The essence of the stone pulsed in the grip of his mage senses, and he shifted it *just so* to release the natural energy trapped within the core of its matter.

No more than a breath had gone by before the entire guardhouse behind him imploded violently. The man-sized stones that comprised the walls of the structure exploded into small shards of stone, propelled inward at incredible speed to eviscerate the defenders within.

Suddenly exhausted from the massive energy expenditure, Emrael stumbled clear of the dust cloud just as his men caught up to him, four abreast with shields up and at the ready, at least ten ranks deep. The Watchers and Syrtsans who had surrendered to Emrael were being stripped of their weapons and apprehended by his soldiers.

He waited as two ranks flowed around him before he moved with them to inspect the guard tower.

Dozens of Watchers and Syrtsan men inside the collapsed guardhouse were barely recognizable as humans after countless shards of stone had torn their bodies to shreds. The whole mess smelled of foul offal, shit, blood, and now the vomit of some of the Ire men who were shuffling across the jumble of rubble and mangled corpses.

Before today, most of the Ire men had only seen relatively civilized fighting, if they had seen any at all. Veterans in his Legion were the men who had seen fighting at Myntar, Gadford, and Whitehall, maybe even some service in the Watchers or a Legion or Lord Holder's guard before that. Most of his recruits, however, had only seen the battle at Larreburgh, or had joined in the weeks since and were as green as could be.

Regardless, none of them had likely seen anything like this, men turned into pulp like meat in a grinder.

They stared at Emrael as if unsure whether he was a hero or a monster. To be fair, he wasn't sure himself. There had been a time when the smell, the sight, of the incredible violence he had just wrought would have sickened him. Now, he only worried about the rest of the men he needed to kill atop the wall. There would be time later to worry about good and evil.

"Half the wall left," Emrael shouted, pushing the laggards forward. "Those bastards are still shooting down on our brothers!"

He let his men pass him by this time, content to let them fight the rest of the battle for the wall. He had just spied some of Worren's men finally gaining the top of the wall to the south, and to the west he could see Timan's force making progress, though not quite as fast as Emrael's had. Between the three groups and the other companies assigned to secure the guard towers like the one Emrael had climbed, they'd take the wall in short order, no need for more of Emrael's heroics.

And a good thing, too. His legs threatened to buckle beneath him and it took significant effort to keep from emptying the little he had in his stomach. Blowing apart the guardhouse had required an immense amount of *infusori*, and moving that kind of energy on top of the fighting had sapped every bit of strength he had. Besides, the gash in his leg wasn't life-threatening, but it hurt like hell.

He limped a few yards back toward where several squads guarded the captives who had surrendered, and sat heavily a little ways apart. His eyes slid shut nearly of their own accord when he laid his head back against the stone of the rampart. He sat that way awhile, focusing on his breathing, feeling some regained energy begin to reanimate his body. This fight wasn't over just yet, and he'd need his strength back.

Soft, sure footsteps clicked on the stone, coming nearer. He opened his eyes to see Jaina approaching. She squatted down next to him, surveying the fallen men along the rampart, the captives, the wreckage that had been a large stone guardhouse.

"Where are Captain Horald and your guard?" she asked without preamble, scorn clear in her voice and expression.

Emrael shrugged and waved a hand to where the fighting still raged on the wall. "Fighting, I suppose. I told them to push forward."

"Fucking amateurs," she grumbled under her breath, then looked to him. "Their orders are to stay with you, no matter what."

"Like you did?"

She glared at him. "Yes, well. Perhaps I'll have to stop taking orders and start planning for your . . . impetuous nature."

He laughed. "Jaina, I know you don't want me risking myself, but if I don't do what I must to win, it won't matter if I'm alive or dead. You felt the Fallen's touch. I saw him. If we don't win this war, and fast, we'll never stand a chance against him and his Malithii. We'll likely die anyway."

Jaina still didn't look happy, but nodded tersely. She squatted to tap the chest piece of his armor. He could see a glint of envy in her gaze. "Have you any charge left?"

"No," he groaned. "Used it all." He waved one hand toward the pile of rubble and bodies.

"So I see," she said wryly. "Impressive, but you could have done the same with one-tenth the power, and you would not feel like you had just drowned and been brought back to life. Keep practicing with my Stonebreakers."

He cursed at her under his breath, but she just chuckled darkly and pulled her canteen from her belt, noticing him patting his own belt where his water should be. She took a long swallow of water and passed it to him. He gulped thirstily, emptying nearly half the container.

"Thanks," he sighed gratefully. "You have any charge left?"

She shook her head as she patted an empty pouch where she kept her *infusori* coils. "Used them all in the fight, but I am still holding a fair bit. I do not have much left, but could pass you some."

"No, save it. I'll get more from the lighting back in the city. What word from below?"

"None yet, but our men have taken the main square and are all inside the walls, save for the reserves which have moved to secure the other gates. The city will be ours before dawn."

He drew a deep breath and lurched to his feet. "Good. Let's go try to keep things civilized."

Back in the guardhouse at the head of the stairwell they had used to gain the wall, they found Timan arranging the transport of the wounded. He glanced at Emrael's leg when he walked in.

"You let them draw blood?"

Emrael started to reply when shouting, screams, and the sounds of steel ringing against steel echoed up the large stairwell behind them.

He, Jaina, and Timan were the only able-bodied people in their guardhouse, though a few of the less-injured Legionmen might be able to handle a weapon.

Emrael and Jaina took up shields and stood at the top of the stairs. Timan moved some of the wounded out of the way and readied himself behind them.

"Get the wounded out of the guardhouse," Emrael snapped at the Legionmen that had been helping Timan. They stared at him in shock for a moment before dragging the moaning soldiers that lay on the floor until they were clear of the guardhouse landing.

The sounds of footsteps in the stairwell grew louder. Four men in teal Raebren uniforms, shields and swords in hand, preceded three Malithii priests with lethal copper cables at the ready. Blood stained their weapons and clothing.

As their attackers reached the top step, he and Jaina stepped forward in unison, putting their shoulders behind their shields to push the Raebren men back before they could gain a solid footing. Jaina and Emrael had trained such maneuvers together often, and both managed to get their shields slightly under the lead attacker's center of gravity while fending off overhand sword strokes. Emrael felt a small surge of *infusori* from Jaina as they pushed at the shields of their attackers. Emrael didn't have any *infusori* left to attempt the same but had considerably more mass and natural strength than Jaina did, and the advantage of momentum besides. A loud crash echoed through the guardhouse as they lifted their opponents from their feet, throwing them back down the stairs into their comrades behind them. All four Raebren men tumbled down several stairs before coming to a stop and lurching to their feet.

The Malithii, evidently more familiar with Jaina's prowess than their Raebren counterparts, stepped smoothly back out of range.

The black-robed priests waited calmly, copper cables and short swords at the ready. They barked orders at the four Raebren men, who regained their shields and came forward again, though much more cautiously this time.

The men in Raebren uniforms moved up the stairs to where Emrael and Jaina waited, but cautiously this time. As they drew within reach, they halted, eyes darting nervously. One of the Malithii priests behind them, a large man with wide shoulders beneath a robe that would have covered Emrael and Jaina both with room to spare, pushed through the rear rank of soldiers to plant a kick in the small of the back of one of the frontmost shield-bearing men. He flew nearly two paces to crash headlong into Emrael's shield.

Emrael took the blow and turned most of the force aside with his shield. The man who had just been kicked hit the ground hard and jerked to his knees in a dazed panic.

Shuffling backward a few quick steps, Emrael swung his sword in a tight, controlled arc, cutting cleanly through nearly half the man's neck. The soldier's body fell to the ground, lifeblood forming a puddle on the stones behind him.

Before the man's head had time to land on the stones with a hollow thump, Emrael had his shield back up and at the ready. Just in time, too. One of the Malithii had used the distraction to whip his metal cable at Emrael, hitting him in the leg.

An immediate surge of *infusori* coursed through him. Exhausted and taken by surprise as he was, the sudden attack threatened to obliterate him. Fortunately, Jaina knocked the whip-like weapon away with a flick of her sword before it could wrap fully around his leg. The *infusori* buffeting his body disappeared as quickly as it had come, and he could breathe again.

Emrael sagged with sudden weariness, his shaking legs nearly buckling beneath him. Jaina raised her shield and moved to cover him as he stumbled backward. She didn't stand a chance against three Malithii, never mind the three remaining Raebren soldiers. Timan scrambled to pick up a shield, readying himself to take his place.

Emrael took only a few seconds to draw a deep breath and stepped back beside Jaina before Timan could. He wasn't going to leave her to fight alone.

The soldiers with the Malithii had now edged to one side of the stairwell, trying to defend themselves on all sides. Emrael took advantage of their distraction and rushed forward with a shout, sword raised, shield in front of him. As he hoped they would, the Raebren men ran, forcing their way past the black-robed priests, who were forced to step aside and let them flee, lest Emrael and

Jaina press the advantage while they confronted their reticent allies. The Raebren men disappeared down the stairwell as fast as they could run without tripping down the stairs.

As Emrael pulled back to where Jaina still stood at the top of the stairs, Timan stepped up beside Emrael, now armed with both sword and shield.

Undeterred by their allies' retreat, the three Malithii stalked up the stairs, their faces set with resolve. The broad-shouldered priest took the lead, a massive blade in one hand, shield in the other. The other two priests flanked him, copper cables at the ready.

Emrael figured that meeting the giant priest's charge shield-to-shield was a very bad idea, out of *infusori* and shaking from exhaustion as he was. He decided to take a gamble instead, throwing his shield at the legs of the Malithii giant as he would a discus. The steel-banded edge of the shield hit the surprised priest in the shins with a gruesome crunch, dropping the man to one knee.

Knowing that one of the other Malithii was likely to strike at him with a long copper-cable weapon now that he was without a shield, Emrael stepped forward and held his now-bare arm up in front of him. Sure enough, a priest snapped a copper weapon at him, making it rigid with a tiny burst of *infusori* once it was twisted around Emrael's arm.

The priest thought he had Emrael trapped, but this time he was ready.

Instead of engaging the Malithii in a battle of wills, each pushing an attack at the other, or even engaging in a physical battle by pulling at the cable, Emrael *pulled* at the priest's life source as soon as the metal cable touched his skin.

The *infusori* with which the Malithii had prepared to attack Emrael, presumably to reduce his flesh to water or cause him to instantly combust or some similarly heinous effect, was swept up in the torrent of Emrael's will. The Malithii was caught completely off guard, and in an instant Emrael had consumed his soul. The priest's body fell to the ground, lifeless.

Emrael now hummed with violent power, *infusori* stolen from another human, and a Malithii priest at that. The scars on his arms glowed, and he suddenly wondered why he had been so afraid a moment before.

With a throat-tearing shout and a burst of *infusori* to bolster his strength, he drove his sword clean through the giant Malithii's shield and into his chest. The huge man toppled backward, and Emrael used all of his weight to drive his blade further into the priest's chest as he landed on top of him. Blood gushed from the Malithii's mouth as he struggled feebly, arms trapped by his own shield. Emrael pushed until his sword grated on the stones of the stairs beneath them.

As soon as they stopped sliding down the stairs, Emrael twisted and jerked his sword from the fallen Malithii. He turned, ready to fight the last Malithii, but pulled up short. Timan stood over the body of the last Malithii priest, his sword still lodged in his ribs as he convulsed with the last strained beats of his heart. Blood ran down the stairs in rivulets.

Jaina stood at the top of the stairs, a Malithii copper-cable weapon in one hand, her sword in the other. She had somehow shed her shield and taken the weapon from the priest without being harmed. That didn't seem fair.

Timan retrieved his blade from the now-dead Malithii with a smooth motion, wiping it clean on the priest's robes before sheathing it.

Emrael quickly checked the Malithii to make sure they were in fact dead, and went a ways down the stairs to ensure that there weren't any more, or other enemies waiting to kill them the minute they turned their backs. He'd be thoroughly investigating how his men had allowed Malithii access to the watchtower.

Back on the landing in the guardhouse, he found Timan and Jaina speaking in harsh tones.

"You consumed the life energy of another human, Emrael," Timan said, his voice hushed. "This thing is not done." He turned to Jaina. "Surely you have taught him this. Why are you saying nothing?"

Jaina took a deep breath and grimaced. "The world is not so perfectly defined as the Order would have us believe. Think to what happened in the temple at Truele. The Book of Ages says that only the Anointed of the Sisters are worthy of such visions. Does he look like one of those old women to you?"

Jaina waited for his slow, unsure nod before she turned her fierce gaze on Emrael. "Do not think that I approve, Emrael Ire. You must be more careful about how you use your power, boy. Even if the Order doesn't come after you, making a habit of consuming the life source of others could harm you severely, in the long run. You know this. You have felt the corrupting influence before."

Emrael shrugged. "Better than being dead. I didn't have a lot of options, exhausted and out of *infusori* as I was. He didn't expect it, and it worked."

Timan stared at Emrael, his face as still as stone, eyes dark and unreadable. "I have witnessed the execution of a full Imperator of the Sacred Order on mere *suspicion* of doing what I just saw him do with my own eyes. It is against our sacred oaths."

Jaina grimaced. "The Silent Sisters and their oaths—that Emrael has not sworn—have never done me or anyone I know a thimbleful of good, but they have gotten a good many of my friends killed. I *do* believe that the Fallen is awake, however, and I believe Emrael is our best chance of defeating him. So does Councilor Maira."

Emrael felt a pang of sorrow. He had only known Timan a short time, but he liked the man. Besides, he was Emrael's kin. It felt wrong to have such a rift between them.

"Timan, I understand that what I did offends your Ordenan sensibilities. We can discuss it later if you wish, but right now we have a battle to win. Either you're with me or you're not. That's for you to decide."

Jaina supported him with a nod.

Finally, Timan grunted a laugh. "I am in deep with you two already. What is a little casual heresy at this point?"

Emrael clapped him on the shoulder. "I'm glad to hear it, cousin."

Before they descended the stairs, Emrael stooped down to grab the almost-severed head of the man in the Raebren uniform by the hair to hack it clean off the body. "We need to ask Saravellin if this fellow was one of hers. The Raebren uniforms could have easily been a ruse, but best to be sure."

On the way down, they passed more dead Ire Legionmen on the stairs and middle landing than had been there during the fight up the tower, but they reached the square without incident. The gate lay in smoldering ruins, and several large blackened craters in the cobbled square marked where Darrain's explosives had wreaked havoc among the waiting Watchers. Hundreds of bodies lying in pools of blood and viscera still littered the courtyard, mostly dead Watchers and Syrtsan guardsmen. The Ire Legion reserves had already recovered their injured and were tending to them wherever they could.

The smell reminded Emrael of a slaughter yard at a hog farm he had visited once with his father and Ban, on a day trip to procure a whole hog for their annual summer solstice celebration. The slaughter yard had been littered with offal and the discarded hooves and heads of hogs had been boiling in a series of large cauldrons. This smelled nearly identical. The parallel memory made Emrael slightly nauseous, but he tucked those emotions away in a quiet corner of his mind. Today was a day for blood.

Timan left them to find a Healer for the men wounded atop the wall. Emrael and Jaina found Toravin to one side of the square, surrounded by a few Captains First and various pages and clerks who carried reports and relayed orders back to the men still fighting deeper in the city. He waited until his Commander Second—might as well be his Commander First, he supposed, now that Voran was settled in Myntar with Elle and his mother—had finished giving orders to a young man with one arm in a bloody sling.

"Tor," he called.

Toravin turned, relief visible on his face as he saw Emrael. "Ancestors, Emrael. We haven't had a report from the wall where you disappeared."

His look turned to confusion and concern as Emrael tossed the severed head near Toravin's feet. The pages nearby took quick steps backward to avoid the gore that splattered from the head.

Emrael's lip curled in a snarl. "Malithii and men in Raebren uniforms ambushed us at the top of the near tower. They probably killed our runners as well. It was a near thing, but three Raebren men escaped. Ask Saravellin if she recognizes this one."

Toravin nodded slowly, eyeing the head. "I'll put this on a pike, ask the Captains to bring their men by to see if any recognize him. All of the Raebren boys were with my reserves, so someone should have seen something."

Emrael nodded, wiping the blood from his hands on his already-bloody pants. "Worren should have the wall cleared soon, but best send a few more companies to help if you've got them. It's hard to gain an advantage on the ramparts. What of the city?"

"The Watchers have a garrison near the southern gate and are holding hard. We've got about two thousand captives already between Watchers and Syrtsan men. Five companies of reserves are policing the streets as you asked."

Emrael was tempted to ask for a full report and to take control of the assault, but he was bone-weary and saw no reason not to let Toravin handle it. "Good. Thank you, Tor. Let me know when we have the city, and send Saravellin to me as soon as you can."

Toravin saluted, and for once there was no mockery or playfulness in the gesture. "Yes, Lord Ire."

"Now, tell me which of these inns has the best food. I'll be in the common room after I have a bath and change," Emrael said.

Jaina spoke up from beside him. "That one," she said, pointing to a four-story white stone building whose large black double doors faced the square. Bold golden letters above the door named it the BLACKSWELL HOTEL. "We'll take that one."

Jaina then took a few quick steps until she stood within easy reach of Toravin, who rocked back on his heels uncomfortably. "Your men abandoned Emrael, Toravin. It will not happen again. I will choose his new guard myself."

And with that, she called to some officer's aides standing nearby as she strode toward the hotel, demanding her and Emrael's things be brought to her immediately.

Toravin was left peering after her in incredulous shock. He looked to Emrael. "Is that true? Your whole squad just left you?"

Emrael waggled his head back and forth. "Yes and no. I ordered them to take the wall, so it's not their fault. Jaina is right, though. These Malithii bastards are everywhere and they seem to find me at will. I should probably keep men with me at all times."

Toravin nodded. "Aye, I'll see to it. Or Jaina will, sounds like."

Emrael chuckled and clapped Toravin on the shoulder. "Now you know how I feel."

He turned to follow Jaina to the hotel but called over his shoulder, "Don't forget, find Saravellin."

As luck would have it, the Blackswell Hotel had hot water piped into several of the bottom-floor suites, a relic of Gnalius's richer trade history, and a product of the relative ease of access to *infusori* from the nearby Wells. Gold coils leak their charge over time, and gold being as heavy as it was, proximity to Wells often meant technological luxury that was hard to find elsewhere. Emrael was surprised that such an opulent establishment had survived the downturn in trade Gnalius had seen over the past decades, but he supposed that there was still plenty of money flowing through these streets due to the *infusori* Wells. Wealthy traders not rich enough to afford their own mansions here likely didn't want to stay at any old inn with the peasants.

When Emrael walked into the lavish black-and-white-tiled lobby, a handsome young Ire Legion clerk behind the ornately carved front desk was looking at Jaina as if she were the Fallen himself. Which, he admitted, she might as well be if you got in her way. The blood that covered the three of them made for quite the specter as well. Emrael only caught the tail end, ". . . or I will tie you like a hog and leave you in the street."

"Trouble?" Emrael asked.

"No," Jaina replied, pointing at the young officer. "I was just explaining to this man that he is whatever I require him to be. He seems to think he is too busy with his ledgers to find us rooms."

The young officer's face went white. "No, no, Mistress. I was only trying to say that there are but a few of us here, working to store supplies."

Emrael frowned. "Leave him be, Jaina. He's not your manservant. He's doing an important job."

"I don't mind, Lord Ire. I searched the entire building, I can show you to the best suites."

In short order, the two of them had been shown to separate rooms, had bathed quickly, and had dressed in clean clothes brought from their trunks by the various aides Toravin had assigned to Emrael and the Imperators. Emrael even had a second pair of boots—he hadn't had more than one pair of boots, and shoddy boots at that, for years. Most importantly, the young aide with Emrael's things had brought him five freshly charged *infusori* coils, with which he recharged the armor Ban had given him. The aide hadn't had enough time to clean the armor properly while Emrael bathed, but he didn't mind a few blood smears and wasn't about to wander around without his armor in a newly conquered city.

When they reached the lobby, they found that Toravin had commandeered the entire building. Ire Legionmen stood guard at the large black front doors, and at every door leading to the large open lobby. Desks had been brought in, and clerks on stools already sifted through papers, receiving and sending orders rapidly via messengers who ran in and out of the building. Toravin and his senior officers sat around a large table in the middle of the room, and had left several chairs open for Emrael and whoever happened to accompany him.

Emrael and Jaina took seats, trying to get caught up with the reports Toravin was receiving in a steady stream, while his Captains updated the large hand-drawn map of the city on the table in front of them. It appeared that the wall was theirs, and the city as well save for the large walled Watcher compound to the south.

"Have you offered terms of surrender?" Emrael asked.

Toravin favored him with a frown. "Yes, Your Lordship. We did think of that."

Emrael threw a paperweight at him. "Have Darrain demolish the place, then. Throw a few of those damned exploding contraptions at them and offer them terms again."

Toravin flashed a pensive frown but nodded and sent a junior officer to fetch Darrain and her Crafters and engineers. Just as the officer went through the doors, a commotion outside drew their attention. A moment later, Timan stomped into the room, covered in blood and gore just as Emrael and Jaina had been. One of his arms was wrapped in blood-soaked bandages, and he limped slightly as he walked. He saw Emrael and headed straight for their table.

"Ire, by the Sisters, you have that Raebren woman in a fit. She's outside with her men, all lined up in the square and ready to fight. They look like they are going to burn you out of here."

"She's what?" Emrael exclaimed, bouncing to his feet. The hour or so of bathing and rest had done him good, but Absent Gods his feet and shoulders ached. "I'll go see her. Jaina, Timan, and Toravin with me. Have everyone who can hold a shield and sword form up and be ready to exit the hotel in formation. Get word to any companies nearby, tell them to form at the edges of the square but not to attack unless I give the order. Send the messengers by the back doors, and send them in squads. Go!"

He had assumed the Raebren uniforms were a ruse, but if Saravellin had readied her men to fight, perhaps she had sent them for him after all.

The room had been busy before, but now it stirred like a kicked anthill as Emrael and his senior officers gathered shields and formed ranks with their men. Emrael only waited until fifty men or so had gathered their shields and weapons before he moved to the doors, Timan and Jaina at each shoulder. Toravin stood at Jaina's other shoulder. All held shields, as Emrael intended to be in the front rank.

"Shields front, pikes behind, crossbows rear!" Emrael bellowed.

Emrael exited the hotel first, shield ready should any crossbow bolts or arrows fly his way, and the rest of his shield-bearers flowed through the large double doors to form around him. Toravin stood immediately to his right, Jaina and Timan behind them with borrowed pikes ready. He didn't look around to confirm, but he could hear shields overlapping to either side of him and the shuffle of boots behind as crossbowmen lined up behind the pikes.

"Forward, slow walk!"

He and his fifty soldiers moved slowly but surely as they stared at a full battalion of heavily armed Raebren guardsmen. Bloody uniforms and bandages dotted the opposing ranks. They hadn't held back from the fighting, then.

Saravellin and her officers sat atop their horses behind the first four ranks of her men, who had deployed similarly to Emrael and his men, but with shields mixed with pikes in the second rank, ready to step into any gaps. Emrael would have done the same had he more men.

"Hold!" Emrael bellowed when he drew within ten paces of the Raebren line. He stepped out of his shield line and let his shield fall to his side, leaving him exposed. He left his sword in its scabbard and walked to within a pace of the Raebren line, just outside easy reach of the pikemen in the second rank. Jaina and Timan followed him, of course, but the rest of his men stayed in a solid formation with Toravin at its head.

Emrael looked to Saravellin. He should have been more careful with his summons, tenuous as their alliance still was. "I just wanted to talk, Lady Raebren. I was attacked by men wearing your uniform and want to know if they were indeed yours."

Saravellin, garbed in armor and wearing a sword like she knew how to use it, glanced obviously at the head Toravin had put on a pole. "I'm only taking prudent measures to ensure my safety, Lord Ire."

Was his reputation really so poor that his allies thought he'd kill them without a second thought?

"I've never harmed anyone to whom I owed my loyalty, Saravellin." He threw his shield to the ground and walked forward, hands raised, until he was right in front of the Raebren shield line. "Let me through. I only want to talk."

Saravellin stared at him from ten or so paces away, face stoic, but the fury in her eyes was unmistakable.

"I have heard about what your *kind* can do," she hedged. Her men nearest Emrael shifted nervously, pike blades from the second rank pointed at him.

He laughed. "Saravellin, I won't survive a pike to the belly any better than the next man. If I try anything, your men can gut me like they would anyone else."

From his vantage, he could see his men beginning to fill the street entrances and alleyways, forming up in shield and pike formations but holding at the edges of the square as ordered. A full company formed up in front of the gate as he watched, four ranks deep. He gestured to his men, who now likely outnumbered the Raebren men and had them surrounded.

"You no longer hold an advantage, and still I offer myself in good faith. Simply take my hand and answer my questions honestly. You will be free to go as you wish regardless of your answers. You have my word."

Saravellin twitched her reins once, but issued the order to let Emrael through. She slid out of her saddle to land on the cobblestones lithely and waited for him with her hands on her armored hips.

Emrael left Jaina and Timan and walked to Saravellin as confidently as he could, though he was keenly aware of the dozens of blades that were within easy reach of his exposed back and sides.

He offered her his right hand, palm up, as if asking Saravellin to dance.

She took his hand after a moment, but her suspicious glare did not ease. "Now what? You call me here to accuse me, and insist on a show first?"

"Not a show," Emrael said, meeting her eyes. "Just relax, and you'll see."

She gasped quietly as he extended his senses to probe her life source gently. Not a full meld, but hopefully enough to learn what he needed. Besides, he thought he already knew the answer.

"Are you working with the Watchers, or their Malithii allies?"

Saravellin's lips curled into a snarl, and he could see as much as feel her genuine anger. "No. No matter my personal feelings on the matter, my father's choice was clear, and I am a woman of my word."

"Four men in Raebren uniforms killed some of my men, and attempted to kill Jaina and me. They were with Malithii priests. Did you send men to kill me?" he asked, pointing at the severed head on a pike near the middle of the square.

Saravellin twisted to frown at the man's head, then shook her head. "No, I did not. I can't guarantee that the men involved were not from Raebren, but they did not act on my orders. My guardsmen are all accounted for. You are welcome to inspect my men, but you will consult me before making any charges."

Emrael nodded, withdrawing his hand gently. "No need. Thank you, Lady Raebren. I believe you. I'm sorry for this," he said, waving his hands, "misunderstanding. I only wanted to hear it from you. I am in your debt."

She eyed him as if she didn't know whether to laugh or stab him, but finally smiled faintly. "Yes. You are. I will collect on that debt."

Emrael raised his eyebrows in mock surprise and met her smile with one of his own. "I look forward to it."

To his men around the square, he called, "Stand down, all of you. They are our allies."

Under his breath, he murmured, "I think," as he strode back to his hotel.

As he came abreast of Toravin he paused to speak close to his ear. "That attack wasn't strong enough to have much hope of killing me, it was always aimed at putting us at odds with Raebren. We still don't have a report from Worren at the south wall, and I haven't seen Tarelle since last night. Someone knew we'd be here, and had Raebren uniforms ready to go. We have a rat, and I want them found *now*."

Toravin pitched his voice low to match Emrael's. "Worren just joined us from his raids in Paellar, I don't think he had time to arrange anything like this. Or motive. Tarelle and his men haven't been seen since this morning."

"Fallen Glory take that lying bastard. Should have killed him when I had the chance. I *knew* he was trying to feed information to Marol and the Watchers."

Toravin's eyes were grave. "Aye, you should have slit his throat, but it would have caused trouble. You couldn't afford to act first. But now . . . if he makes it back to his Holding . . ."

Emrael clenched a fist. "Make sure he doesn't. Send a company after him, and put a bounty on his head. He doesn't know enough to ruin our plans, but I'd prefer the Watchers stay in the dark about our work in Trylla a while longer."

18

Click

"Banron on low frequency. Can you hear me?"

Click

He released the transponder's actuator to fiddle with the Crafting in front of him: a large, complex version of the Observer Craftings. Copper conducting wires, coiled gold reservoirs, and dozens of actuators and other contraptions hummed frantically inside the wooden box frame. The entire thing was connected by copper cables to a copper plate and tall steel pole mounted to the roof above his top-floor workroom in the Crafter's building in Trylla. More cables ran through the floor to the sub-basement, where another long steel rod had been driven into the ground and capped with another copper plate.

He heard only a faint crackling noise from the device for nearly ten minutes before he decided to try again.

Click

"Aelic, can you hear me? Aelic, this is Banron at Trylla Station. Can you hear me?"

Click

Ban had been doing this every first hour of every day for the last three days. Emrael and his army had been gone for nearly a week. The same day, Ban had sent one of his best Crafters, Aelic, back through the mountains with the plans and parts to build a Crafting just like this one in Whitehall. He would then go on to do the same in Larreburgh. Within a few weeks, he should have a communication network operational in this corner of Iraea, at least.

Even better, if the Craftings worked at this distance, with a small mountain range between them no less, his math said that he should be able to build a bigger station to reach as far as Myntar and beyond! Absent Gods, given time, he could probably extend the range to reach Ordena and the Ithan Wilds! Of course, the

Citadel would be ideal for broadcasting, or maybe even a station built on the peaks of the Duskan Mountains behind it.

He wondered for an idle moment what would happen if one of these were installed near an *infusori* Well or even an undeveloped focus point like the Ravan temple. Emrael had been able to cast his voice through the original Observer Crafting over one hundred leagues from a temple west of Lidran, after all, and the frequency had been all wrong to travel that kind of distance. Curious.

A louder crackling noise came through the speaker assembly of the Crafting in front of him, then:

Click

"Banron, this is Aelic! I'm in Whitehall Keep. Well, on top of it, really. Sorry for the delay, there was a bit of a storm earlier and I didn't fancy being roasted alive by a lightning bolt. But by the Faceless, I can hear you! Do you know what you've done?"

Click

The Crafting went back to its quiet hum and crackle. Ban hooted with delight and jumped in the air, but cursed when he knocked his knee on the table.

Still smiling while rubbing his knee, he pressed the actuator on his newest invention.

Click

"Aelic, you beautiful man! I knew you could do it. Does Dorae have what you need to build another? Emrael will want more."

Click

Aelic responded with a choking noise nearly the instant Ban let go of the actuator.

"Ban, I have your plans, but even with the Crafters left here and Dorae's supplies—if he'll give them to me—that'll take time. Weeks, probably."

Click

Ban sighed.

Click

"Make it quickly, Aelic, or Emrael might come after you himself. Send this one with a Crafter you trust—maybe Paia?—up to Larreburgh. It should work there more easily than Whitehall. The next one you build stays there with you. I'll work a big one up here to send to Myntar."

Click

Aelic sounded dejected when he replied.

Click

"Yeah, Ban, I'll try. I'll send this up to Larreburgh and build another."

Click

Ban got a queasy feeling in his stomach at having to pressure his friend. He suddenly appreciated the work Emrael had taken on himself much more. Giving orders put distance between friends, no matter the necessity. The compassion and pride he felt for his brother calmed his nerves as he replied.

Click

"Good, thank you. See that you do, Aelic. You are saving thousands of lives, you know."

Click

Aelic started to respond, but Ban's attention was drawn away by a bell clanging somewhere to the north. Another tolled, and another. Something bad then, to sound that many of the warning bells on the recently constructed outer wall. Middle of the city wall. Whatever.

He hadn't heard whatever Aelic had just said, but he didn't have time. He pressed the actuator in a panic.

Click

"Aelic, the bells are ringing, so I might not be in contact for a while. Get the Observers built."

Click

He disengaged the actuator and disconnected the large Crafting's cables without waiting for a response. These new Observers weighed nearly as much as he did—they were stuffed full of gold and copper and other heavy metals, after all—but he lugged it to the wheeled cart waiting in the hallway himself. He didn't have time to shout to anyone else for assistance. He wasn't sure they would have heard him, anyway. The bells meant an invasion of the city, and everyone was doing the same thing he was—racing down the halls with whatever of their latest research they could carry.

After locking his Observer in a storeroom, Ban hurried from the building and toward the city center square, where he could hear soldiers shouting commands.

He found Captain First Garrus in a command tent near the center of the square, senior officers and runners all around him milling about in near panic.

Ban hung back, staying at the edge of the group for a time, studying the map of Trylla and its surroundings that had been laid out on a large table. Clerks and junior officers bustled about the map, updating it with various shapes of different colors. Ban hadn't spent enough time with the Legion to know all of the particulars but quickly ascertained enough to understand that the hill forts outside the city had fallen and that enemy troops had been sighted at the edge of the ruins. Red triangles pointing southward crowded the map to the north of the city. Far fewer blue triangles speckled the map around the recently constructed wall along the river that cut through the ruins to the north of the city center.

At best, Trylla was about to be under siege. At worst, they had only a few hours to evacuate the city or die.

Ban hurried forward, weaving among the bustle of soldiers to seize Captain Garrus's elbow. Before he could speak, a man with the rounded facial features of a Sagmynan wearing a Justicer's armband shoved him back roughly.

Ban let out an involuntary yelp, but instead of cowering as he might have done not so long ago, he rolled backward over one shoulder and came up on the balls of his feet.

The Justicer stalked forward, the other officers standing back to avoid the sudden commotion.

"Justicer Yudin!" Garrus barked. The cold anger on the Captain's face surprised Ban, but it made the Justicer—and everyone else—stop cold. The man was normally so calculated and composed that when his anger burned through the calm, everyone knew the man was serious.

Garrus shouldered past the Justicer to take Ban by the shoulder.

"My Lord Banron, I am very sorry for my Justicer's behavior. They are overzealous in their duties, at times."

Garrus then turned back to the Justicer, his calm manner already returned. "Yudin, I expect all who serve as Justicers to recognize our senior officers and other leaders. Lord Banron Ire is the brother of Emrael Ire, our future king."

The Justicer's eyes widened with fear. He held out one hand and began stammering an apology.

Ban cut one hand through the air in a dismissive gesture. "Forget it. It was an honest mistake. We don't have time for this nonsense anyway." He pointed at the map, which aides had already resumed updating in a flurry. To Ban's point, more red arrows had been placed all around the city, though none seemed to have moved into the ruins just yet. "Are you confident you can hold the river wall against that many, Captain?"

Garrus's face sagged slightly but his voice was calm when he spoke. "No. When I told your brother that I could hold the city with five thousand men, I didn't think we'd be up against thirty thousand. Honestly, I don't know where they've found the men, and how they moved so quickly. Lord Ire has scarcely been gone ten days! How could they have known?"

Ban shrugged off the question and moved to the table that held the map. "But you could hold the inner wall with your five thousand?"

He and Garrus had worked together in recent days to begin work on a wall that surrounded a much smaller section of the city—the center square and a few blocks of surrounding buildings in each direction.

Garrus eyed him. "Yes . . . but that wall is not complete, Banron. As of this morning, my engineers reported it three-quarters done. But if it were finished, I think we could hold it. For a while."

Ban ran a hand through his long hair and tugged, thinking. "Could you hold the river wall for a day or so? Give me your engineers and craftsmen for that long, and we can finish it."

The Captain First nodded slowly, and so did several of the officers surrounding them. "Yes. We can do that much, I think. With those . . . explosive projectiles you've given my engineers, we may be able to scare them into holding off longer. We'll just have to hope they don't get wise and decide to find a way across the river away from the city to come at us from behind. I don't have the men to defend the wall properly, let alone the river."

"Would a full retreat be any better?" Ban asked.

Garrus's face blanched. "No, I don't think it would. They'd pick us apart as we moved. We'd have to leave the settlers behind if we wanted to survive, or engage for a day anyway to allow them to escape. And I wouldn't want to be the one to tell your brother that we lost the city and everyone in it."

"Nor would I," Ban said with a wry smile. "I don't see that we have much choice, then. Tell your engineers to meet me here in fifteen minutes. I'll gather my Crafters. Hold them for a day, Captain."

19

T hat rat fucking bastard," Emrael growled, punching a fist into the palm of his other hand. "I knew I should have killed him."

He was speaking, of course, of Lord Holder Garan Tarelle, who hadn't been seen since the night before the assault on Gnalius, two days ago. The Watchers that had holed up in their garrison to the south of the city had been burned out yesterday with more of Darrain's explosives, the survivors taken captive. The city was securely his and his plans were proceeding perfectly. Tarelle's disappearance shouldn't have bothered him much, but it did.

"Put a bounty on his head and be done with the man," Jaina mumbled around a mouthful of roasted pine grouse.

Emrael grimaced. "I have, but I'd like to strangle the swine myself."

Jaina shook her head and brandished her eating knife at him. "You have bigger problems to see to, Emrael. Focus on what matters. For example, *you* need to keep yourself out of danger. I will select your personal guard myself, and they will not leave your side. I tire of saving you myself."

"So you've said," Emrael sighed. "Many times. Go ahead and find them. But I won't be kept from doing what I need to, Jaina. I will still fight when necessary. The guard will answer to me."

Jaina just smiled at him as she took a sip of wine, a dark red as was her preference.

After a long day of touring the city and planning its defenses with Saravellin, Toravin, and his other military officers, he and Jaina ate a late evening meal together in a top-floor private dining room as the sun set over the rolling hills to the west. Timan had been with them but was now eating with the other Imperators while Emrael and Jaina dined at their hotel.

"Is Timan upset about what I did to that Malithii yesterday?"

Jaina shrugged. "Many Imperators are quite invested in the Order and their religion. The true believers . . . they adhere to the rules given by the Order without deviation. Besides the stiff and im-mediate penalties, they believe that their future rebirths, and the favorable rebirths of their families, depend on them. If he says he is with you, I believe him. But he may need time to adjust."

Emrael grunted. "And you?"

"Me? I am not so sure. Not anymore. I can *see* the influence of the Fallen God here in this world, feel his power, evil though it may be. The Silent Sisters have ever been just that . . . silent. Perhaps they do not even exist? Or they do and simply cannot be bothered with us?"

He sighed and turned back to his meal. Roasted fowl, ale-soaked barley, and a dark bean and bacon stew that he quite liked. The city was still in chaos after the battle yesterday, but the proprietors of the Blackswell and most of their staff had come out of hiding and had plenty of fine goods stored away, as had many inns and mer-chants around the city. He and his men were paying for whatever they consumed, of course. This was Emrael's city now, not enemy territory to be looted. He had Toravin rotating several companies through peacekeeping patrol duty to ensure his men behaved. Some felt it their right to take what they pleased after seeing their friends, brothers, cousins killed or wounded in the assault. While he felt for them, they would need to learn that their loot would come not from pillaging those who would soon be their countrymen, but from Emrael by way of taxes and confiscated lands when their service was concluded. Funny, how simply calling looting taxation made it acceptable.

They ate in silence for a time, until Emrael thought of something he had been wondering about for a long time but never seemed to have the opportunity to ask his mentor. "Jaina, tell me what you know about the Fallen, and about the Malithii."

She chuckled. "Oh is that all? Where would you like me to begin, Your Majesty?"

Emrael flipped a hand, rolling his eyes at her sarcasm. "Jaina, I mean it. Why are these bastards here? Why are they so invested in this war? Why is the Fallen God himself appearing to me in visions? It doesn't make any sense."

Jaina looked around the room quickly at that, nearly in a panic.

"Please, Emrael, do not say that so loudly. You will turn all of my Imperators against us."

She sighed, then bit her lip as she pondered how to respond. "I do not fully know how to answer your questions, Emrael, but I will tell you what I know. The Ordenan Faith teaches that the Fallen is here to pay for his sins, and that we—the Order, mages who have been taught the Art—are his keepers. His jailers, I suppose. Some time deep in the past, well before even the Ravan Empire existed, the Malithii were once Ordenans, or rather we were once one people. The Fallen corrupted the Malithii and established himself in the Dark Nations, the Hidden Kingdoms. I would imagine, if what the Ordenans believe is true, the Fallen takes great issue with my people and our holy war there."

"Why is he here in the Provinces, then? Why is he bothering with me? Why not fight the Ordenan army in the Hidden Kingdoms, or attack Ordena itself?"

"A small sect of . . . fundamentalists within the Order believe that there's more to our role than just keeping the Fallen God prisoner. The Speakers for the Sisters, as they call themselves, claim that the Fallen can be killed, his power consumed by one chosen by the Sisters to become the new God of this world."

"Oh," Emrael said after an awkward silence. What else was he to say? Jaina stared hard at him, however, obviously expecting something from him. "Wouldn't consuming his power be against the rules of your Order?"

Jaina smiled sadly. "Precisely." She looked at the floor and murmured, almost too quiet for Emrael to hear, "Nothing makes sense, not enough for the pain we are asked to endure. I do not know what to believe, not anymore, Emrael. In many ways, I am as lost as you are."

She gathered herself with a deep breath. "None of that matters to us, not right now. What matters is that the Malithii are here with growing numbers of *alai'ahn*. The Fallen is real, is alive, and has set his forces against us. We must fight them, and we must win, or we will share the fate of their subjected peoples in the Hidden Kingdoms."

Emrael barked a mirthless laugh. "And just how are we supposed to defeat a god, Jaina? You felt how much power he had, and that was just whatever was left in me after seeing a vision of him! Imagine trying to fight him."

Jaina shook her head, again subdued. "I do not know, Emrael. We will likely need the full might of the Order of Imperators if we're to stand a chance, but even then . . . I just do not know. But we must try. We cannot allow the Fallen to turn the rest of the world into the Dark Nations."

Emrael blew out a long sigh. "Well shit." He gulped down the half-pint of ale left in his mug. "I guess we'd better find a way to get the Ordenans involved after all, then. Can you get us a meeting sooner?"

Jaina nodded. "I will send a pair of my Imperators to the Stem immediately to find a ship headed downriver. There should be a Naval Captain, maybe even an Adjunct Admiral on a ship near the mouth of the Sound. They should be able to meet us in here in Gnalius or in Merroun relatively quickly, whether Syrtsan tries to blockade the Sound or not. Say, ten days?"

He nodded. "Ten days should work, but we may still be at Merroun or camped outside Sutwin waiting for Syrtsan's answer. I'm not going to attack the city if I can help it, but I intend to take the town with the shipping yards on the eastern branch of the river. Tell them to put in at the docks in Merroun first, then send a delegate here to Gnalius if needed."

She nodded, but paused with her lips pursed. "Emrael . . . you should know that it will not be easy to get the Ordenans involved. Likely they will want a hefty prize, more than you will want to give. Land, *infusori*, perhaps more."

Emrael smiled sadly. "I may have to give them what they require, Jaina, or I won't have anything left at all when this war is over."

A knock on the door preceded the head of one of two Legionmen guarding the door to the dining room. "The Mayor of Gnalius requests an audience, Lord Ire."

Emrael beckoned at the guard. "Thank you, Legionman. Send him in. Alone, please."

A tall, thin man of perhaps fifty years strode into the room a moment later, a leather-bound notebook in one hand. His hair and pointed beard were finely cut and oiled, his perfectly tailored suit and shined boots immaculate despite the blood and mess that littered the city in the aftermath of the battle. He stopped a few steps into the city and stood stiffly. His eyes flicked to Jaina once, then stayed locked on Emrael. "Lord Ire, I presume?"

Emrael picked up his tankard of ale. "Yes. And who are you?"

The tall man squared his shoulders. "I am Lord Vorot Sunnan, the Lord Mayor of Gnalius. I have come to negotiate terms."

"What terms?" Emrael asked blithely.

"Why, the terms of surrender, of course."

Emrael stared at the man for a moment before responding. "You may as well have a seat then. Will you have any food, or drink?"

The Mayor shook his head stiffly as he pulled up a chair for himself and sat. "Thank you, Lord, no."

"What did you have in mind?" Emrael asked, turning back to his food.

Mayor Vorot opened his leather notebook, withdrawing an expensive mechanical ink pen and gold-rimmed spectacles from a pouch inside the cover. The *infusori* trade paid well indeed. "I, the Lord Mayor of this city and Holder of the surrounding estates and Wells, am prepared to offer you, Lord Emrael Ire, five thousand copper rounds, Provincial, in return for an oath of good conduct until you and your forces depart. You and your forces will leave the city within the week."

Emrael laughed, nearly choking on a bit of rye bread. He couldn't help it. "We what?" When he'd caught his breath and swallowed his food, he continued. "Lord Mayor. You think I'm a Watcher, to be bought off and shipped away? You think I'm a fellow politician, to be bargained with?"

The Mayor looked shocked for a moment, then angry. He puffed up his chest and gathered himself to stand up.

Emrael pointed a finger at him from where he lounged in his wooden dining chair. "Sit," he commanded in a hard voice. "Let me explain the situation to you and make your choices clear."

He waited until the tall man took a chair before he resumed speaking. "I have taken your city by force. Many of my men, and many of the city's defenders, have died for it. There is no negotiation to be had. Either you swear fealty to me as your king, or I confiscate your lands and titles and all that comes with them and give them to someone that will. All that is yours is now mine."

Vorot's eyes blazed with anger. He stood quickly, knocking his chair backward with a crash. "My family has ruled this land since the fall of the Ravan Empire, centuries before the Iraean Kingdom even existed! We were our own kingdom once, you know! You will do nothing more than get me hanged with you when the Watchers put an end to your foolish rebellion!"

Emrael shook his head as he leaned back in his chair to show Vorot that he was anything but intimidated by his outrage. "My men hold the walls of Gnalius, and as we speak are taking possession of the *infusori* Wells in the mountains to the east. We hold all of Sagmyn Province. Gadford, Larreburgh, Whitehall, Trylla, Raebren, and soon all of Iraea will owe fealty to me."

He paused to let his words sink in, then slammed his fist on the table to draw the man's attention again. "I will say this *one* more time. You have two choices. Kneel to me and restore our families' ancient ties. Pledge me your resources. Your taxes and duty to levy soldiers simply transfer to me, all else taken will be paid for.

"Or," Emrael said before the Lord Mayor could respond, standing slowly and picking up his sword, "I'll give you the opportunity to prove your loyalty to Syrtsan, Corrande, and his Watchers." He bared a foot of the blade and idly inspected the runes carved into the steel.

Vorot's face blanched as he eyed the sword. He righted the chair he had knocked down with shaking hands and sat heavily. "I . . . I see."

Emrael looked up to meet his sullen stare. "Shall I call for a clerk to write up your declaration of fealty?"

Vorot now looked at least twenty years older than he had when he entered the room, his face haggard as he nodded his silent assent. When the clerk arrived and had written a short proclamation, both Vorot and Emrael signed it.

Emrael called for more clerks to copy the proclamation and asked them to add to it. "Let it be known that any man joining the Ire Legion will be afforded full rights of citizenship for themselves and their families in the new Iraean Kingdom, and will earn land bounties and standard pay besides. Trained soldiers receive an extra bonus, of course. That includes Watchers and Syrtsan men."

He strode to the dejected Lord Vorot and clapped him on the

shoulder. "Welcome to the Kingdom, Mayor. I expect you in the square at dawn tomorrow for the public oath."

Just after dawn the next day, Emrael tried not to look as tired as he felt as Lord Mayor Vorot Sunnan knelt to swear fealty in the war-scarred square outside the hotel. The tall nobleman looked dazed and none too happy to be in front of a large crowd of the people of Gnalius, kneeling to their conqueror, but he did it. Half the square was filled with Emrael's Legionmen, who cheered as Lord Vorot knelt. The other half of the crowd, civilians from the city, remained quiet.

Afterward, clerks by the dozen rode into the city to read the proclamation aloud and post notices of recruitment in every square. Sergeants and Captains Third would be stationed throughout the city to accept recruits and organize their distribution throughout the ranks.

Emrael could already see dozens lined up to sign for the land bounty at the recruitment station in this main square. They would be needed. Though the assault of Gnalius had been a resounding success, five hundred of his Legion had been killed, with at least five times that number wounded. Worren's battalion had taken particularly heavy losses attempting to scale the wall.

Toravin was due to give him an exact report later this morning, but three thousand out of sixteen thousand fighting men under his command had been lost. Lost to the current war effort, at least. He would never win a long-term campaign this way, not when Marol and the Watchers could likely field three times or more men than he could, not counting any soulbound the Malithii were likely to add to the equation. He needed more soldiers, and he needed to win future engagements with fewer losses.

A ripple in the crowd opened to reveal a half-company of Ire Legionmen escorting—and in some cases carrying—a shabby bunch of their former fellow Legionmen, now stripped of their weapons and armor. Eleven men, accused of serious crimes against innocents by the civilians in the city or by their fellow soldiers, and subsequently convicted by the Captain Second who led each battalion. Many more had likely gotten away with crimes, large and small,

Emrael knew, but he couldn't do anything about that today. He could only make an example of these eleven and bring justice to those who were caught, and hope that it discouraged the rest of his men from disobeying his orders that their conquered territories and their citizens be treated with respect. It served as a warning to the citizens of Gnalius, as well. The nobles and powerful merchants, in particular. Emrael would show them that his laws carried equal weight with everyone, regardless of station or allegiance.

A light rain pattered on the large stones that paved the square as he, Jaina, and Toravin walked to meet the group at a scaffold that had been erected earlier that morning. Timan, freshly healed of his relatively minor wounds after the battle, followed at a few paces with a mixed group of ten of the most dependable Imperators, mage apprentices, and Legionmen he and Jaina had handpicked to be Emrael's new dedicated Royal Guard. Each had sworn an oath to Emrael, a pledge of loyalty to supersede all other ties. Emrael had been astonished to have his cousin Timan and several other Ordenan Imperators swear such an oath to him. Imperators owed their loyalty to their Empire and their Order, and Jaina had told him it was a crime punishable by death for them to swear any oaths of loyalty to anyone else. Jaina hadn't joined them, though he trusted her more even than those who *had* given him oaths.

He had seen more than one of the other Imperators sneer at those who had joined his Guard, but he wasn't foolish enough to think that some of the Imperators sworn to him might not have ulterior motives. For now, Emrael was grateful to have even a few trained mages willingly join him, whatever their reasons.

When the prisoners had been gathered, Emrael paced the line of doomed men arranged in front of the gallows, staring each in the eye. Some of the men sobbed and begged quietly for mercy, others sneered with derision. His stomach roiled with phantom pity and anxiety at the prospect of ordering the execution of these men, but he felt no guilt. He had ordered that only killing innocents be punished with death. He had broken plenty of laws and done morally questionable things in this last year, but even he felt he had moral standing when it came to harming innocents. And besides, he couldn't afford to let his armies rampage through every conquered territory. He had to maintain order, even if it made him a hypocrite.

He stopped his inspection of the doomed men when he saw that one of them was a mage apprentice that had been training with the Imperators. Emrael couldn't remember his name but recognized him from training sessions. He was one of the Iraeans that had first joined the mages in Whitehall. The young man's shaggy brown hair fell in front of his downcast eyes.

"What did you do?" Emrael asked softly.

The boy glanced up at him, surprised at being addressed and obviously ashamed. One of his eyes was black, swollen shut, and crusted with blood. More blood had dried in his hair and in streaks down his forehead and face. He looked back down without answering Emrael. His hands shook in their shackles, his jaw clenched.

"What did you do?" Emrael asked again, more forcefully this time. Toravin started to speak, but Emrael silenced him by putting the back of his hand to his Commander's chest.

The two Legionmen holding the young mage shook him by either arm. The young man stiffened, anger flashing in his eyes and expression. He controlled himself with visible effort and finally looked up, his eyes flicking from Emrael to Jaina and back. He licked his lips. "I killed six men, Lord Ire. Legionmen. Your Legionmen. They attacked me and I defended myself."

Emrael raised his eyebrows and looked at Toravin, who nodded his confirmation but said no more. Emrael looked to Jaina. "You knew of this?"

She shook her head. "I did not. But mages are subject to your laws, same as everyone else. Correct?"

Emrael nodded, but chewed pensively on his lip. "Is he any good?" he asked quietly.

She shrugged. "Ask Timan."

Timan, who had obviously been eavesdropping the entire time, stepped forward without shame. "He has talent in the Art, fights well. Battle-Mage, some Healing. Good combination. Struggles to control his temper at times."

Jaina chuckled. "Like another I know."

Emrael rolled his eyes at her and turned back to the young mage. "What's your name, mage?"

"Daglund, Lord."

"Well, Daglund, I'm going to offer you a chance to get your head out of that noose up there. Give me your hand and tell me what happened. I'll feel whether you're lying. If you lie to me, I'll make sure you beg for that noose before you die."

He extended his hand to the young mage, who stared at the intricate scars that adorned his skin before taking his hand. Emrael extended his *infusori* senses, enveloping the young mage's will with his own without regard for the other man's meager resistance.

"You killed six Legionmen?"

Daglund nodded. "I did."

"Why?"

Daglund hesitated, then spoke slowly, shaking his head. "I told you, they attacked me. I had just eaten a meal at an inn near the center of the city. They were outside, their full squad I would say, walking down the street, drinking. They saw me in my mage uniform—the blacks we've taken to wearing, those of us training with the Ordenans. They ran to surround me, started pushing me, asking how I've got the coin to eat at an inn when they ate from the Legion mess." He glanced at Timan and Jaina furtively. "Said I ought to taste a real fight instead of hiding behind Ordenan pirates and their filthy magic. One of the lads hit me in the back of the head. I don't think they knew I had a sword under my cloak. I drew first, but they attacked me when I did. I only hurt them as I had to, to keep them from killing me. I didn't hurt any but those that came after me."

"How did you come to be in shackles, then?"

Daglund smiled sadly. "They called a nearby patrol. They had crossbows. The Captain believed my attackers' story over mine, and I was alone."

Emrael felt the anger emanating from Daglund as he spoke, his wounded pride . . . and satisfaction at having successfully defended himself against overwhelming odds. He would have done the same in Daglund's place and felt that the boy was telling the truth.

"Does his story match what you know?" he asked Toravin over his shoulder.

His Commander nodded. "More or less. He killed six, wounded

three more. Surrendered easily enough when the patrol arrived to stop the fight."

"Was he drunk?"

"Not that I know of."

"Unshackle him," Emrael told the men holding him as he released his grip. Their eyes widened in surprise, and Daglund gasped with stunned relief.

Jaina put a hand on Emrael's arm and spoke quietly, urgently. "Emrael, you must know that this method of mind melding is not entirely reliable. You cannot discern truth this way, only emotion."

Emrael nodded. "I know," he said, and beckoned to Timan. "Do you think Daglund here would fit in with your Royal Guard, Timan? It's a rare man that can defeat an entire squad by himself, mage or no. I feel he is telling the truth. He, at least, believes he was defending himself."

Timan flashed a dark smile. "Yes, Ire. I think he will do just fine."

Emrael turned to the rest of the men awaiting execution, raised his arms in a questioning shrug, and shouted, "Anyone else here innocent?"

One of the men being held broke down in tears, sagging in the grip of the men holding him. The rest were silent, apparently unwilling to endure Emrael's personal scrutiny, even if it meant a chance at escaping the noose.

"Hang them," he called to the Captain Second in charge of the executions. The wood boards of the hastily erected gallows creaked as the prisoners were lined up and fitted with nooses. A pull of a lever, and ten men fell to their death at the end of a rope.

Emrael's gut roiled as they swung, most rag-doll limp but two black-faced and rasping grotesquely. Funny that he should feel such guilt over these ten when he had caused thousands of deaths just a few days prior.

20

Later that afternoon, Emrael walked into the Blackswell's private dining room to find that Toravin had arrived early for the scheduled war council. Instead of the armor he had been wearing that morning, he was wearing a formal dress jacket in Ire green with the four-stripes-and-single-star insignia of a Commander Second on either shoulder. He lounged in a chair, clean boots on the table, a tankard of something in one hand.

"Thank you for meeting me early, Tor." Emrael closed the doors behind him and unbuckled his sword harness from his shoulders to throw it on a nearby chair. He washed his hands and face in a washbasin, toweled off, and poured himself a glass of water from a pitcher waiting on the table. "I don't think you should be my Commander Second anymore."

Toravin's head lifted sharply, his expression shocked.

"Voran is occupied in the Sagmyn Valley, more Elle's Commander than mine," he continued. "Halrec has been given a Lord Holdership to control. You are leading the core of my Legion for me, in the largest—and most dangerous—campaign of this war. I am hereby promoting you to Commander First of the Ire Legion. I want you to oversee all of it."

Toravin blinked, surprised. "Can you even do that?"

"It's my Legion," he said with a shrug.

Toravin twisted his lips in a wry smile as he snagged a small bread roll from a basket on the table and threw it at Emrael. "You dumb bastard. You should be demoting me. I'd be a much better Captain First. I'm sure someone else could do a better job of babysitting your Legion."

Emrael held up a hand and began counting each point as he raised successive fingers. "A Legion almost entirely comprised of new recruits marched five days' distance in three, with sufficient supplies for an assault and occupation afterward. We took a walled and well-defended city with a quarter of the casualties of the defenders. Other than those ten bastards dangling out in the square, order has been maintained, more or less. As far as I'm concerned, you're doing exactly what needs to be done, and better than any other I could name."

Toravin raised his eyebrows and waggled his head. "I suppose that's true, isn't it?" He frowned again. "And what about you? You like to . . . involve yourself often."

Emrael grinned. "Oh, it's still my Legion. You'll be doing mostly the boring work."

"Fine. I'll be your damned Commander. I'm already doing the work. But it had better be worth it."

"How about I give you the Paellar Holding when this is all over?"

Toravin laughed until he saw that Emrael was serious. He stared at Emrael hard for a moment before his lips quirked in a smile. "Aye, I suppose that'd be worth it," he said with a nonchalant wave of his hand.

They shared a laugh as Emrael stood to throw the doors open. He asked the guards outside to send for someone from the hotel to fetch fresh wash water, food, and drink for the war council that was due to convene shortly.

A quarter of an hour later, the rest of Emrael's confidants arrived. Jaina walked in, deep in conversation with Darrain. From the few fragments of their conversation he heard as they settled in the chairs to Emrael's right, Jaina was interrogating Darrain regarding the explosive devices and how they might be further utilized in battle. He almost pitied his enemies, should Jaina and Darrain combine to further improve the impressive weapons they had used to conquer Gnalius in a single day.

Timan and Captain First Worren were only a few steps behind them, and entered to sit on either side of Toravin at the far end of the table. They greeted each other with smiles and claps on shoulders, and soon had their heads together discussing troop status and the like.

Saravellin entered the room flanked by the Captain of her Guard, who never seemed to leave her side. She spared a hard glance for Toravin before gliding her way to the head of the table to take the chair to Emrael's left, and her Captain, a short but heavily muscled man with a wide, brutishly handsome face, sat next to her. They ignored everyone in the room and sat quietly amid the low chatter, though Saravellin stared unabashed at Emrael as if he were a picture puzzle missing several pieces. Her Guard Captain, named Gorel or some such, listened idly to the Iraean military men sharing reports at the far end of the table.

Hotel cooks and staff entered with steaming dishes of food, allowing Emrael to quietly observe the room.

When the staff had gone and shut the doors behind them, Emrael stood.

"Friends," Emrael said loudly, "Thanks to you and your efforts, the first objective of the campaign is ours." He briefly locked eyes with each person around the table. "Many died or were wounded, and many will yet give their lives for our cause. I expect each of you to keep detailed records of the dead, so we can compensate their families in their stead."

The military folk in the room nodded their approval. Not only was it the right thing to do, but their men still living would fight harder knowing that their families would be taken care of. He hoped to build the military force that he had dreamed of joining just a short year ago, when he was a fledgling Master of War at the Citadel.

"I believe that this is the first step to inspiring more recruits to join us, in numbers that will make the Watchers quake in their boots. It's only the first step, however, and we must continue pressing forward. Even as we speak, Lord Holder Bayr is moving toward Duurn with ten thousand men. Our objective is to pull Syrtsan and his forces as far east of his capital as possible.

"Now," he said, stepping to the large map of the region that he had pinned to the wall behind him. "The Watchers have a garrison in Sutwin, their largest outside of Duurn. Three thousand Watchers, likely as many Syrtsan guardsmen. Too many to attack now, I think, and not worth the men we'd have to station there to keep the city even if we took it. But they can't spare enough men from Sutwin to stop us from taking Merroun," he said, placing his finger on the map where the largest highway connecting Sutwin to the rest of Iraea crossed the east fork of the Teneralle River. "Nor to stop us from bombarding Sutwin's walls if we must, to draw

Syrtsan out of Duurn. Toravin, I need a full count of our forces, and how many we need to leave here to hold Gnalius."

Toravin consulted a notebook on the table in front of him. "Four hundred and fifty-three of our Legion are dead," he said, pointedly looking at Emrael. "That number will climb as the grievously wounded succumb to injuries that even the Mage-Healers cannot heal. One thousand, two hundred and seventy-one of the Ire Legion are under the care of Legion healers. More than two thousand wounded captives and citizens of the city harmed in the attack are also in our care."

Emrael grimaced. "How many of ours will recover within a week or two? Enough to man a crossbow on the wall, at the least?"

He shook his head with pursed lips, then raised his hands in an uncertain gesture. "Perhaps half of them?"

Emrael nodded his thanks. "What about the Iraean mage apprentices, can any with Healing ability be trusted to help the Imperators?"

Jaina pursed her lips. "Perhaps, Emrael, but not without considerable risk to the wounded being Healed. Asking an inexperienced Mage-Healer to heal a complex wound is like asking a farmer to join a shield wall. Technically, they are capable of swinging a sword, but their inexperience will kill more than a few."

Emrael grimaced, knowing many of his men being buried outside the city walls right this moment were dead precisely because he was forced to lead inexperienced farmers to their slaughter in a shield wall. "Use any apprentice mages with Healing ability while they are close to *infusori* Wells, but make sure those being Healed know the risks. Some will accept even poor prospects with our apprentice Mage-Healers, especially if permanent injury is likely without Mage-Healing."

Toravin chuckled darkly. "Most won't. Sentinels and Watchers have put the fear of magic in them, especially Ordenan magic."

He hit Timan in the shoulder playfully. "No offense. But you saw what happened with Daglund."

Timan smiled, a wry slant to the expression. "Yes, we are aware of your prejudices. But I want Daglund and at least one Imperator Mage-Healer to accompany Lord Ire. He has a habit of needing the attentions of a Healer more often than most."

Emrael looked from Timan to Jaina, who nodded her agreement. "How many of our Legionmen do you need to hold Gnalius, Tor?"

"I would need at least three thousand to hold it, and to guard the captured enemy. Five thousand to defend it well, especially if they have anything like those explosives," Toravin said, leaning forward to press his palms to the table. "If the Malithii have their own, we won't hold *any* city for long."

Emrael looked to Jaina, who shook her head and answered Toravin herself. "Even if Malithii arrive with an attacking force, I have never seen this technology deployed so effectively. Such explosives have historically been . . . delicate. Not suitable for use as a projectile, to be sure." She smiled encouragingly at Darrain, who blushed but managed a shy smile in return.

"They could presumably place such a device at your gates or wall by hand or in a wagon, however," Jaina continued, pointing at Toravin. "You must guard your walls diligently."

Emrael's mind replayed the memory of a wagon exploding in a flash of blue light on the bridge on the Kingroad highway between Lidran and Naeran. The blast had put him on his ass and set his ears ringing like a clock bell. A rush of panic, thinking Elle had been hurt. A mad fight with soulbound. Slaughtered Legionmen. Jaina setting the entire bridge alight.

How things had changed in less than a year's time. He felt a sharp ache at the thought of Elle, and wondered how she was doing in Myntar with his mother. He had ignored them too long already. He should write a letter at the very least.

Toravin's response to Jaina pulled Emrael out of his personal contemplation and back to the task at hand. "So five thousand, if you mean to keep it. Three will do if you're willing to take a risk," Toravin said.

"Let's split the difference at four thousand. We're dead if we lose Gnalius, but we'll need every sword available to threaten Sutwin and watch other crossings along the Teneralle. I intend to take the smaller shipping town of Merroun a day's ride east of Sutwin, on the closer branch of the Lys. That should be enough to force Lord Syrtsan's hand. If he doesn't bite, we will reduce Sutwin to rubble with Darrain's explosives."

"Aye, it's a good plan," Toravin said. "Though someone will be left here with four thousand men to keep order, defend the city, and care for the wounded? Poor bastard," he said with a smirk and a wink, obviously intuiting that the task would fall to him.

Emrael smiled. "Correct. I need you to do it, and I want you to find as many recruits in the city as you can. Assign them to existing squads and start training them immediately. We need every soldier we can get, and quickly. We must defeat Lord Syrtsan before the month is out, one way or another. I can't leave Garrus and Ban to hold Trylla alone any longer than that. If the Watchers round up enough boats, they could sail straight down the tributaries of the Lys and be in Trylla with almost no warning. I don't think they have anything close to the vessels they'd need, but better to not take the risk. We can't leave Halrec and Dorae to fight off Corrande on their own forever either."

He left unsaid that he didn't yet trust Saravellin enough to hold a city that was crucial to his plans. It was imperative that he conquer the Syrtsan Holding quickly before turning his attention northward to his own ancestral Holding, and Gnalius provided him a much-needed *infusori* supply close to Trylla as well. If he lost this city, his war was already over.

Captain First Worren had struggled in his mission to capture the walls of Gnalius during their assault, and Emrael wasn't sure he could fully trust the former Watcher yet, either. Not the way he trusted Toravin. Timan would have been capable, but he feared the reaction from his Legion should he place an Ordenan in command. It had to be Toravin.

"We have another problem, sir," Worren offered gruffly. "Supplies. The men lack proper gear, particularly heading into the cold seasons. This city has stores enough for a time, but not for an extended campaign. We'll starve ourselves out of a victory before Syrtsan can even think to attack us."

"What do you suggest, Captain?" Emrael challenged.

Worren frowned in thought, but had his answer soon enough. "Capture the richest cities on the major shipping lanes, bigger the better. If we take Sutwin, we'll feed our men for months."

"Fair point," Emrael responded. Worren was an outstanding field commander, a man soldiers willingly followed on the battlefield, a man of considerable prowess who led from the front. From what Emrael had discerned, however, he was not a man who appreciated subtle approaches to complex situations.

"But," Emrael continued firmly, "Sutwin is a large city, more heavily defended than Gnalius, and they'll know we're coming. We can't afford to capture Sutwin and take casualties on the same scale as we did here. We'll be stretched thin, with no army left with which to threaten Syrtsan or anybody else. Would you still take the risk?"

Worren hesitated now, which Emrael appreciated. Jaina smiled as she met Emrael's eye.

"I suppose not," Worren conceded.

Emrael offered him a smile and a nod. "I agree. The risk is too high, and I think Syrtsan would hole up in his capital if we took Sutwin outright, which is the opposite of what we want. Bayr taking Duurn while Syrtsan focuses on us is the key to the entire plan. So what do we do about supplies? Buy from the Ordenans? Can they get through the Sound and up the Teneralle?"

"My father should have wagon trains on the way, Lord Ire, but they'll be en route to Trylla," Saravellin interjected. "I can send a detachment to route them here, but they will likely take two weeks or more to arrive."

"No," Emrael said immediately. "The supplies you have agreed to send are needed in Trylla as badly as they are here. We'll not steal from them. Unless you have more to offer?"

Saravellin grimaced. "Ah . . . perhaps. There is an old trade route through the Burned Hills just twenty miles north of here, but copper will be needed to buy the supplies and hire the wagons. And guards to accompany them—the old roads can be treacherous."

Emrael raised an eyebrow at her, not sure whether to be frustrated or amused. "Copper again, is it?"

Saravellin's eyes flashed. "What would you have me do? Commandeer wagon trains and storehouses by force? How long would my father remain the Lord in Raebren, acting so? You pay your fighting men, and your civilians. I must do the same, and our coffers are not deep after all the Watchers have taken. I will not profit from our aid, but I will not bankrupt my House and Holding, either."

"I understand," Emrael conceded with a smile. "Merchants aren't likely to take a land bounty or promise of future pay for goods, are they? I'm sure the Mayor of Gnalius will be happy to lend us what we need. I'll have your copper. Please arrange for supplies to be routed here as quickly as possible."

He looked to Toravin. "In the meantime, there must be villages, towns, farms in the area that support the city and its previous garrison. Send out large patrols to ensure that goods still flow to the city. Purchase goods forcibly at the farms and bring it back yourselves if you must, but do not leave anyone without what they need to survive. We will be holding Gnalius permanently, so long-term stores will be essential, as will the goodwill of the people here."

"I'll stay here to manage the supplies and finances, Lord Ire," Saravellin offered. "Under Commander Toravin's direction, of course. I'll keep half of my battalion with me for security and logistics, the other five companies will ride with you to Merroun."

Emrael, surprised, looked to Toravin, who nodded. "Very well. Thank you, Saravellin. We ride for Merroun tomorrow at dawn."

The conquest of Merroun was much easier than that of Gnalius. Word of Emrael's approach had spread ahead of their arrival, and well it should have, as Emrael had sent word ahead to allow for the town's residents to evacuate if they wished.

Most of Merroun's population had fled to the safety of Sutwin's large stone walls across the river in the three days since the Legion had left Gnalius. They were never going to put up a fight, not here. Those citizens of Merroun that remained left the gates to their sprawling, low-walled town wide open, obviously not wanting to invite death and destruction when they had no chance of resisting.

Worren led the forward battalion through the open gates to then fan out by squad to ensure that the myriad side streets, alleyways, and warehouses were clear. They then lined the stone-paved avenue that led to the large bridge that spanned the east fork of the Teneralle, a river wide and deep enough for half a dozen Ordenan warships to sail side by side, just before it opened to the upper Stem Sound.

His soldiers beat their shields with swords and spear butts as Emrael and his retinue rode into the town ahead of the main body of the army. The main portion of his Legion, marching behind those mounted, took up a raucous cheer. This town meant little tactically, but the cheers of his soldiers meant a great deal to him, and to his chances of winning this war. Good morale might not be enough by itself, but lack thereof would surely lose them the war.

The iron-shod hooves of their horses rang on the cobbles of the avenue, the only street that was well-paved. Every side street Emrael could see was of hard-packed and deep-rutted earth that was likely a muddy mess during the region's frequent rainstorms. Other than the typical inns, residences, and other well-off businesses and establishments that lined the main avenue and the stone-paved road that fronted the river, Merroun seemed to be an entire square league or more of shipping yards and warehouses that straddled the river on either side of the enormous bridge. Docks on both sides served trade vessels and a host of fishermen—very few of whom risked working today. Quite a few larger ships had moored in the river, their crews watching Emrael's occupation of the city at a distance. Likely they had pulled away from the docks to stay clear of any fighting, but were unwilling to abandon their cargo and business here in Merroun unless the situation grew severely hostile.

Emrael wrinkled his nose. The place reeked of rotting fish, animal shit, and refuse. No doubt it was far worse when fully occupied by sailors, fishermen, and merchant teams loading up wagons to haul inland to Gnalius and beyond. He and his entourage of senior officers and Royal Guard made for the large clump of boardinghouses and more respectable establishments that lined the avenue nearer the docks while the bulk of his forces set up a camp just outside the city walls.

Toravin had sent nearly a full company's worth of clerks and aides dedicated to the logistics of setting up and running their command post. They handled the work marvelously for a newly formed Legion, and Emrael hardly had to pay attention to the various aspects of appeasing the locals or provisioning supplies. Emrael, his council, and most of the senior officers were given quarters in the largest boardinghouses in the center of the residential portion of town, where they spent an anxious two days waiting for word from their scouts that Syrtstan had taken the bait.

On the third day in Merroun, Emrael and Jaina sat in the common room of the boardinghouse, Jaina sipping a glass of red wine, Emrael nursing a pipe glass of wine brandy.

Worren and the head Ire Legion clerk, Ruval, hosted several consecutive appointments where various aides and clerks read the latest supply and personnel reports. They had carted enough supplies with them from Gnalius to last them weeks, and Ruval was doing his best to make sure it was properly managed.

Few merchants and traders braved the occupation in search of a quick profit selling to the new occupying force, and no new ships had docked in the three days they had been here. Likely Syrtsan had set up a loose blockade near Duurn at the mouth of the river's sound, and probably another near Sutwin as well. They hadn't dared before, as Ordenans would eventually protest violently against such measures—they bought considerable amounts of *infusori* stores out of Whitehall and Gnalius, after all. The Ordenans had the most technologically advanced navy in the world by far, and their appetite for *infusori* was nearly insatiable. Starving Ordenans of contracted *infusori* stores was a very good way to convince them to sink your ships on sight.

Only an Ordenan battleship would risk such a blockade, and Emrael had to hope that Jaina was right to be as confident as she was that her messengers had made it down the Lys to a waiting Ordenan ship. If he couldn't talk the Ordenans into at least keeping the Stem open for them, Emrael's war might end right here in this shithole fishing town.

When the current supply clerk, having assiduously given a report on the quantity of smoked fish bought from local storehouses, finally gathered his papers and strode from the room, Emrael called to the head clerk. "Enough, Ruval, enough for a moment. You'll have to take the remaining appointments without me. I need to see Darrain about her damned machines, it's starting to look like we might need them to make some noise in Sutwin. Just make sure we're ready to move to encampments to the east and north of Sutwin where Darrain can bombard their walls. Only come to me if you find problems that you can't solve yourselves."

He clapped them both on the shoulder as he left and chuckled at Worren's disgruntled expression. The man enjoyed clerical duties even less than Emrael.

Jaina accompanied him silently, and a pair of Royal Guards—Daglund, his bruised eye now an ugly yellow instead of dark purple, and a female apprentice mage he didn't recognize—followed closely behind them as they left.

He had only just reached the building where Darrain had set up her Crafters and engineers when a messenger caught up to him. "Lord! Lord Ire, sir! Captain Third Dirrat with Fifth Cavalry sends a request to meet with him immediately. He is headed to where Captain First Worren is stationed, sir, and says you'll need to hear the report yourself."

Emrael grumbled a few curses under his breath but reversed course to march back to the boardinghouse they had just left. "Thank you, Legionman."

"Syrtsan is on the move," Worren growled as Emrael and Jaina stepped back into the common room. Captain Third Dirrat had apparently already given his report, and now stood at attention next to his Captain First. "He's got ten thousand men—mostly his own guardsmen, but a few battalions of Watchers—headed out of Duurn. He'll cross the west leg of the Teneralle River at High Hill and garrison at Sutwin, most like."

Emrael paced the room, thinking. "Right. We need to keep pressure on him, bring him here to Merroun, but we can't let him catch us on the west side of the river. We'd be annihilated in this little shit town. I want our men on the east side of the river, and I want explosives set under the bridge and ready to fire should Syrtsan get bold and try to cross. Send men to find and destroy any other bridges north of here, have Darrain send Crafters or engineers with them. We'll need our scouts patrolling the river, watching for any of Syrtsan's forces trying to flank us."

Worren nodded. "Captain Dirrat here already saw to arranging patrols. I can send Eighth Company with your explosives, should the scouts find any bridges they can't take down themselves."

Emrael stopped his pacing to fix Worren with a savage smile. "Bayr will have his own scouts to tell him that Syrtsan has left his capital, and he damn well better move soon. We need to keep Syrtsan looking this way until he does, draw him right here if we can. How would you like to lead a battalion or two across the river to attack the garrisons in towns around Sutwin, perhaps even harry

Syrtsan's main forces? Hit them without harming civilians, if you can, but get them to chase you here."

Worren grinned back at him. "I'd love to, sir."

Five days later, Emrael waited at the middle of the Merroun bridge beneath a canvas canopy with Jaina, Worren, and a single squad of his Royal Guard—most of whom were Imperators or their mage apprentices, today. A steady rain pattered on the canvas canopy overhead and turned the surface of the Teneralle to dark bubbled glass.

Worren had just returned that morning with the two thousand men he had led in raids across the river, bearing news that Syrtsan was close behind him with ten thousand men and had requested a parley. Ash, red dirt, and dark spots of dried blood still marred his forest-green uniform.

They watched together as Syrtsan and his own small retinue separated from the main body of his army, which had occupied the western half of Merroun and stood in battle formations, as Emrael's did on the eastern side. Syrtsan's forces numbered at least as many as Emrael's Legion and were all well-trained soldiers. The two battalions of Watchers with him undoubtedly carried *infusori*-Crafted crossbows. It would be unwise to engage them in a fair fight.

Syrtsan's lightly lined face was grim as he swept into the shelter of the canvas, shaking the rain from his cloak with a sharp snap. He threw the cloak to a waiting aide and strode to where Emrael stood waiting, a Syrtsan officer and a Watcher officer flanking him closely.

"You bastard," he spat, stepping close to loom over Emrael. "You pathetic, petty little man. I don't know why these fools"—he swept his arm at Jaina, Worren, and in the direction of Emrael's waiting Legion—"bother with you. But hear me now, boy. I was willing to sit idle while your attempted conquest played out. But now I will finish you, here and now. You have murdered my men, pillaged my lands, and it will not stand." He flashed a murderous glare at Worren before continuing. "I've sent word to Marol and the others, and they've mobilized thirty thousand Watchers to crush you like the worms you are. You'll be dead within two weeks."

Emrael withstood the tirade with a calm face, even nodding along solemnly toward the end, though Syrtsan's professed time-line of two weeks was concerning. Could the man have gotten word to the Watchers so quickly? No matter. Syrtsan was the challenge before him, here and now.

"I understand, Lord Syrtsan," he said calmly. "You did not believe me before, when I told you and the other Lords Holder that there is no middle ground in this war."

Lord Callan Syrtsan took a step forward, shaking with rage, so close that Emrael could smell his fetid breath.

Emrael held up one hand in a stalling gesture. "Now, however, you see the truth. Fighting men and women flock to me because they see that I am strong and you are weak. You have bowed to the Watchers too long, have become used to their chains. I am here to offer you one last chance, Callan. Join me now, today, or share their fate."

Syrtsan's eyes flashed and he tensed, looking as if he was about to draw his weapon, flag of parley be damned. The men who had accompanied him put their hands to hilts.

"Ah ah ah," Emrael cautioned, wagging one finger. He drew *infusori* from the stores in his Crafted armor until his eyes and his scars glowed. The Imperators and Iraean mages behind him shuf-fled as they readied themselves, undoubtedly drawing on their own *infusori* stores. "Do that, and you won't live to see your Watcher masters kill me, will you?"

Syrtsan stood still a moment, a rictus snarl on his face. What-ever else he was, he wasn't stupid enough to fight Emrael and a squad of mages here on the bridge. The Lord Holder spat, then turned on his heel to snatch his cloak and stalk silently toward his side of the river.

"Is that a no, then, Callan?" Emrael called.

Syrtsan didn't look back.

Emrael turned to Darrain, who had been standing with his Royal Guard, though she had stood behind them and hadn't shown her face from beneath the cowl of her oversized rain cloak.

"You can actuate them from here?" Emrael asked.

Darrain nodded, though Emrael sensed her hesitation. She knew what her explosives could do, and was human enough to regret it. "My engineers wired the entire bridge with sheathed copper cabling. Unless they have Crafters looking very carefully, we will be able to actuate from our side of the river. My actuator is waiting for us at the foot of the bridge."

Emrael drew a deep breath, conflicted. The thought of killing so many Iraeans weighed on him. He needed more allies, more recruits, not to turn thousands of Syrtsan families against him. The opportunity to cripple a potentially problematic enemy was too good to pass up, however.

Emrael led his small group back to the foot of the bridge quickly, where Darrain and another of her Crafters readied a series of metal boxes that contained coils and wires and who knew what other components, all connected to strands of copper wiring that ran along the outside edge of the bridge.

"Do it," Emrael commanded with more confidence than he felt.

Darrain and her Crafter pulled levers attached to the Craftings nearly simultaneously. A flash of blinding blue light and giant cloud of dust erupted at the other foot of the bridge, then dozens more in a successive circle, rolling out from the first explosion to encompass the entire western side of Merroun in a cloud of dust and debris. A fraction of a second later, an earsplitting crack and a wave of pure energy buffeted them. Then silence, save for the splashing of debris landing in the river.

Emrael and everyone around him, even Jaina, was stunned by the intensity of what they had just witnessed. The world had never seen destruction so violent and instantaneous, not on that scale. Perhaps not since the days of the ancient Ravans, and maybe not even then. Darrain stood to one side of the group, tears streaming down her face.

As the ringing in Emrael's ears subsided, he heard another sound—the distant screams of wounded men, and a din of confused shouting from those left alive.

Emrael motioned silently for Worren to take the Legion across the bridge. The Captain First shouted, and the waiting battalion of cavalry charged. The foot battalions followed, shields and weapons at the ready. Though the explosions had been impressive, they could still be in for a fight if any of Syrtsan's battalions had escaped the blasts. The explosions had been violent enough and the screams were now loud enough, however, that he was sure it was only going to take a few small skirmishes before the entirety of Syrtsan's army surrendered. The healers and gravediggers would be busy for days.

"I didn't know you had that many," Emrael commented quietly to Darrain. "And those explosions were bigger. You improved them already."

The Crafter flinched at the comment. "I . . . You said you wanted to do as much damage as possible," she stammered between sobs.

"You did well," Emrael clarified firmly, putting a protective hand on her shoulder. "You did exactly what we needed you to, and you saved tens of thousands of lives and likely the war, gruesome though this seems. Thank you, Darrain."

The disheveled, normally cheery Crafter sobbed, burying her face in the shoulder of her fellow Crafter, who looked nearly as distraught as she was.

When he and his Guard—and Jaina, of course—reached the other side, Emrael's suspicions were confirmed. Dead Syrtsan guardsmen and Watchers lay strewn everywhere, their bodies torn to shreds. The explosions had been so violent that the clothes had been torn clear off their bodies. The stench of burned flesh permeated the air, with an undertone of offal and shit.

Jaina stepped up next to him as he surveyed the carnage nearest the bridge. "Many will turn against you when they learn of this, Emrael. Syrtsan's men in particular. They will fear you, now, but revile you as well."

Emrael said nothing for a time, watching as his Legion rounded up the living as captives. Very few were in any shape to resist, and any skirmishes had ended before Emrael had arrived. Nearly two battalions of Syrtsan men and Watchers already huddled in the street, weaponless and unprotected from the rain, guarded by an equal number of Ire Legionmen. The injured limped or were carried to the buildings along the main avenue that still stood, where Emrael's healers had set up their operations.

"I know," he told her quietly, sadly. "I know. They are right to, Jaina." He shook his head. "But I had to do this. We can't win any other way, and we can't afford to lose. The world can't afford for us to lose.

"Besides," he said, stepping from the bridge to walk the debris-strewn street. "Others will join us now that Syrtsan is out of the way. Every Lord Holder we secure or kill will mean thousands of men free to join us without fear of repercussions from their liege lords."

Jaina grunted her agreement and followed without further comment. They found Worren just past the huddled captives, under the stoop of the largest inn. The building right next to it had nearly completely caved in, but this structure seemed solid still, save for missing roof shingles, debris protruding from the wooden siding here and there, and shards of shattered glass stuck in the edges of otherwise empty windowpanes.

Worren and a squad of Ire Legionmen stood in a rough circle around two Syrtsan and one Watcher officer, all of whom had clearly just been rousted from the inn. Emrael recognized Lord Holder Syrtsan almost immediately, though the man understandably looked far more disheveled than when they had met less than an hour before, his hair mussed and his uniform covered in red mud along one side. His eyes were wild, confused, and angry.

"You!" Syrtsan screamed as Emrael joined the group. Though he had been stripped of his weapons, the Lord Holder surged forward in an attempt to attack Emrael. Worren moved before Emrael could even brace himself for the attack. The Captain First's hand whipped out like a striking viper to grip Syrtsan's neck, arresting his momentum and putting the nobleman on his back with a loud thump on the solid wood decking of the inn's stoop. Syrtsan rolled to one side, coughing weakly as he fought to get air back into his lungs.

Emrael surveyed the men calmly. "I regret today's actions, Callan. Your men did not deserve to die for your cowardice, your inability to understand who and what I am."

Syrtsan had regained his breath and lurched to his feet. "You should kill me as well, Ire. I'll kill you, given the chance."

The officers standing behind Syrtsan shifted uncomfortably. Apparently, they didn't share their lord's wish for death.

Emrael smiled at Syrtsan. "I'm afraid I won't be killing you today, Callan. This isn't a petty war of vengeance. I don't hate you. I simply need your land, and your people."

"You want me to swear allegiance to you after this?" Syrtsan said, voice pitched high with incredulity.

"Oh no," Emrael chuckled. "I'm afraid that offer has passed. Now, the deal is this: You order your men holding Sutwin, Duurn, and other garrisons to stand down and surrender to me without a fight. In return, I will personally guarantee your safety and that of your family."

Left unsaid, but well understood judging by the horror in Syrtsan's expression, was the obvious implication that should Syrtsan not agree, his family would not be spared his fate.

"You bastard," Syrtsan growled, his voice cracking with emotion. "You Fallen-damned bastard. I hope the Watchers gut and skin you like a weasel."

"They may," Emrael said gravely. "But not today. Really, Callan, I warned you twice. I would have been a good ally. Maybe even a friend."

Just then, Jaina pushed through the crowd of men to speak in Emrael's ear. "I just received word. The Watchers have attacked Trylla."

Emrael stopped, stunned. His chest turned to ice. Ban. He had let it happen again. He never should have let Ban out of his sight.

"Are they safe? Is Ban safe?"

Jaina shook her head, her expression pained. "I do not know. The messengers left Trylla on Garrus's orders five days ago. Only two of ten survived to reach us, so far."

"Fallen take them," he said, turning to her. "Five days? How did they know? They had to have known very early, to get there so fast."

Lord Syrtsan cackled from behind him. "I told you, boy. Today does not change your fate."

Emrael turned to face the sneering Syrtsan again. He struggled to keep the anger and the bone-chilling fear from his face and failed. He roared in rage and lashed out with a kick to Syrtsan's knee, connecting with a loud pop, much like the sound of breaking a green tree branch. The Lord Holder screamed as he flopped to the ground, hands clutching his ruined knee.

Emrael turned to address Worren. "Offer the captives the same bounty and pay we offer everyone. Watchers and Syrtsan men alike, as long as they're Iraean. And have a mage Heal the Lord Holder. Can't have him dying on us now. We're marching for Gnalius in four hours. Fast march."

"Four hours!" Worren exclaimed. "That's not possible, Lord Ire. We've only just begun to sort the captives . . ."

"The men are packed. We will take the weapons, armor, and supplies from the captives and turn loose those that don't want to join us," Emrael said firmly. "Let them care for their own wounded. Bayr can handle them when he arrives."

Syrtsan, face red with pain, grunted behind him. "Davis? He's a part of all this?"

Emrael sneered at him despite the anxiety tearing through him. "Loyalty ends where opportunity begins, eh, Callan?"

He turned to march back to the east side of the river, his Guard in tow. "I'm bringing down this bridge in four hours, Worren!"

21

A hard two-day ride found Emrael back in Gnalius. He, Jaina, and several mounted companies had ridden ahead, as fast as their mounts could safely travel, leaving the foot with Worren to catch up in a few days. He needed to get back to Gnalius as soon as possible to plan their response, and the foot battalions would be better off marching at a measured pace with the supply wagons anyway. They would need to be ready to march to Trylla straightaway.

Emrael didn't take the time to bathe or even change from his mud-spattered armor before calling Toravin, Jaina, and Saravellin into a meeting at the Blackswell Hotel. He had hardly sat in the high-backed wooden chair at the head of the large dining table when Toravin arrived.

"Bayr was attacked as well," Toravin said as he swept into the room carrying an armful of papers. "He made it as far as Arras before nearly twenty thousand Watchers attacked Skae. Bayr marched back to defend his Holding with his full ten thousand. He's got the Watchers occupied in the hills between Skae and Borrel for now, but they'll have to retreat eventually. And now Syrtsan will be free to attack us from behind as we defend Trylla."

Emrael cursed at the news but quirked a sad smile as he responded to Toravin. "Syrtsan won't be a problem. We captured him after killing most of ten battalions of Syrtsan men and Watchers. We'll need to deal with Duurn eventually, before one of his sons decides they don't mind us killing their father if it earns them an early inheritance. But we should be free to focus northward for now."

Toravin raised his eyebrows in surprise. "You killed ten thousand of his men?" Emrael had moved as quickly as a messenger would have, so this was the first detailed report Toravin would have received.

Emrael nodded. "Near enough. Darrain and her people placed explosives throughout the west side of Merroun, and Worren drew them in. They rejected a peace offer, and we actuated the explosives. Six or seven thousand dead or injured enough that they won't fight again soon, and the rest are dealing with their wounded. We destroyed the bridge and marched straight here. They won't be a problem."

Toravin looked like he didn't know whether to be impressed or nauseated. "Ah. Well. One problem mitigated for now, eh?"

"Yes," Emrael said, not wanting to spend more time on the subject. "Our problem now is Trylla. How many Watchers attacked them, and what else do we know?"

Toravin shuffled through his papers until he found the one he was looking for. "Yes, here is the latest report. Another rider arrived just this morning, says he and several others were sent two days after the siege began, and had to ride around several Watcher patrols that nearly caught him the south of the city. Garrus says there are likely twenty thousand camped primarily to the north of the River Lys. The most recent rider estimates that their numbers may be as high as thirty thousand based on the additional camps he saw. At least ten thousand south of the river. Could be more by the time we get there."

"So they are besieged," Emrael said, closing his eyes and sighing in relief. He had spent the last two days agonizing over the possibility that the Watchers had captured his brother again—or worse. "Garrus has five thousand men and decent fortifications, they may hold. For a time. Thirty thousand is more than I thought they could field. Another twenty in Bayr Holding. Fallen Glory take me."

Saravellin cleared her throat. "They must have stripped the rest of the province bare—stripped the *kingdom* bare," she corrected with a wry glance at Emrael. "I should think that Ire's End, Gallr, even Porshim and High Springs are all at minimum garrison right now. We can't abandon our men at Trylla, certainly not, but there may be an opportunity worth considering."

"Our focus is Trylla," Emrael said firmly. "If the Watchers take Trylla, our entire plan is dead. And I will not leave my brother to die. I won't leave any of our people there to die."

Saravellin raised her hands, clearly not wanting to argue.

Emrael knew he was being curt, but had no patience for anything but getting on the road to rescue Ban. "Did the sergeant note locations and camps sizes, patrols, anything?"

Toravin shook his head. "Not in my report. We put him up in an inn on the next block over."

"Get him here now," Emrael commanded. "I want details."

Toravin blinked in mild surprise at his harsh tone, but complied without comment, opening the door to the private dining room to send a runner for the sergeant.

Emrael turned to Jaina. "I need you to get another message to your people. Their ships will be of little use in Sutwin or Merroun, now. Take the fastest horse you can find, round up any Ordenan Crafting-powered ship you can recruit to sail up the Lys and meet us where the west road from Gnalius meets the river. Whatever that town is called. Atli, I think. I'll send you with all the copper you need."

He stalked to the door without waiting for an answer, throwing it open to shout, "Pen, ink, and paper please! Hurry with it!"

"You want me to go? Personally?" Jaina asked slowly.

Emrael nodded impatiently. "I'd rather keep you with me. Glory knows you've saved my neck more than once in a fight. But I need the Ordenans to help us cross the Lys quietly and where the Watchers won't expect. I trust you more than anyone else to get that done."

Jaina shook her head, glancing at Toravin and Saravellin uncomfortably. "I cannot, even if I wished to, Emrael. There is a significant risk that not only would I not be listened to, I might be apprehended as well."

Emrael looked at her, taken aback. "What do you mean? The Imperators here follow your lead. You'll have the backing of my mother, and mine. What could you possibly have done to anger them? You've been with me the whole time."

Jaina smiled. "That is precisely the issue, Emrael. Ordenan politics are not so simple, any more than Provincial politics are simple. There are many in the Council and elsewhere who oppose your mother, and therefore oppose you and what you stand for. Many do not want to become involved in Provincial affairs, but others are acting to protect personal interests in *infusori* contracts and other trade."

Emrael gestured at her in confusion. "And this means that they'll abduct you, but be fine negotiating with someone else we send? I don't understand, Jaina."

Jaina's smile turned sour. "My . . . opponents in the Council, they have made their displeasure known. They sent an Imperator to apprehend me in Whitehall. They will not likely risk angering you or an official emissary, but I might be a prize worth the price, now. They will consider me an Ordenan first, your emissary second."

Emrael rubbed his eyes with one hand. "Fine. Send whoever you wish, just make sure they can get the job done, and quickly. I figure it will take us five days to reach the Lys. If your people can find an Ordenan ship near Merroun, they should be able to meet us in time. I want to be able to cross the river where the Watchers won't expect us, and they can move us faster than any other ship on the water, even if it's just one, and we can be sure they won't talk to the Watchers about it after. I want you to send to Ordena for more as well. I need enough ships to move at least ten thousand men quickly, whenever I want. Five ships?"

Jaina wagged her head. "Three to five, depending on the ships. But Emrael, they will not send them for free. They might not send ships at all, no matter your offer."

"My letter will tell them I'm willing to pay five thousand copper rounds for transport."

Jaina raised her eyebrows. "That sum should attract the Councils' attention. Do you have five thousand rounds to give?"

"I have it somewhere. Between Tarelle's coffers and my own in Sagmyn, I should have far more than five thousand to spend winning this war. For now, we'll take it on loan from the banks and lords of Gnalius. There's plenty of money here, I can smell it. Lord Mayor Vorot might have five thousand for us himself."

Saravellin chortled in disbelief. "That's enough to buy a small fleet of your own, Emrael, or feed your entire army for months. Is that a wise expenditure?"

Anger surged through Emrael, but he forced himself to take a breath to calm himself before responding. "I don't have time to build a fleet, and I don't have trained sailors like the Ordenans do. Our army will all be dead within the month without the ability to transport across the river without the Watchers knowing about it.

Chances are, we'll all be dead anyway. But hitting them from the north is our best chance at evening the odds."

Jaina and Toravin nodded at that, and Saravellin made a surrendering gesture with her hands.

"I assume then," Saravellin said, "that we're abandoning Gnalius? If you've got Lord Holder Syrtsan, there's no need to spend troops here."

Emrael pursed his lips as he considered. "We'll leave a skeleton force here. We'll need the Wells soon enough, and we can't afford to let Syrtsan's sons or lesser lords like our dear Mayor Vorot think they can organize a resistance. We'll hold Lord Syrtsan hostage here as well."

"Let me do it," Toravin offered. "I've already learned the fortifications and the surrounding area. Give me the same four thousand men and we will hold here as long as you need."

Emrael stood from his chair to pace the length of the room. "I could use you at Trylla, Tor. It's going to be ugly, and the men respect you."

Toravin smiled. "I can think of someone else who has commanded more men in more battles—in just the last year—than nearly anyone alive in all of the Provinces. You're a trained Master of War, for Mercy's sake. You are the only commander they need, Emrael."

Emrael flushed a bit at the praise but shook his head doggedly. "It won't be as simple as leading our men straight at an unsuspecting foe or assaulting a small city like Gnalius. The Watchers will have spread out around Trylla, they outnumber us heavily, and we can't just attack and run. We have to kill them all, or enough to force them to retreat. I'll need several people I can trust to lead smaller groups without needing constant orders."

Toravin shrugged. "You've got Jaina. Worren. Timan, if he'll leave your side."

"And me," Saravellin said.

"You?" Emrael asked, surprised. "You want to fight?"

"Yes," she said, lifting her chin. "I've trained a good bit more than most of the men in your 'Legion,' and my men have proven loyal to you, have they not? Tell me what needs doing, and we'll do it."

"Why?" he asked simply.

She rolled her eyes. "Whether I like it or not, my fate is now firmly tied to yours, Emrael Ire. If you lose, the Watchers will dismantle my Holding, and probably execute me and my family besides."

Emrael raised his eyebrows. "But you volunteer more men now, when I'm at my weakest. I'm sure the Watchers would be quick to forgive you if you turned against me."

She smiled broadly, showing her straight white teeth. "Don't think I haven't considered it," she said, leaning forward onto forearms planted on the tabletop. "But now I've seen what you're capable of, what you're willing to do to win. Even if I helped the Watchers kill you, I'll be stuck in a small and languishing Holding, beholden to the Watchers and other Lords Holder that have no love for us. Less, now. If I fight with you and we win, there will be considerable gain for me and my House. Correct?"

He gave her an appraising look and shared a small smile with Jaina. "Yes, that's fair. What's your price then, Lady Raebren?"

Saravellin's expression turned coy. "We will speak of prices later, after we do what needs to be done at Trylla."

He laughed. "You'll have your reward. But you're not coming north with me. Send to your father for more men. If you send a messenger with spare horses ahead of your thousand, you should be able to meet whatever forces your father can muster at North Ford. Your task will be to hold the attention of Watchers to the south of Trylla. Keep them occupied by causing as much damage as possible. Classic hit-and-run tactics, only attack when you can do so without taking heavy casualties."

Saravellin nodded, her face calm. "I'll take care of the south. You handle the north."

She reached her hand out to seal the agreement with a handshake.

He took it, gripping her hand tightly as he met her eyes. "We'll meet in Trylla."

Absent Gods, he hoped he could trust her.

Emrael sat atop his horse on a bluff overlooking the muddy bank of the Lys River, watching as a giant Ordenan vessel dropped her anchor several hundred paces from shore. The crew lowered a small whaleboat from the main deck, which then rowed to shore. When it beached, Emrael, Jaina, and Worren dismounted to walk through the knee-high grass to meet the four men who hopped out to trudge through the mud and grass at the river's edge. Timan waited with a full squad of the Royal Guard some fifty paces away, and their entire army camped not half a league away after a grueling five-day march.

"Lord Ire, I presume?" the man leading the small group of Ordenans asked, as if anyone else would be waiting for him on the empty riverbank several leagues from the nearest town, Atli. The Ordenans wore plain black clothing, but their posture and demeanor clearly marked them as military of some sort. Emrael wondered whether they might be Imperators—Jaina had warned him that they would run into an Imperator or two, as they were typically stationed on all official Ordenan ships.

"Yes, that's me," Emrael said. "Thank you for coming." He offered his hand to the man, who looked at him with a calculating stare for a moment, then accepted the handshake. Emrael sent a nearly imperceptible pulse of *infusori* into the man through their touching hands and felt the man's defenses spring into place immediately. The Imperator stiffened, pulling his hand away roughly, clearly caught off guard. His companions put hands to sword hilts.

Emrael raised his hands and smiled. "No harm intended, honored Imperator. I'm sure you know that I am a friend to the Ordenans," he said, gesturing to Jaina and Timan.

The Imperator had recovered his calm, astute demeanor, though his jerky movements belied his continued discomfort. "Yes. Well. I have a missive for you from the Captain of our ship. She asks for a portion of payment before services are rendered, and I am on orders from the Council of Imperators to interview several of the Imperators believed to be with you. Their names are on a list included with the missive. We will row you out once you have the money and the Imperators I need to speak with." He held a paper envelope out to Emrael, which he accepted and passed to Jaina. She flipped through it quickly and nodded.

Emrael turned back to the Imperator. "We'll have your money shortly, and Jaina has gone to fetch your Imperators."

The Imperator's eyes twitched to look at Jaina briefly at hearing her name. A slight narrowing of the man's eyes told Emrael that he didn't know her on sight, but that her name meant something to him.

Emrael didn't like it.

"What's your name?" Emrael asked.

The Imperator's gaze snapped back to Emrael. "Marco," he replied tersely.

"Well, Marco," Emrael said, stepping closer. "Jaina is my close friend. I don't care if she's on that list of yours, she doesn't leave my sight unless she wants to. Same goes for all of the Imperators with me. I will take any aggression toward them very, very personally."

Marco raised one eyebrow, clearly not impressed. "Very well, Lord Ire."

Jaina returned shortly, several Imperators following her. She handed Emrael a small chest filled with coins—one thousand copper rounds, to be exact—and stood at his side.

Emrael hefted the small fortune in coin and made a mental note to review his ledgers personally. Toravin trusted their head clerk, Ruval, a friend from his time in the Watchers, but Emrael wasn't comfortable trusting his money to a relative stranger. Ruval clearly knew his business and was well compensated, but that didn't mean he could be left with sole oversight of his finances. Emrael would have been tempted to filch at least a bit, had the roles been reversed.

He opened the chest and turned to show the Imperator the coins, a deposit to show the Ordenan Captain that they intended to secure his services in good faith. "One thousand copper rounds, Provincial."

Marco stared flatly. "You offered five thousand rounds. In writing."

"I also requested three ships, Imperator."

Marco frowned. "She won't be happy." The Imperator turned without another word and led the way back to the rowboat.

The small boat took Emrael, Jaina, Timan, and two other Imperators across to the waiting Ordenan cruiser, a massive steel and wood ship at least twice the size of anything Provincial forces had ever put into the water. In addition to large masts that supported sails to propel the ship, two large engines mounted aft turned a series of propellers that churned the water behind the ship to a froth when in use. A large hatch in the midship must have housed the *infusori* storage array. Emrael had seen schematics, and knew that a ship like this would carry thousands of enormous insulated coils, all connected to the propulsion system that could carry a ship like this thousands of leagues before it needed to replenish its charge. There would also be large *infusori*-Crafted ballistas under the deck that would shoot from hatches in the side of the ship. They were not unlike the one that Darrain had used to blow down the gate of Gnalius, though as far as Emrael knew, the Ordenans had not developed reliable explosive projectiles. Their simpler incendiary bolts were more than effective enough to allow them to dominate the seas, however. Only the bravest captains ventured far from the coast without having paid the Ordenans their annual tax.

And this wasn't even close to the largest ship in the Ordenan Imperial Navy. They had dozens just like this or bigger. No wonder their appetite for *infusori* was nearly insatiable. He couldn't hope to contend with the Ordenans in a naval war, or any war for that matter, but he might be able to exploit their greed for *infusori*.

When they reached the ship, a cantilevered beam swung over the side, and the sailors there cranked large metal wheels that lowered ropes with hooks on the end. The hooks attached to large rings on the front, the back, and each side of the small rowboat, and the sailors cranked their wheels the opposite way, lifting the rowboat out of the water.

The Captain, a uniformed woman with high cheekbones, olive skin, and wings of grey hair at her temples, greeted them as they stepped onto her ship. "Lord Emrael Ire, son of Maira Tinoas Ire. Welcome to my ship, *Dark Shore*. I am Captain Vairi Boane. You have payment for the requested transport?"

Emrael handed her the box, which she opened to inspect but handed quickly to one of several junior officers standing at attention behind her and to either side.

"One thousand rounds?" she asked simply.

Emrael shrugged. "A deposit, but perhaps fair payment. I need quick transport for ten thousand men, supplies, horses. I requested no fewer than three ships, preferably five. You are only one ship, as far as I can tell."

Captain Boane didn't respond to him; rather, her gaze turned to Jaina, Timan, and the others stepping aboard. The muscles of her jaw flexed once. "Imperators. A representative of your Council requests your presence in the aft cabin."

Emrael stepped forward, stalling her. "We sent an Imperator to you with our offer. Yuuran. Where is he?"

Her face hardened as she turned back to Emrael. "Imperator Yuuran was called back to his homeland by the Council of Imperators, Lord Ire. The affairs of the Empire are not subject to negotiation."

Captain Boane's grim expression grew darker. Marco and two of the male Imperators who had been summoned to the ship walked wide of Emrael to take positions to either side of the Captain.

Emrael stared into the Captain's eyes. "I claim these mages as my own. Any who wish to stay with me, that is." He looked pointedly at the two who had just defected, Imperators he hadn't seen often and whose names he couldn't remember. "If you threaten my people, Captain, I'll take my money back and negotiations will be over."

Captain Boane hesitated. To Emrael's surprise, he felt Marco and the two Imperators draw *infusori*. He felt only a slight tingle at this distance, but the fact that he could feel anything at all from several feet away—and the slight glow in the irises of their eyes— told him that they likely held all the power they could.

He laughed and drew deeply from the *infusori* stored in his armor. Thank the Absent Gods for Ban and his brilliant mind. Power flooded him in an instant. The scars on his hands began to glow, and he was sure his eyes and scars on his face glowed as well. He reached into the pouch at his waist where he kept spare *infusori* coils and drained them as well. He let the empty coils fall to the deck with a dull clink, one after the other. Glory, why didn't he hold power like this all the time? The world seemed so much simpler when he knew he could reduce the ship beneath him to cinders with a touch.

Another Imperator, a handsome man just short of middle age, exited the aft cabin and crossed the deck with swift, sure strides. "Captain, Imperators, stand down. We will not spill blood during a negotiation, certainly not with Lord Ire. He is a friend of the Empire."

The new Imperator turned to Emrael, extending his hand in an offer to shake, seemingly unperturbed by the massive amount of *infusori* coursing through him. "Jeric Alloda. Pleased to make your acquaintance, Lord Ire."

Jaina growled, "Don't touch him, Jeric," and stepped forward in an attempt to keep Jeric at a distance. Emrael took his hand anyway, mental defenses up and ready. No attack came, not even a slight buzz of power.

They released their handshake and stepped back, eyes still locked. Emrael could feel Jaina next to him, wound up like a wolf ready to leap at her prey. Jeric pointedly avoided looking at her. They clearly knew each other.

Emrael put a hand to Jaina's shoulder, keeping his eye on the group of Imperators facing them. Marco and the others still glowed with *infusori,* and the Captain of the ship looked as if she still expected bloodshed. Now that Emrael paused to look around, he saw that dozens of inconspicuous sailors had retrieved small crossbows—sleek and compact, almost certainly an Ordenan *infusori*-Crafted design—and held them at the ready.

"We are here to negotiate only," Emrael said, loud enough for the bystanders to hear clearly. "Even with one ship, you should be able to ferry my army across the river in a day or two, correct? My engineers can construct a temporary dock here and on the other side of the river when the first party lands, and perhaps a barge of sorts. I would have liked more ships to prevent my forces from being split for so long, but I am still willing to pay for your services. Perhaps half of the original price, Captain?"

Captain Boane licked her lips, then nodded. "Agreed. I will begin as soon as your engineers have completed their dock. I will not bring my ship into water shallower than twenty feet, mind you. And no more than five hundred men per trip. Fewer if there are equipment or supplies."

Emrael nodded. "They'll have it done by tomorrow at dawn. We'll move a forward party first, with an outfit of engineers. I'll have the destination ready for you when we board tomorrow. The remaining fifteen hundred rounds will be delivered when the last of my people are safely across."

The Captain nodded in return and gestured at the rowboat, still hanging from the cantilevered beams, a rowing crew still aboard. "My men will take you back to your camp."

As he turned to board, Jeric finally looked to Jaina and Timan. "Jaina, my dear. Nice to see you. And Timan, the Tinoas boy. Should have known where you'd stand."

Jaina spat in Jeric's direction, but Timan remained silent. Emrael locked eyes with Jeric as the rowboat was lowered smoothly to the water. That man would be trouble.

Emrael joined the first group to cross on the *Dark Shore*, boarding the huge ship via a rough timber dock that Darrain and her engineers had miraculously constructed overnight. The rising sun lifted itself above the Duskan Mountains to turn the Lys a shimmering orange, and the myriad animals that made their home along the river woke to chirp and croak and splash in the water. This far outside Atli and this close to the forbidden territory of Trylla, the land and river had grown wild.

He took four companies of his best soldiers to dig in fortifications and to protect a company of engineers as they constructed a dock where they landed just northeast of the mouth of the Sael River, a tributary that flowed into the Lys from a small mountain range in the Bayr Holding and the lowlands of the Ire Holding. They were nearly fifty leagues from Trylla itself and unlikely to be discovered by the main force of the Watchers attacking from the north. Ten thousand men do not travel quietly, however, so Emrael deployed his cavalry in squads to scout the surrounding area as soon as they arrived.

Darrain had her Crafters and engineers placing pilings for the dock that would hopefully be constructed by the time the *Dark Shore* returned with the next load of his soldiers. Large pines and low brush were cleared from the highest hill near the riverbank, tents were erected in surrounding grassy clearings, trenches were dug, and makeshift palisades were built. They wouldn't stay here for long, but Emrael would rather spend the effort to build defenses that would be abandoned than be attacked and not have them.

Emrael occupied a large canvas pavilion erected on a high hill near the riverbank where he, Jaina, Worren, and Timan could watch the construction of their camp and take reports from the scouts as they returned from their assigned routes.

The Royal Guard took shifts guarding the pavilion and the tents reserved for Emrael and his officers, keeping a squad of mages and soldiers nearby at all times. Emrael was pleased to see that the rest of the Imperators that had chosen to stay with them had joined Timan in the Royal Guard. For better or worse, he wanted to keep them close.

Late in the evening of the second day, Emrael and Jaina walked the rock-strewn riverbank to watch as the last load of his men and wagons disembarked from the Ordenan cruiser. Timan and Daglund followed closely. The river-tumbled stones clinked beneath their boots as they strode to the newly constructed dock, and the roiling churn where the clear mountain water of the Sael tributary met the murky water of the Lys mirrored the anxiety and impatience stewing within Emrael.

Undoubtedly, merchant vessels traveling upriver toward High Springs would have seen the huge ship cruising back and forth along the short stretch of the River Lys, but Emrael couldn't do anything about that for now. He simply needed to move faster than the Watchers could react.

As the last of his Legion and wagons cleared it, Emrael and Jaina made their way down the dock and up the gangplank before the Ordenans could cast it off. Emrael waited at the top of the walkway, not setting foot on the ship.

Captain Boane noticed him standing there with his three companions and made her way over to him with brisk, confident steps. "You have my money?"

Emrael waved to Daglund without turning around, and his Guardsman stepped forward to hand a large leather satchel to a man who had followed Captain Boane to meet them. "Fifteen hundred rounds, as agreed. And another hundred rounds besides, because I'd like you to deliver this to your Councils with my compliments."

Emrael pulled a parchment envelope from his belt pouch, as he had no pockets in which to keep such things when he wore his armor, which was almost always these days. Captain Boane accepted the envelope and looked at Emrael expectantly.

"It's an offer that I think they'll want to see for themselves," Emrael replied with a smile. "Assuming I live to retake Trylla, I'll have considerable *infusori* production under my control. I propose an alliance—*infusori* guaranteed to flow to the Ordenan Isles from my Wells in exchange for ships, and men. Bring five ships—five this time!—and someone who can speak for your Councils to Trylla in one month's time. We can sign the deal then."

"I'll deliver it," Captain Boane said simply. "We will moor here for the night, and sail for the Isles at first light."

They nodded to each other, and Emrael turned back the way he had come. His plans were beginning to come together. Now he had a war to win.

Well after nightfall, Emrael stripped his armor and pulled off his boots at the entrance to his large carpeted tent. Toravin had hired a servant for him in Gnalius, a plump older man named Jorim. Toravin had been insistent, said something about maintaining an image.

Jorim took the armor and boots as soon as they hit the floor, already brushing off mud and dust from the day's work as he walked toward his own tent nearby. The quiet, genial man now did his laundry, fetched him meals, and even shaved his face for him. It felt . . . awkward. But he had to admit that it did save him a great deal of time.

"Be careful with those, please, Jorim," he called after the man. "The armor is very precious."

The man didn't bother to respond, obviously not impressed with the admonition. Or perhaps he was hard of hearing; the man was rather old. Emrael wondered sometimes if Toravin hadn't been playing a prank on him in hiring the man.

He washed quickly with a rag and a bit of scented soap in a basin of warm water Jorim had prepared and settled into his cot, determined to get some sleep before the raid to the north he had planned for the morning. Just as his mind began to calm from the frantic pace of the day and anticipation of battle tomorrow, he heard a rapid scuffle of feet followed by a heavy thump on the grassy ground outside. Plenty of activity still buzzed in the camp, but something about the cadence made Emrael's heart race.

He rolled out of his cot and to his feet in an instant. He crouched, eyes darting around his tent for sign of a threat. When his eyes had adjusted to the dark and he decided that he was alone, he snatched his sword from behind the washbasin and crept smoothly from his tent, ducking low in case someone was waiting for him to exit.

Nobody was, but neither was there any sign of the pair of Royal Guardsmen assigned to watch his tent through the night. He couldn't see past the circle of light cast by a single *infusori* coil hung from the flap of his tent, however, as the night was pitch-dark due to heavy clouds that had filled the sky that afternoon.

Something was definitely wrong.

The heavy canvas of his tent had muffled the sound, so Emrael had no way to know which direction the earlier noise had come from. He had a hunch that any trouble would have come from the Ordenans moored at their makeshift dock, however, being that they were newly camped in the middle of nowhere, dozens of leagues from any major settlement. And if he wasn't the Ordenans' primary target, Jaina likely was. She had decided to pitch her tent with the other Imperators in the Royal Guard, as she had personally assumed the role of overseeing their training, teaching both swordcraft and the mage Art. Timan was a fierce fighter, a skilled Battle-Mage, and a capable battle leader in Emrael's opinion, but apparently Jaina found him lacking as an instructor. She found most people to be lacking in one way or another.

A few lit torches stood near the pavilion, atop the hill between his tent and the river. He skirted the hill, staying to the darkness of the overcast night. His bare feet made nearly no sound on the trampled grass as he wove his way through the few tents that had been erected between his and Jaina's: Worren's, Jorim's, and a few supply tents he had wanted close to the command center. The cool night air pebbled his bare skin; he only wore his underbreeches, and wasn't about to take time to dress for propriety's sake.

He held his scabbard in his left hand and his hilt in his right as he ran, ready to draw but keeping the blade covered to keep the firelight from reflecting off of the ancient steel.

He abandoned his caution as he neared Jaina's tent and heard sounds of struggle inside. Large dark lumps lay on the ground nearby, but he didn't pause. Jaina had a tent even larger than his own, and the glow of an *infusori* lighting coil emanated from within, as did periodic grunts of pain. He sprinted, drawing his sword just before he leaped through the flaps of the large tent.

Inside, he found Jaina facing two armed figures in the full copper-alloy scale armor of Imperators, blades in hand. Jaina was dressed only in her thin silk nightdress, and blood ran down one side of her face from an apparent injury on her scalp. She had her back to the closed rear of her tent, feet set squarely. Her blade tip hovered low, almost daring one of her two assailants to attack. One Imperator already lay on the ground clutching a horrible wound in his stomach, intestines spilling from between his fingers as he moaned. Emrael recognized him as one of the Imperators who had been with their army but had stayed with Jeric and Captain Boane after the brief altercation at their first meeting aboard the *Dark Shore*.

"You okay, Jaina?" he asked, not taking his eyes from the two Imperators left standing, a man and a woman who turned her attention to Emrael. He realized with dismay that it was Cailla, the Mage-Healer who had healed him in Trylla not long ago.

"Fine," Jaina replied tersely, launching an attack on her now single assailant. Within three strikes, she put the tip of her blade into the man's thigh, then had to dance to the side and out of range as the Imperator responded with a desperate overhand swing.

Emrael couldn't pay attention to Jaina any longer, as he had his own fight on his hands. Cailla rushed at him with a flurry of strikes, which Emrael only just managed to evade by parrying and stepping back into the dark of the night. Gods, she was fast. Every Imperator he had known was nearly the equal of a Master swordsman in the Provinces, and an adept mage in at least one discipline of the Art besides.

He decided that negotiating was worth a try, as he was far from certain that he'd best her in a swordfight. "Cailla, don't do this. Nobody else has to die."

"*She* does," she hissed, surging forward again. She used a series of feints and a final lunge that Emrael recognized from his years of training with Jaina. He slid smoothly to the side, his bare feet nimble on the grassy earth. Anticipating her attack as he had, he could have dealt her a killing blow in return, but opted for a one-handed throw that would leave him in control of her sword arm.

As soon as he grabbed her wrist and began to twist, however, a sudden shock of *infusori* burst through him like nothing he had felt before. His entire body felt as if it had momentarily been turned to jelly, numb and weak. His grip broke and he stumbled away, though the momentum he had created with the start of the throw carried her over his hip to land headfirst on the packed ground. He stooped to pick up his sword with fingers that felt like sausages and backed away as quickly as he could manage, still struggling to recover from the *infusori* attack. The strength seemed to be returning to his limbs, but his extremities still tingled, and Cailla had already rolled to her feet.

"Don't let her touch you!" Jaina shouted at Emrael from within the tent. "Healers can kill with a mere touch!"

While Emrael would have liked to know that well before this moment, he didn't have the energy to respond. He stepped back farther from the Mage-Healer, using his longer blade to keep her at a comfortable distance, trying to let his hands and feet fully regain feeling.

Cailla wobbled slightly as she regained her feet, clearly disoriented by her hard fall. She looked from Emrael to Jaina, who had managed to turn her opponent and back her way out of her tent to fight on open ground. Jaina's back was now to them, and she was hard-pressed with her own opponent.

The Imperator Healer sneered at Emrael again before she turned from him to sprint toward Jaina.

Emrael lurched forward, running as fast as he could. "Jaina, behind you!"

Jaina dove to one side just before Cailla's blade swept through the space where she had been an instant before. She still hit Jaina in the calf as she adjusted her swing, but Jaina rolled to her feet with her sword at the ready.

A split second later, Emrael planted a kick with all of his momentum behind it at the small of Cailla's back. She flew forward, crashing into the male Imperator hard enough that both tumbled to the ground. Emrael followed them closely as they fell, lunging with his blade to stab the man pinned beneath her in the throat.

Screaming with rage, Cailla rolled away and whipped her blade at him without bothering to regain her feet. Emrael blocked the blow with his scabbard, which he still carried in his left hand. Her sword cut through the tanned hide to bite into his forearm as he spun away from the attack. Blood immediately began to seep down his arm to trickle from his fingers and into the dark grass.

She rolled to her feet once more, and Emrael let her.

"Put down your sword, Cailla. I'll grant you quarter. You'll get back to your ship, I swear it."

Her eyes darted from her dead companions to Emrael, and then in the direction of the waiting Ordenan ship. She hesitated, then shook her head, shifting her grip on her sword.

Just as she and Emrael stepped toward each other for another clash of blades, Jaina appeared out of the night, sword flashing to pierce the Mage-Healer's back, the blood-streaked blade exiting the right side of her rib cage. Jaina pulled her sword out smoothly and stepped back, leaving her former comrade to fall to the ground, choking as blood filled her pierced lungs.

Other Guardsmen and Ire Legionmen were shouting now, running to gather around them in various states of undress.

"She was our last Mage-Healer, Emrael," Jaina said quietly when Cailla finally lay still.

Emrael tore his eyes away from Cailla to look at her. "We have Daglund, right? And Dairus is still at Trylla."

Jaina shook her head again. "Daglund was on guard duty at your tent. If he is not here with you, he is likely dead."

Emrael growled in frustration.

Jaina limped to him and held his wounded arm, inspecting it carefully in the dark. "You need a Legion healer, even if all they can do is stitch you up."

He nodded mutely, planting his sword in the turf since he now had no scabbard from which to hang it. "Are you all right? I saw you limping."

She grimaced, but before she could say anything, Timan arrived.

He was stark naked, sword in hand, hair a mess. He had obviously been asleep or otherwise occupied when he heard the commotion. "What in Glory's bloody name is going on here?" he asked, looking from Emrael and Jaina, who were both barely dressed and covered in blood, some their own, most not. His eyes widened as his gaze took in the Imperators littering the ground. The two outside were dead, but the man Jaina had eviscerated in her tent still groaned in pain.

"My Guardsmen?" he asked.

Emrael simply shook his head.

Timan grimaced, then stalked over to Jaina's tent, apparently completely unabashed at having his genitals dangling about in front of the entire Legion. He threw the flaps to Jaina's tent open and grabbed the wounded Imperator by one ankle to drag him out of the tent. The Imperator mewled in pain as his intestines and other viscera spilled on the ground.

When he was clear of the tent, Timan put a bare foot lightly on the man's chest. "Who gave the order, Dam?" he asked in an oddly calm tone. The Imperator gasped in pain, but shook his head.

Timan stabbed his sword into the man's open gut wound. The Imperator screamed until he had no air left in his lungs.

"Was it Jeric?" Timan asked, again calm. The wounded Imperator nodded frantically as he drew a choking breath.

"Good," Timan murmured, then said more softly, "May the Sisters grant you passage," as he slid the point of his blade into the man's exposed throat, leaning on the sword momentarily to punch through the man's spine. Dam spasmed, then went still save for his mouth, which continued to gasp for air for a moment.

Timan checked on the still forms on the ground, likely the bodies of the Guardsmen that had stood watch near Jaina's tent, then stalked back to Emrael and Jaina, already shouting at nearby Legionmen to fetch a healer for Emrael and Jaina. "I'm going to look for the Guardsmen who were supposed to be at Emrael's tent. You did not see them on your way here?"

Emrael shook his head. "I didn't see them, but I didn't have time to look. We'll be fine, go on. And for Glory's sake, put some pants on."

When a Legion healer, a grizzled man wearing a white armband, finally jogged up to them, Emrael nodded toward Jaina while he held his forearm wound with his good hand. "See to her first. I'll be fine for a moment."

The healer nodded, kneeling and calling for a torch and some stools.

Emrael locked eyes with Jaina while the healer worked on her, cleaning and sewing up the gash in her calf. To her credit, she didn't even flinch.

"Want to help me pull Jeric off that ship and gut him?" Emrael asked, voice rough with anger.

Jaina hesitated, drew a deep breath, then shook her head. "No. He can claim that these Imperators acted on their own. They were technically assigned to me. Captain Boane will back him. If you do not want a war with the Ordenans—and you do not—you will pretend this never happened, and so will the Ordenans. It is how their politics work. You should, however, send a squad to guard the dock. Nobody on or off that ship again."

He nodded and called a nearby Captain Second over to give him the order.

An hour and many stitches later, Emrael and Jaina walked together toward Emrael's tent, where Jorim, placid as ever, had prepared a large tub of hot water for them to wash in.

"You first," Emrael said, giving a mocking bow as he held the flap of his tent. Jaina rolled her eyes but entered with a small smile, then shrugged out of her blood-soaked nightdress immediately. Emrael averted his eyes and closed the tent flap quickly. "Absent Gods, Jaina."

She laughed, exhaustion and emotion heavy in her voice. "I do not have the energy for your proprieties right now, Emrael. Stay out there if you wish, but I am bathing this instant."

Timan found him only a few minutes later as he waited outside the tent, sitting in a wooden camp chair, nursing his wounded forearm.

"I found your guards in the grass about ten paces that way," Timan said. "Alive, by the grace of the Sisters, though Daglund is still unconscious. Nasty lump on his head, someone hit him hard enough that they didn't care whether he woke up or not. Lilan is already awake, though she'll have a headache for a few days."

Emrael pursed his lips in thought. "Why, though? They didn't attack me, only Jaina."

Timan shrugged. "Perhaps you left your tent as they were dragging Daglund and Lilan away, to keep anyone else from noticing them? They may have wanted you alive."

Emrael chuckled incredulously. "They were going to subdue me and just carry me out of camp?"

Timan nodded matter of factly. "Easily done with only rudimentary defenses such as these. Some Imperators I know can use *infusori* to keep light from touching them, to some degree. Malithii do it too. Particularly effective in the dark. Better by far to keep you and anybody a mage might target behind walls from now on. It would be easier on my men and women of the Guard, to be sure."

Emrael sighed and nodded, though it felt wrong to hide behind a wall when his Legionmen were left to fend for themselves outside. "Very well. Do you know anyone that can teach me this trick with the light?"

Timan shook his head. "It is rare, and difficult. Only a few I can think of know it, though others likely hide that they can. Keeping your abilities secret can be a great advantage."

"Like Healing?"

Timan grimaced. "No, not that. I can't think of a reason anyone would hide that their entire life. If we want a Healer, we will have to send to Ordena or hope that more of our Iraean magelings develop that talent on their own. Like Daglund, if he survives. That, or send for your mother. Or the Lady Arielle?"

He shook his head. "I need my mother right where she is. And Elle and I are . . . She has other duties."

Timan smirked. "You are making friends with everyone."

"If I had the energy to stand up, I'd kick your ass."

"Of course you would," Timan laughed.

Jaina, now wrapped in Emrael's soft wool robe, opened the tent flap to raise an eyebrow at them. "Your turn."

Jorim and a small swarm of servants hauled the tub out to dump it in the grass, and others warmed more water in the large pots over the newly rekindled cookfires.

Jaina turned to Timan. "You. Send someone to fetch my travel trunk and my bed. I will be staying in Emrael's tent tonight."

"You'll be what?" Emrael asked, incredulous.

"Don't be a fool," she replied with a smirk. "My tent is full of blood and offal, and you will be safer if I am nearby. I will not rest easy while that ship is still moored here."

22

Sweat rolled down Ban's forehead to sting his eyes as he hoisted stone blocks and roughhewn beams into place between two buildings at the outer edge of the main square. Teams of his Crafters, engineers, and various craftsmen that had followed Emrael to Trylla did similar work at various points all around the square, building a large ringwall along broad avenues that traversed this part of the city while the bulk of the Legion defended the river wall to the north. All of the civilians had been gathered in the inner fortress with the Legion, and many had volunteered to help put a barrier between the invading army and their families.

They stacked stone from buildings that had already fallen on the other side of the avenues—or that Garrus's engineers had pulled down to create more clear space on the other side of their wall—to build walls with steps leading up the interior that the defenders could use to fight from, like a bulwark.

Ban and his Crafters weren't exactly used to this level of physical activity, but the threat of imminent death spurred them to their task right along with the men and women who were accustomed to such labor. The distant sounds of fighting—crashes of steel on steel, the shouts and horns sounded by the defenders, and an occasional scream—were a constant reminder of why they worked themselves to the bone. Building fortifications suited Ban far better than fighting Watchers in the streets.

Of course, their makeshift defenses weren't nearly as good as the sheer walls a true fortress like Whitehall Keep or the Citadel would have, but they had effectively turned a square mile of city into the next best thing. Unless there were Malithii who had replicated Darrain's explosives in large numbers, Ban reckoned that their five thousand should be able to hold it against even overwhelming numbers. They just needed another hour or two to finish this last wall on the north side and two or three other spots on the southeast side of their pseudo-fortress. Ban had deemed the southern walls lower priority, seeing that the enemy was almost certain to attack from the north, where they could cross any of several bridges across the River Lys that split the ruined city. Garrus hadn't had the opportunity to take down the bridges with so little warning, and Emrael hadn't wanted them taken down earlier because he would need them for his imminent campaign against Marol and the Watchers in the north. With no viable fords or bridges for leagues in either direction, the battlegrounds were well set.

A horn sounded nearby, much closer than any had before, maybe just a few streets from where they were working. The wall was only built about half as high as they needed it to be. Ban's crew redoubled their efforts, exhausted though they were.

The crash of steel on steel and screams of wounded men erupted nearby. Very near. Ban had just looked up from his work when a squad of Ire Legionmen ran from a nearby alleyway and into the cleared avenue, panic clear on their faces. The unfinished barrier Ban and his crew were working on was their best chance at escape back into the fortifications, and they sprinted straight for it, some of the men even dropping their shields to run faster.

The Ire Legionmen standing on building rooftops and atop the finished stone barricades to either side aimed their crossbows and conventional longbows, but held their arrows until men in the blue coats of the Watchers boiled from nearly every alleyway in sight. There were hundreds of them running after the ten poor Iraeans fleeing from what must have been a massacre at the river wall.

"Shoot!" a soldier overhead roared, and hundreds of crossbow and longbow strings slapped in a rolling wave, sending bolts and arrows streaming from rooftops, empty windows on street-facing buildings, and from behind the stone barricades.

Dozens of Watchers were struck and crumpled, folding around their wounds to squirm and twitch on the ground. Their comrades who had survived the volley hesitated, looking from the fortifications in front of them to their fallen friends in shock. The Iraeans in their makeshift cityscape fortress continued shooting as fast as they could reload their weapons. More Watchers dropped to the

muddy cobbles, and within seconds the surviving Watchers retreated to the cover of the few buildings still standing on the far
side of the avenue.

Ban was left gasping for air, shaking with adrenaline. The avenue was quiet save for the moans and cries of the wounded who
squirmed in growing puddles of their own blood. The small group
of retreating Iraean soldiers had climbed over the wall right next
to Ban, pulled up by several of the workmen who still labored to
finish the wall even during the skirmish. They now sat in a small
cluster, breathing heavily. One of them began to sob.

Ban approached to ask them quietly, "What happened?"

One of the soldiers, a solidly built older man with iron-grey hair
and bright blue eyes, closed his eyes as he responded in a voice
raspy with emotion and exhaustion. "We just didn't have enough
men. We shot hundreds of them, maybe thousands. But we ran out
of crossbow bolts, even ran out of arrows. The Watchers and their
priests brought those . . . monsters. Those things that look like
people, but all grey and half-rotted. We killed so many, but they
took one of the buildings in the wall that hadn't been all bricked
up. . . . We ran when they got through. There were just too many,
Lord Ire. Too many."

An Ire Legion officer, an Iraean Captain Second Ban didn't
know but had seen in Garrus's meetings, had arrived to hear most
of the man's report. He asked from behind Ban's shoulder, "And
the rest of our men, Sergeant?"

The older sergeant opened his eyes to stare at the Captain
Second for a moment before answering with a shake of his head.
"I don't know, Captain Withan. I don't know. There were a lot
of us still up on the wall, and plenty in reserve. But . . . well, you
saw. There were at least twenty thousand between the Watchers and
Marol's men, not counting those monsters. They came through
damn quick, sir. Damn quick."

Captain Withan cursed, then called a page over to him. "Tell
Captain First Imarin that we are holding for now, and that the
holes in the wall to the south need to be finished immediately.
We're about to be surrounded. Minimal survivors from the battalions
on the wall."

"May the Ancestors welcome their souls," the Captain muttered as the page ran off with the message, then looked to Ban. "There were three thousand men on the river wall," he said quietly. "We're going to need whatever tricks you and your engineers can cook up for us, Lord Ire. Do you have any more of the explosive devices?"

Ban smiled sadly back at the officer. "We have a few surprises for them, hidden in those buildings across the street and in larger buildings all between here and the river wall. When you give the word, I can bring most of the buildings in sight down on their heads to buy us some time."

"All at once?" Captain Withan asked.

"Yes. I'm afraid I only have a single actuator for the explosive Craftings. They will all explode at once."

Captain Withan nodded. "We'll let them fill those buildings up, then. Let them start their next assault. I imagine it will come tonight, or sooner. We'll want to kill as many of the bastards as we can with your magic, maybe scare them into a temporary retreat so we can look for any of our men that managed to hold out. Be ready to bring them down on my signal."

Then louder, he called to his men, sergeants and a few Captains Third that had gathered for orders in the aftermath of the first repelled assault. "I need scouts! One hundred men to look for survivors and tell me what in Glory's dark name is going on out there. A half-round to each man for a day's work! Have them ready in ten minutes."

23

Emrael sat atop his horse, squinting through the late-morning sun at the stone-paved road nestled at the bottom of the gently sloped hills on which they waited, nearly ten leagues from his base camp at the junction of the Sael and Lys rivers. The stone-paved road was in poor shape from half a century of neglect and disuse, but the stones had kept most trees and brush from growing, leaving a relatively bare strip through the dense forest that was clearly visible for leagues from this vantage.

Countless towering evergreens and an occasional hulking hardwood carpeted the sea of gentle hills here in the heart of the Ire Holding. A farmstead or small village interrupted the sea of deep green with patches of brighter green or rich brown here and there along the old road. This was the old country, thousands of leagues of land in any direction full of hardy Iraean folk who had likely rarely seen a Watcher before this campaign on Trylla. Folk who held to the old ways.

He flexed his left hand, testing his injured arm. The deep gash to the outside of the forearm hurt, to be sure, but what concerned him most was the persisting numb feeling and weakness in his hand. Daglund might have been able to do something for him, but had taken such a knock to the head that he still couldn't see straight. He and everyone else had to settle for the services of ordinary Legion healers back at camp, who thankfully had the necessary apparatus to accelerate healing with *infusori* coils, but were a far cry from being able to perform the nearly instant miracles of an Imperator Mage-Healer.

Emrael hadn't been willing to delay his planned raids to undergo such treatment. He would just need to strap a shield tightly to that arm when it came time to fight. There would be time to heal fully when Ban and the people in Trylla were safe.

Jaina sat on her horse next to him in the trees next to a hilltop clearing that gave them a clear view of the road for nearly a league to the north. Their scouts had captured a small Watcher foraging party, and those prisoners had revealed that reinforcements were due from Torrevahle in the north any day now.

Emrael had four thousand of his men arrayed in battle lines all along the road, a ways back into the woods to remain out of sight and to muffle sound. His scouts and several companies of cavalry were positioned in full squads to either side of the road in a broad radius with orders to intercept any Watcher scouts. He couldn't afford to let any of them give warning.

Worren led another four battalions twenty or so leagues farther to the east, similarly planning an ambush on any forces going to or from Trylla by way of Vahle, Torrevahle's twin city. They had left Captain Second Durmac Faerwin in charge of the remaining two battalions, tasked with further fortifying and defending the camp back at the mouth of the Lower Sael River. Emrael was taking risks splitting his army into three parts, but outnumbered as he was, risks were necessary.

Just as he was thinking about heading back into the trees to wait with the main body of his troops, ten or so men on horseback appeared on the horizon, traveling the old road at a fast canter. As they drew nearer it became obvious that they wore Iraean green. Emrael sent a Captain Third down to the road to flag them and bring them to where he waited with Jaina, Timan, a squad of Royal Guards, and two more Captains Third who waited to relay commands to the Captains Second who led Emrael's four waiting battalions.

In short order, the ten scouts made it up the hill and dismounted to rest their horses, who breathed heavily, clearly exhausted. Their sergeant stepped forward to salute as he reported.

"Sergeant Yorley, Lord Ire, First Battalion scouts. Watchers are moving south. Three leagues or so behind us. Near five thousand of the bastards, and a wagon train half a league long. Their scouts should reach here in an hour or so."

Emrael nodded his thanks. "Excellent work, Sergeant. How many scouts, and in what formation? How is the main body arrayed?"

The sergeant shook his head. "Hard to say about the scouts, Lord. We saw two pair riding less than half a league from their main force, to either side of the road. They have a company riding vanguard few hundred paces in front. The rest of 'em are in ranks marching down the road as easy as you please. Ain't even carryin' shields."

Emrael smiled. "Thank you, Sergeant. One of these Captains Third here will record that you and your squad will each be awarded a copper mark for your success."

He turned to the Captains Third attending him. "Tell the battalion Captains to line up every bow we have in the trees along the west side of the road just there before it reaches this clearing. They're to keep at least thirty paces back from the tree line, out of sight. They will hold their weapons until the Watchers are fully stretched along our formation. We need to kill a lot of them with that first volley if we want to even the odds."

He paused for a moment, looking to Jaina. She surveyed the spot Emrael had chosen and said, "Put soldiers with shields ten paces behind them for cover, they can retreat after the first two volleys and shoot from behind a shield wall."

Emrael looked back to his Captains Third. "Three ranks ten paces behind them with shields on both sides of the road, pikes every second man in the second rank. Two volleys from the bowmen on the west side of the road, then the ranks advance. I want every crossbow and longbow we have on that line. Third Battalion will have their horse ready to charge the vanguard, First Battalion horse will cut off the retreat. We're killing or capturing the lot of them."

The Captains Third saluted and jogged off into the woods. Emrael turned to Sergeant Yorley and his squad of scouts. "I want you to wait here, spread out in pairs across this little valley. Capture any of their scouts that come near, fast and quiet. Put on their uniforms and ride ahead of the Watchers' main force. Let them see you, but not up close. If they send anyone to fetch a report, ride away calmly. We need to lead them into the trap without letting their scouts find our main body."

The sergeant saluted and his squad jumped back in their saddles, nudging their poor horses back down the hill and into the trees on the other side of the road.

Emrael and his company of Royal Guards—Timan had been recruiting heavily to bolster their numbers—took position at the northern end of the ranks of foot soldiers that formed up quietly in the dense woods beside the road. The trees nearest the road were newer growth than the giant conifers that dominated the ancient forest farther from the road, and that thick new growth made a perfect screen to hide them from the Watchers riding south on the old road.

A hush fell over the Ire Legion as the sounds of hooves and boots on stone reached them. Soon Emrael could see flickers of motion through the thick brush. The dust kicked up by the column rolled over them, tickling his nose and throat. His scouts had done their job. Or at the very least, the Watchers' scouts had failed to do theirs.

Emrael held up a hand to remind the men to wait in silence, and his officers relayed the silent signal down the ranks. He grew anxious, waiting for a Watcher to look too closely to either side. The Watcher column continued unabated, however.

The Captain Third who led a company of crossbowmen and regular archers crouched in the bushes just a dozen paces in front of where he and his Royal Guard waited. The Captain Third finally signaled for his men to ready their weapons and they stood, tensed and waiting. He brought his arm down sharply and shouted, "Release!"

The cascade of snapping strings was met quickly by a cacophony of screams and curses. A second snap of strings and wave of screams, and the archers shuffled to get behind the shield wall.

It was time for action.

"Forward ranks!" Emrael shouted. He took a place in the second rank and followed the line of shield-bearing Guards.

They moved through the brush and crossed the shallow trough next to the ancient roadway at a fast walk. The Watchers hadn't fully recovered from the volleys, which had hit with brutal efficacy at such close range. Hundreds lay bleeding on the ground. Most still standing had stowed their shields with the supply wagons for the march, though a few had retrieved theirs and now tried to cover their friends. Not enough of them, however.

Emrael's shield wall met a disorganized line of Watchers who, though they outnumbered the Ire Legionmen nearly two to one, had no choice but to retreat. Unfortunately for them, a wall of Ire shields also advanced from the opposite side of the road.

Ire swords and pikes skewered the defenseless Watchers who had now been herded together on the far side of the roadway. Crossbow bolts and arrows still flashed overhead from where the bowmen had remained uphill, now sowing death and panic among the milling Watchers with calculated shots rather than volleys. Some turned to flee back up the road to the north, where the Iraeans had left an open escape route, but most stayed and died as they tried to fight off the ambush.

Battle joy sang in Emrael's veins and was amplified by the *infusori* he pulled from his Crafted armor. From his position in the second rank, he thrust his sword through the overlapped shields of his men again and again, stabbing the Watchers that hacked and pushed at the shield wall in vain. His sword soon dripped blood.

He pulled back from the battle line to catch his breath, walking back behind the lines to shout orders to his bowmen who maintained their position on the hillside, calling for them to direct their bolts at the Watchers mounting a resistance to either side of the attacking Iraean shield wall.

As the battle progressed, the shrinking numbers of Watchers contracted into two groups, cut off to the south by the Ire shield wall that had come together and fused ranks to corral the Watchers north, back along the road they had traveled.

The Ire lines pressed forward, using what was now a significant advantage of numbers and support from bowmen still shooting from the hill to wreak havoc on the Watchers. Emrael could tell that the day was theirs, and many of the Watchers had obviously realized it as well. They desperately moved to retreat. Some ran clear of the Ire lines and continued running down the road or into the forest, anywhere they could escape the slaughter Emrael had unleashed on them. Most, however, ran only long enough to get clear and seemed to be trying to form up again, despite being severely outnumbered.

Emrael raised a flag, a signal to the mounted companies on either side of the road to charge the routed Watchers. They slashed with their long sabers as they clashed with the disorganized and shieldless Watchers at the rear of the enemy formations. Men screamed in pain and panic, and suddenly the Watchers lost their nerve. Slowly at first, and then in a wave, they threw down their shields and weapons to run into the trees or dropped to their knees, crying for surrender.

His men were forced to kill a few more Watchers who didn't realize their comrades had surrendered, but soon the battlefield was quiet save for the screams, sobs, and moans of the wounded. It felt wrong to Emrael to not have fought more himself, but he had to admit that it had probably been for the best. Blood trickled down his forearm in a steady stream from the wound he had taken fighting the Imperator days earlier. It must have torn open during the brief time he had taken part in the battle.

When the wounded had been tended to and the captives had been rounded up, Emrael called for his Captains Third to join him under a small canvas canopy while a Legion healer set up a folding table to restitch his bleeding wound.

"Casualties?" Emrael asked his three battalion leaders without preamble.

The officers exchanged looks before the bearded Captain Second Selvin Varlut, an experienced former officer in the Norta Guard, stepped forward. "One hundred and fifty-seven dead, four hundred and twelve wounded, Lord Ire. Best estimates put Watcher dead at over three thousand, fifteen hundred captured."

Emrael winced as the man tending his wound cut away the cloth bandage and began to pick the thread out of his torn wound. The edges of the deep gash were swollen and inflamed, especially where the stitches had torn, but thankfully did not smell foul.

He looked back to Captain Varlut. "Excellent, thank you, Varlut. And how many of them fled?"

"Five hundred or so, I'd say, some likely to be wounded. We've already sent four parties of cavalry after them, five squads to a party. We'll make sure they won't be a problem for us anytime soon, sir."

Emrael smiled, trying to ignore the pain radiating from his left arm as the healer did his work. "Perfect. And the supplies captured?"

Another of the Captains Second stepped forward. Derril Gunnard, a former Watcher, if he remembered correctly. "Our clerks are still searching the wagons, but it looks like rations. Lots of them. Salted fish, venison, pork, beef, beans, millet, barley, oats, wheat, the usual. Probably meant to feed the entire Watcher army for several weeks."

Emrael nodded, thinking. "Good. Let them go hungry. Our people trapped in Trylla are probably going to starve first, however, so it doesn't help all that much. Any weapons, *infusori* stores, money?"

Captain Second Gunnard shook his head. "Not much, Lord, besides what the Watchers were carrying for themselves and a few wagons of *infusori* coils meant to recharge their Crafted crossbows, no doubt. We've given our men leave to take armor and weapons from the dead and captured as they see fit. The rest will be loaded in the wagons."

"Well done. See that our bowmen are all outfitted with any *infusori*-Crafted crossbows recovered, whether they want to trade in their bows or not. Train them quickly. Crafted crossbows are too valuable, too effective to let them go to waste."

The three Captains Second nodded along with him. They knew their business.

Captain Second Varlut shuffled his feet. "Sir, what do we do with the prisoners?"

His officers knew that they didn't have plans to stay in any one place for long. This ambush had been designed to draw the Watchers' attention northward, and to secure supplies. They didn't have time to deal with prisoners. They were obviously worried about the measures Emrael was willing to take.

He met each of their eyes. "Wounded will go on wagons as needed. We'll march the rest back to our camp. If any of them lags on the march, take his boots and turn him loose."

The Captains nodded in speculative appreciation. Gunnard smiled. "I think by the end of the war we'll have a lot more volunteers from their ranks, Lord Ire. Our boys will have a chat with them on the way, I'm sure. Many of the survivors are Iraean folk. Was the Corrandians who kept fighting the longest."

Emrael hissed in pain as the healer probed his now-unsutured wound, but then forced himself to match Gunnard's smile. "I hope so, Captain. Get the men ready to move. I want to be on our way within the hour."

24

Ban shuffled through several Observer devices arrayed on his desk, powering each one and connecting it to a similar device to ensure it functioned properly. He'd been locked away in his office for hours, feverishly working to give Garrus and his Legionmen any advantage he could in the fighting that was to come.

These modified Observer Craftings were far from his best work. Ugly and simple, but functional. They would transmit more or less within line of sight, which should work for what he had planned.

Finally satisfied, he placed each one carefully in the cloth-lined wooden case he had prepared, secured the lid, and hurried out of the Crafters' Hall. As soon as he stepped out the door into the afternoon sun, the smell of feces and unwashed bodies nearly made him retch, as it always did. One of his more practical Crafters had worked with an engineer to build a device that drew air from the roof of the Crafters' Hall to create positive pressure inside the building, keeping the stench at bay.

Their soldiers had taken heavy casualties when the Watchers had broken through the river wall, but even still they had nearly four thousand Ire Legionmen and almost an equal number of camp followers, tradespeople, and farmers crammed into their hastily built fortress. Ban had done his best to design trenches that emptied outside the walls for sanitary use, but they had quickly proven insufficient—and getting people to use the public latrines had proven more difficult than he would have believed. He just hoped that the water wells inside the fortifications didn't foul. Nobody had gotten sick from the water that he knew of, but it was just a matter of time, most likely. He made a mental note to have a team of engineers work on a water-purification system . . . assuming they had any *infusori* and other materials left to make one.

Garrus, his officers, and Ban's own officers from his newly formed company of engineers and Crafters waited for him in the main square, where Garrus had erected a large canvas tent that served as their command post. He certainly could have used one of the large buildings surrounding the square—Ban had even offered his own that Jaina and Emrael had used, but Garrus wanted the people trapped with them to see that he was working to protect them.

When he arrived at the tent, he set his case on a table and nodded to the Captain First, who called in the ten Legion volunteers waiting outside. Ban handed his box to one of his trusted Crafters, Lerran, who in turn handed the Craftings out.

Ban waited until each volunteer had an Observer in hand before he began his instructions. "These Craftings are rather simple. The actuator is the only part you need to know—a lever, just here," he said, holding up the device he had kept for himself. "Press the lever until you feel it click, and hold it while you speak. My receiver in the Crafters' Hall will pick up the transmission, where my people will be ready to record your report and take the information to Captain First Garrus and his officers. Questions?"

One of the men raised his hand timidly. Ban nodded at him. "Yes?"

"I was just wondering," said the young man, probably only eighteen or so. "Can you talk back to us through them? Tell us when the blue bastards are near our position, that kind of thing?"

Ban hesitated. He could have built the Craftings to do that, but had rushed to complete these transponders as quickly as possible. "No, Legionman, I'm afraid not. Your Craftings can transmit sound, but don't receive."

Captain Garrus cut in. "The extra coin you'll receive when the job is done is because this is dangerous work. And it *is* dangerous, make no mistake. But we'll do what we can to keep you safe. We'll have maps marked with grids for each of you, like this one, and you should move as needed to stay clear of any Watcher forces moving through. None of you will be stationed where there is likely to be fighting."

Garrus turned to the map hung in the tent, where the city surrounding the fortifications had been marked over with numbered sections. Each number corresponded to a section of a ring around the fortifications in any given direction. The grid marked with the number five, for example, was a section of the city between one thousand and two thousand paces from the wall of their fortification, directly north from the northmost wall.

"Each of you will be assigned a grid number to occupy. When you get into position—and remember, get high where you can see, but stay hidden—relay your position as closely as you are able. We'll avoid targeting your immediate surroundings with Lord Ban's explosive Craftings," he said, gesturing to nearly a dozen catapults stationed nearby, each aimed in a different direction. Crews still surrounded each, finishing construction or conducting training with dummy loads.

Captain First Garrus paused, and his face grew grim. His voice was lower, heavier when he spoke again. "If we are to survive this siege, you boys are going to have to do extraordinary work. Our supplies are almost gone, and we likely won't survive another assault unless we know precisely where and when to strike. Let the blue bastards gather in close, in large numbers before you give the signal. We'll only have one shot at this."

The volunteers looked somber, but determined. The Captain gave them each a silent nod of gratitude. "They'll likely be planning another attack for tomorrow, so you'll go over the wall tonight, one by one, in dark clothing. Get in position, then call out your targets in the morning when the Watchers move in. Take enough supplies to last for several days in your positions, just in case. Staying put will be key to you staying alive."

Ban took a deep breath to steady himself as he surveyed the gathered scouts to make sure they had the right of operating the Craftings.

Tomorrow would be full of fire and blood, one way or another.

Darmon Corrande stood next to the shell of a relatively whole stone building in the ruins of Trylla, using his telescoping looking glass to study the fortifications at the city center. The Iraeans still manned their makeshift barricades and the buildings they had reinforced to create a rather formidable wall around their encampment.

Though the meager predawn light made it difficult, he spotted dozens of bowmen and other soldiers ready to loose on the

Watchers if they drew close. Hundreds of decaying corpses in blue uniforms already littered the hundred paces or so of cleared area immediately outside the fortifications, proof of the price that would be paid to take those walls and kill the rebels within. Whoever held command of the fortifications knew their business.

The Malithii priests who effectively led this army were insistent that they take the city today, however. Word had just reached them yesterday that their supply wagons and reinforcements had been ambushed, with only minimal survivors. Rather than try to hunt down a roving band of rebels, the priests wanted to end the rebellion here and now. They saw Trylla as the only real threat, despite the fact that someone had just killed or captured nearly ten thousand men fewer than twenty leagues to their north. Darmon was sure it was Emrael himself, despite reports that he and his forces were engaged somewhere in the Syrtsan Holding.

Even still, the dark priests were hesitant to commit any of the soulbound monsters they had brought with them, preferring to send Watchers or Corrandian Legionmen to their death. They were saving the foul beasts for something Darmon didn't intend to stick around for.

"We must move closer, boy," the Malithii priest next to him hissed. "Your orders are to be on the edge of the cleared lane, and to attack at the signal! Not hiding nearly five thousand paces from their walls!"

Ostensibly his "advisor," the stocky little tattooed bastard clearly thought he was in command.

Darmon ignored him, still peering at the fortifications through his looking glass. "They have men using looking glasses in the highest windows of the outer buildings," he murmured to the Watcher officer standing next to him, Captain Second Teuri Vaslat, a native Corrandian. Vaslat grunted his acknowledgement. He and Darmon had become fast friends in the last weeks. It turned out that Darmon wasn't the only one who wanted to be rid of the Malithii. Far from the only one who wanted them gone, in fact.

"Did you hear me, boy?" the Malithii priest demanded, his accented voice louder. The priest—Darmon had just met the ass this morning, and couldn't tell the Malithii names apart anyhow—

stalked toward Darmon, his face wrinkled in a furious snarl. "You listen, I will—"

Darmon calmly collapsed his telescope using the stump of his right arm, pointedly ignoring the priest as he slipped it into a leather case and then into a pocket sewn into the inside of his coat. As the priest drew within striking distance, Darmon pulled the dagger from his belt and lunged at the dark-robed man in one smooth motion. The priest moved to the side lightning-quick, securing Darmon's good arm with both hands to disarm him.

Darmon felt a painful tingle where the priest touched the bare skin of his hand, then an instant later, Darmon was racked with pain. His vision turned white around the edges as he sank helplessly to his knees.

What the priest hadn't counted on, however, was Captain Second Vaslat, who stabbed the Malithii bastard through the heart with his short sword, twisting the blade as he pulled it out of the priest's back.

The pain coursing through Darmon disappeared. The Malithii priest sank to the rubble-strewn ground, gasping and croaking as the life bled from him to sate the parched dust of the crumbling city.

"Right," Darmon said breathlessly as Vaslat helped him to his feet. "That hurt. Let's just shoot the next one."

Vaslat smiled grimly as he stooped to clean his blade on the dead Malithii's robes.

Darmon turned to walk back to where their battalion waited in the ruins. "We need to get out of here, and quickly. Send men to Durit and the other Captains. Any who want to join us must do it now. We're riding back the way we came, across the river and then west. That's where Ire will be."

"We're leaving already?" Vaslat asked, surprised. "I thought we were going to wait until the battle had well and truly begun."

Darmon waved his hand back at the fortifications without stopping, though he began visually scanning the taller buildings around him. "Those men aren't just watching for attackers. There are too many for that, and they're not even looking at the ground. They're looking at the rooftops, or perhaps the horizon. I don't know what tricks they have up their sleeve, but I don't want to be the ones to find out."

Captain Second Vaslat looked at Darmon askance but relayed the orders to move the battalion out of the city. None of the officers asked where the Malithii priest who had been with them had gone.

By the time Darmon reached a large building near the river, two squads of his men had apprehended a man hiding in the upper floors and held him in the street, one man on either arm and a third with a sword drawn and held lightly against the man's chest. The man himself was young, hardly more than a boy, and his mismatched black woolen clothing had seen better days. Odds were good that this lad was a follower of Ire's.

"Men, please," Darmon said soothingly as he reached the group. "There's no need for the weapon. Is there, friend?"

The Iraean's head snapped up, hope suddenly bright in his eyes. He had clearly thought that his life was about to come to an end. He jerked his head from side to side violently. "No, no need for weapons, Lord," he said breathlessly.

"Good," Darmon said. "My men and I are leaving shortly, and I'll let you scurry back up that tower when we do. But only if you tell me exactly what you're doing out here."

The boy's eyes flicked to and from Darmon's face as he clenched his fists nervously. "I'm sorry, Lord, but I can't. I can't." His voice nearly broke, but his jaw was set with determination.

Darmon fought to quell the anger that surged inside him. He couldn't question the boy properly if he was to maintain goodwill with the Ires, and that had to be his primary aim.

Darmon sucked his front teeth irritably, but finally waved his hand at the Watchers holding the poor Iraean boy. "He has something in his hand. Get it for me."

The young Iraean Legionman struggled, but not so hard that Darmon's men were forced to hurt him. Not badly. In short order, they handed a small piece of metal over. A short lever stuck out from one side of a complicated Crafting. He depressed the lever, but nothing happened.

"What does it do, boy?"

The Iraean Legionman squirmed again, but when Vaslat moved toward him, he squealed, "It's to talk to the camp. To Lord Ire."

"Emrael Ire is inside the fortifications?" Darmon asked, surprised.

The boy shook his head. "No, no. The younger Lord. Banron."

"I just press the lever and speak into it? He will hear me?"

The boy nodded mutely, tears rolling down his ruddy cheeks.

Darmon considered a moment, then depressed the lever and held the Crafting close to his face.

"This is Darmon Corrande. I understand that Banron Ire will be on the other side of this Crafting."

He paused, looking to the Iraean boy again.

"It doesn't speak, Lord."

Darmon grimaced but pressed the lever again. "Banron, I apologize sincerely for any previous . . . animosity. We have a greater enemy in common now."

Silence.

"I propose an alliance. I'm taking your man with me, but he will not be harmed. I've arranged for a sizable contingent of United Provincial Legionmen to join me in abandoning the Malithii priests. My hope is to find your brother somewhere to the north and join my forces with his."

He turned to ask Captain Vaslat why the men weren't marching yet—the Malithii would not stay ignorant of his betrayal for long. Before he had uttered a word, however, the ground shook and an incredible sound tore the air around him. A blinding flash of blue light preceded a massive cloud of dust and rubble that enveloped them. Next he knew, he was picking himself up from the ground, choking as he tried to breathe in the cloud of dust.

He ducked into a nearby ruin and pulled his shirt over his face, straining to breathe for several minutes while the dust cleared outside. When it did, he stumbled into the street to assess the situation. He stopped when he caught sight of the Ire fortifications, stupefied. The ring of buildings closest to the Iraean fortifications were gone. Not knocked down—they no longer existed! There had been thousands of Watchers lined up in those streets, waiting for the order to assault the fortifications. Thousands dead in an instant. What could do that?

"Gods ascended," he murmured to himself.

Captain Vaslat ran to him from where he sheltered with a group of men in the cavernous first floor of another nearby ruined stone building. "Lord Corrande, you're hurt," Vaslat said, reaching his hand toward Darmon's head.

Darmon frowned, pressing his forearm to his scalp. His dusty sleeve turned muddy red with blood. "It's nothing. No pain. I'll see to it when we're out of the city."

A flying piece of rubble must have grazed him. He hadn't even noticed, shocked as he had been. Some others had not been so lucky. Here and there a blue-uniformed lump lay in the street, covered in rubble and heaps of fine dust. Their comrades already moved to help them, and Vaslat now stalked the street, calling out orders to his officers.

"What in Glory's dark name was that?" Vaslat asked, taking a break from barking orders to stop next to Darmon and peer around in nervous wonder.

"Banron Ire," he said simply. "That little bastard is the most talented Crafter since the Ravan Empire. Better than the Ordenans or the Malithii, probably. We don't want to be here when he shows his next surprise. Send word to the other Captains who want to leave, if they're still alive. We're going now and will not wait for stragglers. And bring me the head of that Malithii we killed."

Ban covered his ears and ducked behind a stone wall as the order came to actuate the hidden explosives. He counted to thirty to allow time for the signal to reach everyone in the compound and allow them to seek shelter.

"Cover!" he called loudly, then depressed the lever on his transponder. He had seen plenty of these explosives detonated, but this particular explosion surprised even him. A wave of pure *infusori* energy washed over him with an accompanying clap of thunder, followed quickly by a cloud of thick dust and raining rubble.

He had tweaked a few aspects of Darrain's design for the explosive Craftings, but he hadn't expected *that* much of an increase in output.

When the dust had cleared, he raised his head to peer at the outer fortifications and was relieved to see that the buildings and stone barricades still held. For the most part. Large stone blocks had been blown from the tops of barricades here and there, and a few deteriorated spots on buildings had collapsed in the blast, though the explosives had been placed several hundred paces from the fortifications. The damage to the city—and the Watchers preparing to assault them—must have been massive.

He jogged to the building on the outer ring that served as a lookout point, taking the stairs two at a time to reach the highest floor, where recessed windows provided a protected view of the surrounding city.

The blocks of buildings nearest to the fortifications were gone, flattened by the blast. Large craters marked each spot where an explosive had been placed. He was too stunned to count them precisely, but it looked as if every one of his Craftings had detonated. He felt a surge of pride and a sick sense of awe as he turned his attention to the human cost of his work.

Before the blast, the lookouts had estimated that a full ten thousand Watchers were lined up in the surrounding streets, preparing for an assault. None were visible in the wreckage now, though here and there he spotted a ragged pile of blue cloth or glint of metal amid the rubble and dust.

As he watched, a few Watchers in dust-covered uniforms stumbled to the edge of the blast radius to blankly stare at where ranks of their comrades had stood just minutes ago.

"Sir. Lord Ire. Sir." A Legion runner pulled at his elbow, trying to get his attention.

Ban turned to stare at him a moment before shaking his head and blinking to clear his thoughts. "Yes, what is it, Legionman? Repeat everything, I wasn't listening properly."

The runner nodded patiently. "We've had a message, Lord Ban, from one of our spotters out in the city."

Ban frowned. "They aren't supposed to call in catapult instructions until the Watchers move in for a second assault. That might not happen today, after the blast," he said, waving his hand at the wreckage below.

The runner shook his head. "No, Lord, it's not that. One of the men, Yren, transmitted just minutes ago. Or rather, Darmon Corrande did using Yren's Crafting. He had a message for you and Lord Emrael, sir."

Ban felt a pit in his stomach, remembering the brutal beating he had suffered at Darmon's hand. "Go on," he said, face solemn.

"Darmon Corrande said he apologizes for past animosity, and

that he wants an alliance with you and your brother, Lord Ban. He says he's taking some Watchers north to join Lord Emrael."

Ban frowned, puzzled. That didn't sound like Darmon, not at all. It was likely a trap of some sort, but he couldn't for the life of him think how Darmon might be trying to lay it. He couldn't believe they'd let their guard down so easily. And why would he say that Emrael was to the north?

"Thank you, Legionman. Record the transmission and get back to your post."

25

At dawn two days after their ambush on the Watcher reinforcements, Emrael, Worren, Jaina, and their senior officers convened at the apex of a large hill a few leagues to the north and west of Trylla that provided a good view of their planned approach. After the successful ambush, Emrael had met up with Worren, who had led a successful raid of his own, though the Watcher party he had ambushed had been smaller. Their combined captives were now under guard at their camp at the mouth of the Lower Sael River, while the bulk of their ten thousand moved toward Trylla.

The hill they occupied was too far from the city to see anything but clumps of tents and vague hints of motion at the very limit of human vision. Even with a looking glass, they could only guess at troop types and numbers, but it appeared as though a large portion of the Watchers' forces had crossed the river to the south side of the city and had torn down large sections of the river wall that Garrus had constructed. Even so, the reserves left in the large Watcher camp at the northern edge of the city numbered at least as many as the men Emrael commanded, maybe more.

The biggest mystery, by far, had been the flash of blue light near the center of Trylla, and the accompanying blast that had been audible even here, leagues away.

Garrus seemed to have created fortifications of a sort around the grand square they had first occupied, and as far as they could tell from here, those were still standing. A good sign.

That the blast had been caused by some sort of *infusori* Crafting was obvious, but Emrael could only hope that it had been Ban's doing.

Now that they were within eyesight, Emrael had tried over and over to hail Ban on the Observer Crafting he still wore around his neck, but all he could get was a strange crackling noise through the device. He wondered why the thing was normally silent and now made this odd noise, but what mattered was that he couldn't contact Ban to coordinate plans and make sure they were all okay. Perhaps when they drew closer.

Just as Emrael was about to give the order to continue their march, an entire contingent of Watchers came into view on the forest road they currently occupied, headed straight toward them. They were far enough away that his forward scouts wouldn't have encountered them yet.

With the aid of his looking glass, Emrael saw that the Watchers carried a large white flag out in front of them and were less than five thousand strong. No sense in taking chances, however.

Emrael called over the two Captains Second that had accompanied them to the hill. "Battle formations. Ten ranks deep across the road at that clearing there. Fan the bowmen three deep in the trees with three ranks of shields and spears in support. Send scouts out in all directions to make sure we aren't being flanked. Do it now."

Worren approached him as the Captains Second saluted and ran the orders back to the waiting men. "Even if they're truly surrendering, how did they know where we'd be? And why would they surrender to an inferior force in the first place? There are tens of thousands still in Trylla."

Emrael shook his head. "I don't know, but I suspect we're about to find out. Have our bowmen ready but stay their weapons unless given the order."

Their men formed a shield wall ten ranks deep across the road and a large grassy clearing to either side where they had stopped to rest. Bowmen and their escorting battalions fanned out to either side to take positions all along the approach. Emrael, Jaina, Timan, and two squads of the Royal Guard stationed themselves with the front ranks.

Emrael watched curiously and with not a small amount of relief as the Watcher army halted out of bow range to send a sole squad of men forward under their white flag of truce. As they drew nearer, Emrael was shocked to see Darmon Corrande leading them. He put a hand to his sword and took an angry step forward, an involuntary sneer of rage on his face. "You!"

Darmon stopped ten paces short and held up his hands—well, only one hand, being that the right arm ended in a pinned sleeve rather than a hand—in a placating gesture. "Peace, Emrael. We've come to seek peace, an alliance."

"What do you really want, Darmon?" Emrael called back.

Darmon's mouth pursed in a tight grimace. "I understand your caution, Emrael, but I swear to you, there is no trickery involved. These men here have all chosen to follow me rather than the Malithii foreigners. They have subverted the lawful leadership of my own province and of the United Provincial Legion. We will fight with you to be rid of them. Look, I brought proof."

The three severed heads his men tossed onto the soft dirt of the roadway looked to bear the tattoos of Malithii priests.

Emrael scoffed, still filled with so much anger that it threatened to blind him to reason. "You expect me to forget that you and your father are responsible for bringing those bastards to the Provinces? That you enslaved students and Masters of the Citadel?"

He paused, then said through clenched teeth, "You beat my brother half to death."

Darmon held up his missing hand again, his face now tight with worry. "I know our past has not been . . . amicable. I would not be here if I had any other choice. But would I put myself here in front of your line of archers"—he gestured to the woods on either side, where he apparently had seen Emrael's bowmen—"if I had a better option? I know you won't trust me, not yet, but even if you turn me away or kill me, please take these men. Most are native Iraeans with no love for their new Malithii masters."

Darmon motioned to one of his men, who pulled forward the horse of a scared-looking young man in worn black woolens.

"We have one of your scouts from Trylla. He can attest, we killed our Malithii handlers and fled without attacking your encampment. We have not fought against you."

The young man in Ire greens nodded, wild-eyed. "Yes, Lord Ire. Lord Corrande didn't join the others that died in the explosion. Lord Banron sent us out to the city to report Watcher locations using this." He held up a metal contraption smaller than his palm and babbled on. "I swear to you, Lord Ire, I didn't tell them a thing. Not one thing."

Emrael held up one hand to silence the boy. He recognized the

Crafting. Even from this distance he could tell that it was very similar to the Observer he himself still wore. "Enough."

If he let these Watchers join him, he'd potentially be allowing his enemy a position at his back. If he refused, he'd likely have no choice but to fight this force, which numbered more than half of his own, here and now. He'd likely win, but his army would be crippled just when he needed them to be at their best if he was to liberate Trylla and save his brother. As always seemed to be the case lately, he had no good options.

A summer breeze rippled the leaves of the trees around them and kicked up dust that flew into the faces of the Watchers across from him. He could see the tightness in their faces, the worry. Some of their mounts, picking up on the unease, pranced or threw their heads, wanting to get moving. These were men who knew they were in a poor position.

After a tense moment, Darmon spoke again, emotion lending a quaver to his voice. "The Malithii have taken everything, Emrael. My family. My people are slaves. As are the Iraeans to the north. I know it sounds crazy, but the Fallen himself leads them."

That made Emrael pause. "The Fallen himself leads them, you say?"

Darmon's face blanched, his gaze growing distant. "Yes," he said, a hitch in his voice. "I saw him with my own eyes. An image of him, at least. I could *feel* his strength. Like the power the Malithii wield, but . . . vast."

Emrael nodded despite his misgivings. He breathed deep, trying to calm himself. He knew Darmon to be a spoiled, immoral rat. He wouldn't trust such a man no matter the circumstances . . . normally. But they were not living in normal times. His gut told him that Darmon was sincere, and he knew firsthand that seeing the Fallen up close could change even Darmon's heart.

While Emrael pondered in tense silence, Darmon fidgeted nervously. Finally, he walked nearly to Emrael's shield wall and dropped to his knees on the dirt road. "Please, Emrael. Please see reason. I'm begging you."

Emrael stared at his longtime adversary, trying not to show his shock. The Darmon he knew from the Citadel would not have been capable of such humility, even as a ruse.

Finally, Emrael turned to Timan and Daglund, who led the two squads of Royal Guards that had accompanied him. "You know how to check for mindbinders and other Craftings the Malithii might have planted on them?"

Timan nodded. "I can show Daglund and the others easily enough."

"Check them."

Emrael still felt uneasy about it, but walked forward to extend his hand to Darmon while his mages checked the Watcher officers waiting behind him. He helped his enemy—former enemy, perhaps—to his feet, but kept his grip on Darmon's hand. He pushed a pulse of *infusori* into Darmon, breaking past his innate defenses quickly. He didn't do anything sinister this time, however—he simply swept his senses through him, feeling for a mindbinder or other Crafting. He knew that accessing the emotions of another via his *infusori* senses couldn't help him ascertain anything as complex as enduring loyalty. But he could check for Malithii Craftings and any overt signs of subterfuge.

When he was as sure as he could be that Darmon wasn't planning anything sinister, he broke his grip. "I don't trust you, Darmon. I will watch you carefully, and will kill you without hesitation if you fail to obey my orders exactly. Understand?"

Darmon nodded, and Emrael surveyed the rest of the Watcher officers. "My mages will be searching each of your officers to make sure none of you are under Malithii control. Normally, I would take you and your men into my Legion by putting you all into different squads and companies. Today, however, you'll keep your current commands and ride vanguard. I don't trust you yet, to be frank. Help me defeat your former comrades, and then we'll take you into the Ire Legion for good."

26

Emrael, Worren, Timan, and Jaina rode their horses just behind the lead ranks of Ire Legion as they marched into the outskirts of Trylla, where the dense forest worked to reclaim the outermost reaches of the ruined city. A hot summer sun just at its zenith beat down on them as soon as they left the trees, instantly causing Emrael to start sweating beneath his armor. He took a swig from his water can before offering it to Jaina, who waved him off.

"You'll go weak from the heat," he said with a smile.

Jaina glanced up at the sky, then frowned at him. "This is not heat, Ire. The Westlands are so hot in places, people travel only at night because an hour in the sun will cook you alive. Besides, you will have to piss every mile we travel. No thank you."

Emrael shrugged and took another swig and went back to watching the empty buildings around them.

Darmon and his five battalions of Watchers rode vanguard ahead of the Iraeans, leading the way through the abandoned streets. So far the intelligence he had provided had been good. They hadn't run into any Malithii or Watchers, not even scouts or sentries. Darmon claimed he had cleared this portion of the city of such sentries on his way out of the city.

Despite word of Emrael's attacks in the north having reached the Malithii and Watcher leaders here, Darmon said that the Malithii had insisted on taking Trylla, depriving Emrael of his only real base of operations.

The Watcher attack hadn't gone quite as planned, however. The *infusori*-fueled blast Emrael had seen earlier in the day had in fact come from the Ire forces inside the fortifications. Darmon said that thousands of Watchers had likely died.

And so Emrael and his forces had left their supplies in the forest with a mere company to guard them and now rode straight to where the Malithii had made their camp in the northern portion of the city. Troops from the Malithii's native lands and the soulbound they had brought with them were still being held in reserve, apparently too precious to risk on a first assault. Darmon was confident that he could convince more of the Watchers to desert the dark priests and join them if the Malithii's loyal troops from their homeland—and the terrifying soulbound, of course—were killed.

Emrael felt a chill run through him as they moved through the abandoned streets. It felt too easy, and trusting Darmon Corrande felt wrong. Worse than wrong. It felt suicidal, and worse, nearly ten thousand of his men would die with him if he was leading them into a trap.

But truth be told, Darmon's information had only confirmed what Emrael, Worren, and Jaina had already decided to do. Attacking while the Malithii and Watcher forces were divided offered their only real chance at victory, and they had no choice but to act immediately.

Darmon had sent squads of Watchers out into the city to intercept any scouts the Malithii had posted around their encampment, but so far this part of the vast city was quiet. Broken stone buildings loomed over the dirt-and-rubble-strewn streets, timeworn skeletons of a city that had once been the hub of the western world. Their army could probably traverse the entire city without catching a glimpse of the Watcher and Malithii forces, if they wanted to.

As they marched through the eerily quiet streets, Emrael's Observer pendant began making noise from where he always wore it around his neck. At first, it was so quiet that he hardly heard it over the clopping of the horses' hooves and the quiet jangle of thousands of men marching in leather and steel armor. When he finally realized what he was hearing, he frantically grasped the pendant, holding it to his ear. At first, he could only hear more of the same crackling noise he had heard back at the hill outside the city where they had met Darmon and his Watchers.

Slowly, however, he accustomed to the noise and was able to pick out a distinct voice.

"Crafter command, this is Durcan. I mean, this is overwatch three. Watchers are marching through sector seven. Probably a full battalion. Maybe. They're moving away from the fort, sir."

Emrael tried using his own Observer to respond, as his was

Ban's original design that could both receive and transmit, unlike those given to the scouts that had been sent to monitor Watcher movements. Both Craftings stayed silent no matter how many times he tried to contact his brother.

He growled in frustration, then furrowed his brows as he considered what he had heard. Someone had obviously been using another of Ban's Observer Craftings to scout out the attacking Watchers, though Emrael had no clue where sector seven was. The Iraean scout Darmon had handed over only knew that his own sector had been number twelve and that Ban and Garrus planned to bombard the Watchers using the information gleaned.

Watchers marching north away from the fortifications could be a problem for Emrael and his army, however.

He turned quickly to Worren, holding up the Observer. "I think whatever men the Watchers had committed to attacking the fortifications are headed back this way. We need to attack quickly or come up with a new plan."

Worren grimaced as he gave the Crafting an appraising glance. "If they are regrouping, we could try to make our way across one of the river bridges to hold the fort with Garrus and your brother."

Emrael shook his head. "I don't think we could get our supply wagons and sneak across in time, we'd be an easy target. Besides, the last thing they need is to cram more men inside that fort, they're likely swimming in shit as it is. Best thing is to attack now while they're still divided. If Darmon is correct, eliminating the camp might bring more Watchers to our side. We could secure Trylla today and turn the tide of the entire war in our favor."

Worren, always in favor of aggressive tactics, bared his teeth in a savage grin. "Let's kill the bastards, then."

Within the hour they had halted just half a league or so from where the Malithii had made their encampment. Darmon and his second, Captain Vaslat, trotted their horses back to where Emrael and his own officers rode.

Darmon bowed his head briefly to Emrael, then pointed down the wide avenue on which most of their forces traveled. "The camps are just ahead, where those buildings up there give way to a clear space. There will be soldiers from the Westlands standing guard, probably some sentries posted at regular intervals around the perimeter of the camp. They are more interested in keeping people in—soulbound especially—than they are in any threat. Still, we'll need to move quickly to overwhelm the defenses before they can organize themselves."

"How many soulbound are there?" Emrael asked.

Darmon shrugged and shook his head. "I don't know. I wasn't allowed into the Malithii encampments."

Emrael nodded. "Nothing for it but to attack decisively, then. Form a shield wedge. I'll have my foot form ranks to cover your flanks once we enter the square. Bowmen will shoot from the third rank until contact, then withdraw to the reserve. Cavalry will be held in reserve until you break through their lines. Press your wedge forward as quickly as possible, we can't get stuck fighting in streets like this one. Punch through hard, we'll do the killing in your wake."

Darmon frowned but nodded without comment, then moved quickly to arrange his men in tight ranks that would fan out to form a giant wedge once they reached the square. Emrael issued orders and formed his soldiers up behind him. They started at a fast march, the sounds of thousands of boots and hooves on the broken cobbles of the large avenue now thunderous.

A loud baying horn sounded somewhere ahead of them, then another, and another. A milling mass of soldiers in odd armor all painted black suddenly appeared at the mouth of the avenue, each carrying a large black wooden shield and a pike with a slender, wickedly curved blade.

"Press forward!" Emrael shouted, and then Darmon's Watcher battalions slammed into the front ranks of the soldiers from the Hidden Kingdoms in the far-off Westlands. Their wedge formation parted the surprised, disorganized Westland soldier ranks like the hull of a ship through water. Watchers in the second, third, and fourth ranks of the wedge used their shields to support their fellows in the front ranks as they pushed forward, continuing their advance even as they used spears and long swords to skewer the Westland soldiers. The rear ranks used their short swords to finish off the enemy that fell underfoot.

Before long, however, the Watcher advance slowed as more and more blue-uniformed men fell to the curve-bladed spears. The black-clad warriors had recovered from their surprise and had already formed into ranks of shields and slender pikes three or four deep.

"Push the flanks!" Emrael called to his officers, who repeated the orders. There was only a space about one hundred shields wide on either side of the back end of the Watchers' wedge formation. The bulk of his army was still trapped in the wide avenue, rendered useless in the battle. If they didn't push forward enough for the rest of their men to engage the enemy, they'd be overwhelmed in minutes. Darmon and his Watchers already took heavy losses, surrounded as they were.

Emrael called orders again. "Engineers! Explosives twenty paces beyond the ranks! Now! Now!"

He had hoped to save the few of Darrain's explosive Craftings they had left for a truly dire situation. Without additional materials and *infusori* stores, she and her Crafters couldn't make any more. But he had to do something.

Darrain and her company of engineers hurried forward, loading the explosive Craftings into six small catapult-like contraptions that could be carried by two men together. After a brief moment of fiddling with the catapults and the timing controls on the Craftings themselves, the engineers launched the first Craftings to tumble over the heads of the Iraean and Watcher ranks.

Balls of blue flame preceded concussive explosions in the rear ranks of the gathered Westland soldiers, incinerating men inside a ten-pace radius and knocking those within twenty paces off their feet. Many were set alight where they had flammable clothing or hair exposed.

One Crafting had either been poorly aimed or shot from a faulty catapult, and it landed directly in front of the Ire Legion ranks where they had joined the end of the Watcher shield wall to the left. Iraeans, Watchers, and Westland soldiers alike were enveloped in a flash of blue flame that Emrael could feel from where he sat on his horse one hundred paces from the fighting.

"Seventh Company forward!" Emrael shouted, though Seventh Company's Captain Second already had the men moving to fill the gap. One of the reserve squads assigned to recover the wounded ran forward with them, trying to beat the flames off of their fallen comrades, pulling them back to safety before the Westland warriors could recover and attack.

The explosives worked, despite the one malfunction. The Malithii's soldiers had reacted much as he had expected, recoiling from the blasts and leaving their front ranks unsupported. A massive ball of flame erupting in your midst had a way of disrupting focus and unnerving even the most hardened warrior.

"Push, push!" Emrael repeated, and his men moved forward quickly, slaughtering the disoriented Westland soldiers by the dozen. The Ire Legion ranks finally pushed into the square, far enough that they were able to deploy four ranks deep stretched across the width of the large open square—really an entire block of the city that had been demolished, the stones carted off somewhere or another, leaving only bare dirt and cobbles. Emrael, five companies of cavalry, and one battalion of foot held in reserve waited anxiously behind the fighting line as the battle turned to an ugly melee. The Westlanders fought well, but caught off guard as they had been, simply didn't have the numbers to stand against Emrael's forces. Some of the foreigners even fought bare-chested or in loose black clothing not unlike that of their Malithii priest comrades, and some lacked shields. Emrael watched with grim satisfaction as the Iraeans and Watchers cut through their lines methodically.

Just as Emrael started to wonder whether they were going to have to kill every last one of the black-clad soldiers, the baying horns they had heard earlier sounded once more. A chorus of dozens of horns emanated from somewhere just beyond the opposite side of the square, and immediately the Westland soldiers broke away from the fight to retreat north and east toward the horns. After a few moments, they were gone, scurrying back into the warren of crisscrossing streets like wasps retreating into their nest.

They let the few survivors go, too tired from the intense battle to give chase. The sun had been near its noonday peak when the army had entered the ruins, but it now sat low in the sky, no more than an hour away from twilight. Emrael thought about ordering his cavalry to pursue and put an end to the enemy here and now, but if there were horns farther back in the city calling to these troops, there could be another army waiting for him. Starting such a conflict just before sundown would be madness.

As if his thoughts had summoned them, half-dead soulbound monsters boiled out of the streets and alleyways on the far side of the large open square. Thousands of them arrived within minutes, herded by dozens of Malithii priests. Emrael could see their copper-cable weapons glinting in the late-afternoon sun as they whipped at the soulbound, exerting their control over the horde.

"Absent Gods," Emrael cursed as he watched the horde continue to grow. There must have been nearly ten thousand of the beasts already, with more pushing into the square from the rear. At even odds, he wouldn't risk a confrontation with those monsters if he had any other choice. As best he could determine, fighting soulbound two to one was the minimally acceptable tactic. Jaina and Timan agreed with him and said that three to one would be better with troops unused to facing the implacable half-dead beasts.

"Reserves load the wounded on horses," he screamed, panic in his voice. "Square formation pull back into the avenue, pull back! Eighth Battalion form ranks to the east, three hundred paces back from the square. First to the north, Third to the west. Cavalry leads the rest to the south. Move move move!"

Darmon and his Watchers pulled back first, and Emrael didn't stop them. The square was littered with bodies in blue uniforms, and nearly every Watcher left unharmed helped an injured comrade back into the safe space behind the battalions assigned to form deep ranks in the avenue to cover their retreat. They were fortunate that the Malithii and soulbound in the square behind them seemed to be waiting for something rather than attacking immediately. Perhaps they wanted to gather greater numbers to ensure their victory? Whatever it was, their opportunity for escape wouldn't last long.

Emrael stopped Darmon as he drew near where Emrael, Worren, and Jaina had gathered to supervise the retreat. "Can we get to the fortifications across the bridge? Will the other Watchers attack us if you are in the lead?"

Darmon shook his head and panted his reply. "Not all of the Watcher Captains are sympathetic. They may follow Malithii orders."

Jaina nodded. "We will not make it that far anyway, not even close. *Alai'ahn* are difficult to outrun in formation. They do not move quickly, but they can march for days at a time."

Emrael swore under his breath, his mind racing. They could retreat all the way outside the city, to the encampment where they
had left the bulk of their supplies. The camp only had a shallow
trench and hastily placed stakes for protection, however. Thousands of soulbound would run right through such defenses. And
that assumed Emrael's battalions would make it that far before
being overrun—it would take nearly as long to reach the camp as
Ban's fortifications to the south.

Everyone was watching Emrael as he deliberated. Finally, he
asked, "Where do we go? We need walls, and quickly. Did any of
you see anything we could use on our way here?"

All of them stood silent, shaking their heads. Fear and dread
shone in their eyes. All save Jaina.

"The temple compound," she said with authority. "It has head-
high walls, enough to slow the beasts and give us a chance. We can
put men with bows on the buildings inside. And the temple will
give you, at least, an opportunity to recharge some of our stores."

Darmon looked at Jaina oddly; he wouldn't know about Emrael's ability to pull *infusori* directly from an *infusori* Well, or an
ancient Ravan temple that sat over an untapped Well. Emrael and
Timan, however, nodded. It would work. It had to work.

"Can you find it?" he asked.

Jaina nodded in reply.

"Good. Take command of the cavalry, lead the way. Quickly,
please."

At that moment, the horns behind them blasted once more,
their low reverberating sound physically palpable. The thunderous sound of thousands of shuffling feet replaced the sound of the
horns as the soulbound finally began their charge.

"Timan and the Guard on me, we'll support Eighth Battalion.
Tell the engineers to bring every explosive we have left. Throw a
few in the buildings at the mouth of the avenue, throw the rest
well back into the soulbound's ranks. Worren, lead the main body,
make sure we have shields in tight ranks to the sides, and a battalion in reserve. Eighth is about to lose a lot of men."

Emrael raised his voice to shout orders to the Legionmen of
Eighth Battalion nearby. "Quick march to the rear! Now! Bowmen
face rear to cover the retreat, shoot at will!"

Orders given, Emrael strapped a shield to his wounded arm and drew his sword before he stalked toward the rear ranks, where Eighth Battalion had locked shields in preparation to meet the soulbound charge. Timan and the hundred or so Royal Guardsmen were quick to follow. To his surprise, Darmon and two companies of Watchers joined them as they found places to join the shield wall.

Emrael nodded solemnly to Darmon as they both jogged toward the impending battle line. He nodded back. Darmon had obviously participated in the battle himself, despite not having what had once been his sword hand. Blood smeared the front of his blue uniform, and accompanying tears in the material likely meant that some of it was his.

"We'll earn our place," his unlikely ally said grimly. The Watcher Captain Second that seemed to follow Darmon around like a shadow nodded his agreement.

They reached Eighth Battalion's commanding Captain Second when the shuffling soulbound were perhaps a few hundred paces away, pouring into the avenue with a shambling gait. The Ire men had packed the avenue with a wall of overlapped shields that spanned between broken stone buildings on both sides.

Emrael returned the Captain Second's salute before rapidly giving his commands. "Send orders for the first and second ranks to lock shields and hold the line at all costs. Second rank will need to hold up the first, those soulbound will hit like an avalanche. Third rank will use spears. These soulbound bastards won't defend themselves, but won't stop fighting until they bleed out, so cut off their hands if you can, and aim for the neck or heart to kill them quickly. Hold until you see explosions in the enemy ranks, then we all retreat as quickly as possible. Understood?"

The Captain Second nodded and shouted orders that echoed down the lines. Spears were passed forward to the third ranks as the first two pressed their shields tightly together. Bowmen used boulders, the steps and windows of buildings to either side of the avenue, and anything they could to gain a vantage from which they could continue shooting over the heads of their comrades. Any damage they inflicted on the enemy was imperceptible, however. There were just so Fallen-damned many of them.

Emrael made his way to the engineers that had accompanied him. Darrain's nose was smudged with dirt—she had been among the engineers who had volleyed the first round of explosive Craftings at the enemy. She was supposed to have gone with the main body of the Legion, but Emrael didn't have time to argue with her. "When my mages throw your Craftings, run as fast as you can back to the reserves. Stay close to me. Timan and Daglund will take care of you."

She nodded mutely, staring at the oncoming soulbound with her lips pursed, resolute. Timan and Daglund hovered nearby.

"Hold the explosives until my command!" Emrael shouted to his Royal Guard, who had formed a rank of their own just behind the Legionmen. There were only a dozen or so of Darrain's explosive Craftings left, each in the hands of an Imperator or Iraean mage from Emrael's Guard.

The bowmen stopped shooting as the soulbound neared, running back down the avenue to form tight double ranks just behind where the main body marched away.

The soulbound finally collided with the ranks of Iraean Legionmen with an earsplitting crash, like a hundred buildings collapsing at once. Some of the men in the first rank were knocked flat on their back upon impact. The soulbound wasted no time in savagely hacking them to bloody pieces with their heavy swords and giant axes. Iraean Legionmen and some of Darmon's Watchers from the second rank filled the gaps quickly, using short swords to rend horrible wounds in the soulbound's unprotected bodies.

After recovering from the initial clash, the front two ranks of Legionmen huddled behind their shields, straining to hold the line against the crushing press of the mad-eyed soulbound, keeping their heads low as the grey-skinned monsters hacked with inhuman strength at the tops of their shields. Men in the third rank lunged with spears to stab over the top of the shield wall in front of them, trying in vain to slow the soulbounds' vicious attacks.

The soulbounds' strength was too much for the Legionmen to handle for long. Wooden shields began to splinter, rendering them useless to the soldiers hiding behind them. They screamed and fell before the onslaught, shield arms ruined as soulbound weapons found their marks.

"Now!" Emrael shouted at the men of his Royal Guard, who depressed the actuators on the Craftings and heaved them overhead. Emrael began a slow count to ten in his head, then held up the shield strapped to his arm to shelter Darrain, who still stood next to him, staring in horror.

Again, a searing flash of blue light preceded a massive concussive blast that shook Emrael so hard he almost lost his feet. Others around him did, though luckily those in the shield wall were pressed so tightly together that most had stayed upright.

The mages in his Royal Guard that had lobbed the Craftings overhead had done a better job this time, and the balls of fire had each obliterated dozens of soulbound and set more still alight. Several of his mages had thrown their Craftings into the huge stone buildings that loomed over the mouth of the avenue where the soulbound milled in a seething mass. Those Craftings tore the stones apart as if they were made from sand, propelling chunks of debris outward in a lethal arc, obliterating the nearby soulbound and their Malithii masters that had sought shelter in the ruins. The buildings themselves groaned after the blast, then slowly toppled into the avenue, crushing hundreds more soulbound and isolating those fighting Emrael's men from the larger part of their force, just as he had hoped. The Ire Legion was left facing a mere hundred or so of the half-dead monsters rather than thousands.

A few surviving soulbound had caught fire and apparently didn't have even the presence of mind left to them to try putting out the flames. They still fought even as they burned alive, compelled by their Malithii masters via their soulbinders despite the agony apparent in their screams.

The stench and the all-too-human screams coming from the burning beasts were enough to drive a man mad. Emrael could see the effect they had on his soldiers, who hesitated even in the midst of a vicious battle. The wooden shields they used to fend off the continued attacks of the burning soulbound were beginning to catch fire, further threatening to collapse his ranks.

He himself shuddered. "Rear march! Hold the line! Slow retreat!"

Most of the men obeyed the order, retreating from the attacking soulbound while holding the shield wall. Where the soulbound had caught fire and still pressed the attack, however, men began to panic and pull back too quickly. Soulbound that had escaped the blasts of Darrain's Craftings charged into the gaps, hacking mindlessly at Legionmen who were now exposed by their comrades who had fled the line. Legionmen began to scream and scatter before the pressure of the soulbound attack, despite now having superior numbers. The wild, powerful swings of the soulbound that had been mostly contained by a tight shield wall now wreaked havoc among the disorganized battalion.

"Timan!" Emrael shouted. "Ready the Guard to charge!"

He signaled to Eighth Battalion's Captain Second, who sounded a full retreat. As soon as enough of the Legionmen were clear, Emrael waved his Guard forward, jogging with them in a loose line to meet the soulbound.

As he passed his weary Legionmen and neared the shrieking soulbound, Emrael pulled his shield tight to his body and put his shoulder behind it, ignoring the pain that lanced through his arm. He used the shield as a battering ram, colliding violently with the first soulbound in the remnant horde. Soulbound might be inhumanly strong and immune to the effects of pain, but they weighed roughly the same as normal humans and seemed to be no better than an average person at keeping their feet.

The soulbound rebounded from Emrael's shield to crash to the ground. He thrust his sword into the beast's gullet and moved on quickly to make sure he was out of range of the axe the soulbound flailed as it died.

He hit another soulbound with his shield, just barely getting inside a wild swing of a sword to knock this one backward as well. Pain flared again in his wounded shield arm, so bad that he flinched involuntarily. He stepped backward quickly, letting his Guard pass by him to engage the soulbound in his stead.

Timan stopped at his side, a concerned look on his face. "The arm?" He shouted to be heard over the din of battle.

Emrael nodded mutely, sucking breath between gritted teeth.

Disappointment flashed in Timan's expression. "You should not be fighting injured, Emrael. There is no need, one man will not win this battle."

Emrael grunted his agreement but didn't pull back any further. The fighting still raged on a mere twenty paces away. Timan, his eyes constantly surveying the fighting, positioned himself to cover Emrael. Then the insufferable Imperator began pushing him forcibly back toward where Eighth Battalion still loaded their wounded on supply wagons, preparing to retreat with the rest of the Legion. The pain in his arm continued pulsing, feeling as though it had been cut to the bone all over again, or worse, so he let himself be herded. His Guard were making short work of the remaining soulbound anyhow. Getting to the temple compound was what mattered now.

He might not have been in proper condition to fight with his men in a shield wall, but he balked when Timan tried to get him to climb into one of the supply wagons that now held scores of their dead and wounded.

"I can walk, Glory blind you," Emrael said irritably, shrugging off Timan's attempts to get him into the wagon. "Just get these wagons moving, and make sure the Guard is prepared to cover our rear. Moving quickly is what will save us now."

He sheathed his sword and pulled desperately at the straps of his shield to finally get the damned thing off of his aching arm. As he set it in one of the wagons holding their dead, however, he spotted a body that made him numb again, though with shock rather than physical pain this time. Darrain lay dead in the wagon next to armored Legionmen, blood still oozing from a mess of a wound in her chest. A crossbow bolt protruded from her back.

Emrael closed his eyes and bowed his head briefly in grief. Legionmen losing their lives for him was bad enough. But Darrain . . . people like her weren't supposed to suffer the same fate as simple soldiers. She was so intelligent, had so much promise. Ban would be devastated. Emrael was devastated, and was ashamed that it was for practical reasons as much as personal. Next to Ban, Darrain had been their best Crafter.

But how had she been killed? She had been near Emrael until he charged the soulbound with his guard. None of the enemy had penetrated their lines so deeply.

Timan came over to see what had caused Emrael's reaction. "Ah, shit," he cursed, his voice full of emotion.

Emrael looked up to meet his gaze. "Find out how this happened, Timan. She was behind our lines. She should have been safe."

"Westlander arrow?" Timan guessed softly, pressing one hand tenderly to Darrain's forehead. He had spent considerable time with the serious little Crafter, coordinating between the mages in his Guard and the Crafters in Darrain's company of engineers.

Emrael shook his head. "No. I saw her after the Westlanders retreated. The Malithii and soulbound didn't use any arrows."

"The Watchers?"

Emrael bared his teeth in a snarl. "Could have just as easily been one of your Imperators using a stolen crossbow, Timan. You know as well as I that the loyalty of Ordenans is fickle. There are many in our midst who could be our enemy. And now they've killed one of our own. This *will not* happen again."

Timan's eyes glittered hard and dark. "I'll find them."

27

Jeric Alloda stood before the assembled Ordenan Councils, sweat dripping down his back, soaking his shirt under his arms. The Council of Imperators and the Council of Citizens did not hold joint audiences unless the business at hand was particularly grave. Even the two High Judges were here, trying to mediate the quiet but fierce rumblings coming from the various huddles of old Councilors. He was in deep shit.

Jeric stood silent in the center of the chamber floor while the Councils deliberated among themselves. He had arrived just that morning and given a full report of everything that had happened with Jaina and the Ire boy. Well, almost everything. He had left out the part where Jaina had kicked his ass.

But the Councils now knew that Ire had taken portions of the Iraean territory, that Jaina and Maira had already allied themselves with him despite the cautions of the Councils, and that Imperators had died due to Ire's foolhardiness.

Jeric had also failed to mention that Cailla and the others had died attempting to do what Jeric couldn't bring himself to in killing Jaina to keep Ordena out of Provincial affairs—and out of Provincial wars, especially. Yaris and others on both Councils favored controlling the Provinces and making alliances via economic means. They argued—correctly—that the Ordenan people could not fight their holy war in the Westlands and a war in the east at the same time, no matter that the Malithii had at last found their way to the eastern continent. The war in the Westlands had taken a turn for the worse besides, from what Jeric had heard from his Imperator friends who had been deployed there recently.

He met Councilor Yaris's eyes briefly. The stately older man with huge, bushy eyebrows merely pursed his lips, then looked away. Jeric had met with his patron before this meeting, and Yaris had been less than pleased that Jaina still lived to further Councilor

Maira's agenda in the Provinces. The two had been bitter rivals for years, and now that Maira was trying to pull Ordena into a war in the Provinces besides the war in the Westlands . . . well, blood had now been spilled between followers of the different factions, and it was unlikely to be the last Ordenan blood shed by their own political infighting.

Abruptly, the Councils began to shuffle their way back to their assigned chairs, one Council arrayed in an arc to one side, the other Council arrayed the same way to the other side, the High Judge of each Council seated next to the other in the middle.

"Imperator Alloda," the High Judge of the Imperator's Council intoned. "You have given us much to consider here today. Your report, and those of Councilor Maira Tinoas, detailing the presence of Malithii priests—and *alai'ahn*!—are of critical importance. It seems that Emrael Ire, Councilor Tinoas's son, has mounted a significant resistance to the Malithii and those that have allied themselves to them. It is the will of both Councils of the Holy Empire of Ordena that an alliance be formalized with Emrael Ire. We accept his offer of *infusori* stores from the Wells of Gnalius in the amount of one thousand standard coils per month, and will provide him transport for his troops plus ten thousand men of our own. You, Jeric, will lead them."

Jeric was shocked, nearly speechless. "Me?"

The High Judge stared at him with unblinking eyes. "Of course, Imperator Alloda. You have the most current information, tenure in the Order of Imperators, and a personal relationship with Jaina Lanrona. Do you not?"

He froze momentarily. Jaina would kill him if she saw him again. There was very little he could do to stop it, and he knew it. Even if she didn't, Emrael would never strike a deal with him. But he could hardly tell the Councils that now. He would be demoted, likely sent back to the Westlands to die. At best.

He couldn't for the life of him come up with another excuse as to why he would turn down the honor of leading ten thousand of the Imperial Army, and a small fleet besides.

"Yes, Your Honor. I will be blessed to lead the men and women of the Empire in fulfilling the wishes of the Councils."

Councilor Yaris glared at Jeric from his seat. Jeric might have just lost his patron for accepting an Imperial assignment that would likely end in his own death, most likely at the hands of one of his oldest and closest friends.

Sisters save him.

28

Halrec stood on the highest balcony of the mansion that had recently belonged to Lord Holder Tarelle, surveying Larreburgh and the surrounding land. The outer walls had long since been repaired after Emrael's assault of the city, and had been strengthened significantly besides. The Malithii priests could tear down a stone wall just as easily as the Ordenan mages had done, so the Imperators and Crafters assigned to Halrec had erected a series of steel stakes and lighted fixtures outside the walls, all around the city perimeter. The bastards wouldn't sneak up on them without one of their patrols or watchmen sounding the alarm first.

That wouldn't help Halrec with the challenge that faced him today, however. He had just received a letter from Emrael, telling him that Lord Holder Tarelle had defected, and that he was offering to give the Tarelle Holding to Halrec—if he could hold it. Holding it was the issue.

"Commander Syrtsan, sir? They are waiting for you downstairs." Captain Third Karran stood at attention in the doorway that led back to his study.

"How many came?" he asked.

Karran pursed his lips in thought before responding. "Fifty or so, sir."

Fifty minor holders represented perhaps two-thirds of those he had summoned. More than he thought would come, given the circumstances.

The Watcher raids from the Paellar Holding in the north had grown more frequent and had ranged farther into the Tarelle Holding. A month ago, the Watchers had fled after only minor skirmishes. Twice in as many weeks, Halrec had fought brief pitched battles and had been fortunate to turn back the raiding parties after only minor damage to farmsteads in the north. He suspected that Emrael held the attention of the bulk of the Watchers and their Malithii allies for now, making a full attack on Larreburgh unlikely, but an attack from the north would come soon. He wasn't sure he would have allied with someone in such dire circumstances.

"Have any of the scouts in the Tarelle Gap returned?"

"None, sir."

Halrec cursed. "It's been ten days. Something is wrong. If Corrande has sent an army across the Duskans . . ."

He stared at the giant canyon that wound its way through the looming mountains directly east of the city. Was that smoke wafting above the peaks that separated Iraea from the Corrande Province, or just a dark tendril of cloud?

If Corrande decided to march an army through the pass, there was little Halrec could do but retreat behind the walls of the city and prepare for a siege. Even with the reinforcements from minor holders he'd convinced to join him, he only had fifteen thousand men at his command, and perhaps half of those would have been up to Barros Legion standards. Many were middle-aged, or teenagers, or simply hadn't been in so much as a brawl at a tavern. He had his officers training them night and day, but he knew that they would be a liability in a real battle.

"Commander Syrtsan, sir? They're waiting for you in the grand hall."

"Thank you, Karran. Lead the way."

When he walked in, all fifty holders—the minor lords that with their oaths granted the Lord Holder of a Holding his title—rose to their feet to stand in silence as Halrec took his place at a small table set in front of the rows of chairs.

Halrec waved them back to their seats as he settled into his, embarrassed but pleased at the show of respect. "You all know the odds we face," he began, surveying the room and finding mostly grey-haired men staring back at him. "And I think by now you know what I represent, and what Emrael Ire represents. What we fight for, and who we fight against. Many of you have already stood with me and my men, fought back the Watcher raids from the north."

Halrec held up the letter from Emrael. "I've received a letter from Lord Ire. Lord Holder Tarelle has defected, betraying us all. Lord Ire has offered me the Tarelle Holding."

He paused to gauge the reaction of the holders in the room. Those that had fought the Watchers with him had irrevocably thrown their lot in with him and Emrael. But supplanting a Lord Holder with hundreds of years of history as the ruling noble in the region was bound to raise a few eyebrows even still.

"With your support," he continued, "I will accept, making this not just a military assignment, but my home as your Lord Holder. What say you?"

The room was silent for an awkward moment in which Halrec began to fear he had misjudged the intent of these lords who had come in response to his summons.

But then a small, slender man in the front row—Luran, one of the first to bring his entire garrison from his holding to the south—smiled and said loudly, "Aye."

A chorus of deep voices echoed his, and Halrec didn't hold back his smile. "Thank you, Lords. That's enough for now. You should also know that our battle is soon to become a war. Bring your people here, all of them, and any stores you can transport quickly. You will be given space, wherever we can find it. I suspect we have weeks, months if we're lucky, before Corrande leads a sizable force into Iraea. I think we will be his first target. They'll try take Larreburgh, perhaps more, before the first snows fall. Count on it."

29

Maira Ire leaned back in the chair in Arielle Barros's study, rubbing at her temples, half her mind on the mountain of documents she needed to tend to back in her own office. Fool she was, thinking that this voyage would be a chance to relive the glorious adventures of her youth. It seemed that her inescapable destiny was to be buried in paperwork. She would be up well into the night sorting through it all.

The papers weren't the source of her headache at the moment, however. Arielle had asked to see her urgently despite the late hour, and the letter she had read aloud was enough to give anyone a headache.

"What should I do, Maira?" Arielle asked for at least the fifth time. The girl's eyes were red and puffy, but to her credit, her voice was strong and clear. She did not let even Maira see her tears.

"Child, I have told you already. This decision must be yours alone. But if your father is truly dead, it represents an opportunity for you. Should you gain control of the Barros Province, our chances of surviving this mess would increase considerably."

The letter was from the girl's sister, Samille. Ostensibly from her sister, that is.

"Why would they send this?" the girl asked finally.

Maira smiled. "That, my girl, is the correct question. Now. Either your sister is in need of help—she speaks only of problems, never solutions—or she is a pawn in what is almost certain to be a trap laid by Malithii priests."

"It is almost certainly a ruse," Elle agreed. "I saw the mindbinder on Samille myself."

"Yes," Maira said carefully, "but why would they be trying to lure you into a trap? Besides your relationship with Emrael, what is your significance to them?"

Arielle grunted. "Not much of a relationship anymore, probably. I saw to that."

Maira laughed. "Do not fault yourself, dear girl. My son is not easy to live with. You are worth more than your relationship with Emrael—"

She was interrupted by the door to Arielle's rooms being thrown open. She whipped around to see Voran striding through the doors. She relaxed slightly, but still intended to reprimand her old friend. What was he doing barging into Arielle's private quarters like this, at this time of night? Manners were important.

She got her answer as two Malithii priests dressed in ordinary Provincial clothing swept into the room a moment later.

"Oh, Voran," Maira said, rising to her feet. Fool that she was, she had not come properly armed. She was just a mere hundred paces from her own rooms and there were supposed to be guards in every hallway, after all.

An Imperator was never without some form of weapon, however. She put a finger to the *infusori* coil she carried in a pouch on her belt, drew the energy into her in a flash, then pulled two thin copper-alloy rods from a pocket specially sewn into the calf of her pants. Confident, she settled into a ready stance, putting herself between the three men and the girl.

Voran looked surprised to see her. When the shock melted from his face, he simply looked sick. "Lady Ire," he blustered, "why are you here?"

"I might ask the same of you, Voran Loire," she said calmly, keeping her eye on the two Malithii priests. They had probably passed through the Citadel easily, hiding their intricate tattoos with high-collared coats and the cloth-brimmed hats favored by merchants during the hot summer months. The priests seemed content to wait on Voran, so long as their quarry did not raise an alarm. Likely they had not counted on an Imperator standing in their way.

Voran stared at the floor and mumbled, "You weren't supposed to be here, Maira. I didn't know."

Scorn made her voice rough. "So you would simply have delivered this girl to them and been done with it? I should be grateful I was spared?"

Voran looked up, angered. "I tried to protect you, for the love I have for you and your dead husband. But this is business, and a much smaller price than you and your son ask of others for your own gain. How many thousands have died so you can rule, how many more will die?"

Maira shook her head. "You do not know the Malithii like I do, Voran, and I certainly do not know you as I thought I did. So be it. Arielle," she said without looking over her shoulder at the girl, "stay back behind the desk. Scream for help as loud as you can."

At that, the Malithii priests glided forward on nimble feet, already drawing short swords and copper-cable weapons from their belts. Voran, coward that he was, slipped out the doors as Arielle screamed for her guards, her voice shrill.

The Malithii attacked in a frenzy, eager to get through her to Arielle before help arrived. That they attacked instead of fleeing like Voran said much about their resolve. She knew that these men would fight to their deaths rather than fail in the assignment their elders had given them.

A slight sidestep let her avoid a lunging strike from the Malithii on the right. She whipped her copper rod into the Malithii's tattooed wrist with a quick, controlled downward strike. As the copper touched the dark priest's skin, she released a lightning-like burst of *infusori*.

Nobody she knew of had her combination of power and unique skill when it came to using the bursts of power favored by Battle-Mages. It wasn't so different from Healing, really, save in reverse.

This Malithii had not been ready for it either. He reeled backward, body in a taut arc as every muscle in his body seized at once. She left him convulsing on the floor and started toward the second Malithii, who now had a wrinkle of caution around his eyes.

The priest feinted with his blade before whipping his copper-cable weapon at Maira. She knew this trick well; this priest intended to do to her what she had just done to his friend.

The copper-alloy weapons that both Malithii and Imperator mages favored conducted *infusori* energy both ways, however. If one knew precisely the phase of the *infusori* energy that was being transmitted by the mage, it was possible to completely neutralize that energy and its intended effects.

This was far from her first encounter with the Malithii.

She allowed the cable to touch her, neutralized the priest's attack, and blasted an enormous amount of *infusori* back up the Malithii's own weapon, manipulated just so. The priest shuddered and his eyes grew wide just before every inch of his skin sloughed from his body. He flopped to the ground, dead. She picked up the short sword he had dropped and plunged it through the heart of the other Malithii she had paralyzed.

Arielle vomited noisily on the floor behind her desk.

Maira frowned as she surveyed the room. "Ah. My apologies for the mess, dear. We will have someone clean it all up, I promise. Come with me, we need to find out just how much damage Voran has caused. He likely was not expecting to be found out today, but who knows how deep the rot has seeped."

She hurried into the hallway, Arielle just behind her. The hall was empty, nobody in sight. There should have been a full squad on duty tonight. Doubtless Voran had arranged for her to be unguarded.

Several hallways and two short staircases brought her to where her squad of Imperators kept their rooms. Two of them loitered in the hall, ostensibly playing a game of cards, but she knew they were on watch duty. Even here in the Citadel, they knew to be on their guard. She should have had them watching Arielle from the beginning.

"You two," she said with a wave of her hand. "Fetch the others, please. There has been an attempt on Lady Barros's life—and my own—by Malithii priests. This will be a long night."

The two Imperators, Yman and Droan, tall young men with sandy-brown hair, saluted her and ran from door to door. In a matter of minutes, Maira and Arielle were surrounded by ten fully armed and armored Imperators as they stalked the halls toward the Legion command offices.

When they arrived at the small dining hall repurposed as their Legion's command office, an aide assigned to staff the front desk was the only one still there. At a command from Maira, he blinked the tiredness from his eyes and left at a dead run to rouse the officers of the Sagmynan Legion. Within minutes, the three Captains First and several Captains Second had assembled in the room, and they had even managed to put their uniforms on. Maira nodded in approval at the display of discipline. Voran had done something right, at least.

"Your Commander has betrayed us," Maira stated simply, her voice hard and crisp. "Voran Loire led two Malithii priests to Arielle Barros's rooms this evening in an attempt to abduct or kill her. Voran is now a fugitive, one I expect you to find before the night is dead. Five hundred copper rounds to the men that bring him to me, alive. Half that if he's dead."

The officers had listened intently, their faces becoming more and more surprised with every word. Now, however, they erupted nearly at once with exclamations of surprise and outrage.

Captain First Bari Rynan, a Sagmynan Legionman who had joined Emrael early after the conquest of Myntar, waved the rest to silence. "What of the Malithii attackers?"

"Taken care of," Maira said simply. "Voran is the primary concern, now, though your men should ensure that any other Malithii that may be in the city are dealt with. I suggest you shoot them with crossbows."

He nodded solemnly, as did many of the officers in the room. They had seen what the Malithii could do in the battle for the Wells above the city some months ago. "We will see it done, Lady Ire. I suggest we secure the city walls immediately, and send men to strengthen the East Pass and the harbor at Ladeska. Voran has issued odd orders these last few days, pulling men from our garrisons there for various reasons."

Maira frowned at not having heard this from Rynan sooner, but soon calmed herself. If she herself had not seen through Voran's treachery, how could she expect it of anyone else? "Thank you, Captain. See it done." She turned to meet eyes with the rest of the officers. "The Captains First here will all report to me directly. I will be approving all troop movements, and I want a full report of current deployments as well as anything the lot of you see as risks. Fetch me all of Voran's orders in the last month as well. Within the hour, please, Captains. Now go rouse your men."

The Captains saluted, faces serious as they marched from the room. When they had gone, Maira turned on her heel to hike down the hall to the nearby tower that had been the astronomy observation tower when the Citadel had still been a school.

The Imperators took up positions in the doorway to the staircase without being asked, leaving Maira and Arielle to climb the stairs alone. Giant glass windows built into the thick stone walls surrounded the room at the top of the tower and had even been built into the roof, bathing the observatory in the blue light of the half-moon. Pinpricks of white light from distant stars blanketed the open sky above. Maira had always loved gazing at the stars—the Academy in Ordena had several observation towers like this one, and she had spent considerable time there during her years of study.

The peaceful scene did not last long. The sound of shouting came from below just as they stepped to the windows to see the faint glow of a distant fire in the pass to the east. For them to see the fire from here, the entirety of the barracks and various supply and administrative buildings that comprised the Legion compound there must be burning. Perhaps the surrounding town of Cyaco that served merchants as well.

"They've already taken the pass," Maira said quietly, cursing herself for a fool. "They will not have done that unless they have the requisite forces to attack the city."

She turned to put a bloodstained hand to either side of Arielle's face, gripping tightly as she stared into the girl's eyes. "Your choice has been made for you, child. I will try to hold this city, but you must go. Go to Emrael, do what you must to secure your home province. I'll have four of my Imperators and a full company of cavalry ready to escort you within the hour."

Maira turned and ran back down the stairs to the Citadel proper, already shouting orders to the Imperators and the gathered Legion Captains as she exited the tower. "Barricade the city gates and light the walls! Post your men on the battlements in rotations. We will have a battle by morning!"

30

At first light a day later, Elle Barros rode her horse along the Kingroad just outside of Lidran, surrounded by a full company of Sagmynan and Iraean Legionmen—all Ire Legionmen, she supposed. It was still odd to her that these men, and so many others, owed their loyalty to Emrael. To think that less than a year earlier, she and Emrael had been riding this very stretch of road together. Emrael injured and delirious, Yamara on the brink of death after being captured by Corlas, Darmon Corrande, and a squad of Watchers.

She cleared her sleep-deprived mind of memories and focused on the task at hand as Lidran's walls emerged from the morning fog. They approached the gate just as it was being opened at sunrise. The sergeant in charge of the squad guarding the gate took one look at one hundred armed men not in Barros grey, and immediately began shouting for the gates to be closed. Within moments, the alarm bell above the gate rang loudly and Barros Legionmen with crossbows ran to take positions on the ramparts. They no doubt thought that Emrael had come to raid the city, though a single company would never ride straight for the gates like this if they meant to attack.

Elle continued ahead of the company of Iraeans as they called for a halt. She walked her horse slowly toward the gate and waved a white cloth over her head. Thankfully, no crossbow bolts or arrows flew her way, and as she reached the gate, the sergeant in charge drew a small side door open.

"Who are you?" he demanded. "Don't come any closer."

Elle stopped. "I am Arielle Barros, Sergeant. I would like an audience with whoever commands my father's garrison here in Lidran."

The sergeant paused. "That would be Lord Holder Gerlan, Lady. I can send a messenger," he said doubtfully, obviously unsure what to do with a strange woman riding up to the gates with a full company of armed men, claiming to be the daughter of the governor.

"Be quick about it, Sergeant. Tell the Lord Holder that Arielle Barros has been refused entry to the city."

The Legionman's eyes widened. "Ah . . . you're welcome to enter, but your men will have to wait outside. No armed men that ain't Barros Legion, by order of the Lord Holder."

She shrugged. "I'll bring five men with me, a mere honor guard. They will leave their weapons with you, Sergeant, so you won't be disobeying any orders."

The Legionman hesitated again, clearly uncomfortable but pacified by the offer to leave their weapons. Elle took his hesitation as being close enough to acceptance and turned to shout for the four Imperators and the Captain Third of the Ire Legion company to accompany her. In short order, they turned over their weapons and rode with her to the Legion compound while the rest of their men made camp in the forest outside the city.

When they arrived at the compound, Elle was met by a man in armor adorned with the two riveted steel shoulder straps of a Captain Second. Two full squads of Legionmen stood behind him, ten of them with loaded crossbows. They clearly did not trust Elle and her companions. Considering Emrael's attacks months earlier and the political instability undoubtedly rife in the province after her father's death, she couldn't blame them.

Belatedly, she realized that the Captain Second was none other than Prilan, the man who had been tasked with seeing them to the capital earlier in the year.

"Prilan," she greeted him warmly, ignoring the armed men behind him. "A Captain Second, so soon?"

Prilan flashed his handsome smile—he seemed to be in a much better humor than when she had last seen him. To be fair, he had been caught up in quite the fiasco, attacked by soulbound and then effectively taken prisoner by the very prisoners with whom he had been charged.

"My Lady Arielle," Prilan said with a bow. "I was sorry to hear about your father."

A pit formed in Elle's stomach, but she kept a neutral expression on her face. "I was too. What can you tell me about how he died? My sister's letter was sent urgently but said only that he was attacked."

Prilan's eyes hardened. "Yes. We know only that he was attacked in his own palace. Most think it was the doing of the southern Lords Holder, as his death coincided perfectly with their march on Ridgetop and Naeran. I myself think that the Ire bastard and his Ordenan ilk are more likely to be responsible."

Elle's smile quirked into a frown. "Captain Prilan," she admonished gently. "Whatever else can be said of him, I am quite sure that Emrael did not kill my father. I will find the truth, but I'll need your help to see it done."

Prilan's smile this time was tight-lipped, but he gave her another bow. "Right this way, my lady. Your men can wait in the entry room, I'll take you to the Lord Holder. Your father tasked him with overseeing operations here in Lidran after his nephew, Captain First Luere Gerlan, was murdered. Reports say that Emrael Ire himself took part in the murder, with an Ordenan accomplice."

"And if that's true, we will ensure that Lord Ire pays a price for that injustice, and for his intrusions on Barros lands. But it cannot preclude an alliance with him, and even the Ordenans. We have a greater enemy, for now. You know that as well as anyone, Prilan. You've seen them."

Prilan nodded thoughtfully as they walked the halls of the command building where the Lord Holder had his office. "You may be right, but it won't be easy. Not for me, and especially not for the Lord Holder. Good luck."

He stopped next to a large set of arced wooden double doors and knocked politely.

"Come in," a scratchy but deep, strong voice boomed.

Prilan opened and held a door for her while she swept into a room that smelled of dust and old leather. The gleaming wooden shelves that covered every wall were stuffed full with books. More books littered the two sofas and various side tables in the room.

An old man with a large, strong frame that had once likely held considerable muscle but was now mostly sinew sat in a leather-upholstered chair behind the large desk near the window at the far side of the room.

"What do you want?" he rasped.

Elle strode to one of the chairs on the opposite side of the Lord Holder's desk and sat without waiting for an invitation. "What I want, Lord Gerlan, is for you to do your duty."

The old Lord Holder looked up at her over the paper he had been reading through heavy spectacles, forehead wrinkled and eyes wide with astonishment.

"Excuse me?"

"I want you," Elle said loudly and slowly, clearly pretending to be talking to an invalid, "to do your duty. If my father is dead, your duty is to see his heir assume his place as governor. Has my sister declared herself Governor of Barros?"

Lord Holder Gerlan growled in anger. "I ought to have you arrested, colluding with the bastard that killed my nephew, invaded my lands, killed our people. Listen here—"

"No," Elle cut in firmly with a toss of her head. "I'm done listening. All of that is regrettable, and will be reckoned with. But it does not change the path we must take. Has my sister assumed the Governorship?"

He grunted. "No."

Elle stared into his watery blue eyes. "Then I must assume that I am my father's only remaining capable heir. Your allegiance, and that of the Legionmen left here with you, is owed to me."

He stared at her for a long while. The room was silent save for the ticking of a clock and the quiet rasp of Lord Holder Gerlan's breathing.

"Did you know," he rumbled, "that the southern bastards besieging Naeran have allied with Emrael Ire?"

Elle's stomach lurched. "What?"

Lord Holder Gerlan nodded, a sad frown sagging his weathered face. "Ordenans just like the ones who walked in with you delivered an offer of alliance from the Ire boy to the Lords Valantes, Erlene, and Sumraec. They tried to get me to join them, even after what they did to my nephew. Ire goaded them into attacking your province, and as far as I know could be behind your father's death as well."

Elle paused as the sinking feeling in her gut amplified. She hadn't known about Emrael's communication with the southern

Lords Holder, but it was plausible that he'd seek an alliance after her father had rebuffed his offer. It felt like something he would do.

She shook her head sadly. "Emrael is a fool at times, and a dangerous one at that. But we must be pragmatic about the situation. We cannot afford to fight him and the foreign Malithii who have joined with the Corrandes at once, and I have seen for myself that the Malithii are the more pressing enemy. They have just attacked the Sagmyn Valley again, and we are undoubtedly next."

The gaunt old man across the desk from her sighed. "What issue is that of ours? We are allied with the Corrandes and the Watchers. Why should we now fear them and ally ourselves with rebels that have wronged us? They hold Gadford even now! I for one will welcome the Watchers. We'll see how the rebels like fighting the full might of the Provinces."

"Damal, it's not as simple as that anymore. The Corrandes have allied with the forces of the Fallen. They turn men and women into half-dead monsters called soulbound."

"Do not speak to me of the Fallen or any of your religious nonsense," Damal replied gruffly. "I'll not be tricked into your foolishness as easily as that."

Elle frowned at him in disapproval. "I assure you that these monsters are very real, and that their Westland masters will be the end of the Provinces if we fail to defeat them. Ask Prilan if you don't believe me."

She paused to calm herself and focus. If the man didn't even believe that the threat they faced was real, pleas for reason would be of no use. "That's beside the point, though, isn't it? You are alone, Lord Holder. Emrael Ire and his allies are to your north, east, and now south. Regardless of my motivations—or your beliefs—I am your only hope. Give me your loyalty and send men from the Barros Legion compound here to get me to the capital. I alone can negotiate peace between the southern Lords Holder, Emrael Ire, and his mother in the Sagmyn Province who represents Ordenan interests."

Damal sat back in his chair, staring at her in silence, so she continued in a soft, sinister voice. "Or, you can take a chance on Corrande and the Watchers. It's possible that they'll defeat Emrael's forces in Iraea and Sagmyn. It's possible that they have finally devised a way to defeat the Ordenans, who have allied themselves with Emrael Ire. It's even possible that the southern Barros Lords Holder let you live long enough to see it."

The Lord Holder sank back further in his chair, his eyes sunken and haunted now. "Hmmmph," he grunted noncommittally.

"You have something like ten thousand Barros men stationed here, correct?" she asked, standing as if the Lord Holder had agreed to support her. Nerves made her stomach flutter, but she let none of that show on her face or in her voice. "I need four thousand of them to get me to Naeran safely, and to bolster whatever men my father had in the capital. You'll keep six thousand, and your primary concern will be to hold the West Pass against any intruders. In return, I'll see to it that Emrael Ire returns Gadford to you, and I'll increase your share of the tariff on goods flowing through Lidran and Gadford to fifty percent of net proceeds for ten years."

"Fifty percent?" Damal raised his eyebrows, sitting forward to rest his forearms on the desk. He was clearly interested now. "The Ire boy will just give Gadford to you, easy as asking?"

Elle put on a soft smile that she hoped hid her lack of certainty. "I believe I have the answer to that riddle, given proper support from my Lords Holder. Starting with you, Lord Gerlan."

"And what of your sister? She's the rightful heir to your House, is she not?"

"She is. Or would be, if she were capable of such. The Westlander priests have placed one of their . . . *magic* devices on her," Elle said, using a term for mindbinder Craftings that the no-nonsense old Provincial Lord would understand. "Even if she can be recovered, I am the right Barros to lead my House and this province. I am the effective governor now. Our articles allow for such, and my sister will agree with me, one way or another."

Lord Gerlan harrumphed. "Better you than those southern bastards or your daft sister, I suppose. You'll not get any open declarations of support from me, however! Not until you have settled the southern Lords Holder and given Gadford back to me."

Elle smiled. She had really done it! "That will be fine, Lord

Holder. For now, the Legionmen will be sufficient. I will contact you as soon as I've settled things in Naeran."

Lord Holder Damal Gerlan swept one hand across his mostly bald pate and sighed throatily. "Absent Gods send you do, girl. I wish you luck."

31

Emrael lost count of the number of skirmishes he and his men had fought on their way to the Tryllan temple. What he did know was that nearly a third of his men were dead, left to rot in the streets as they retreated.

The summer sun drained their legs of energy as they ran for leagues. Sweat ran down their faces beneath padded helmets and armor. Only the injured lagged, however, and were loaded quickly into wagons when they did. The soulbound weren't particularly fast, but never seemed to tire, and Emrael's wounded could only march so quickly. By the time the Iraeans had marched a league, the soulbound would catch them and force another fight. Once or twice, a contingent of Westlanders had fought with the undead monsters.

Emrael led each battle himself, fighting until he was delirious with exhaustion. Most canteens had long since run dry, and stopping to refill from the water barrels in the supply wagons was out of the question. At least half of his company of Royal Guardsmen were dead or riding the wagons with the other seriously wounded.

He laughed in exhausted relief as he finally caught sight of Jaina up ahead, waving to them from the entrance to the timeworn but still-solid walls of the temple fortress. He heard many sighs of relief all around him, and they all picked up their pace without needing encouragement. Legionmen from Jaina's advance party manned the walls with crossbows as the wagons bearing their wounded and supplies went through the stone archway at the corner of the compound. Emrael's bowmen and the bulk of the foot soldiers followed while Emrael, his Guard, and Third Battalion formed a loose shield wall behind them. Nearly an hour had passed since they had last been attacked by soulbound, but Emrael didn't believe for a minute that they had given up the chase. In fact, it might have been his imagination, but he thought he heard a rumbling shuffle of thousands of their tireless feet pounding their way down a nearby avenue. Absent Gods send they didn't have any Westlander bowmen with them this time.

"Hurry through!" he shouted at his men. "Push, push. The bastards are almost on us!"

Sure enough, less than five minutes later, a small cloud of dust preceded a horde of soulbound charging down the avenue directly at them. The monsters howled and screamed as they ran in their shuffling gate, wildly swinging their heavy, rusted weapons. The greater part of Emrael's men had made it inside, but there was no way they'd all make it in safely without another fight. Trying to hide behind wooden shields only worked so well against the fearless, inhumanly strong soulbound. And now that the majority of his men were inside the walls of the temple grounds, those outside the wall would be cut into mincemeat—including Emrael himself. They had no more explosives, and dragging the rest of his forces back out of the safety of the walled temple compound to fight a pitched battle was out of the question. Emrael would have to do something himself.

As Emrael stepped out from behind the protection of the shield wall, he shouted to the twenty or so mages that had followed him. "Timan, give me Yirram and a few more, and you take the other Stonebreakers to the other side of the avenue. We'll bring down enough buildings to block the road. That should give us time to retreat and secure the walls of the compound."

Timan nodded and assigned Daglund and seven other men and women to Emrael quickly, leading the rest down the avenue in the other direction. Emrael and Yirram, the blocky Imperator Stonebreaker who had trained him often in recent months, wasted no time in finding the largest stone building on their side of the street, a huge six-story edifice made of white limestone.

Yirram immediately began inspecting the stone walls at the ground level that supported the enormous structure, running his thick, meaty hands over the stone the way another man would touch his lover. "The trick will be weakening the stone just enough that it will tumble, but not immediately. These rotten buildings could collapse any which way, crushing us all if we are not careful." He gave Emrael a long look, a sardonic slant to one corner of his mouth. "Which means that you should stand back while I work."

Despite his exhaustion and the impending danger, Emrael chuckled. Yirram wasn't wrong, but they didn't have time for one person to bring down the entire building. Already they could hear the stomping feet of soulbound drawing nearer.

"No time for you to dally, Yirram," Emrael joked. "You start here, I'll begin weakening the other side. If we cut clean through the front wall here, weaken the sides, and leave the rear wall intact, it should collapse right into the street like we want. Leave a good bit solid toward the back and I'll give it a push when we've got everyone clear." He jogged to his side of the building and called out to the rest of the team of mages—two more Ordenan Imperators and six Iraean apprentices—asking them to watch the perimeter of the building.

Emrael put his hand to the pouch on his belt and drew on a charged coil he had snagged from a supply wagon in their hasty retreat to the temple compound, as his armor had long since been depleted. Demolishing a wide swath of stone at the front of the building was simple enough, though the building groaned ominously each time he destroyed an arm's-width portion of stone. Weakening the stone on the side of the building was far more difficult. Weaken even one section too much and the whole building would crash down on their heads. Much of the sweat now rolling down Emrael's forehead had nothing to do with physical exertion, or even the physical toll of working with so much *infusori*.

Yirram finished well before he did—the man had been practicing the mage Art for decades, after all—and helped him on his side. Finally they finished and Emrael called to the other mages as they exited the gaping rectangular entrance to the building where large doors would have once stood.

Soulbound were just visible down the avenue, perhaps two hundred paces to the north and west. Screams and the clash of steel on shields told them that fighting had already started to the south where their men had formed a shield wall to block the wide street. They didn't have much time.

Emrael led the way down a side alley to the rear of the enormous building they had just weakened. He issued quick orders for the rest of the mages to stand back while he and Yirram prepared to bring the building down for good.

As Yirram put his hands to the building's rear wall, his large muscles bulged and rippled as if he were going to push the building over with brute physical force.

"Wait," Emrael barked. Yirram looked at him quizzically.

"Listen," Emrael said.

The shuffle of the soulbound grew louder and louder, but because they traveled as a mindless herd, they kept to the main avenue where their Malithii masters drove them. The mages were relatively safe in their alleyway.

"Wait for the Malithii to reach the building. Might as well take out some of the bastards while we're here."

They hardly breathed as they watched a dense mass of soulbound begin to pass the other end of the long alleyway to the side of their building. When they judged enough had passed that their Malithii masters were likely nearby, Emrael nodded to Yirram, who put his hands back to the stone wall. An instant later, Emrael felt a burst of *infusori* flow from the Imperator's hands. A loud crack made them all flinch involuntarily, and then the building in front of them groaned ominously.

"Run!" Yirram shouted, putting a hand to Emrael's back to give him a shove. They sprinted back toward the temple compound, but a few of the mages were too slow. A pretty red-haired young woman Emrael didn't know by name and Daglund had been at the far side of the alleyway farthest from the temple compound and thus had the farthest to run.

Most of the building collapsed into the wide avenue just as they had planned, undoubtedly crushing hundreds of soulbound and hopefully their Malithii masters with them. A large portion of the rear wall had stayed intact, however, and now rebounded as the rest of the building snapped away from it.

Emrael felt as much as saw the large section of stone wall begin to tip back toward them. Daglund and the redhead had no chance to outrun the thousands of pounds of falling rock.

Emrael turned as quick as thought, already pulling the last of the *infusori* from his coils as he reversed course. He met Daglund and the redhead just before an enormous stone block fell on them.

Emrael stretched his arms above his head and poured *infusori* into the stone at the exact moment that it made contact with his fingers. *Infusori* washed through the falling stone in a wave, turning it to sand even as it fell on them.

He was buried to the neck in the resulting enormous pile of powdery sand, and Daglund to the shoulders. Only a shock of auburn hair showed where the pretty young mage had been. Daglund struggled free and began digging her out frantically as Emrael thrashed, trying to create room to dig himself free. The other mages were there in a few moments that felt like years.

"Alsi!" one of the other Iraean mages cried as she leapt to help unbury the redhead. They finally uncovered her face, which was covered in snot, drool, and caked sand as the poor girl coughed and struggled for air. At least she was alive. That was a win in Emrael's book, considering that the alternative would have been a puddle of gore under a large heap of limestone.

Now exhausted nearly to the point of delirium, Emrael stopped struggling as Yirram and another Imperator dug him free, yanking him out by the shoulders when they dug down far enough to get a grip on him. He stumbled as he climbed down from the small hill the sand had created, and finally his legs gave out.

Yirram was there to lend a hand again. "Sweet Sisters, lad. I have never seen anything like that," he said as he hauled Emrael to his feet. The bulky Imperator waved one hand over his head to mimic what Emrael had done. "Do you even know how stupid that was?"

Emrael smiled through the exhaustion that made him want to empty his stomach. "No, not really. Guess this makes me the best Stonebreaker in the group now, eh?"

Yirram chuckled. "Long way to go yet, boy, but you will be showing me that trick again if I have to throw rocks at you every day for the rest of your life."

Emrael grunted a chuckle and turned to where the others had just freed the red-haired girl, Alsi. "She okay?"

Alsi herself nodded even as she continued to cough and retch. "Just need some water," she rasped.

"Let's get back to the compound then," he said. "Four-rank formation, Alsi in the middle. There are going to be stray soulbound and perhaps a Malithii or two between us and the gate." He waved a hand tiredly at where the alley they were in ended in a stone wall. They would have to venture back into the main avenue to get to safety, as the walls of the compound were too high to scale quickly.

When they reached the main avenue, they found dozens of dust-covered soulbound lurching about in a rage. Many of them sported several crossbow bolts shot by the Iraeans guarding the temple compound but still wandered about looking for something to kill, not yet having bled to death.

Emrael let the others take the lead, content to be in the second rank, tired as he was. They moved swiftly and quietly, striking down soulbound only where they had to.

As the group emerged from the haze of dust fifty paces or so from the temple gate, several crossbow bolts flew toward them as a cry of alarm was raised.

"Don't shoot, you Fallen idiots!" Emrael screamed hoarsely. "Don't shoot, we're friendly!"

Another bolt flashed in their direction as he shouted. A jolt of panic coursed through him as he thought it would take him full in the chest, but the Iraean mage just in front of him moved just enough to take the bolt instead. It hit the man in the upper arm and stuck there, likely having struck the bone.

Emrael caught the injured mage as he fell, but stumbled and nearly fell himself. The man cried out in pain as Emrael lowered him to the ground, and quickly lost consciousness. He would probably lose the arm, if he didn't die before they got him to safety.

Fallen Glory, what Emrael would have given for a Mage-Healer.

The commotion caught the attention of a group of soulbound that had been hacking away at the ranks of Iraeans still defending the gate in a shield wall. A dozen or so of the beasts turned and lumbered straight at the mages with him, who had no shields to protect themselves. The mages in the front ranks parried the powerful soulbound blows desperately as they met their charge, and in the blink of an eye the soulbound were right in the middle of their formation.

Emrael was forced to abandon the injured mage as a soulbound charged straight at them. He didn't have time to draw his weapon, so he ducked the wild swing and used its momentum to redirect it, tripping the soulbound with one leg as it passed him. He had his weapon out in a flash, battle rage giving his spent muscles renewed strength. His sword cut cleanly through the soulbound's neck as it tried to regain its feet. The monster collapsed, its spine severed.

A scream to his left made him whip his head around in time to see one of the Iraean mages spitted on a soulbound's sword, its vicious thrust having punched straight through his leather and metal plate armor. The soulbound tried to shake the mage's body from its weapon with powerful heaves of its arm. The fatally wounded mage gasped in pain, blood flowing from his mouth and the wound in his gut. Emrael screamed in rage as he swung his own blade.

His tired body wasn't obeying him perfectly anymore, and his aim suffered for it. Instead of taking the soulbound through the neck as he intended, the last two inches of his sword lodged in the soulbound's skull. The soulbound dropped instantly, taking Emrael's weapon with it.

He dropped to the ground, reaching for his hilt. A whoosh of a weapon slicing through the air above him made the hair on the back of his neck prickle. He had just avoided being chopped in half by pure chance. When he couldn't shake his sword free, he rolled as quickly as he could to regain his feet, drawing the short sword at his side. The soulbound that had just tried to split him in two lunged to grab Emrael with an impossibly strong two-armed bear hug, tackling him back to the ground.

Emrael's nostrils filled with the fetid stench of the half-dead soulbound as he struggled in vain to free his arms from the monster's grip. The soulbound atop him no longer tried to use its weapon either, opting instead to bite with broken, yellow teeth at Emrael's neck, where only a thin collar of chain mail protected him. He pushed with all his might, even dredging up the last vestiges of *infusori* left in his body to fuel his strength, but couldn't break the monster's hold on him. A piercing pain and warm wetness on his shoulder told him that the soulbound had broken skin.

A calm came over him, Jaina's years of training kicking in when he needed it most. Rather than try to fight with brute strength, he elevated his hips, put one foot under him, and twisted violently so he was now on top of the soulbound. He was still locked in its arms, but now he was free to pull his head and neck away from his attacker. He spun to the side, finally freeing one arm, though he had to drop his short sword to do it. He put his free arm into the soulbound's neck, keeping its teeth away from him. Its tight grip limited his breathing, however, and was so powerful that he thought his ribs might break. He needed to get out of this thing's grasp, and evidently nobody was going to do it for him.

Desperate, he touched the soulbound's bare skin with his hand, opening himself to its life source, intending to kill the monster by absorbing it as he had done occasionally with human opponents.

When he opened himself to the soulbound's life source, however, he recoiled involuntarily, shutting off all contact as quickly as he could. Even still, he began to retch at even the brief exposure to the creature's putrid, corrupted life source. Worse, he was left with the distinct impression that the person within this twisted creature felt everything—felt its own body decaying, felt the pain of every injury, sorrow at what it was forced to do by the Malithii controlling its soulbinder. It was still a person, trapped in a living nightmare.

Emrael snapped back to reality. He didn't have time to pity the soulbound, who was still squeezing the life out of him and attempting to sink its cragged teeth into his exposed flesh.

A boot stomped near Emrael's head and a sword flashed just to the left of his face, spearing the soulbound through the eye. The grey-skinned creature sank back to the ground with a sigh, finally releasing him.

"No time for lying about," Daglund said, pulling Emrael to his feet by the collar of his armored vest. All of the soulbound who had attacked them were dead, but there were more already clambering over the enormous heap of rubble behind them. Daglund began to pull Emrael toward the safety of the temple compound, where all of the Iraeans had finally made it inside the walls, but Emrael resisted.

"Wait!" he barked, pulling free of his guard's steadying grip. He stumbled back to where he had dropped his sword, wrenching it from the soulbound's skull with a whip of his arm. He secured his short sword as well and resheathed both quickly before he jogged back to where the mage who had taken an arrow to the arm still lay unconscious. Emrael felt his pulse to make sure he was still alive and called Daglund and another Iraean over to carry the man to safety.

He followed them to the gate, where three ranks of shields still held, waiting for the party of mages to make it back to the compound, which encompassed dozens of buildings that surrounded the ancient Ravan temple.

Jaina, a concerned expression on her face, met him as soon as he was through the ranks of shields. "What took you so long?" Then, when he stumbled on one knee, she put a hand to the blood running down his arm and said, "Where are you bleeding?"

"My neck," he said, lurching to his feet. "One of the soulbound *bit* me. Can you believe that? Is there somewhere I can rest? I can barely see straight."

Jaina, however, was already shouting for a healer to bring boiling water, distilled alcohol, and some bandages. She pulled him into a nearby building and sat him down on a crate while she continued shouting until two Legion healers came running with the supplies she had demanded. Emrael's serving man, Jorim, came running as well, fresh clothing and travel rations in hand.

"It's only a minor wound, Jaina," Emrael said, confused at the ferocity with which she was removing the armor and clothing covering his bite wound.

She looked at him, her dark eyes haunted, her mouth set in a worried frown. "No, Emrael. Soulbound can transmit terrible diseases with their bite. We must disinfect it immediately."

He grimaced. Disinfecting was going to hurt. "The alcohol will take care of it?" he asked hopefully.

She pulled the cork from a glass bottle of distilled alcohol that the healers kept for just such an occasion. "No, but we have to try. If we do not get you to a Mage-Healer within three days, there is an even chance you will die of a terrible fever. Even if you do not die, your mind might be ruined forever. It happens every so often in the Imperial Army. Most often, those that are stupid enough to wrestle with soulbound do not live to worry about the illness."

"Daglund seems to be fine now," Emrael suggested. "Couldn't he just Heal it?"

Jaina shook her head. "He is a decent battlefield Healer, but nowhere near experienced enough to burn away a disease safely. Not until we have no other choice."

She pulled Emrael's armor from him and accepted a stiff-bristled brush from a healer, while the other healer bathed the wound with a cloth and warm water.

"You will not enjoy this," Jaina said, pity in her eyes. She turned to the two healers. "Hold him still."

"I'll be fine, Jaina," he said, waving them away. "I don't need to be held."

She raised one eyebrow skeptically, but shrugged and poured a good quarter of the bottle of alcohol over his shoulder before starting in with the brush.

Emrael had to choke back a scream when the alcohol burned its way into his shoulder, but when the brush began scouring the chewed-up flesh, he felt his head spin and his vision faded.

Emrael jerked awake to find Jaina tenderly dressing his neck, his shoulder, and the forearm that had been wounded days earlier. She put a warm hand to his chest, pressing him back down on the cot he had been moved to while unconscious. "Lie still a moment."

The smell of distilled alcohol still permeated the air. Jorim and the healers were gone—they were alone in a small tent that had been set up away from the fighting at the gate, judging by the now-muted sound of bowstrings snapping. He no longer heard the crash of weapons on shields, nor the chorus of shouting that accompanied close quarters battle, so his men must have succeeded in blockading the gate opening.

Emrael sat quiet for a moment as his friend tended to his wounds, which now throbbed with a deep, burning pain, reliving the recent battle and his unfortunate encounter with the soulbound's life source.

He looked up sharply as he recalled the crossbow bolt that would have hit him square in the chest had it not hit the mage in front of him instead. "Did Timan make it back?"

She nodded. "Yes, but he's being treated. Took a cut to the leg. He will need to rest for some time."

Emrael grimaced. "Jaina, I need you to find the man who shot at me as we approached the gate."

She glanced at him, mildly surprised. "It was an honest accident, Emrael. We could hardly see and had been shooting at soulbound. Your troops are far from experts, besides."

Emrael began to shake his head, but stopped as it caused a searing flash of pain in his neck. "Check the bolt lodged in the mage's arm . . . I don't know his name, but he took that bolt for me, Jaina. It was aimed directly at me, in the middle of the formation. Someone within our forces killed Darrain earlier, as we retreated from the square. Shot in the back. Looked like a Watcher bolt to me."

Jaina's jaw clenched and her eyes narrowed. She hadn't known about Darrain. "I'll look into it," she said, her voice hard. She had liked the clever Crafter.

"Now," she said, standing. "Keep your bandages clean and dry, and rest. I am going to look around the Ravan temple. Perhaps I can find something like Crafted healing aids."

Emrael smiled. "I thought temple Craftings were too dangerous to go sifting through?"

She frowned and arched an eyebrow. "Assumption of risk is warranted in this instance." Her eyes flicked to his bandaged neck. "You will die without intervention."

Emrael's smile faded. "And a Crafted healing aid would do the trick?"

She shook her head and shifted her weight from one foot to the other. "I do not know, but we should try. It will be difficult to reach a Mage-Healer in time."

"Don't bother, then. I'll go down into the temple later. I can pull enough *infusori* from the Well to do more than a Crafting could."

She wagged her head, thinking. "It is not the same, and will not heal you. It may, however, buy you a little more time, or keep you functional longer at the very least. The excess *infusori* may purge some of the illness the soulbound has passed to you, keep it at bay. It is worth a try."

Emrael tensed his muscles in anticipation of pain and rocked himself out of the cot and to his feet. Sure enough, his neck and shoulder felt like they were on fire, and his forearm throbbed with a dull ache. He had almost forgotten about his arm.

"Let's go take a look at the crossbow bolt in our friend's arm first," he said gruffly as he breathed deep through the surging pain.

He used his good arm to pull his boots on and shrugged on his armor with Jorim's help, then walked out of the tent after stamping his feet a few times to make sure his legs would hold him. Absent Gods, he was tired.

As he followed Jaina out of the tent, a few nearby men—the injured and those tending them, mostly—raised a quiet cheer. Emrael waved to them as he passed.

Jaina finally stopped next to a large tent and held the flap aside for him. Inside, the poor Iraean mage who had been struck in the arm lay on a cot of his own, still unconscious. One of the Legion healers had cut the mage's uniform away to expose the wound, the crossbow bolt still protruding from a puckered, swollen gash. Sure enough, the bolt looked like those the Watchers carried, dyed pure black.

Timan limped into the tent as Emrael and Jaina discussed treatment options with the healer, who wanted to amputate the arm to prevent infection and death. The mage's arm had swollen significantly, but even still it was obvious that the bone had been broken by the crossbow bolt.

"You are not taking Boran's arm," Timan told the healer gruffly. "He is one of our best swords. Dairus can heal him, we just need to get back to the main compound. Assuming Dairus is still alive." He looked to Emrael. "We have a plan to get across the river to your brother, right?"

Emrael grimaced. "Not yet, but we will."

"And it has to be soon," Jaina added.

Timan's eyes flicked to Emrael's bandages. "Why? What happened?"

"An *alai'ahn* bit him," she replied.

"Shit," Timan growled, eyes now pinched with worry. "I will gather the Captains right away. We will be at the temple in an hour to plan the next move."

He turned to leave immediately, but looked back once as he reached the tent flap. "I have two of the Guard tailing you today, even in the camp. Make it easy for them, would you? And do not allow them to take Boran's arm. I will let Daglund have a run at him before we resort to that."

The Legion healer didn't look happy. "I can keep him alive a few days, but he'll need to ride in a wagon with the other seriously wounded."

Emrael grunted. "Begin planning a move, please, for all of your patients. We'll likely move again sometime during the night."

As he and Jaina strode out of the tent, something occurred to him and he looked to Jaina, his eyes wide. "Soulbound can't see any better than we can in the dark, can they?"

She shook her head. "No, and it's common practice in the Ordenan army to move at night, as the Malithii struggle to organize their Mindless in the dark. They can do it, but not easily."

Daglund and Alsi—still covered in stone dust from the mishap with the collapsing building—turned out to be the members of the Royal Guard assigned to follow Emrael today. Emrael and Jaina walked the perimeter of the compound so Emrael could see the measures they had taken to barricade several gaps in the compound wall. Most had been shored up with blocks of stone piled into the gaps, but here and there holes had only been stopped up with broken supply carts, camp equipment, anything that had been on hand. Such poor defenses would never hold against the mindless ferocity of the soulbound, even with men stationed all along the walls, crossbows ready to decimate the enemy. Even with solid walls, however, they had no supplies and wouldn't last long. Their best hope lay in moving across the river before the Malithii could herd the bulk of their army here.

They reached the portion of the compound where Darmon and his Watchers had set up their tents and were seeing to their hundreds of wounded. Rows and rows of cots filled with men wrapped in blood-soaked bandages filled the broken buildings, streets, and small square where they had set up their camp. Darmon himself walked the lines, a bandage around his head. When he saw Emrael approaching, he bowed deeply, and the Watcher officers with him followed suit.

Despite his show of humility and the Watchers' valiant efforts in the earlier battle, Emrael had to suppress a surge of anger when he saw his old enemy. He of all people knew that their war with the forces of the Fallen would require him to ally with anyone willing, but that didn't mean all was forgiven. Certainly not forgotten.

A Watcher crossbow bolt had been one arm away from punching through Emrael's heart a few hours ago, after all.

"One of my mages has a Watcher crossbow bolt in his arm, Darmon."

Darmon's eyebrows drew down in concern. "It has been an awful day, Emrael. Thousands of my men are dead, thousands more wounded," he said, waving his hands in a wide arc. "Mistakes happen, Emrael, but I assure you—"

"It was aimed at me, Darmon," Emrael growled, stepping closer to stare up into Darmon's eyes. "My best Crafter is also dead, a bolt in her back. A suspicious man might wonder whether a bastard like you has ulterior motives in forming an alliance with an old enemy."

Darmon's face blanched as he saw the rage in Emrael's eyes. "Emrael—"

Emrael's mouth tightened.

"Ah . . . Lord Ire . . ."

Emrael nodded slightly, and Darmon continued, eyes wide with caution. "I'll look into it myself. I swear on the Faceless Gods and on my life, my pledge was made in good faith. But . . . it's possible that the Malithii have an agent among my men. I've seen devices they use, Craftings that give them a measure of control over their victims."

Darmon had the grace to look embarrassed. He had used variations of mindbinders when he had helped the Malithii take the Crafters at the Citadel hostage.

Emrael took a deep breath, breaking his stare to look around at the Watchers. Nearly everyone had some wound or another. They had fought well, Darmon included.

"We call them mindbinders," Emrael allowed grudgingly. "I'll assign a pair of my surviving mages to you. They'll know how to check your men for such Craftings. Have you seen the Malithii use them often?"

Darmon shook his head as he ran his hand along his jaw. "They seem to have very few. I only saw their most senior priest use them, and usually on high-value targets."

Emrael looked over at Jaina. "As you suspected."

Darmon looked worried. "I wouldn't have thought to see one

here, particularly on a soldier. Whoever placed it would have had to do so well ahead of time and would have had to anticipate that I'd be here, with you. Either that, or—"

"They're still here," Emrael finished grimly. "Inspect your men carefully, Darmon. I will hold you accountable for any further incidents, mindbinders or no. Darrain was a friend."

Darmon looked like he wanted to say more, but wisely held his tongue. Emrael was in no mood for anything but agreement from Darmon and his ilk.

"I want you and your officers to meet me and mine at the temple building at the center of the compound in an hour. I'll have orders."

Darmon saluted sharply, and the Watcher officers with him followed suit.

Jaina immediately shepherded him to the temple itself, obviously anxious to search for a Crafting that might be of use in healing Emrael's wound. The temple's outer foyer had been left unoccupied and the door to the temple itself remained closed—only a mage could open it, after all, and those who weren't injured or otherwise recovering were undoubtedly assigned to the walls. Daglund and Alsi silently took up positions at the single door leading into the foyer from outside while Emrael crossed straight to the *infusori*-activated doorway.

"We do not have much time, Emrael," Jaina said as he opened the doorway with a quick pulse of *infusori*. "Stay in the temple as long as you can, and hold as much *infusori* as you are able. Perhaps I am wrong. Perhaps it will heal you."

They descended the stairs into the ancient Ravan temple. The inscription in the walls began to glow before they reached the bottom landing, almost as if the ancient structure were greeting them. As soon as he entered the temple, he felt the tingle of *infusori* all around him. He started down the hallway of the temple, pulling *infusori* in greedily, letting its energy wash through him. The immense amount of power coursing through him didn't take away his pain and soul-crushing weariness, but it made them easier to live with.

"What is your plan to get across the bridges?" Jaina asked as she followed him down the temple hallway. "The Malithii and Watchers still obeying them will undoubtedly move quickly to secure them, or even destroy them. If that happens, we will die."

Emrael slowed until he could see Jaina as she walked beside him. "We'll move as soon as it's dark. Standard box and wedge, five ranks deep, bowmen then horse in the center. When we get to the bridges, we'll have the bowmen hit them with crossfire at angles while our pikes push theirs. We'll have to move fast to keep from being taken from behind by soulbound, but I don't see what else we can do. If we stay, we die. If we run, we die. And our men trapped to the south die as well. A lot of us will die anyway but it's our only option that entails some chance of success, so we'll hit it hard. Or did you have a better plan up your sleeve?"

When Jaina glared at him silently, he grumbled, "Exactly."

Though he already had the pulsing power of the temple's *infusori* Well flowing through him, he walked purposefully down the long hallway to the last room, where he knew the book of visions waited for him. He could not have said why he felt the need to go so far into the depths of the temple—he didn't plan to spend time perusing the book of visions. His Captains would be waiting for him, not to mention the preparations for the impending battle. The power within him seemed to grow in intensity as he walked deeper into the structure, however, and he figured that if a little *infusori* might help him, a lot of *infusori* had a better chance still.

He locked eyes with Jaina as he stopped at the doorway to the chamber that held the book of visions. "How long do you think I need to stay down here?"

She shrugged. "Hold as much *infusori* as you can. If it is going to work, ten or twenty minutes should be sufficient."

He pulled harder at the *infusori* surrounding him, filling himself with so much that he felt every element of his being vibrating in time with its pulse. Jaina watched, and though she showed no obvious emotion, he knew her well enough to see that she was nervous. Why should she be? He felt better than he had in ages, injuries or no.

He smiled, touching her shoulder briefly as he stepped into the room holding the book of visions. He was already here, he might as well take a quick look.

The moment he stepped through the doorway, a solid metal door he hadn't known existed slid out of the doorframe behind him. Jaina sprang back into the hallway with a yelp as it slammed shut, only narrowly avoiding being crushed.

Emrael was left in the room, alone with the book of visions. He looked around with wide eyes, a sudden surge of fear pushing him to a state of heightened alertness. The copper-inlaid script in the walls stopped glowing, plunging the room into darkness. Only a small pattern of angular script in the ceiling continued to glow, but did almost nothing to light the room.

"Absent Gods," he muttered to himself as he edged back toward the door.

This felt all too much like one of the visions, particularly the one of the Fallen himself that had been forced on him by way of the mad Prophet, Savian. If Jaina was making any noise on the other side of the wall, he couldn't hear it. He put his hand to the cold metal surface of the door after he backed up into it, sending a surge of *infusori* to open it as he would have any of the other doors in this place.

Nothing.

32

"My Sisters will not answer you, my Son," a voice rumbled out of the darkness. "They do not care for this world as I do."

A small patch of the same angular script as adorned the walls of the temple began to glow softly near the far end of the large rectangular room, illuminating a huge man-like figure that bore those marks. The Fallen God of Glory.

How had the Fallen come to be here, now? The room had been empty before he stepped in, he was sure of it. Could this be just another vision? Did it matter?

Pure panic ripped through Emrael. His last encounter with this Being had left him shaken, nearly emotionally crippled. "Why do you call me that?" Emrael asked, his voice raspy and shaking. He was proud he had been able to speak at all.

The Fallen, lit clearly by the now-fierce glow of the scars that adorned his ashen skin, rumbled a powerfully deep laugh. "You continue to fight the truths I have shown you. You will understand, in time. Oh yes, there will be plenty of that, I think."

Emrael regained his senses quickly, though he surmised that it might be impossible to become totally accustomed to the deep reverberations of power that rolled through him each time the Fallen spoke.

"What do you want?"

The Fallen tilted his head, peering at Emrael silently for a time with eyes that glowed with *infusori*.

"I want revenge. I want peace," he said quietly, now calmly approaching Emrael with powerful strides. "I am here to make you an offer."

The Fallen reached out his giant hand to touch Emrael's shoulder. As before, the power of the Fallen God surged through him, threatening to obliterate him, to burn the soul clean out of his body. He felt as if he were trying to consume the entire world's worth of *infusori* at once—immense, achingly deep pain intertwined with a feeling of unstoppable power. The power to shape the world however he wished.

"All can be yours, Emrael Ire," the Fallen purred. "Submit to me, become my disciple, and all will be yours in time."

Emrael was tempted. A better man would not have been, but he was tempted. As he grappled with his own ambition and with the unspeakable power and pain coursing through him, however, his mind flashed back to his fight with the soulbound earlier that day. He recalled with perfect clarity the agony it experienced, the putrid corruptness of the soulbound's life source.

The Fallen had created the soulbound, had created the Craftings that enslaved humans in a never-ending state of torment. No God such as this deserved his loyalty, no matter the power he held and promises he made. Emrael would not be a part of subjugating the world for this monstrous Being, even if refusal cost him his life.

"No," Emrael growled defiantly through the pain.

The Fallen smiled again, just as he had the last time Emrael had defied him. "It is good that you cannot be bought so easily, my Son. It is good."

He removed his massive hand from Emrael's shoulder. The pain, the ecstasy of the Fallen's power ceased completely. Where Emrael had felt drained, barely human the last time he had survived such an encounter, he now felt perfectly fine—far better than he had when he had stepped in the room, in fact. He rolled his left shoulder, astonished to find it completely healed of the soulbound's bite wound. His forearm had been healed as well—not even a blemish remained on his skin.

"Now the test begins in truth, my Son!" the Fallen crowed. "Only when you have sacrificed everything you hold dear will you be worthy of my Glory."

Emrael had no idea what that meant, but it didn't sound good. Before he could even think to ask the Fallen anything further, however, the chamber was flooded with blue light as the copper script in the walls began glowing with an immense amount of *infusori* energy. He shut his eyes reflexively against the sudden brightness, and when he opened them again, the Fallen was gone.

The door opened suddenly behind him, causing him to jump in surprise and whirl around, crouched in a fighting stance. He pulled a flood of *infusori* into himself in a flash, but Jaina stood at the door looking as surprised as he was.

Despite the enormity of what had just happened to him—or maybe due to relief from the intense encounter—he couldn't help but laugh at his friend, who glared at him from outside.

"What did you do to the door?"

"Absent Gods, Jaina, he was here. The Fallen himself." He reached up to pull the bandages from his neck, probing with his fingers to be sure that there were no longer any wounds.

Jaina now looked at him askance. "You have only been out of my sight for a second. Maybe less. The door slammed shut and opened almost instantaneously."

"I don't know how, Jaina, but he was here. Take a look at my neck, my wounds are entirely healed. He was talking about his sisters, then tried to make me his disciple. He offered me power."

She took a quick step toward him, her eyes flicking to his newly healed shoulder and neck. "How did you answer?" she asked in a low, intense tone. He could see her body tense.

Emrael had to fight the urge to step back from her just as he had from the Fallen. "Glory, Jaina, I told him no. He touched me, and it felt like an avalanche of *infusori*, but pain—deep, soul-crushing pain—all at the same time."

She touched his now-healed shoulder, her face pinched in an expression of deep concern. He felt her open herself to his *infusori* senses, and he did the same, letting her feel his life source, his soul.

"You seem perfectly well," she murmured. "He did not affect you as he did last time."

Emrael nodded, distracted by his connection with her. "I feel great, but he said something about a real test, and sacrificing everything I care about—"

He cut off the conversation and his connection with Jaina to leave the room at a run. "He's going after Ban!" he called over his shoulder. "That's why we haven't seen any of them since we holed up here. We need to get the men ready to move now!"

Emrael left the room at a jog, digging the *infusori* coils from his large pouch and charging them with the energy he pulled from the natural *infusori* that flowed through the temple itself.

"Here, take these," he prompted Jaina, shoving half a dozen glowing coils at her as they ran together back toward the temple entrance. She looked at him like he had lost his mind but took the coils in her arms without complaint. She knew they'd prove handy in the coming battles, and he had his Crafted armor that he had already charged.

"Why are you suddenly so sure they're going after Ban?" she asked.

"He—the Fallen—said something about me sacrificing everything I care about," he said over his shoulder as he ran. "Kept calling me his son. I think he's playing some kind of game with me, and that game apparently involves trying to kill everyone I care about."

Jaina stopped dead in her tracks. "He called you his son?"

Emrael slowed to a stop to look back at her in confusion. "Yeah, but we can figure that out later. We've got to get to Ban."

Jaina started jogging with him again but as they neared the stairs that led back up to the outer chamber, she stopped again. "Emrael," she began hesitantly, "the Malithii believe that men are not destined to inherit Glory's power to join the Silent Sisters, but rather to join Glory in waging war against them. The artifacts our Order has found in the Westlands all have one thing in common: they refer to the Sons of Glory who will liberate the Fallen and fight the Silent Sisters with him. Most Imperator factions assume that it was the Malithii referring to themselves, but one faction of my Order believes that the phrase 'Sons of Glory' refers to something else. . . . There are ancient records that mention such figures, but the accounts don't provide any clear conclusions."

"And which are you?" he asked, meeting her green eyes briefly.

"I do not know, not anymore. The Fallen could almost certainly control you directly if he wanted to, but seems to want your cooperation. You are clearly not giving it to him. Beyond that . . . I believe we have no choice but to fight. I am still with you, Emrael. To the end, if needs be."

Emrael stepped close to her, and as both of her arms were full of brightly glowing coils, he grasped her shoulders and leaned down to settle his forehead against hers. "Thank you, Jaina. You have no idea how much that means to me."

They stood together for a time; how long, he could not have said.

"Enough of that," he said with mock gruffness and a smile as he straightened and took a step back. "Let's get moving."

They emerged from the temple to find Darmon, Captain Second Vaslat, Timan, Captain First Worren, and many of their Iraean Captains Second and Third, perhaps two dozen in all. They stood in loose ranks, and most had looks of uncomfortable surprise on their faces as Emrael emerged from the temple, scars glowing brightly, Jaina with an armful of glowing coils. They hadn't had time to get used to all of the oddities of a commander who was also a mage, let alone Emrael's other quirks. They would learn.

He addressed his gathered officers unceremoniously. "Get everyone who can fight ready to move in one hour. We can't wait until nightfall."

The room was silent for a confused moment before his officers erupted in protests.

Emrael held up his hands and was pleased when the room quieted quickly. "I've just learned that the Malithii are going to attack our friends south of the river. They may have already."

"Your brother's Crafting?" Timan asked, glancing at the pendant still hanging around Emrael's neck.

Emrael wasn't about to tell his officers that he had just spoken with the Fallen God. Half would think he'd lost his mind, and the other half would think he had been fooled, tainted by him. And he might have been fooled, he had to admit, but it was a risk he'd have to take. They had planned to move by nightfall anyway, and he couldn't let Ban and his other men face the full Malithii forces alone.

He shook his head and walked to the doorway rather than answer. He scanned the sky and sure enough, a faint haze of dust to the south was just visible in the afternoon sun. Men were on the move, and the dust-caked streets of Trylla betrayed their movements. If he hadn't known what to look for, however, he might have missed it entirely.

"Look for yourself," he said cryptically.

Timan gave him an odd look, but his officers murmured their surprise when they saw the haze of dust.

"I'll be damned," Worren grunted, squinting. "It could just be a stiff wind kicking that up, but I think you're right. How in Glory's dark name did you know? You've been down in that dungeon for the better part of an hour."

Emrael again ignored the question. "Send scouts right away. Cover half a league in all directions, make sure we aren't running into an ambush. We're leaving in an hour. Go now."

33

Emrael stood atop the south wall of the temple compound, staring at the column of smoke that now billowed from the city south of the river, staining the summer evening sky. He could only hope that their fortifications hadn't fallen already. How had the Fallen coordinated this attack on his brother so quickly after Emrael had surprised and hurt the Malithii forces, and why? Why was he trying to hurt Ban and others close to him?

They were questions for another time, when he wasn't staring a battle square in the face. His path today was clear, but he couldn't shake a feeling of uneasiness. Jaina might be able to help him piece it together. If not, Ban would. If they got to him in time.

He turned to survey his men. The seven thousand Ire Legionmen and three thousand Watchers who remained able had suited up and stood in ranks. He knew that many of them bore injuries, some serious. They had chosen to fight on anyway, rather than be left with the thousand or so grievously wounded that would stay behind the walls of the temple compound. He tried not to think about the thousands of men they had already lost in the battle with the Westlanders and soulbound earlier that day.

Worren gave him the signal that all was ready. Emrael drew his sword and lifted it over his head to draw his men's attention. The ranks below occupied so much ground that not all would hear him, but his men would pass the message back. Not for the first time, he wished he had a voice-amplification Crafting with him.

"Men of Iraea. Watchers that have joined our cause," he shouted, resheathing his sword. "Many of our brothers and sisters have died today. More of us will yet die. But we fight to save our brothers and sisters who are trapped south of the river, facing the full might of the Malithii forces we fought earlier today. I will not let them die alone, and I am proud to have you join me. We fight for the cause of Iraean freedom and the freedom of all Provincial peoples from the tyranny of foreign invaders. A cause worth more than my life, or any of our lives. We will win today, and when we do, the Provinces and a shared freedom will soon be ours."

A ragged, tired cheer emanated from the ranks. Emrael smiled. For these men to be cheering at all after the day they had meant a great deal.

He descended from the wall to fetch his horse and lead the way out of the temple compound, riding in the front rank with Worren, Jaina, and Darmon this time. Save for Timan and twenty or so of the Royal Guard, of course, who insisted on riding in front of Emrael.

Their scouts had found no sign that any Malithii-led forces were in the area, and the smoke still rising in a thick, dark column to the south told a clear story. They pushed as quickly as their tired men behind them could march, crossing over one of the river bridges and through a section of toppled stone where the river wall had stood just weeks ago. The silence and lack of contact with the enemy was welcome but eerie after the harried flight from the soulbound just hours before.

They rounded a bend onto one of the main avenues that led to the city center and there they were. Organized ranks of black-clad Westlanders and blue-clad Watchers backing a milling mass of soulbound that surrounded the city center compound. The grey half-dead creatures hacked with heavy weapons at the stone fortifications and tried in vain to scramble with their inhuman strength over the low walls constructed between buildings, but it appeared that the defenders were successfully fending them off. For now. Emrael guessed that his people inside the crude fort were outnumbered at least five to one.

As they came in sight of the fortifications, Emrael heard a voice coming from the pendant at his chest. He held it up to his ear to find that several people were now relaying information and commands through Ban's devices. As he listened to one of them call out a number, a volley of huge stones soared over the compound walls to crush scores of Westlanders who had been busy constructing catapults and siege engines of their own.

The large column of black smoke rose from what had once been a large building near the cleared space around the fortification.

It was now a deep crater with chunks of stone and Westlander corpses strewn on the ground in a circle nearly a hundred paces wide. Wagons and other equipment still burned and smoldered all around the crater, sending greasy black smoke skyward. It was obvious that Ban, Garrus, and the men inside the fort had found a way to target the Malithii forces with deadly accuracy, and had saved or built more of Darrain's explosives for the occasion.

He raised his Observer to his mouth, actuating the lever to try to contact his brother or those using his brother's devices.

"Banron. Ban, are you there? This is Emrael, we're here in the city. I have nearly ten thousand men ready to attack the Malithii forces from the rear. Ban, please answer."

After an uncharacteristic moment of silence and a series of odd clicks and crackling noises like rustling of dry leaves, a voice asked over the Crafting, "Lord Ire, please repeat. We didn't hear all of it. We've sent for Lord Ban."

Emrael nearly laughed with relieved joy. "We've got ten thousand men and will attack the Malithii from the rear. Just keep those soulbound occupied."

Ban's voice responded, nearly bringing Emrael to tears. "Oh Absent Gods, Emrael. I'm glad you showed up when you did. We only have three or four thousand men left. The Malithii and Watchers have nearly thirty thousand, even after all we've killed. They'll be through our walls soon."

"We'll show them that numbers aren't everything," Emrael replied with forced conviction. He had maybe one-third that many soldiers and knew he was likely marching to his death. "We'll hit them from both sides, make them wish they had never heard of Iraea."

"Sure we will," Ban said. Emrael could hear the strain in his voice.

"Have you heard from Saravellin?" Emrael asked hopefully.

"No, we haven't. Should we have?"

"No, it's nothing." Emrael forced himself to make his voice upbeat as he actuated his Observer to respond to his brother. "We'll give them all we've got, Ban. If we hit the Westlanders and Watchers hard enough, they might retreat. At the very least, we may be able to lead them on a chase back to the north side of the river to buy you time to escape. We'll have to kill all of the soulbound, though."

"I may have the solution to that particular problem," Ban responded distractedly, as he did when he was trying to think and talk at the same time. "Is Darrain with you? I want to ask her a few questions."

"Shit," he muttered to himself before responding to his brother. "Ban, Darrain is dead. We've been fighting nearly the entire day. I've lost thousands already."

Ban was quiet for a moment. They had been close. "I see. Whatever you do, Emrael, don't let your men into the cleared area around our walls. You hear me? Don't go into the cleared space. We're just about out of *infusori*, but I think I can arrange one last surprise for them. If it works, our wall and the buildings along the perimeter should fall and crush the soulbound if they're close enough."

Emrael looked to Worren, Jaina, and Darmon to make sure that they had heard. He could tell by the encouraged light in their eyes that they had. "That might just give us a chance, Ban. We'll hit them hard, push as many as we can next to the walls, and let you do your work. Just be sure you're ready, because we'll take heavy losses if we have to fight them on even ground for long."

"I'll go now. Be careful, Em."

"You too, Ban. I love you."

Ban didn't respond, obviously already off to work on his explosives. Worren, Jaina, and Darmon were already issuing orders by the time Emrael looked back to them, anticipating exactly what he wanted them to do. They were relatively confined in this avenue, but would separate and fan out to attack from as many of the major streets as possible, which radiated out from the city center like the spokes of a wagon's wheel. Darmon and his Watchers set off to the east while Emrael and his men took this wide avenue and the surrounding streets. Worren and the other half of the Ire Legion marched away to attack from the streets to the west.

As they drew near, the Westlanders and Watchers ahead noticed, as Emrael had known they would. The rear ranks turned, presenting a solid wall of shields and pikes.

"Bowmen, aim just over the shields! Shoot!" Emrael shouted as his men lined up in a shield wall of their own. As instructed, the half-battalion of bowmen left to him aimed and loosed a volley with a chorus of snaps, highly tensioned crossbow strings releasing nearly in unison. A few bolts hit the enemy shield wall with a resounding thud, but the majority flew true, hitting the mass of Westlanders still trying to turn their ranks. Hundreds fell, writhing. The ranks of Westlanders around them whirled around in panic.

"Keep shooting! Make them huddle up!"

His bowmen loosed a volley every twenty seconds or so, which was quite impressive even with *infusori*-Crafted crossbows. After four more volleys, the Westlanders had positioned shields to shelter most of the men in their ranks. Many had switched their pikes out for crossbows of their own, which they now shot at the Iraeans with surprising effectiveness. These troops knew their business.

Trading pikes for bows was exactly what Emrael had hoped for, however. He left his five hundred bowmen with an equal number of men to cover them as much as possible with large shields while they continued to shoot, keeping the Westlanders grouped tightly.

Meanwhile, he bellowed commands for the rest of the four thousand men left to him to move forward at a quick march. Pikes were gripped tight in the second and third ranks while the front rank loosed their short swords, ready to deal death in close quarters. A few men in the second rank carried heavy broad-faced axes for chopping at the opposing shield wall as well. They knew their part, now all that was left was to play it.

The Iraeans closed the distance quickly and didn't slow when they reached the line of Westlanders, who now scurried to switch their crossbows again for long pikes with their slender blades. A thundering crash like a hundred trees falling at once echoed through the avenue when the shield walls met. As Emrael had hoped, the Westlander ranks were pressed backward into their already tightly packed comrades, making it nearly impossible for them to maneuver.

The Iraeans took advantage. The front rank thrust their short swords through whatever gaps presented themselves, or swiped low to slash the Westlanders' legs. The pikes in the second rank stabbed mercilessly at the seams between shields, rending flesh and spilling blood as the Westlanders were pinned against the shields of their own ranks behind them.

Emrael's men killed hundreds in a few short minutes, stepping over the dead and dying Westlanders to press the attack. Finally, the Westlander ranks rippled as they pushed their own men into the cleared space beneath the walls of the fortifications to give the ranks facing Emrael space to fight properly.

Their ploy had worked. Westlanders now shared the space beneath the fortification's walls with the soulbound, whom they kept at bay with their shields. He could see to the west that Worren had similarly pushed his opponents into the clearing, but couldn't tell whether Darmon had succeeded with the enemy to the east. It would have to be good enough.

Emrael looked expectantly at the walls of the fort, expecting them to come tumbling down any moment on the heads of the tightly packed soulbound and Westlanders.

Nothing happened.

His men fought on, now taking as good as they gave. The Westlanders now had room to maneuver, which meant that spears and blades flashed into the Iraean ranks. As he watched, an Ire Legionman in the front rank was disemboweled by an expert thrust of a Westlander blade. The man fell screaming, and all his friends around him could do was pull him back to the relative safety of the rear ranks while another from the second rank pushed forward quickly to fill the gap in the shield wall before the Westlanders could press an advantage.

"We can't keep this up long," he shouted at Jaina to be heard over the din of battle, though she sat on horseback right next to him, their legs touching. She nodded.

Then it got worse. A group of Malithii working with the Westlander crews to salvage their ballistas and catapults finally succeeded, sending three large boulders crashing into one of the fort's stone barricades. Rubble sprayed in every direction as the barricade and portions of the buildings to either side collapsed.

The soulbound that had been beating at the barricades for the better part of an hour now poured through the small opening like a flood. Ban and the people trapped inside would be overwhelmed and slaughtered if many more got in. Emrael had to stop the Malithii from opening any more gaps in the wall to give Garrus's men a chance to push the soulbound back.

He stood in his stirrups to signal Timan, who had what was left of the Royal Guard fanned out in a loose circle around Emrael.

"Fetch all the cavalry we have here," Emrael shouted when Timan drew near. "We're going to lead a charge at the Malithii engineers, just there. The Guard will fight the Malithii while the rest of the cavalry makes a loop through the enemy ranks. Just tell them to get us there, then turn back here."

He turned immediately to the two Captains Third attending him. "Send orders to the reserve ranks. They are to follow in our wake to pressure the Westlanders' flanks. Go."

Timan and the cavalry officers had already gathered to one side. Emrael nodded to them and drew his sword.

"There are too many," Jaina said urgently at his side. "Killing ourselves won't do Ban and the others any good."

Emrael smiled sadly. "If we don't win here, we're all dead anyway. There will be no chance at a second retreat. I won't leave Ban or any of the others here to die alone, and I'd rather die fighting than fleeing. We have to give Ban a chance to do whatever it is he has planned."

He raised his sword and swept it forward. He let the first cavalry company pass before he, Timan, Jaina, and the fifty or so Royal Guards left alive fell into formation. As they drew near the left flank of their battle lines, the Iraean infantry shuffled backward quickly to let them through.

The five hundred cavalry plunged through the Westlander ranks. Charging horses collided with the Westlander shield wall, throwing black-clad men backward like leaves blown in a gale. A few of the Iraeans or their horses were hit by the enemy's wickedly barbed spears and flopped to the ground thrashing and screaming.

Fortunately, the enemy hadn't expected such a fast, violent attack and hadn't had nearly enough pikes or crossbows ready to stop the charge. To be fair, Emrael wouldn't have expected it either. This charge made little tactical sense, as it was almost certain to end badly against superior numbers tightly packed in the space beneath the walls. But letting the Malithii take the fortifications would be far worse, and they didn't know about Ban's plans to bring the wall down on top of the Westlanders and their soulbound.

The column coursed through the enemy like floodwaters in a

dry streambed, first using spears to skewer the Westlanders before drawing their swords to slash at the enemy as they lost momentum.

When the company ahead of him slowed due to the press of tightly packed enemy ranks, Emrael signaled his Guard. They followed as he veered right, turning their column into a wedge formation. Men around him fell screaming but he urged his horse onward, slashing opportunistically as the animal trotted through the madness of battle.

Finally, he broke through the Westlander ranks to the relative calm of the burned-out square in which the Malithii had set up their siege machinery. Ban's catapults had reduced much of their equipment to scrap, but at least a hundred Westlanders and twenty Malithii priests still operated a dozen machines that had escaped the barrage.

Emrael could feel as much as hear his Royal Guard following him as he charged straight at the crews preparing their catapults for another shot. A slash of his blade cut through a Westlander's throat, spraying blood all over him and the rump of his horse as he rode onward. When he reached a high stone wall at the edge of the square, he was forced to dismount, as the Malithii's machinery and supplies left him little room to maneuver. He pulled a small round shield from where he had tied it to his horse and quickly strapped it to his arm.

He was relieved to see Jaina and Timan among those that still rode with him. They and perhaps thirty of the Royal Guard looked to have survived the charge.

While the rest of the mounted Iraeans continued eastward to where Darmon and his Watcher battalions presumably fought, Emrael and his Guard formed a loose half-circle to face the two dozen or so Malithii that were already gathering several squads of Westlander infantry. Emrael and his friends would be outnumbered and only a dozen or so of the Guard were mages—and poorly trained compared to the Malithii, besides.

He drew from the *infusori* stored in his Crafted armor until he could see the scars on his hands and the exposed parts of his arms glow clearly even in the full light of the afternoon sun. He felt Jaina and the rest of the mages with him do the same as they eyed the

Malithii a few short paces away. Emrael beat his sword against his wood and steel shield. His Guard took up the cadence but stopped quickly as the Westlander shield wall shuffled toward them.

"Iraea and freedom!" Emrael shouted, abandoning the safety of his own shield wall to sprint at the Westlander directly in front of him. He wasn't about to wait for the priest behind the front rank to whip his copper-cable weapon over the top of their shields. Overwhelming the Malithii was their only hope.

Jaina sprinted with him. He dipped his shoulder behind his shield at the last second, knocking the surprised shield-bearing Westlander off his feet to fly backward into the Malithii behind him. Both went down in a heap.

Jaina darted in, her sword whipping quick as lightning to take both through the throat. Knowing she was at his back, Emrael turned to hack forcefully at the Malithii to his left, who was trying to whip a copper cable at Timan while the Imperator grappled with two Westlanders at once, protecting a fallen Guardsman at his feet. Emrael's sword crushed the back of the Malithii's skull.

Something hit Emrael's midsection hard—a Malithii copper cable. Pain seared through his whole body as a Malithii unleashed a torrent of *infusori* that threatened to tear the very fiber of his being apart. Nearly as soon as it began, the pain disappeared. He ducked and held his shield over his head in a defensive posture while he tried to blink the pain-blindness from his eyes.

When he could see again, he realized that Jaina, Timan, Yirram, and several other of the Royal Guard had closed together around him, protecting him behind a wall of shields and hacking swords. The three Ordenan Imperators held off twice their number in Westlanders and Malithii, their weapons crackling with expertly weaponized *infusori* anytime they struck an enemy.

He climbed to his feet, head still pounding with waves of residual pain. Without hesitation, he pushed his way back into the Iraean shield wall. He caught a Westlander's sword strike on his upturned shield, then punched his own blade through the man's chest with a savage thrust.

He was fully in the throes of *infusori*-fueled battle rage now, but the desperate, feral fear that filled his chest spoke the truth. If

Ban and those inside the fortification didn't pull off a miracle, and quickly, he and everyone with him would be dead inside the hour.

"Run up a white flag with the Watcher standard below it," Darmon commanded, staring across the hundred-pace distance between his rebel Watchers and the ranks of the Watchers that still obeyed the Malithii. Both sides waited silently behind ranks of shields, crossbows ready but held at ease. He hoped to avoid killing men he had ridden with just a few days earlier but strapped a shield to the stump of his right arm all the same.

In the two seasons Darmon had been practicing the blade with his left hand he certainly hadn't managed to regain his former prowess, but neither was he afraid. He reckoned he had little to fear from any but those few like Emrael who had both studied the sword for a lifetime and had the advantage of two working hands.

He suppressed a surge of resentment and old hatred. He couldn't afford to indulge those feelings. Like it or not, Emrael represented his best chance at expelling the Malithii from his province. His people, his family, had to be valued above his pride. Besides, if there was a "right" side of this conflict, he certainly hadn't been on it.

A Watcher Captain First near the rear of the enemy ranks turned to talk to three Malithii priests who had just arrived. The Watcher Captain pointed at the flag Darmon had raised, then continued to move his hands wildly as he spoke. Though he could hear the din of battle happening to the west where Emrael and the Iraeans fought, the standoff here was quiet enough that Darmon could clearly hear the Captain shouting nearly two hundred paces away.

The three Malithii stood still for several seconds, until one of them lunged forward with a lightning-quick thrust of a short sword that gleamed for an instant in the afternoon sun. The Watcher Captain slowly toppled from his horse to fall on the dust-caked cobbles of the wide avenue in which they faced off, clutching his gut.

Darmon stared, shocked. None of the Watchers around the fallen Captain First moved either.

"Crossbow, now!" Darmon barked. "Crafted."

A sergeant pulled one from the hands of a nearby bowman and handed it to Darmon, who dismounted to aim carefully. As good as he had been with a blade, bows and crossbows had always been his weapon of choice.

He breathed in, then out slowly as he squeezed the trigger. The crossbow bucked as the string released. The quarrel raced in a gentle arc to pass cleanly through the chest of the Malithii who had stabbed the Watcher officer. He crumpled to join the Watcher Captain in the dirt.

"Kill the Malithii! Kill the priests!" Darmon shouted, running through his lines and into the open space between the opposing ranks. "Join us!"

He knew the Watchers there could see and hear him, and that they knew who he was. He could only hope that they'd have the courage and the morals to turn on their Malithii masters in the face of overwhelming odds. Even if these five thousand Watchers joined his three thousand and Emrael's seven thousand, they'd be outnumbered nearly two to one. And that was counting on the Iraean troops to fight as well as the highly trained Westlanders and their soulbound—a tall order.

He sighed in profound relief when the Watchers nearest the two remaining Malithii swarmed the black-robed priests, hacking them to death in seconds. The opposing Watcher ranks turned as their officers bellowed orders, forming a shield wall to their rear as they pulled back from the Westlanders facing the stone walls of the fortification.

Three Captains Second and a squad of Justicers rode to where Darmon waited with Captain Second Vaslat and a squad of his own men assigned as a security detail. They saluted him, though they did it as they'd salute an equal. He'd have to settle for what he could get.

"Lord Corrande," a small Captain Second with a narrow face said. "What now?"

Darmon saluted back from where he stood in front of his ranks with a wry smile. "We don't have a choice, do we? We fight with the Iraeans."

All three of the Captains Second nodded. They knew that they faced long odds now, especially against a horde of the soulbound monsters. But they had also seen as much as he had of the Malithii and their barbarism. Villagers rounded up by the thousands and fitted with soulbinders. Watchers and Provincial Legionmen thrown into battle with no regard for life on either side of the conflict—both here in Iraea and eastward in the Ithan Kingdoms. Their entire society taken over by force and coercion. The men under Malithii control just needed an excuse, an opportunity to rebel.

"Let's hit them hard before they realize what has happened," he replied, climbing back into the saddle of his horse. "Tell your men we've got nowhere to go if we don't win here today. There will be no retreat. Only victory or death."

The paving stones beneath Ban's feet shook as something exploded to the north and east of where he stood in the central plaza. At first, Ban feared it was a premature triggering of the explosives his engineers were setting to bring down the buildings that made up the fortification's wall. In theory, the large buildings would fall on the heads of the soulbound and Westlander soldiers who now pressed the attack, trying to scale or destroy their barricades by brute force.

But it couldn't have been his explosives. He had deactivated the actuator for this very reason. As dire as the situation was, he couldn't risk bringing down the buildings on his own men. That meant that more of the Malithii catapults had survived than he had thought.

The screams and shouts of battle—and death—grew louder and louder. The soulbound must have made it inside their defensive wall.

He sprinted from where he had been working on building more explosives with a group of his engineers to where Garrus had already formed up his meager reserves to form a shield wall at the mouth of the avenue where the Malithii's forces had breached.

Ban grabbed Garrus's shoulder. "We don't have all the explosives in place. How long can you hold?"

Captain Second Garrus shook his head, a grave look in his eye. "No way to tell how many got in. We'll find out soon. I reckon we can hold for ten, twenty minutes at least."

"Call your men back from the wall if you can. We've got to blow it now."

Garrus's face blanched. "If we bring down the entire wall now, we'll be overrun, Banron. Everyone inside the fort will die."

Ban smiled sadly. "We don't have a choice, Garrus, not now. Emrael and his men are out there fighting to give us a chance, and soulbound are inside the walls. We've got to do it now."

Garrus ran his hand over his stubbled face. Ban thought he might have seen a tear on the man's cheek. "Absent Gods help us. Do it. Just give us twenty minutes to get everyone clear. We can hold them that long."

"Twenty minutes," Ban agreed. "Be sure you hold them."

Garrus saluted before following his men down the avenue, where the bestial sounds of soulbound fighting with shouting Iraean Legionmen already echoed.

Emrael and the two dozen or so of the Royal Guard that still lived now stood in a rough circle, shields tightly interlocked. Jaina stood to his right, a cut on her forehead making her face a mask of blood. Timan crouched to his left, now dragging his injured leg every time he moved. Daglund stood somewhere behind Emrael, their backs nearly touching. Most of Emrael's Guard were dead or missing, including Alsi.

They had killed all of the Malithii here in the square in their initial attack but were now surrounded by hundreds of Westlanders. Luckily, they were no longer eager to press the attack now that their masters were dead. Scores of Westlander dead also littered the courtyard, a testament to the deadliness of the Ordenan Imperators and their apprentices in the Royal Guard Timan had created. Emrael himself had lost count of the men he had slain, the *infusori* coursing through him fueling him past the point of natural stamina and into a frenzy. He simultaneously felt that he was on the verge of vomiting with exhaustion and that he could fight forever. He would certainly pay for the effort later, if he lived.

Emrael's cavalry had managed to set fire to the remaining Malithii catapults, but if they still lived, he didn't know where they were. His infantry had tried to follow their charge, but must not have been able to press through the ranks of Westlanders.

Just as the Westlanders inched forward for what was likely to be their last clash with those who remained with Emrael, a cacophony of clashing blades, battered shields, and screams erupted just to the east of the square. The Westlanders hesitated, looking around to see what was happening.

Within moments, a tide of Watcher blue swept into the square behind an immaculately aligned shield wall. The surprised Westlanders fell to the Watchers quickly. As he watched, the men in blue paused, turned their shields aside for the crossbowmen in their ranks to loose among their enemies, then closed ranks again to push forward with spears bristling between overlapped shields.

Before the Watchers had covered half the square, however, the disciplined Westlanders had formed ranks and halted their progress with a thunderous clash of wooden shields. Emrael and his small group were still isolated, separated from their unlikely allies by dozens of Westlanders.

Emrael shuffled closer to Timan, pushing him back inside their circle. The Ordenan tried to resist. "I'm fine," he growled.

Emrael turned quickly, slamming the edge of his shield against the face of Timan's. The Imperator stumbled backward into the sheltered center of their formation, unable to hold weight on his injured leg.

Emrael took a step backward, pulling Jaina and the Iraean mage apprentice who had stood next to Timan with him to keep their shields tightly locked. Just as they set their feet, the Westlanders shuffled forward with their black shields while men behind them hefted thick-hafted spears with barbed blades.

Emrael met two black shields with his, and the impact knocked him backward. Only quick feet and Timan's hand on his back kept him standing. A spear blade flashed over his shield while he was off balance. He recoiled as searing pain consumed his left eye and spread across his face.

His world turned red. He blinked and shook his head, keeping his shield in front of him as he tried to adjust to only being able to see from his right eye.

The Westlander directly in front of him lowered his shield

slightly to slash overhead with a sword. Emrael caught the strike on his shield and frantically thrust his own sword at the gap between the shields, releasing a burst of *infusori* as his blade found purchase. The soldier on the other end of his blade burst into flames, sending greasy black smoke into the sky and filling the air with the putrid stench of burned flesh. The Westlanders shrank back quickly as their comrade screamed, giving Emrael and Jaina a momentary reprieve.

Emrael watched the man burn, half in shock, when a jolt shuddered through the very stones beneath their feet. Jaina screamed in his ear, and something slammed into his shield, knocking him onto his back. His ears rang, the back of his head hurt, and his vision was now white in his right eye and black in his left. He moaned in confusion and terror, thinking himself completely blind, but his vision soon returned to his right eye. The ringing in his ears, however, remained.

He sat up slowly, choking as he tried to breathe dust-filled air. Each cough sent a flare of pain through his skull. He could feel hot blood seeping from his eye socket to run down his face.

The courtyard was littered with rubble and bodies. Those closest to the fortification—where the fortification had just been, anyway—weren't moving. Ban had finally brought down the wall, and it looked to have worked. Nearly all the soulbound had been crushed, and many of the Westlanders besides, leaving less than half of the black-clad foreigners alive.

Jaina scrambled to him using both feet and one hand, while the other arm held her shield up just in case.

"Fuck," she muttered. Then, louder, "Emrael?" she shouted. "Emrael, can you hear me?"

The relief was obvious on her dust-covered face when his remaining eye tracked to her.

"How bad is it?" he croaked.

Jaina grimaced as she looked him over. "Bad enough. Only a Mage-Healer will be able to tell us more. Can you stand?"

No amount of soldiering could prepare a man to be so near such an explosion. Most of the Westlanders had been very near the wall of the fortified compound, and so even the ones that had survived were heavily wounded, disoriented, or both. The Westlanders still able to were already starting to regain their feet, however, picking up shields and swords, looking all around with wild eyes. Rather than move to attack, they retreated carefully into a defensive position.

"Help me up," Emrael grunted at Jaina through the pain, getting to his feet with her help. His head swam and he was still disoriented by only having one working eye, but he could stand. Jaina stepped closer so he could rest his shoulder on hers. He saw Daglund help Timan up and hand him the shield he had dropped. A few others of the Guard still alive joined them, backs to each other, shields up, blades ready. It was utterly futile; there was no way for their small group to fight through the thousands of remaining Westlanders who even as Emrael watched seemed to be regaining their nerve.

Just then, a roar erupted from the south. Emrael nearly shit himself in panic until he realized that the cacophony came from inside the fortification. He watched in profound relief as a flood of soldiers in Iraean green and Raebren teal climbed over the rubble where a wall of buildings had been just moments before. Thousands and thousands of them charged the disorganized Westlanders and the few soulbound left alive after the blast. The Westlanders put up a good fight for several minutes, but where they had once held a strong numerical advantage they were now outnumbered.

The Westlanders gradually began to fall back, then began to flee en masse like a herd of black sheep fleeing from a pack of wolves. The few soulbound left alive were cut down quickly as the stampede began in earnest.

Emrael and the remaining Royal Guard had a new problem. The Westlanders no longer cared to fight them, but they stood in the middle of the thousands trying desperately to escape. They huddled together again, those with shields doing their best to ward off any Westlander who got too close.

"Follow me!" Jaina shouted, guiding Emrael by the hand to a nearby mostly intact building. Daglund continued to half-carry Timan, battering the occasional running Westlander with his large teardrop-shaped shield as they hobbled in tandem. Emrael was glad to see that more than a dozen of his Guard still lived to reach the safety of the ruined building with them.

Daglund eased Timan down next to Emrael as Jaina issued

orders to the men and women who had joined them, stationing two on each doorway and broken-down wall where Westlanders might gain entry.

Emrael sank to the rubble-strewn floor of the ruin next to Timan. "How bad is the leg?" Emrael asked.

Timan grunted. "Nothing a Mage-Healer cannot fix." He leaned closer, inspecting Emrael's face. "I cannot say the same about your eye, Em. I've never seen a Healer manage anything like that."

A wave of grief washed through Emrael. All things considered, today had turned out far better than he had dared hope. He was alive, and he had reason to hope that Ban still lived. But so many of those who followed him had died. Thousands of people who had trusted him to lead them to a better future now had no future at all.

And losing an eye . . . for a warrior like Emrael, it was nearly as bad as losing a hand.

Jaina made her way back to Emrael, bandages and waterskin in hand. He nearly fainted from pain when she poured water over his face to rinse away the worst of the grime before securing a bandage to the left side of his face. "I can't do any more without risking further damage, Emrael. We need a Mage-Healer. Sisters send Dairus still lives."

After an hour or so, the din of battle outside subsided to the nonurgent shouts of soldiers, and the moans and screams of wounded. The Westlanders had either died or fled.

34

Emrael sat on the steps of the old mansion in the central square of Trylla, hands balled into fists to bear the pain as Dairus the Imperator Mage-Healer poked and prodded at his ruined left eye. Ban and Jaina stood nearby, looking down at him with pity in their eyes.

Hundreds of their wounded littered the square in ragged rows of moaning, screaming men and women. Dairus wouldn't be able to Heal them all, not even a meaningful fraction. Emrael felt guilty for accepting the Imperator's Healing, but knew it was necessary. They'd all die if he became incapacitated now.

Dairus shook his head sadly. "I lack the skill to repair your eye to working condition, young mage. The best I can do is to heal over the eye socket so you do not risk infection."

This was not the news Emrael had hoped for, certainly. To his shame, his thoughts turned to his recent visit with the Fallen in the Ravan temple. The dark God had healed him of his wounds once.

His mind then turned to his mother and Elle. Could one of them have Healed him properly, if they were here? No matter. What was done was done.

He tried not to let any of his inner turmoil show, to keep a straight face and smooth voice as he responded, "Do it. Thank you, Dairus."

The Mage-Healer nodded, moving closer. "I am sure you have noted that each Mage-Healer's process is different. My Healing is not gentle, I am sorry to say. Hold *infusori* if you have any, and bite down on something."

Ban quietly handed him a strap of leather to bite. Emrael pulled the last of the *infusori* from the armor suit he still wore and held it while the Imperator put his finger right in his injured eye socket. He screamed around the leather strap as *infusori* coursed through him, a river of ice-cold agony. His eye and the deep wound that stretched from his scalp to his cheekbone itched and ached intensely. The pain of healing was worse than the pain of the wound itself.

When it was over, Emrael stood, panting, running his fingers over the freshly healed wound. Smooth scar tissue now covered the entirety of his eye socket, and he was surprised to find that an eyeball was still underneath.

Dairus saw his surprise and shrugged. "Better than tearing it out, no? I do not trust myself to be able to control the bleeding in these conditions."

Emrael stood on shaking legs to clap him on the shoulder. "See to Timan next, please. I need him."

Ban and Jaina followed him to where Worren and Garrus coordinated the men that remained in repairing some semblance of a defensive perimeter. Foodstuffs hauled from the temple compound and the supply wagons they had left north of the city were being distributed, and more wagons had been sent to retrieve the injured there. The two Captains First had things well in hand.

Just as he reached them, the sound of clattering hooves filled the square as Saravellin returned at the head of a few thousand mounted men in teal Raebren uniforms. They had been out pursuing the dregs of the Westlanders, making sure they didn't have time to regroup and attack them again.

Saravellin spotted them and walked her horse over, a squad of Raebren men tailing her at a polite distance. Blood splatters adorned her armor, her face, her horse. "The bastards are marching out of the ruins as we speak, fifteen thousand of them left alive. Maybe more we didn't see. They're likely retreating to their nearest stronghold, wherever that is."

Emrael nodded and motioned for her to join them. She started as she drew near enough to see his newly healed-over eye but recovered quickly and a sly smile cracked her serious face. "I see you've been taking care of yourself."

"I wasn't all that handsome to begin with," he replied, matching her small smile. "We all owe you our lives, Saravellin. Where did you get so many men? Did Dorae send the men in Ire green?"

She laughed, drawing a letter from one of her saddlebags. "No, I'd say not. Those were Garrus's men. Dorae sent this, though."

Emrael broke the seal on the letter and read it. A knot formed in his stomach.

"You read this?" he asked without looking up. He knew as well as any that wax seals were easy to pry with a hot knife and replace the same way. She seemed the type to want all information available to her. He would have done the same.

"I did," Saravellin murmured.

"And you still came?"

She just shrugged.

He turned to Worren, Jaina, Ban, and Garrus, who waited to hear the news. He told them.

Dorae hadn't sent any men, and wouldn't be. Sagmyn had fallen to the Malithii, his mother and their Legion there besieged in Myntar. Elle had abandoned him, abandoned them, and had somehow taken control of a portion of her father's province—and the Barros Legion. Rather than offer support, she had demanded the Iraeans vacate Gadford. Dorae had been forced to keep his Guard at Whitehall and wouldn't be helping anyone anytime soon. He ended the letter asking Emrael to negotiate with Elle over Gadford, as Dorae didn't have resources to hold it and defend Whitehall should the Watchers attack again.

"That crafty girl," Jaina murmured.

"Indeed," Saravellin agreed. "I thought you and she were . . . ?"

She trailed off, her gaze boring into Emrael's eye. He shook his head. "It's complicated."

She guffawed. "Wonderful. We are all caught in your lovers' spat."

He shook his head again, remorse and anger warring in his chest. "No, this is something more. I offered an alliance to the rebellious Lords Holder in the south of her province, who then besieged her father in Naeran. If she controls the province now, something happened to her father and likely her sister besides, and she likely blames me. She could be a real problem. I need to speak with her immediately."

"How will we get to Sagmyn to relieve the siege there?" Garrus asked, blunt as always. The Sagmynan Captain First's family lived in Myntar and he had extended family spread throughout the province. "We cannot leave them in the hands of these cursed Malithii."

Emrael held his gaze a moment, and could only be honest with him. His Captains had certainly earned that. "I don't know, Sub-commander Imarin. We don't have enough men or resources to do much of anything. For today, enjoy being alive—which is more than many of our sisters and brothers can do."

He swept his hand toward the teams of men beyond the fort who loaded wagons with the dead. Their Iraean brothers and sisters would be buried. The Westlanders and soulbound were being piled onto pyres for burning.

"For now, we rebuild here. Subcommander Worren, I have an assignment for you, my friend."

Both Worren and Garrus looked at him with curious looks. "We are . . . only Captains First, Lord Ire," Garrus offered, as if afraid Emrael had lost his mental faculties.

Emrael laughed. "You've both earned a promotion and more. Garrus, I expect you to pick men for promotions, take Darmon's Watchers into your battalions. Watcher officers will keep their ranks."

Garrus saluted, his face stoic.

"Worren, pick a battalion and go to Gnalius. You're going to take command of the men there and send Toravin and Lord Syrtsan to me. I'm going to try to negotiate with the bastard, but if we can't come to terms, you'll be going to war with the Syrtsans. Be ready to leave in two days. I'll have detailed orders ready for you, but hold everything east of the river at all costs."

Worren saluted, his grin malevolent. He was not one for re-building. War was his calling. "I'll see to it."

When he and the others had finished reviewing the plans for treating the wounded and repairing the defenses, he headed for his rooms to get some sleep at long last. He felt ready to collapse after a very full day of fighting and *infusori* expenditure. His building now housed wounded in nearly every room, but his personal quarters were still his. Ban and Jaina followed him, of course, but he was surprised when Saravellin walked beside him.

"I see what you're doing," she said in a low, throaty tone. "Rotating your Commanders so none of them cement enough power to threaten you. Do you fear them so much?"

Emrael looked at her askance. "Is that what you think I'm doing?"

"Isn't it?"

In truth, Emrael had considered it, but only as a fringe benefit. Truth was, Worren was exactly the field commander he needed to secure Gnalius and the eastern Syrtsan holdings quickly and with finality. Toravin was the man he needed to help him coordinate what would be a complex and arduous campaign to rebuild Trylla, recruit new soldiers, and expand northward as they expelled the Malithii and their ilk.

"I trust my officers, Saravellin."

She shrugged, still smiling. "I've heard. We'll see."

Darmon and his Watcher confidant, Captain Vaslat, approached them as they headed across the square. Emrael slowed, allowing them to intercept. He hadn't debriefed with the Watchers, and certainly owed them that much after they had risked so much to trade alliances.

Darmon pursed his lips as he took in Emrael's scarred-over eye. "We're quite the pair now, eh, Ire?" He held up his stump of an arm.

Emrael's lip twitched in a small wry smile. "Pity you blue bastards couldn't take care of those Westlanders any faster. That was my favorite eye." He now felt an odd kinship with the man, despite their past, despite his misgivings. He knew that Corrande was only here because he had no other choice, and trusted him little even so. But there was something about having fought a desperate battle on the same side that softened Emrael's heart.

"How many men do you have left, Darmon?"

"Four thousand or so."

Emrael nodded. "Good. With your leave, I'd like to take them into my Legion. Your men will be spread among the companies, your officers will retain rank and take command of the reorganized groups."

Darmon hesitated. "I have no rank," he said finally. "What am I to do?"

"I have something in mind," Emrael replied, waving a hand vaguely. "Arrange your men with Subcommander Garrus there, and we'll talk specifics tomorrow."

Darmon moved to salute as Emrael continued his tired walk to his residence. Captain Vaslat moved as well, but what Emrael had taken to be a salute turned into a lunge, a dagger in his hand.

At first, Emrael thought the Watcher was coming for him, but he aimed just behind instead, where Jaina and Ban walked.

Emrael sprang without thinking, twisting to put himself between the attacker and his friends. His family.

Vaslat's dagger sank into the flesh of Emrael's forearm. Emrael flexed and twisted his wounded arm, ignoring the pain as he used his other arm to punch at Vaslat's face. The dagger slipped from the Watcher Captain's grip.

Before he could even move to draw his own weapon, Darmon's sword flashed to skewer the Watcher Captain in the back, right through his heart. Blood splashed to the stones at their feet.

The heir to the Corrande Governorship threw his sword to the cobbles and sank to his knees instantly. "Please, Lord Ire. I swear to you, I had no part in this. Vaslat was a man of his word as long as I knew him. I joined you in good faith, as did my men. Please, I mean you no harm. None of us do."

Rage coursed through Emrael in parallel with the pain in his arm. He knew that he needed Darmon, needed his newfound unlikely alliance if he wanted to win not only the war for Iraea, but the war to defeat the Malithii and the Fallen God who commanded them. But his anger didn't want to listen. It wanted to eat Darmon's heart raw. The only thing that stopped him was a hand on either arm—Jaina and Ban had stepped forward to restrain him, to calm him. Ban moved to wrap Emrael's wounded arm to stem the bleeding.

Emrael stood silent, still shaking with rage as Jaina knelt next to the dying Watcher. She stood, a grim look on her face, a small ring in her now blood-soaked hands. "Mindbinder," she growled.

Saravellin looked confused, Darmon shocked.

Jaina spoke. "We checked all of the officers before we rode for Trylla, Emrael. This should not have been possible. I do not believe Darmon to be capable of this."

"How did this happen?" Emrael asked Darmon harshly.

Darmon looked like he was going to be sick. "I don't know, Emrael. I swear it. I've only seen one man who had these Craftings. A bastard Malithii named Savian."

"Their Prophet."

Darmon's eyes widened. "You know him? How?"

Emrael stared hard. He still shook, though he now had control of his emotions. "I know him. He's here, in Iraea?"

Darmon shook his head. "I don't know. I last saw him in Corrande Province."

"He's here. And you're going to find him."

Emrael stalked back to where Dairus the Healer still worked without further discussion, leaving Darmon on his knees with his friend's corpse.

Emrael's eye was locked on Darrain's face, her body wrapped in the cleanest cloth they could find. The blue glow of the copper script inlaid on the walls of the Ravan temple made her pallid skin look even paler than it was, like she had become an ephemeral being.

A ghost.

He squeezed Ban's shoulder and pulled him close. His brother's body shook with quiet sobs. The two Crafters had been close. How close, Emrael didn't know exactly, and didn't ask. He couldn't bear hearing the answer.

More corpses occupied the other stone biers in the room—in truth, they were the magical bunks like the ones they had slept on in the temple in the wilderness of the Barros Province. They had wanted to honor their dead somehow, and this was the best Emrael could come up with. Flame-haired Alsi and many others from the Royal Guard rested here, as did four Ordenan Imperators who had died in the fighting. Other spots had been given to Garrus and Worren to choose, honoring particularly valiant men and women who had fallen. Already the corpses stank, but their party lingered after the last body had been laid to rest. Jaina, Timan, Yirram, Daglund, Worren, and Garrus stood quietly in a rough semicircle just outside the door to the chamber.

Finally, Timan took a half-step into the room. "These Imperators, and indeed the lot of them, have died so all of us might live, and for our freedom. May the Sisters grant them a measure of Glory."

Jaina and Yirram tapped their chests in response, evidently an Ordenan custom of some sort. Emrael cleared his throat. "Time to see to the living."

He ushered everyone out and turned back to the doorway when they had all exited. A pulse of *infusori* actuated the door's mechanism. After it clunked shut, Emrael frowned in thought and put his hand back to the door. He drew a huge amount of *infusori* from the ambient power of the Well and pushed it into the door, using his senses to guide the power through the stone just so. The imperceptible cracks around the perimeter of the door sealed shut, and the Crafted mechanism inside the wall burst with a violent explosion.

"No one will disturb their rest," he said simply, tears now leaking from his eye. Odd that he would cry now. Yirram nodded and put a hand to his shoulder.

They walked through the war-torn ruins back to their fortifications in silence.

The main square was still filled with hundreds of tents that housed their wounded. Many died daily despite their efforts. Such was the cost of war, but Emrael wished desperately that he had more Mage-Healers. When he knew that most of these people could have been saved by one with the proper abilities, their deaths were a particular insult.

He spotted Saravellin on the steps of his manse. He had given her his rooms, opting to bunk with Ban again while usable rooms were scarce.

Saravellin paused briefly in her conversation with Garrus to look Emrael's way, but immediately resumed her conversation as if he didn't exist. She had all but taken over reconstruction of the city, even personally arranging the teams that loaded the enemy dead into wagons to dump in the large pyres on the outskirts of the city. She had hardly even wrinkled her nose at the putrid stench of the soulbound corpses, which seemed to decay at ten times the rate of a normal body. An odd woman. Odd but impressive. Garrus thought the world of her and gladly let her handle nonmilitary matters.

Emrael was just glad the two got along. He was in no mood to negotiate peace between allies.

Ban led him to the Crafters' Hall, which hadn't changed materially since Emrael had last been there except for the copious amounts of scrap material strewn about the hallways and in just about every room Emrael saw.

"This is almost as bad as your workstation back in our room at the Citadel was," Emrael quipped.

"Things got . . . hectic," Ban said apologetically. "My Crafters worked some miracles for us, Emrael."

Emrael smiled. *His* Crafters. Ban hadn't asked for power, hadn't yearned for leadership. But it had found him anyway.

Ban continued. "I don't know if you realize, but the damage we did to the Malithii and their men with our projectiles—"

He stopped to purse his lips and scrunch his eyes. He was trying not to cry. "Darrain saved us all with her design, Emrael. She deserved to be here."

Emrael put his hand on his brother's shoulder as they walked up a large granite staircase to his workshop on the top floor. "I'm sorry, Ban. I tried," he said, his voice rough with emotion. "I am to blame. I should have kept her safe. She wouldn't listen when I tried to keep her back, and I wasn't expecting one of our own to be shooting at our backs. But I should have kept her safe."

Ban shook his head. "No, Em. You had no way to know. Glory, we were almost killed right on our doorstep. This burden is mine. I'll have something built by the end of the week. Mindbinders won't plague us any longer."

They arrived at Ban's workshop, and Emrael stopped just inside the doorway, staring at a giant metal contraption that nearly filled the large room. "Where in Glory's dark name did you get the materials for this?"

Ban looked sheepish. "I looted the temple. Don't tell Jaina. Or that shaman of yours. I took the copper from a room I don't think anyone will look in, and kept the circuit whole so the inlay still glows just fine."

Emrael laughed from deep in his belly, the first real laugh he'd had in weeks. "Your secret is safe with me. Jaina really would whip you bloody, though, you know."

Ban turned to his copper spire, which seemed to extend through the roof. He fiddled with some boxes and various Craftings he had connected to the spire, then motioned Emrael forward. "This is like the Observer I made for you, but it can broadcast much farther. Receive, too. My Crafter Aelic had its twin working in Whitehall weeks ago, but I had him send it on to Larreburgh with Paia—

figured Halrec would need more help, and Aelic can build one more easily in Whitehall than he could in Larreburgh. We have been broadcasting on higher frequencies to reach our scouts here in the city more clearly to target the Malithii machinery, but I've just reconfigured it for distance and we hailed Paia early this morning. She said Halrec wants to speak with you."

Ban looked at him expectantly. Emrael waved his hands at his brother impatiently. "Go on then, get Halrec for me."

Ban turned back to his work, chewing on his tongue as he twisted knobs and finally pressed a lever near an array of hundreds of steel pins connected to a wire that led to the spire. "Paia, this is Banron at Trylla Station. Please respond."

He let go of the lever and waited. Five minutes or so later, he repeated himself. Emrael took a seat and began fiddling with a half-finished project on a nearby worktable. Several attempts later, a voice responded.

"Ban? Is Emrael there?"

The voice emanated from one of Ban's boxes, corrupted by a series of pops and crackles. It was more than clear enough for Emrael to recognize Halrec's voice, however.

Ban depressed a lever and beckoned Emrael over to a device that looked like a bird's nest of looped wires. "Go on, speaking into this."

Emrael couldn't help but smile as he responded. "I'm here, Hal."

"About damn time. We're in real trouble here, Em. Just more than half of the minor holders answered my call to gather in Larreburgh and accepted me as Lord Holder."

Emrael grunted. "Seems okay to me. Half is more than I would have expected."

"That's not the bad part. Whether those absent fight against me or not, I think I'm going to have upward of fifty thousand Watchers and Malithii and Absent Gods only know who at my gates within weeks. Days, maybe. Most of my scouts don't return, and those that do report large groups of soldiers moving to the east up the Tarelle Gap, and north in Paellar."

"Fallen Glory," Emrael sighed, closing his eye. "Hal, we just lost at least half of our men just to keep Trylla, and it was a close thing. Sagmyn is under siege, and Elle has abandoned us in an attempt to take over Barros Province. She's threatening Dorae. I don't have more than five thousand men that could march right now. You've got to get out of there. Take any who will leave and come to Trylla."

Halrec was quiet long enough that Emrael looked to Ban, thinking that the Crafting had malfunctioned. Ban shrugged, his hands in the air. "It's working."

"Hal?"

His friend finally responded, his voice low and hard. "These people just accepted me as their Lord Holder, Emrael. That means something to me."

Emrael sighed. "I know Halrec, but we'll get Larreburgh back at some point. We can retake a city. I can't replace you, or the men the will die with you."

"Thousands will die if I leave them, Emrael. Tens of thousands. I can't do that."

"Halrec, see reason. *All* of you will die if you don't leave. Take any who want to leave with you. Come to me in Trylla. Or go to Whitehall. I don't give a shit. Dying in Larreburgh is not the answer."

Halrec guffawed, causing the Crafting to crackle and pop loud enough to hurt Emrael's ears. Ban scrambled to adjust some knobs.

"Emrael, these people can't travel hundreds of leagues ahead of an army of Watchers and soulbound and who knows what else. Many don't have a horse or wagon to their names. Children, Emrael. Is becoming king really worth leaving them to die?"

Emrael sank his head into his hands. "Hal, what do you want me to do? I can't get there in time, or with enough men. And I have my own battles to prepare for here. We haven't won the war, not even close."

The Crafting sat silent. He sighed again, then pushed the lever down one more time. "I love you for staying, Hal, I do. I'll send to Dorae and even to Elle, asking them to send men. But please, consider sending any of your people who can travel to safety while you still can. Get our men out to fight another day. I can't help, and the others likely can't either."

"I can't leave, Emrael. This is the fight I choose. Help me if you can. I'll update you this same time tomorrow."

Silence.

Emrael cursed, quiet at first, but crescendoed to screaming profanities. Ban watched calmly.

Emrael finally stopped, breathing hard, wanting to lash out, to break things. He knew how much Ban's Craftings meant to him, however. He nearly turned to stalk out the door in search of something to break, someone to fight, anything on which he could vent his frustration. His brother's calm eyes stopped him.

"You done?" Ban asked quietly.

Emrael flopped into the chair again and folded himself to rest his head on his knees, his hands gripping his hair, which had grown in the weeks since he had last had time to think about cutting it. "What am I supposed to do, Ban? It's too much. Mother, Halrec, Dorae, Elle, the people here. I can't save them all, no matter how hard I try. And how am I supposed to beat the Fallen God himself? I can't do it."

"You must accept that the people you love control their own destiny, Em. You can't control what others do without becoming as bad as the Fallen himself. So why do you think you are to blame for everything that goes wrong?"

Emrael didn't respond, so Ban stood. "Come with me, I want to show you something."

Emrael slowly unfolded himself from the chair and followed, his rage quickly settling into a deep melancholy. They climbed a metal ladder at the end of the hallway to stand together on a railed balcony on the roof of the building. The Crafters' Hall was likely the tallest building left standing south of the river now that some of the largest had been brought down on the heads of the soulbound and Westlanders that had assaulted the fortifications. He could easily see the river from here, and beyond to the ruins where the temple lay.

They stood there for a time, watching the thousands of men and women that had followed them to Trylla. Rebuilding the outer wall, caring for the wounded, cooking, hauling water, riding out on patrols. Their shared dream had been wounded, but was once again bustling with life.

"You did this, Emrael," Ban said finally. "You have paid the price as much as any but the dead." His brother touched his scarred-over eye gently and kept an arm around his shoulders. "All of these people believe in something greater than what they were born to, just like we do. And you've given them a chance to fight for it, to build it with their own hands. Whatever we have to do, that's worth something. Whether the Fallen is real or not, we can't stop fighting. We can't leave these people to languish."

Emrael, still staring northward, started laughing.

Ban pulled his arm away and punched his shoulder. "Ass," he grumbled.

"Not you," Emrael said, punching his brother back. "Look there," he said, pointing to the river. "I can see it even with one eye."

"Is that a ship?"

Emrael gripped the stone railing of the roof balcony. His melancholy now warred with anger. Anger and, oddly, hope. "Ordenans."

The Ordenans were dangerous bedfellows, but he didn't have much choice at this point. "I'm either going to start another war with the most powerful nation in the world, or make them our ally. Let's go find out which."

ACKNOWLEDGMENTS

My wife, Kailey, will always come first, especially when acknowledging the privileges that allow me to spend the time I do writing Emrael's story. She is a true partner to me, the enabler of all my mischief. Thank you for making me your trophy husband.

I have been delighted to work with a new editor (and dare I say, friend) Robert Davis, whose insights and candor I value very much. The copy editor of this volume, Terry McGarry, deserves enormous praise for helping me keep my shit together.

To the "boots on the ground" at Tor: I don't know most of you personally, but I know you exist, and you all deserve huge raises. Thank you for kicking ass.

I would be very remiss if I did not mention Sunyi Dean, my marvelous *Publishing Rodeo* podcast cohost, and the rest of the secret discord gang. It's a wonderful thing to have friends.

Thank you for reading. Your kind comments and reviews mean the world.

ABOUT THE AUTHOR

Jennie Brown, Jennie Brown Photo

SCOTT DRAKEFORD is the author of the Age of Ire series. He's also the cohost of the Hugo-nominated podcast *Publishing Rodeo*.

Drakeford is a former mechanical engineer and tech person turned full-time trophy husband, father, and writer. He currently lives in the PNW with his badass wife, their tenacious children, and two dogs.